THE

BACK OF BEYOND

Travels with Benjamin

THE

BACK OF BEYOND

Travels with Benjamin

Martin Vopěnka

Translated from Czech by Anna Bryson

Plamen
Press
Where Words Ignite

Washington, DC

Plamen Press

9039 Sligo Creek Pkwy, Suite 1114, Silver Spring, Maryland 20901
www. plamenpress.com

Printed in the United States of America

10 9 8 7 6 5 4 3 2 1

PUBLISHER'S CATALOGING-IN-PUBLICATION DATA

Names: Vopěnka, Martin, author. | Bryson, Anna, translator.
Title: The Back of Beyond, Travels with Benjamin / Martin Vopěnka;
[translated by] Anna Bryson.
Description: Silver Spring, MD: Plamen Press, 2021
Identifiers: LCCN 2021938152 | ISBN 978-1-951508-01-2 (paperback)
ISBN 978-1-951508-13-5 (Epub)
ISBN 978-1-951508-14-2 (PDF)

Subjects:
LCSH: Czech Fiction--Translations into English.
European literature—21th century. | Central European Literature.

BISAC: FICTION / European / General.
FICTION / World Literature/ Czech Republic
FICTION / Family Life / General

Edited by Rachel Miranda Feingold
Edited by Nicole Suozzi

Photo copyright © 2021 by Luka Kostovski
Cover Design Copyright © 2021 by Nikola Kostovski

Contents

Chapter III:
The Journey to the Back of Beyond Starts in Earnest

Chapter IV:
The Journey Moves Further from its Starting Point

Chapter V:
The Journey is Lost in a Mist of Forgetting and Re-Emergence

Chapter VI:
The Hell of Loss and the Purgatory before Entering the Paradise of the Heart

Chapter VII:
Epilogue

THE

BACK OF BEYOND

Travels with Benjamin

Chapter I

A Painful Liberation and Challenge to a Journey

THE BACK OF BEYOND

The Burial of a Wife and Mother

I kept my arm round Benjamin's shoulders, and he instinctively huddled into me. A few steps in front of us, at the bottom of a shallow grave, lay the coffin containing his mother. The gravedigger had lowered it in before our arrival, and so, apart from the two of us, the only person present was the elderly priest in his crumpled cassock.

A warm, late spring breeze was wafting through the small cemetery on the wooded hill above the city. This was definitely the kind of scene she had imagined, the way she would have wanted it. Always preoccupied with death, she had once told me about her ideal funeral, but she couldn't have had any inkling back then that, one day in May, she would drive through a red light at a busy intersection and a moment later would cease to exist.

The crowns of massive beech trees rustled softly above our heads. Their leaves already unfurled, they kept the thirsty sun from drying up the paths beneath them, sodden from yesterday's rain. The air was saturated with smells of different kinds but above all the smell of turned clay.

A burial like this had taken a lot of arranging, and over the last few days I had often worried that I was wasting time on it just when Benjamin needed me most, but now I mentally acknowledged that all those difficult negotiations with the authorities, the funeral home, the gravedigger, and the church had been worthwhile. If nothing else, I owed this to her—a leave-taking of the kind she had wanted. (Living with her had made me realize that there are people in the world who have been getting ready to leave it since before they were born).

The priest mumbled the words of the prayer with a humility that sounded genuine. He looked back and forth between the grave and us; he must have found us a touching sight as we stood there, silent

1

and alone. Benjamin didn't move at all, just pressed his head harder and harder against my chest. He didn't cry. Maybe it hadn't yet sunk in, or maybe he just accepted the death of his mother—naturally, the way children accept things.

What I was feeling, if I remember rightly, was a mixture of boundless grief and relief. Anyone who has ever lived with someone who finds living a burden will understand why I was relieved. And no one who has ever understood people like that, and caught a glimpse of the futility that stares them in the face, will be surprised at the tears springing to my eyes.

Just like her, I had quite often thought about the possibility of her death. Not because I wished her any harm. More because I had considered her death an acceptable way out for both of us. I had thought that if she would only die while we were still together, then her life would have some meaningful culmination, but if I were to leave her, perhaps taking Benjamin with me, I would absolutely destroy her. Except that now, when the prospect I had conjured in my mind had actually become a reality, my feelings were different.

The terrible certainty that I would never talk to her again, that her face would never brighten again, her hands never stroke Benjamin's fair hair again—it made me want her to come back. I wanted to talk with her at least one more time and apologize for all my roughness and lack of patience. I wanted to explain that my behavior had been nothing more than a refusal to accept her state of mind, so painfully out of tune with the world that it undermined all my certainties and brought my sense of order crashing down.

I had a thousand reasons to reproach her. A thousand reasons to blame her for the decline of our relationship: her sexual apathy, her selfishness, her lack of interest in my needs. Instead, I remembered just one little episode from a holiday by the sea, back in the days before we had Benjamin, when we were looking to the future with hope and were completely devoted to each other. I had jumped off some rocks into the foaming waves (they were high rocks, and I knew I'd only have the nerve to do it once). She was supposed to take a photo of it but hadn't managed to click the shutter in time, and so I shouted and swore at her—God, really terribly. She loved me and I acted disgustingly. She must have forgotten it long ago—other days had come, grey and sad. But recalling it now, what I most wanted was to throw myself down into the grave, put my arms around her cold body, and beg her forgiveness. That was out of the question, and so all I could do was hope there was life after death, and her soul was looking down on us from up there, and she realized I would have wished her happy with all my heart.

Benjamin's first words when I told him she was dead had been, "Dad, are you going to be with me now?" The question suggested to me that he was taking it as realistically as I was. I had assumed I would have to get him excused from school, but in the end, he didn't lose a single day. At least it meant he hadn't had so much time to think about it and get overwhelmed by grief and self-pity.

The priest finished the ceremony and asked us to come up to the grave. I leaned towards Benjamin, "We're going to throw a little earth on Mom's coffin. You go first."

We had talked about that before, but he gave me a surprised look, and I saw that he was all choked up. "Already, Dad?"

I realized that as long as he could still see the coffin with her body in front of him, he could keep on believing he hadn't lost her yet. That moment would come when the coffin disappeared from view. With my arm round his shoulders, I led him to the edge of the grave. "Take a handful of earth and throw it down," I told him.

He clung to me desperately, "I don't want to, Dad!" All his composure of the last few days was gone.

"Benjamin!" I hunched down to his level and squeezed him, "Benjamin, Mom isn't down there anymore. Her soul is floating around us. She's looking at you, and she loves you a lot. She'll never leave you."

He ducked his head even further down my chest. "But Dad, if her eyes aren't open how can she see us?"

"A soul doesn't need eyes to be able to see," I answered, "a soul sees us completely—just as we are. She just knows about us."

"And a soul never ever dies?" he mumbled tearfully.

Although I believed there was some kind of spiritual dimension to our existence, I had never been convinced about life after death. But it was hard to remain a skeptic face-to-face with a grieving child, "Benjamin, that's a thing nobody knows for sure," I said, nonetheless. "Nobody knows exactly how it is, but I hope that something like a soul is still there when we die."

"Because thoughts can't go away, can they?" He brightened and raised his voice, "thoughts can't fall apart like bodies, can they?"

I stroked his fair head. "You're right, our thoughts, and our feelings too, our love, can't just disappear. I'm sure they keep going. So, come on; let's take handfuls of earth and throw them down to Mom in the grave. And while we do it, we'll think about her soul, and how it's going to stay with us."

"Okay," he agreed, even though he was still reluctant. We squatted right down together, and each threw a clod into the grave, releasing an even stronger scent of wet clay. Benjamin started to enjoy it. He plunged his whole arm into the heap and used it to rake the earth over the edge. Then he jumped over to the other side of the grave and started on the opposite heap. He was shoveling it down like crazy, and the coffin was beginning to disappear. Benjamin's pants, shoes, and sleeves were covered with a layer of earth. It doesn't matter—I said to myself, it isn't important, but I had to make an effort to hold back and let him be. No, I'm not going to stop him, I kept assuring myself. I'm not going to slow him down with even the slightest hint. At that moment, I noticed the priest was standing a little distance away, unable to take his eyes off the scene. I went up to him with an apologetic smile. "His mom couldn't have wished for a better burial, don't you think?"

The priest gave me a chilly look, "A final leave-taking isn't a football match," he said witheringly, "You ought to be bringing him up to show more respect and obedience."

The blood rushed to my head. It always winds me up when I try

4

to be friendly to someone and get a rebuff. "Why don't you leave it to us how we say goodbye?" I snapped. "We didn't need you. You were only here because that's the way she wanted it."

"We all belong to God," said the priest with surprising detachment, and he turned and walked slowly away. I was already regretting my outburst, for anger was out of place here, and the real reason I had lost my temper was that I wasn't even sure about Benjamin's behavior myself. Somewhere inside, I had probably been ashamed of it, and that was what made me so irritable.

I went back to the grave. In the meantime, Benjamin had covered almost the whole coffin, and only one shorter side was still showing. If any of the relatives had been there, they probably would have fainted at the sight of Benjamin, ruddy-faced and digging with his bare hands in his filthy best clothes.

The coffin had disappeared, but plenty of earth remained on the sides of the grave. I caught Benjamin's hand. "The gravedigger will finish it. Come and clean up."

"The flowers, Dad, we've forgotten to throw in the flowers," he remembered.

"You're right." (I had laid the flowers on a neighboring grave at the beginning.) "We'll throw them in now."

"But we'll have to cover them up with more earth, Dad."

I was glad that the earth-throwing was over. "No, let's leave it like it is," I urged him, "I like it that way."

"Okay." He gave a conciliatory shrug.

We each threw a flower into the grave and went to the tin sink by the wall of the cemetery. "You look a real old mess. Come here." I tried at least to brush down his pants, but the earth was wet from yesterday's rain.

Benjamin looked at me guiltily. "Don't be mad at me, Dad."

I put my hand on his head—I liked doing that, I did it often. "But I'm not mad at you at all."

I saw his relief.

We set off back to the city. When we had walked thirty or forty meters

5

downhill, the hum and roar of congested roads and accelerating buses rose to meet us. I was thinking of myself at his age. How would I have reacted if my mother had died? I couldn't imagine it. It was true that I hadn't much appreciated my mother—she had spent several months of every year in the main Prague psychiatric hospital in Bohnice. Pure, radiant maternal love was something I had never really experienced. On the other hand, if she had died, my whole world would still have collapsed. The communist regime that ruled the country back then hadn't provided much room for maneuvering. For a start, everybody had to go to work. They had called it the "right to work" and immediately added "the duty to work." How would my father have looked after me?

My situation today was different. Over the last few years, I had made a lot of money through short-term investments in stocks, and by the time of Benjamin's mother's death, the only work commitments I had were ones I imposed on myself.

We arrived back at the car. Before the burial, I had parked in the shade, but the sun had moved round and was now scorching the glass and the shining hood. "Wait!" I said, "Take those things off!" I pointed to the muddy trousers and shirt. "It'll be hot inside anyway."

I helped him off with them, making sure he didn't get even muddier in the process. He slipped into the car barefoot, just in his vest and underpants. "Where are we going Dad?"

"Where can we go like that?" I pointed to his bare legs. "I don't think they would let you into a theater."

He burst into childish laughter.

We rode through the Prague streets, and I drove self-confidently, aware that from now on how we lived would depend on me alone. I gripped the steering wheel with both hands and felt like a wheelman and a captain all in one. From now on, I wouldn't have to take account of her anxious neediness, and there would be no more endless quarrelling. My life was my own again, opening up towards the horizon like an avenue of tall trees. Maybe it was then, somewhere on the three-lane city loop, that my long-shelved idea of setting out on a journey came back to me. At that point, it was still only a glimmer, a feeling. It was something to do with the need to fulfill a life with Benjamin—father and son—the way I had imagined it ever since his birth. Perhaps because he could never completely rely on his mother, his trust in me was boundless. For the same reason, I felt absolute responsibility for him. He seemed immeasurably dear and fragile to me. When he was two years old, he had caught a childhood illness and started to look like he was choking. That night I had been with him in our log cabin under the mountains, and freezing rain had fallen. The car, the road, and the trees around us had all been covered in a layer of ice as I drove him through the foothills, while he babbled something about fairy lights through his wheezing. Afterwards, I had often imagined us walking along the wagon track across the side of a nearby hill, hand in hand. We would set out early in the morning, and by noon the local people would see us high in the sky, climbing up through the white clouds. That was the kind of journey I had dreamed of, over the hills and faraway and never to return…travelers passing out of sight and out of mind, to the back of beyond.

The House of Sick Souls and the Graveyard of the Nameless

Our apartment on the outskirts of Prague was not at all luxurious. I could have afforded much better. It was just a slightly larger-than-average apartment in what had been a state housing project, but living with Benjamin's mother, I had never had the will or the desire to change anything. It is only worth creating a beautiful living space if you have a beautiful life.

As soon as we were back in the front hall, I realized just how hard it was going to be for us here. Her coat was still hanging on the coat stand, her shoes still lying by the door. The still air was stale with the sediment of years. We were both about to disappear into our respective rooms when the telephone rang. It was her father. "I'm assuming that now you're willing to tell us where you've stuffed her into the ground." His tone was hostile—I hadn't told them where the burial would be because they refused to respect my wish to be alone with Benjamin there, and they would have turned up and spoiled everything.

"Of course." I adopted the same kind of chilly controlled tone, "The easiest route there is…"

"Thanks a million for not inviting your wife's own parents to their daughter's funeral," he said after I had told him the way, and he hung up.

Less than two minutes later, the telephone rang again. This time it was my own father. "Get me Benjamin, please."

Dad's tone was cold and even imperious, and I could hear the fundamental disapproval in his voice. He thought that cremation was the only suitable form of funeral from Benjamin's perspective. Apparently, it was socially obligatory these days, and an actual burial would give Benjamin outdated ideas. Meanwhile, Mom had been worried about Benjamin's strung-out feelings—she would have been happiest if he hadn't been taken to the funeral at all.

"What are you going to talk to him about?" I asked Dad.

"Kindly leave that to me," he retorted. He had a fixed notion that he played the decisive role in Benjamin's life, and I was just in the way.

"I'd like you to bear in mind," I told him, "that the funeral was just as it ought to be. There's no need to go back over it."
"Look here…you've got no right to interfere in my relationship with Benjamin. Anyhow, one day I'll tell him everything."

"What d'you mean, everything?"

"Well, that it's…it's because of you his mother's worm food."

As always, I was enraged by the self-assured stupidity of his opinions. I looked around to check that Ben wasn't listening. He was now in his room with the door shut, but I still dropped my voice. "Are you saying I should have had her mummified?"

"You know perfectly well what I'm talking about," he said, evasively.

"No, just a minute." I wasn't going to let him off the hook, "If you want to be mummified when you die, don't forget to put it in your will."

I had hit a nerve and could sense Dad's fury, but as usual he converted it into self-pity. "What kind of son did I raise?" he lamented. "You don't have the slightest respect for me, not an ounce of consideration. One day you'll let me die on the street."

"So, I'll go get Benjamin for you." I put the receiver down next to the telephone and went into Ben's room.

He was sitting at his desk and scribbling something, but probably wasn't really doing anything. "There's a call for you," I told him.

He gave me an annoyed look, and I understood his fears of having to go back over the funeral.

"It's Grandad. Come talk to him."

"If I have to," he said.

From a short distance away, I tried to catch what they were

talking about. But it was only Dad doing the talking—I could hear Benjamin's bored, "Yeah…hmmm…yeah…"

When he finally hung up, we both went off to mind our own business. All at once I felt very down. Just a little while before, behind the wheel, I had felt great. My life had been beckoning to me with all its new possibilities, and it was all just up to me. Now I hunched in my study and felt as if another of those new possibilities was passing me by every second, never to return. I had no plan, no idea of what to do.

Somewhere, out of sight and not yet quite conscious, the idea of leaving was ripening inside me, but for the moment I was unaware of it. Instead of feeling relieved to have the funeral behind me, I was crippled with anxiety. I knew I would have to fill up Benjamin's time, hour after hour. The few days between the death and the funeral had been so full of tension that there had been no room in my head for thoughts like this. Now they came in an avalanche, and I was starting to have doubts about myself. Was I really the maternal type? Could I really devote myself body and soul to a child—help him with his homework, wash his clothes, play idiotic games with him? How could I have felt like a winner when in fact I was a normal selfish man, who needed space for my pleasures, free time uninterrupted by the claims of others. And of course, if possible, at my back a patient woman, ready to get up for a sick child, take care of everything, to smile, to cook…

I tried to come to my own defense by recalling that Benjamin's mother had been far from ideal, and I had learned to do plenty by way of childcare. Quite apart from the fact that I could afford a lot of help; I was rich.

Suddenly, the study door opened softly. "Dad…?" Not waiting for my permission, Ben slipped inside. A moment later he was beside my armchair. "Dad, I don't know what to do." I could see the anxiety in his eyes.

"You don't know what to do? How come?" I feigned surprise. "Well, one thing we're not going to do is sit here when it's so nice outside. Come on, let's go and find some food."

"Okay," he agreed. "What clothes should I wear?"

"Just choose something. You know what it's like outside."

He went off but soon came back. "I can't find any socks."

"Socks? Aha." I went with him into his room. I opened the top drawer of his wardrobe. It was full of tiny, neatly folded flannels from Ben's infancy. It was the same in the next drawer down. That was just like her—that clinging to the past, to the small things. "Where did you get your socks from yesterday?"

He gave me a guilty look, "I didn't change my socks."

"Benjamin," I said, "You're eight years old. You should be able to think of such things by now."

His terrified expression disarmed me. I hugged him. "It doesn't matter. You'll learn."

We found socks in the living room under the bookcase. Underpants too; he had been wearing the same ones for a week). We got into the car, and I hastily tried to think of a destination. The nearest restaurant was just around the corner, but I wanted us to have a little bit of an excursion. I headed for the Vltava riverbank. I had already sat with him there once before, when I had excused myself from a family Sunday walk and taken him for a ride on the pedal boats. Today was an ordinary workday in May, and the terrace was empty. We found seats where we could watch the water flowing past. Soon we were talking about how the water would end up in the sea and then evaporate and then rain down again, and a lot of things like that. In the meantime, two girls had sat down at a neighboring table, just in my line of sight. They were both pleasant to look at, not too glamorous but not slovenly either, and my eyes kept sliding towards them more and often. I even failed to register Benjamin's last question and answered just "Mm..." While Ben talked up a storm, I was drifting off into the realm of dreams. I imagined hiring one of the girls to take care of the household. I would behave in a friendly but correct manner and soon impress her with how I was looking after my son and how I was rich but still managed to be normal despite the wealth. Sexual play would soon develop naturally, alongside the cleaning and cooking. Not that I would have to go out with her or marry her. Our relationship would be unequal, a service affair, but unlike regular prostitutes, she would be putting her real self into the sex, even if it was only an act of convenience and not the union of two souls. I imagined some of the various forms that this convenience would take, and suddenly I was aroused under the table.

The food came and brought me back to earth. I had to cut up the tough meat for Benjamin. I realized this was still the day we had buried his mother. And we were sitting here as if nothing had happened and chatting about the natural cycle of water. And it was only three in the afternoon, still plenty of time to go before evening. Maybe we should go on the boats again or to the zoo or to the Castle and Petřín Hill. Except all of that somehow lacked a story, a reason for going specifically there. After all, this was an exceptional day.

Then the idea came to me. It was the story of my own mother. She wasn't dead, but there had been a time when I had buried her several times a year, whenever she had been admitted to the psychiatric hospital in Bohnice.

"Let's go and look at a big park," I said.

"But why? Why a park, Dad?"

"Wait and see."

I paid. As we were leaving, I met the eyes of one of those girls. She didn't avoid my gaze, but seemed a bit startled, as if pulling back a little. She must have had an inkling of my imaginings; I wasn't quite a complete nobody to her.

The embankment was one long traffic jam; we inched forward for about half an hour, and I felt the city draining me dry. It had probably been a stupid idea to start on this trip, and we should have gone to the playground instead.

"Are we still going to the park?" Benjamin kept asking impatiently.

Eventually we got out of the center, and the rest of the drive only took about fifteen minutes. I parked by the hospital wall. We walked along a pavement lined with lilacs shedding their fading blossoms and found ourselves in front of the reception building. Tiled pathways converged on it symmetrically from both directions, as they often do in stately homes. The modern housing estate around the hospital was now more or less softened with greenery and was less of an eyesore than in past years. When I was a child, it hadn't been there at all. Back then, the hospital and its large park had been way beyond the city limits and only a single bus had stopped there. That was the bus we used to take, me and Dad, since we didn't have a car. There had been fields in all directions, apart from a small hedge protecting a big well—a working source of water, just in front of the gate. There hadn't been many cars in Czechoslovakia then; nothing to compare with the traffic today. I couldn't help feeling a pang at how much the world had changed even in my lifetime, and how much we had managed to destroy in just the last few decades.

"Is this the park?" piped Ben.

"Yes, it is. Actually, it's not just a park. It's a hospital."

"A hospital? Are we going to a hospital?"

"Yes, Benjamin. But it's not an ordinary hospital, where you go when you break your leg or need an operation. The people here have minds that are ill. Or they just don't know how to live in our world. When I was your age, and when I was much smaller too, my Mom—your Gran—spent several months being treated here every year. We used to come visit her, but back then, children weren't allowed inside, so most of the time I used to wait here by the entrance. Sometimes there was a nice porter on duty, though, and he would let me through."

Why am I telling him this, for God's sake? I checked myself. And I didn't add that, when I had found Mom in a strange building with barred windows and a bunch of really weird women, it was even worse than being kept out.

"So are children allowed in today?" asked Ben.

"Today, yes. You'll see. No one will even notice us."

"But why couldn't children go inside back then?"

"Because back then, people thought it wasn't good for children to see a mentally ill person. Those people often behave differently to the way we expect. And apart from that, our country was ruled by communists, and they banned all kinds of things."

We had reached large glazed doors with heavy wooden frames. Here, under a stone archway, we walked into the entrance hall. For a whole century, two worlds had met here. The entrance hall was part of both worlds; solitary patients would stand around here, but at the same time, anyone could come in from the outside. It surprised me how little had changed inside. The same smell, the same dimmed light, the same echoing steps and voices. On the other side, a smaller door led into the park. "Come on," I gave the hesitant Benjamin a little push, and we went out into an open green space. Once I had cracked my knee here, rushing to greet Mom. It was here I had always seen her coming, and here that she had always left me again, seeming unreadable to me, a stranger, changed beyond recognition. For years to come I had failed to understand it, just as it would probably take Benjamin a long time to comprehend what today—the day of his Mom's funeral—would mean for the rest of his life

"Hey, there's a church here too," he said, surprised. "And benches." "There's absolutely everything here," I assured him, "so some people can spend almost all of their lives here."

"Like in prison?"

Yes, I thought to myself. In their own prisons. Not that I could say anything so complicated and mysterious to Benjamin.

"No, this isn't a prison. People are getting treatment here. It's just that some of them simply don't know how to be like us. For example, they're scared of cars, or they're scared of going shopping, or they're always frightened and don't even know why. And so, they'd rather be in here. But it's true that one pavilion here is like a prison. It's where people are locked up when they've committed a crime, and it's turned out that they're not okay—that they did it because they were sick."

"Can we go and look at that pavilion?" Benjamin was keen.

"Okay," I said. "It's right at the back. On the way, I'll show you

14

where your grandmother stayed most often."

We set off. Oh, that marvelous, peaceful feeling you get from immense trees, I thought. The park was dominated by a red beech with branches so massive that it was as wide as it was tall. There was a chapel on a little hill, with only a little sandy path leading up to it, as if the architect had wanted people to get a sense of distance from all the rush and bustle of ordinary life, and give themselves up to Mother Earth, or else to feel like someone making their way to a sanctuary beyond the boundaries of their native village, ready to receive comfort, hope, and salvation. At the time when I had visited my mother here as a child, the church had been closed; the communists had turned it into a dump.

As we walked on, we saw grasshoppers jumping about in the tall uncut grass and bumble bees flying around. It struck me that the tiny creatures had found a good refuge, hidden away from the deadly breath of the city. Benjamin also looked invigorated by this sandy path full of sun, and he broke into a run. He ran up a grassy bank and jumped back down again, and did it again, several times. In the meantime, two shabbily dressed patients approached and stared at Benjamin with wonder. Both were quite young. One couldn't have been more than twenty, and the other around thirty, but I judged from their slouched figures and empty eyes that their lives had most likely taken a permanent turn for the worse. They would wither away here, becoming institutionalized, resigned. They seemed to realize that Benjamin, with his childish enthusiasm did not belong here, and something about his behavior attracted them, as if they were vainly trying to recall their own childhoods. At this point, Ben noticed them too and nervously ran back to me. In an excited whisper, he asked, "Are those sick people who live here?"

"Yes, they are," I nodded, "but there's no need for you to be afraid of them," I added quickly.

"I'd like to go now," he said.

"Let's keep going. You wanted to see the prison."

He hesitated, "But maybe we could go there another time. I'm

15

not really looking forward to it that much."

"Just come on, there's nothing to be scared of." I put an arm round his shoulders, and we went past the two patients.

"Good afternoon," they said politely.

"Dad, Dad," Benjamin was excited. "They know you!"

"No, they don't. They greeted me because they weren't sure I wasn't a doctor."

"No, Dad," Ben insisted, "I think they know you."

"How on earth could they know me?" I laughed.

"Because you used to come here to see your Mom."

I was pleasantly surprised how fast he had absorbed the information and even used it.

"Benjamin, when I started to visit Mom here, those two weren't even born. But that old lady," I pointed ahead on the pavement, "might already have been here back then." She was dragging herself along on swollen legs, but in fact, she wasn't necessarily that old. Just strangely rigid in her every movement, as if someone had trapped her soul in glass. I knew that kind of rigidity all too well and wondered about what it must be like to get stuck there. How much hidden pain it must involve for anyone whose longings, despite everything, were still directed outside, to the life he had lost. But then again, how much comfort and calm for anyone whose desires had already been compressed within this place forever. After all, what is ultimately so sad about hobbling along the asphalt paths here day after day, down avenues of leafy trees? Do we on the outside do anything more meaningful? It came to me then that my own longings were directed beyond the confines of my life. For years, I had never felt a sense of fulfilment. I had been living behind walls that I myself had built, and only now that my wife was dead, would I find out if I was really capable of leaving those walls behind.

We passed the church and utility buildings and made our way to the furthest part of the park. We passed the pavilion where my mother had often stayed as a patient. As a young boy, I had gotten this far once. Mom had been standing in the open door of a room, and some unpleasant woman had shouted, "He's ashamed, look how ashamed he is!" I couldn't understand why Mom wasn't coming with us, and why she would rather live here, in the company of such weird people.

"But Dad, there are bars on the windows there," Ben observed. "Is this the prison?"

"Not yet. The prison is right over there at the back."

As I spoke, a heartrending female shriek came from somewhere inside. It struck me that I probably shouldn't have brought him here at all.

"What's that?" He was startled, afraid.

"Although it's hard to imagine," I tried to explain the inexplicable, "having a sick mind means a lot of suffering. It hurts, maybe more than a leg or a stomach. It hurts in a different way that no one can imagine if they haven't experienced it for themselves. The bars are there so that someone like that can't hurt herself, maybe by jumping out."

"Did it hurt Grandma that much?"

I swallowed hard. "Definitely," I said. I knew that I had known only a tiny fraction of it. My mother must have suffered far more than I would ever be able to imagine. It was a real miracle that she had always managed to come back and live with us as if nothing had happened.

The prison pavilion turned out to have been closed long ago. The barbed wire had disappeared and the only reminder that convicted prisoners used to live here was the high wall around the yard. Benjamin and I turned around and headed for the exit. "Is that all?" he asked, disappointed.

It occurred to me that I could also show him the old hospital cemetery. It was about two kilometers away on the edge of the forest, high above the Vltava, and overgrown with ivy, quiet and deserted. Of course, I thought at once that it might not be a good thing to drag him to another cemetery today, but I had the feeling that the reverse might be true. When you have already met death, you shouldn't try and run away. "Not all," I said mysteriously.

"Are you going to show me something else?"

"Wait and see."

Before we reached the way out, I told him there had once been a pond here. The patients had caught fish in it and had grown rushes that they had then woven into baskets. It struck me as amazing that the park had a history like this and had witnessed so many human lives. How many other boys must have visited one of their parents back then, just like me? How many love stories had reached their last chapter here? Other hospitals didn't have this fateful character; people got there by chance or, at least, their illnesses had less of a clear relationship to their own selves. By contrast, it was oversensitive people—men and women whose perceptions were too sharp, and whose minds were too fragile to bear the emptiness of everyday life— who tended to end up here. The park was steeped in their souls.

We were back in the area between the church and the reception building. "So, what are you going to show me, then?" asked Benjamin.

"We'll drive just a little further." Now we were walking through the entrance hall. "See how nice and peaceful it is here," I told him, "But in a moment, outside, that will change."

Back in the car, I started to have doubts. The world of souls in pain was now behind us and there was no guarantee we would enter it again at the abandoned hospital cemetery. We had changed back into practical people, people of today.

"Can I watch the soccer game tonight?" Ben asked, as if confirming my thoughts.

I wasn't annoyed with him. He might have buried his Mom today, but that didn't mean the world stopped turning. I knew I would watch the game too. We both needed our dose of mass entertainment. It was everywhere, after all, and gave shape to the course of our existence: from qualifier to qualifier from championship to championship. "We'll watch the game tonight together," I said, "but first we're going to take a look somewhere else."

"I don't feel like going any place else today."

"But it's an interesting place. You'll see."

I drove to the furthest corner of the park and then up the opposite slope. Here there was a pleasant huddle of small houses, while high on the next hill the tower blocks of the projects loomed up incongruously. I parked by the stone wall of the former hospital garden and led Benjamin around an abandoned children's playground on a wooded bluff above the Vltava valley. The sun was already setting, and the twilight was gathering on the path below. Birds occasionally rustled in the thick spring undergrowth. They must have brought the coffins this way, I thought. The people who ended up in the hospital cemetery must have been the most abandoned of the abandoned, poor and nameless.

"A bit further on in the woods there's a small cemetery, where patients who died at the hospital were buried." I told Ben where we were going to stop him from being impatient.

"Can you die of a sick mind?" he wondered.

"I don't know. It wasn't necessarily the sick mind that killed them. Some patients just grew old here, and had no family, and so when they died, they were buried here. They might have just died of old age."

"Mom wasn't old, was she?"

"No, she wasn't. Mom was young."

"Not completely young, though," he corrected me, "More like somewhere in the middle."

"You're right. You put it nicely. In fact, that's what people call it. It's called *middle age*."

We went around a set of gardeners' allotments that had been laid out here in the last years of communism and had robbed the place of its sense of inviolable peace. Particularly on weekends, when the crazy gardeners had been enthusiastically digging beds to the sound of radios and cheery conversations, roasting sausages on fires, and shitting in the surrounding forest, all the sanctity that usually surrounds last resting places had been banished.

This evening, the allotments were empty of people. We could

already see the original cemetery wall. The cemetery was rectangular with two gates set opposite each other: one from the north and the other from the south. The gates had been locked for years, so the only option was to climb over. I lifted Ben up and set him on top of the wall and swung myself up beside him. In front of us was a twilit and initially unreadable expanse of complete silence, depth, and mysterious rest. "Where are the graves?" Benjamin asked.

"Can you see those almost invisible little mounds between the trees? They're overgrown with ivy and so hard to make out. The dead here didn't have tombstones. Just iron signs with numbers."

I dropped to the other side and saw him hesitate. "Maybe we'll find a sign or two," I said to tempt him.

"Seriously?" He jumped down into my arms.

My fear that we wouldn't be able to surrender ourselves a second time to that asylum atmosphere of sanctuary was unfounded. I knew of no other place where you had a better sense of what it meant to be abandoned. Nobody had wanted, or known, these dead, or waited for them. Relatives had stripped them of their property, if they had ever had any, and stripped them of their legal independence, and then consigned them to the furthest corners of their minds until in the end they had truly forgotten them. There must also have been people who had never had anyone in the first place, who had been found God knows where: lost, incapable, disabled. And here they all slept the sleep of the just, which must have been a relief to them. Nature had opened her embrace to them here—had accepted them for what they were.

We headed down a path to the left alongside the green ivy. "So you see, Benjamin, these people were sick, and on top of that, they had no one who loved them. We are never going to forget Mom. She's in our hearts; we'll carry her with us everywhere. She'll live with us."

In the evening we watched the soccer. The Czech Republic took an early one-to-zero lead, but in the end, lost two-to-one and was knocked out. We went to bed disappointed.

They Have to Live Together Every Day

In the days that followed, I felt like I was in a trap. Taking Benjamin to school in the morning, hurriedly dealing with some work stuff before picking him up in the early afternoon, then maybe going with him to his sports practice, helping him with his homework, and fitting in phone calls, washing dishes, even doing the laundry. What comes next? I asked myself. After a week, a year, ten years? I was afraid the everlasting round of tasks would swallow me whole. I would sink; I wouldn't even have time to stop for a moment and realize it was all sheer insanity. Although every day I reassured myself that I didn't actually have to work, and that we had enough money if not for the rest of our lives then at least until Benjamin left home, the work still kept piling up, and I couldn't bring myself to refuse it. My life was a crazy stampede in a circle, just like most people's lives.

In those first days, Benjamin became a lot less lively; maybe he sensed the pressure I was under. His eyes lost their penetrating spark; he slouched, and his head drooped between his shoulders. When he waved to me from the door of the cafeteria after school, he was no longer the old wild Ben I had known before, a boy full of curiosity and restlessness. Now he just quickened his pace a little when he saw me. There was no eager rush, no little jump or sign of joy that might have encouraged me in my self-delusion that things were as they ought to be.

One night when I was sitting by his bed, he caught my hand and gave me a searching look, as if afraid to ask me something important.

"What is it, Ben?" I encouraged him.

"Dad, if there's a God, will bad boys end up in Hell?"

I had been expecting something else completely, something to do with his mom. Now my first thought was that he'd probably misbehaved somehow. "I'm sure there's no Hell of the kind people used to imagine," I told him. "Even if God exists, that doesn't mean

21

there's a Hell with demons and torments for people who've been bad. Maybe Hell might mean something different, because there ought to be some justice, after all, and good and bad people shouldn't end up all the same. Maybe Hell might mean that the people who've been bad won't get to God after they die, and they'll be all alone, lost somewhere in the darkness with all the evil they've done. But that's not something you need to worry about. You definitely haven't done anything so awful that God would stop loving you for it."

"It's a pity that bad boys won't go to Hell," Ben grumbled.

I realized I'd probably gotten the wrong end of the stick. "And what have these boys done that's so bad you want them to end up in Hell?"

"They throw books at me, and they kick me, and they're always laughing at me."

It was like a knife in my heart. My fragile, darling Ben, whom I'd always wanted to protect from anything bad, was now the victim of bullies. Yes, I could well imagine it. Other boys his age were already cynical, talking and playing tough—about girls, movies, computer games, weapons. I wouldn't have encouraged softness in a boy, definitely not, but it wasn't my place to dictate his path in life, and I could see that he wasn't at all to blame. If he was thoughtful and sensitive, if he was holding on to his childhood world, if he was different in any way, it all meant that his peers would make him pay. It's only when you're an adult that you can get away with being different. As an adult, you can avoid a lot of trouble by choosing your path carefully. You don't have to accept the judgments of the crowd, or get involved with thugs, or pour out your heart to cynics. But even so, it's not easy, and few people can really manage it.

"They shouldn't do that," I said.

"I keep telling them they shouldn't."

"If they're really bullying you and doing it often, you'll have to tell your teacher," I advised.

"But I already told her. She said I shouldn't be a tattletale, and we kids should settle it among ourselves, and she wasn't going to tell us how we should behave to each other."

The stupid cow, I thought to myself. How well I knew that old fake egalitarian spirit, that "sort it out for yourselves, don't bother me with it" attitude. That kind of adult would never warm to a child with a problem and would never have the guts to face up to something she didn't know how to resolve. I knew what Ben was going through from my own childhood. At grade school, it had been hard for me to find a friend to spend school breaks with. On the other hand, with many years of hindsight, I had to admit I hadn't been a reliable friend myself. I had been pretty clever when it came to survival. I had known how to get in with various gangs and often avoided a beating by making sure that someone else—someone dumber and more helpless—took the fall. I had known how to butter up the teachers, too, and once, when I had tempted the bad boys in the class into holding a bigger boy's hand down on a burning hot radiator, nobody believed I could have been involved, not even the victim himself. Yes, I had been pretty clever. All the same, I had often been scared at school, mainly in the bathrooms and the locker rooms before PE.

So, what should I say now to my own dear son, who on top of the bullying had lost his mom? Should I tell him I had no way to protect him? That the dad he trusted so much didn't know how to deal with it? On the other hand, was I really supposed to come to the class and deal with it for him? Was I supposed to scare the brats off? Threaten to slap them so hard that not even their parents would recognize them? Provoke an endless round of payback?

"You know what, Benjamin, I'll go and talk to your teacher. She can't ignore me like she ignores you. Then she'll keep an eye on those boys."

He gratefully cuddled up to me, "Will you go there tomorrow, Dad?"

"Tomorrow I'll call your teacher and arrange a meeting with her."

"So, the day after tomorrow then?" he gave me an imploring

look.

"Most likely the day after tomorrow."

Two days later, I took Ben to his gym class and went back to the school for the meeting. The teacher was a tall woman of around fifty, with the air of a feminist. She assured me that she was aware of the problem and was making sure that the boys didn't hurt Ben—especially when he had suffered such a tragedy, she did not forget to add. I pointed out that it was important right now for Benjamin to feel supported and to believe in justice. She pretended to understand, but I sensed that she actually found the stronger tough boys appealing, because they already represented the masculine element, and she liked being their queen bee. Still, we parted on cordial terms. At that moment, there was nothing more I could do.

I still had an hour to burn before picking up Benjamin, and so I went for a walk. It was another pleasant day in May, with no suffocating heat, but not for the first time I was assailed by skeptical thoughts. I looked at the windows of the houses here and wondered whether the people behind them ever asked why they were alive. Surely everyone should remember that question every day and be conscious of it always hanging over them. I tried to tell myself I was being too abstract, and that ultimately what was important was every cooked supper, every loving act, kiss, or caress. But then I immediately countered my own argument with the thought that it might be that way if only a few hundred or a few thousand people were living on Earth, but when there were seven billion people… not even God could invent seven billion meaningful lives. At the same time, I was very conscious that I shouldn't communicate this skepticism to Benjamin, because children ought to grow up with the feeling that life has meaning and is beautiful.

After an hour, I went to get Ben from the practice field and immediately saw that he was somehow fed up. He blurted it out right away. "Dad, I don't want to come here anymore."

"What's the trouble?" I didn't understand. "What happened? You've always liked sports."

"It's too much work. It's no fun anymore."

That really made me mad, and I might have shouted at him if I hadn't remembered my own skeptical thoughts. So, there you are, I thought to myself—when push comes to shove, you're no skeptic, and it's irritating you that your son should be bored with something as absurd as practice.

"But do you think you'll get anywhere in life if you don't want to make an effort?" I said in a calmer voice. "In life you have to get past a lot of things that can seem like too much work: unpleasant, or pointless. But once you get past them—if you grit your teeth and keep going, then eventually you get the real reward. Because one of the best feelings a man can have in life is when he's satisfied with himself."

Internally I made a face at myself, thinking of all the objections that could be made to that statement, even though Benjamin would not be able to come up with them. But at the same time, I felt I was telling him something that was true, or that was good for him, and so valid. "Don't you want to make three meters in the long jump anymore?" I continued. "You used to want to jump three meters. Don't you want to now?"

"Yeah, I do. But we don't jump anyway. All we do is work out and run, run and do squats…"

"Do you think you're smarter than the coach? That you know better than he does? Haven't you realized that squats make your legs stronger and that's good for jumping?"

"I guess so," he agreed, without enthusiasm.

"But mainly, Benjamin, you need to realize that nothing in this world is free. Nothing important, anyway. And what comes free doesn't have value. If you could jump three meters right now, if any boy could jump it, what would be the value in jumping three meters?"

"You're probably right Dad," he said. "D'you think I'll be able to jump the three meters before the summer vacation?"

"I don't know, Ben. It's not for me to guarantee it. Only you can

25

do it. You've just got to persevere and be patient."

If anyone had said that to me, I thought, I would have told him to get lost. If I had really wanted to tell the truth, I would have had to tell Ben that his sports, just like every other entertainment, was just a way of driving away thoughts of the meaninglessness of our existence.

Dad Seeks out Physical Love

As the vacation approached, restlessness was getting the better of me. The grandfathers on both sides were calling almost every day, trying to get me to tell them what Benjamin was going to do, and when, and where. I was cagey. I still didn't have any clear idea myself, but one thing I knew: I wasn't going to stumble along under their supervision and with their help.

On one of the first days in June, I headed for the psychiatric hospital again, this time by myself. It was a weekday morning, and I had taken Benjamin to school. I took the metro and then a city bus in the opposite direction of rush hour traffic, so there were plenty of seats, and I sat comfortably by a window. I wondered what I actually expected from another visit to the place. What was I looking for there? I had no real answer. Maybe I was hoping for some kind of encouragement, inspiration. Maybe, somewhere inside, I was asking myself how I could live a life between walls, already built and impossible to climb. But while, for the patients, the hospital was surrounded by a wall they had already built around themselves, it actually gave me a sense of getting beyond my own walls. It stirred my soul with memories of childhood. These were memories of one ruined life, memories of helplessness, but now more recent memories of how Benjamin had been there with me.

I got off the bus by a concrete shopping center from communist times. The shops were not doing well and had no real chance of prospering. Apart from the supermarket, they had been changing—a boutique had become a bakery, a bakery into a betting stand, a betting stand into a furniture store. Those cheerless little stores in the middle of all that concrete only confirmed my lack of faith in the main pillar of our modern civilization, which is the production, sale, and consumption of unnecessary things. I was struck by the futile destiny of the retailer of unattractive chairs, which showed no trace

27

of art and had been designed and made without interest, without joy. I couldn't understand what anyone dependent on selling them could ever expect from life, and I was completely baffled to think that somebody would probably buy them. Those dusty chairs cast a grey shadow over the whole young day.

I walked around the former well, where a very pleasant little park area had been created. Only a few lime trees and thujas remained from the old times. The sun was rising through a clear sky; the day threatened to be sultry, summery. When I was a child, the conventional wisdom had been that, on such warm summer days, you just had to be by water at all costs—whether a swimming pool, a river, or just a muddy pond. Anyone who happened not to be by water inevitably felt out of step. Maybe communism was to blame for giving people so few creative possibilities. The trouble was that ever since then, such sunny days had made me uncomfortable. Somewhere inside it all was an insistence on consumption, like—hey you! Quick, finish whatever you're doing, throw on some suntan oil, grab a blanket, the wife and kids, and make sure that at least in the late afternoon you sink into something that can still be called water.

Today the hospital was busy. A lot of patients were on morning outings, in groups or individually. Doctors and nurses were hurrying between the pavilions. I set off in the opposite direction to the one I had taken last time. It was here that my mother had been housed in more recent years. I was waiting for the moment when I would calm down and would see whatever I had come for. But it never came. I realized there was nothing for me to find here today. I turned left, and left again, and returned to the entrance by the shortest possible route. I called my assistant to tell her I needed to meet with her that very morning.

We met in a cafe in the Old Town. "I'm probably going away with Benjamin for a time," I started.

She nodded approvingly, "I assumed you would."

"Why did you assume that?" I was surprised.

"Summer vacation is coming up. Whatever would you do with

the boy in Prague?"

It was my turn to nod now, although she hadn't quite understood what I meant. I had meant... But no, actually no. At the time it wasn't at all clear in my head. I wasn't thinking anything. Maybe I was starting to sense what it was I didn't want, but why upset my assistant with something that wasn't yet a fully formed decision? "I'll arrange standing orders for regular tax deductions and your salary," I said bluntly to get over the awkward moment. "And I'll also give you enough blank signed checks to pay the invoices. Those will just be the routine payments for services. In about two weeks, I'll give you more precise instructions."

She gave me a searching look. A certain excitement had raised her pulse. She was very capable, but also hungry for power, and I knew she wouldn't be averse to being in control for a while instead of me, even though it was just a small brokering firm with no permanent staff. The greed I had already noticed lurking behind her devotion to the firm, as well as the ugly eczema on her face, had been a perfect barrier to any non-professional relationship developing between us. It suited me that way. I was just a little worried that she might somehow financially abuse my absence. But I had two accounts and had craftily shifted most of the money from my business to my private account to ensure that she couldn't get an overview. She had access to the records for the business account but not the private account.

It was time to pick up Benjamin. In recent weeks he had stopped complaining that his classmates were hurting him but had once come home with a bruise under his eye. He claimed it was an accident, but offered a pretty unlikely explanation for it, which I couldn't even understand. I sensed that behind the walls of the school and the pretense that he was fine, he was going through something I probably couldn't enter into. He was fighting his own battle and facing his own suffering. I tried to give him opportunities to tell me about it and did so again now, in front of the school cafeteria, asking as if surprised, "Has something happened to you? You look upset."

But he shook his head, "No Dad. I'm not upset."

He didn't even like going to his sports team anymore. For a while he made an effort, and once wanted me to go with him to the field to measure his performance in the long jump, but otherwise he showed no enthusiasm. I was starting to have serious doubts about my ability to bring him up effectively. Maybe I was too much of a skeptic to motivate him. Maybe he somehow sensed my detached view of everyday human efforts, and though in my case it was just a philosophical attitude that didn't prevent me taking pleasure in life, in his case there was a risk it might lead to indifference to everything, to total apathy.

We walked home, and I knew he was experiencing something unpleasant that he wouldn't tell me about, and that this inexpressible experience might divide us in the future.

"Dad…" he started, back home on the stairs, but didn't continue.

"What is it?"

"Dad, do I have to go back to school in September?"

Aha, I thought. Now maybe I'll learn something. "Why are you asking? Are you scared of something at school?"

"No, I'm not," he answered irritably. "I'm just asking if I'm going to have to go back there when I don't like it? It's no fun."

"Benjamin, everyone has to go to school. Without school, you'd stay ignorant. You wouldn't know anything, and you wouldn't be able to do anything. And you wouldn't be happy."

"Yes, I would, Dad. I'd be happy."

"But what would you do all day if you didn't go to school? And what would you do when you grow up?"

"I'd help you with everything. And I'd play, I'd go shopping…"

"But Benjamin, you can't really believe you'd enjoy it, just playing. Don't forget that in the meantime the other children would be at school. I'd have to work, and you would be alone most of the time. And what happens when you grow up? You'll want to achieve something. Believe me, Benjamin, you simply have no clue. When you're grown up, it won't even occur to you to want to help me in my work. You'll have your own work."

Inside the apartment, I had already removed almost all traces of her, but it was obvious we couldn't go on living here in the long term. I had started to look around for another place, but I still had no clear vision of our future, and so my interest in buying another place was only sporadic.

On the other hand, I was starting to feel the lack of sex. Not that my marriage had brought me sexual enjoyment. Absolutely not. I had been secretly buying physical love for years. In the first days after her death, my sex fantasies had retreated into the background, but now that burning desire was making itself felt again. I started imagining all kinds of exciting scenarios, but instead of getting any relief from them, they just stirred me up even more. Now, I was seeing almost every woman as a sex object, and it even started to get in the way of my business negotiations. My only thought was when, where, and how I would fuck that woman. I bought a small classifieds magazine and read through the ads for prostitutes. But, of course, I was aware of my responsibility for Benjamin. Every meeting with a prostitute always made me afraid of trouble. What if it got me mixed up with blackmailers or gangsters? What if someone filmed me or even killed me?

In the end, I found an ad from a girl called Gabriela. I had already been with her and remembered her as a young woman who had managed to retain her individuality. She had even seemed to like her work—to enjoy it. In the past, I had left her place with a pleasant sense of fulfillment.

The very next day I arranged to go to her apartment on a busy Prague street. She welcomed me warmly and even remembered me. She escorted me to the shower and offered to shower with me. Compared to the ideal, she had a slightly sagging ass and her breasts weren't out of the magazines either. In the shower, we gently felt each other up, and she asked about my wife—whether she was still so depressive and difficult. I told her about the car crash, and she was at a loss for words. She might have suspected that my wife's death had been a relief for me, but she would never have had the nerve to say so.

"What about children?" she asked, "Do you have children?"

I boasted about caring for an eight-year-old boy and felt her sympathy. Our sex was passionate then; gentle and wild, almost genuine. She didn't hurry things as most of the girls did, and when I had climaxed, she aroused me again after a few minutes. I was unimaginably turned on. We made love for more than an hour. And she wasn't even expensive. I saw it as a kind of solution.

A week later, I visited her again. I asked her what she wanted from life, and she said she had a boyfriend who knew about her work and wasn't bothered by it. I thought he couldn't care for her much if that was the case. She told me she could easily find other work in childcare or as a nurse, but that the money wasn't enough. She wanted the security of always being able to buy what she needed, and so peace of mind. I hinted that I already had enough for that kind of peace of mind, but that so far, I didn't know what to do with it. I couldn't deal with that meaningless everyday banality—the way everyone lies, and pretends that what they are doing is something meaningful, and forgets that it isn't and could never be an answer to the really fundamental question—the question of why we are in the world at all and how we can fulfill our lives in an era when we're not struggling just to survive, because this civilization is based on people wanting more and more. Gabriela didn't seem to understand but asked with a smile if I had anything against just having a good time this morning. As soon as she said that, I got hard and we went for it enthusiastically, at an hour when most people had to be at work. In the end, we lay beside each other, dripping with sweat, and a friendship had started to grow between us.

I called again after another week; it was already June, and unbearably hot days bore down on the city. She didn't pick up; I told myself she must have gone out for a while. When she hadn't picked up for four days in a row, I went to her apartment. I slipped into the building with a man walking a dog, and upstairs I was puzzled to find that her name card was gone from her door. It had been replaced by one that read, "Dr. Dudek, Attorney." I rang the bell and my heart thumped in my chest.

A huge man opened the door. "What you want?" he asked gruffly, with an eastern accent.

"I'm looking for Gabriela," I mumbled quietly.

"Gabriela? No one with that name here," he said, and slammed the door. I stood there alone, helpless.

I tentatively called another few times, but I knew it was no good, and that I wouldn't see Gabriela again. Maybe she had decided to live with her boyfriend; or was the big man her boyfriend? She wasn't cut out for prostitution anyway—she was too kind and personal. Although I tried to explain away her absence in this way, I couldn't entirely shake off my fears for her. What if she was in the hands of pimps, and they had killed her or sent her God knows where?

A Son Misses His Mom

So the days went by. One evening, Benjamin snuggled up to me when I was wishing him goodnight.

"I miss her."

Actually, I had been expecting it. I knew it had to come, and been surprised it had taken so long. Whatever his mother's problems, she had loved him and given him maternal love. I lay down next to him on the bed and stroked his hair. "I know, Benjamin, I know."

"Couldn't I see her for just a little while? Just a minute?"

I shook my head sorrowfully. "When someone dies, sadly, it's forever. There's nothing anyone can do about it. I mean, we people can't do anything. Maybe God could…"

"Could God arrange for me to see Mom again for a minute?" Ben brightened.

"Even if God existed, he wouldn't—"

"I know God exists," he interrupted. "I know it."

"But not even God would change the laws of nature," I told him. "And one of those laws is that we all only live once, and death ends our lives on earth forever."

"But I need to tell Mom something."

Oh, I understood him, all right. He used to talk to her every day, boasting about his successes, confiding when something hurt, when he felt sick. Every single day must be full of moments when he wanted to tell her something. "You know what? You talk to her. You could whisper to her under the covers, or somewhere you're alone, or you could write to her and mail the letter on the water, or we'll take it to Mom's grave together."

"Will she read the letter?"

"Well not directly, like we read letters. But she'll be with you when you write it, because her soul is definitely everywhere that you are…And what do you actually want to tell her?"

"I'm probably going to get an "A" in Czech. That's what I wanted to tell her. My teacher praised me and said I've improved."

"It's nice that you want to tell Mom that, but why not tell me as well?" I smiled. "I'd be pretty happy to hear a piece of good news like that." I stood up.

"Wait, Dad," he held out his hand, caught my sleeve and pulled me back. "Stay a little longer with me."

"It's late and you have school tomorrow. You need to go to sleep now."

A month had passed since her death, and we went to visit her grave. Once again, I parked in the shade under the chestnut trees, and once again we set off for the small cemetery. Beneath us the city roared, but I was moving out of it in my mind. I had been born in Prague and attended school here, but the city of my childhood was gone forever. Today it was becoming a modern European city; more and more houses had been renovated, and the atmosphere of communist times lingered only in the aging prefab housing projects. The project where I had lived with my parents as a boy now seemed to me desperately grey: all those badly fitting windows, cracked panels, and behind the facades the greyness of thousands of identical flats. The children's playground was desolate. The children had disappeared as the inhabitants of the houses grew old, and today there was no one here to play. As a child, I had felt fine there; all of us had been pleased to be able to live right here. We hadn't known it, but the way we saw the world back then was very limited. Communism had permeated our minds and didn't allow us anything more—ambitious demands or even fantasies. It was enough that there was running water, that the toilet flushed, that the heating worked, and we were grateful. Especially the grandparents, who were part of a whole generation that had come from rural poverty and saw it as a real step up. They didn't notice that they were no longer masters of their own destinies in this communist would-be affluence and had allowed themselves to be robbed of the most important things that made their lives unique. They didn't want to hear about the progress of the free Europe, that was also dealing with poverty and discomfort, but doing so naturally and freely. All the same, in the housing project of my childhood, where I spent most of my time outside in the playgrounds with plenty of boys of my age, in all kinds of cliques and groups, with hockey sticks and sometimes skates in winter, and with balls and tennis racquets in summer…I had been happy.

The little hill with the cemetery on it was one of those places where time had stood still. There had been no bold innovations here, and there were big old trees that linked each new day with the pre-communist past. But at the same time, it was not a historically appealing place, fortunately. Prague attracts hundreds of thousands of tourists, who get high on history and the city's famously unique atmosphere, as packaged and sold on every corner. I had never really felt it, or perhaps only as a student, coming back slightly drunk through the deserted streets of the Old Town. Yes, back then there was an atmosphere—back when a trumpeter might play long into the night on the Charles Bridge even though nothing like that was officially allowed, and so it was a secret shared by the listeners. Today harmonica players, trombonists, and violinists play there openly, not for that wonderful reason, but to entertain tourists. Despite its reputation, Prague had nothing to say to me. I had no reason to live here.

We passed through the gate on the path between the graves. Benjamin ran ahead. In his hand, he held a flower and several letters, and as he ran with them—with such unaffected sincerity—I was so moved that the tears sprang to my eyes. My beloved unhappy Benjamin.

I approached the fresh gravestone as he was already bending down and tucking in the letters. "Dad, Dad, look, Mom's name is on the stone! How come someone's carved it there like that?"

"Because I told the stonemasons to do it. I ordered this stone from them."

"But Mom won't hear me if she's under the stone."

"But she's not under the stone. Remember how I told you that

36

her soul is wherever you are? Do you want me to leave you alone here for a while?"

"But where would you go, Dad?"

"Don't worry, nowhere far. I'll just take a walk around the cemetery."

"All right then. I'll run and catch up with you."

I was still finding it hard to hold back tears. I was all too conscious of my beloved Benjamin as a boy who had lost his mom and all too aware that everything was temporary, ephemeral. It was borne in on me that I wouldn't be here forever, and even Ben wouldn't be here forever, and not even a father's love could hold out against eternity. I longed to embrace Benjamin, take him away from the cemetery and from this city—somewhere clean and tranquil, where we would walk over grassy hills, close to the clouds in the sky. Close to God, in whom he believed because nothing else was left to him, and in whom in fleeting moments I had also believed, when I thought of my Ben as a child whom God would love and protect.

I walked slowly beside the cemetery wall and, after a moment, he caught up with me. "Dad, we've got to go now."

He seemed to have done what he wanted to do and now needed to get away fast. "D'you know what I think?" I said. "I think that you and I ought to go off somewhere—to the back of beyond. Just as soon as the holidays begin." (Later I often wondered why I had put it like that, "the back of beyond," when I could have just said we would take a long trip. But I liked it. There was something mysterious about it.)

"Okay, Dad." He looked eager, but then he frowned, "But we have to tell Mom."

"All right. Let's tell her." We went back to the grave. This time I concentrated my thoughts mainly on her, telling her wordlessly that I would be going away with Benjamin for a time, although I didn't yet precisely know where and for how long. I promised her I would protect him.

Ben gave me a questioning glance, waiting to see what would

happen. And when I was silent, he said, "So I'll tell Mom, okay?"

"Tell her."

"So, Mom," he began, as if he was really announcing an important, surprising thing, "Dad and I have decided," he looked at me to make sure it still applied, "to go somewhere together far away. Will we be going to the sea too, Dad?"

I shrugged. I didn't know myself. "Maybe to the sea, maybe the mountains…I don't know yet."

As I said it, I realized that I didn't want to go anywhere if it was just going to a normal tourist thing. It had to be different. We would start off and then we would see.

Relatives Try to Talk Them Out of the Journey

The next day, I met with my assistant. She could hardly contain her excitement, masking it with a show of eagerness to please: off you go, boys, and don't worry about a thing. I warned her that I didn't know myself yet how long we would be gone. Maybe we would be back in a few weeks, but it could turn out to be longer. I wanted to leave secure in the knowledge that there was nothing that I would need to come back for. I described everything in detail and gave her a four-page plan setting out what she should do in various situations that might arise.

"So, I'll be having to take care of absolutely everything," she said craftily, "That's going to be a lot more work than usual."

I said nothing, and so she continued. "What will I get for that?"

I disliked anyone trying to push me. I preferred giving of my own free will rather than having someone make demands. "I'll make sure you're properly remunerated later."

"Later is later," she laughed, having obviously worked all this out in advance and calculating that now, two weeks before the vacation began, she was irreplaceable. "But to have some security, and to motivate me to up my game so you can have some peace of mind, I think you should give me a fifty-percent raise for the time you're away. If you're satisfied when you get back, then maybe more."

I had reckoned with thirty percent but her fifty percent annoyed me, especially with her pretense that there was nothing she wouldn't do for me. But I had no choice. "I suggest a thirty percent raise now and twenty later, when you've shown you can cope."

"I was thinking that then I might get a special bonus." But she saw the disgust in my face and hastily added, "No, it's fine, really.

We'll do as you suggest. I'm sure you'll give me that bonus when you see the results."

My biggest problem, much bigger than my assistant and her demands, was the relatives. The grandads and grandma called almost every day. Benjamin had boasted to them that we were going to the "back of beyond," and it stirred up a storm. "First you keep the funeral a secret from us and now you're taking our only grandchild away?" blustered her father. "We thought he'd be spending at least a week of his vacation with us. And what does this "back of beyond" business mean, anyway? What's it all about?"

"I never thought you'd behave like this," her mother added, "We were mistaken about you, that's for sure," and started sobbing into the telephone. "Now I guess all we can do is die."

My father was more sophisticated. "I've thought about it, but in my view, it would be an error for you to go anywhere with him this year. He should stay here, calm down. You know you can count on me to help with him. I could take him for week."

My mother was the only one to leave me alone. She had been back in the Bohnice mental hospital for the last couple of weeks.

It wasn't that I didn't understand the grandparents. They had invested all their hopes in Benjamin. He was their one and only, admired and loved. If they had wanted to be with him for his sake, and not their own, I would have been more patient with them. Only it was all too obvious that concern about their own genes, their line, was behind their interest. Of course, I too loved my son because he was my son. Every day reminded me again how special and irreplaceable it was—the feeling of having someone like that. But I never forgot that it didn't make me immortal. In the third and fourth generations, my genes would be watered down, and one day not a single person who had met me, or a single person in whose memory I had left a trace, would be walking the earth. My life had to take its course here and now, and if I messed up, I wouldn't get another chance. Sympathy whispered in my ear that I should let the grandads have their time with their grandson, but I knew that I couldn't and mustn't suppress my need and longing to leave because of them. This time I wasn't going to be the slave of sympathy, and I was going to do what I was convinced was best for Benjamin and me. Even if it meant hurting someone.

Father and Son Get Ready to Leave Despite All the Doubts

The last week of school began. The heat receded and the long-expected rain arrived. I opened all the windows and aired the apartment. The scent of raindrops and steaming streets wafted in. In the last month, I had hardly done any cleaning and tidying; the place wasn't fit to live in. And now we had started to put together piles of stuff for the journey, me in the living room and Ben in his bedroom. I gathered sleeping bags, a tent, and camping gear even though I still had no clear idea of where I would go. I began to have doubts about myself again. On the journey, I would be with Ben all day every day, and here I was getting bored just playing *halma* with him. Would I be up to keeping him entertained the whole time? And wouldn't I eventually get annoyed with his constant interest and presence? But Ben's eagerness dispelled my doubts. He was always running up to me with a new suggestion. "Dad, Dad, what about goggles for the sea?" I shrugged, "I haven't promised you the sea. I'm not saying we're going to the sea, and I'm not saying we're not going. But you can take the goggles."

I tried to endow our departure with some deeper dimension—to make it more than just the ordinary beginning of the vacation. And so, I wrote him a letter: "Dear Benjamin: This is a ceremonial announcement that you have been chosen for a great and difficult task. You have to set off with Dad for the Back of Beyond. Where we are going in the Back of Beyond nobody knows for sure. You can gaze into the misty distances, but it is possible that the Back of Beyond is quite close and is all around us. Come with Dad on the journey, dear Benjamin, and you will see." I used a match to singe the letter along the sides and put it under Ben's pillow one night. In the morning he flew into my room crazy with excitement. "Dad, Dad! I got a letter. D'you know who wrote to me? Look, it's all scorched."

Friday was the last day of school, the day when report cards were handed out. I excused Ben from school until then and sent him to the grandads for two days. One of them was supposed to pass him on to the other. When I was driving him to my father-in-law's out of Prague on the Wednesday, I was overcome with breathless anticipation. I had felt the same eagerness once, long ago, when I had still been living with my parents and had invited a girl to stay one time when they were away. On the drive back, my excitement only increased. I was looking at forty hours of freedom and I wanted to exploit it, whatever the cost.

First, I considered my old girlfriends and lovers. Only one of them, my old love Petra, still had a place in my heart. Actually, she had never left it. When we met, she was married, which is why it didn't work out. Later, she divorced— but although we loved each other, she only wanted to be friends. I was already married by that time anyway. Now the situation had changed, but I knew she wouldn't change her mind. So, I dug a two-week-old classifieds out of the trash. Compared to the difficult and often painful creation of a relationship, the ads had one indisputable advantage: whatever I chose, I could have today.

I tore out five ads offering threesomes. A soft female voice answered the first number I tried. "Yes, of course there can be two of us," she said, as if she had been in the middle of meditation. "Both at once? Sure, just as you like."

I wrote down her directions and the code on the doorbell. "I'll definitely be there," I assured her.

"Come over, no problem," she said, as if she really didn't care in the slightest. I was sure that a lot of men got their rocks off just by arranging a meeting and then never turned up. I guessed she reckoned with that.

Pleasantly aroused, I still had time to stop by the bank, where two weeks before, I had arranged to have my private account divided in two and ordered another bank card. On the way back, I felt so contented that I couldn't help asking myself if I wasn't a bit of a pig. After all, everybody at least pretended to think that prostitution was something dirty, so what did that make men who had sex with prostitutes? It was just that my body needed physical love. It needed it and didn't ask whether I happened to have a lover or a wife, and if I was with someone or alone. Of course, deep inside, I too had an unfulfilled ideal of reciprocal harmony in love, but fate had made me first an unsatisfied husband and now a lonely widower—and all in my best years, when I still had strength and an appetite. Despite all my wish for penitence, I couldn't find it in myself to condemn my need. (The Old Testament heroes were encouraging in this respect, for unlike the New Testament ones, they had their needs, but were loved by God even so). The moralizers tend to be the ones that jack off bent over in the toilet or can't get it up.

At one o'clock, I rang a bell with no nameplate by the door of a shabby apartment block. A curvaceous woman with a sleepy look came to open it, and I was sure she was the woman I had spoken with on the phone. She quietly greeted me and led me down some stairs. For a moment I was gripped by alarm, remembering my beloved Benjamin. I would probably be wise to leave. The woman sensed my hesitation and turned back to me with friendly eyes. "This used to be the cellar, but we've got it fixed up very nicely." Her tone reassured me. I followed her down into a small basement apartment. What came next was familiar: a quick consultation on what I wanted, payment in advance, a shower. The other woman was a young girl with a charming ass, and the first woman set her up for me beautifully. They saw that I wasn't experienced and put me at my ease. In an hour, I managed it with both of them. The girl just did as she was told, and was really only a kind of mannequin, but the creative element was the older woman. There was something very tranquil and steady about her. In the end, she let me take her the normal way, from in front, stroking my back and hair to encourage me, to spur me on. She knew how to give men what they had lost long ago and mostly didn't even know they were missing: a maternal embrace.

At three o'clock, I was walking down the wet streets of Vršovice feeling self-confident and relaxed. I was now savoring every step and looking to the future without fears. I stopped at the edge of a small park with a few benches and a sandpit. There were still drops of water on the branches from the morning rain, but a child of about three was already playing in the sandpit. His mother stood at the edge. I knew nothing about her family, nothing about the contents of her life, or her thoughts. Maybe a man was happy with her, made love to her each night, and had plans to save for a new television. It was so banal that it made a lot of sense. The trouble was that this kind of life had somehow passed me by, and maybe my constant tendency to dwell on its futility just showed my frustrated desire to live that way, to conform. I was also a little sad to be setting off on a journey without having a permanent place to which I could return. It suited me that it should be that way—that the place would be the journey itself and my love for Benjamin on that journey, and his trust in my wisdom and ability to protect him. But on the other hand, I was afraid of this departure to the Back of Beyond. Yes, here in this little city park on a slope between houses, I realized I had formulated it correctly to Ben that time: we weren't going somewhere far from home, and we weren't going somewhere near home. We were off to the place you go when you have no fixed point to go back to, and no faith to light your way; when you have nowhere you can call home.

I bought nonperishable groceries for the first few days: powdered soup, powdered drinks, biscuits and sweets, but it was only for form's sake, since I knew it would be easy enough to get anything along the way. It was still only the afternoon of first of my two days of freedom, and so I also bought two bottles of French wine and called a friend to invite him to come and drink them with me. We met in a park by the river, a place where we used to drink as students, but back then, it was the cheapest fruit wine. The water below the falls smelled the same, although the Vltava was in fact cleaner than before. We had to laugh at how much the surroundings had changed since our student days, and how our lives had changed and how our possibilities had multiplied, but how little had changed inside us. The evening was warm, if wet, and we started back in high spirits. Before he got on the tram going in his direction, I almost told him that many years before, I had wanted to lure him into sex with me. It was a time when I hadn't scored for around half a year and he hadn't scored for even longer, and I wanted to experiment. But in the end, I didn't have the nerve, and I didn't mention it now either. I also said nothing about the planned journey. I didn't know how to explain my intention to him, and in fact there was nothing to explain. I only said I was leaving Saturday.

I woke up Thursday morning with no more than a mild hangover, but into a different, utterly stifling world. I lay helplessly in bed, and the mere idea of having to sit up, get on my feet, and go to the bathroom filled me with despair. I knew this reaction very well: a revenge on me for the optimism of the previous evening. Sometimes, the better my mood was one day, the harder it was the next day for me to even think of getting up and walking, the simplest human tasks. And today I had one more important task—to bring the car in for service before the journey.

After long minutes of hesitation, I pulled myself up and managed at least to sit on the edge of the bed. Everything I had lived through with Benjamin's mother, the good and the bad, seemed to be streaming past me and setting off a nostalgia for a time that was already vanishing, because the possibility of repairing our relationship and restoring its original innocence was finally gone. After twenty minutes or so, I staggered into the kitchen and the feeling of impotence started to dissipate. I managed a normal breakfast and got into the car without much sense of hope or curiosity but also without the complete feeling of being walled in that might have led to my failure to go anywhere with Ben. I spent the day on a series of little errands: buying maps, medicines, playing cards, getting the car serviced, packing. It all seemed to take longer than usual, but I got through it. And in the afternoon, I started to look forward to Benjamin's return.

He came in with my father, who seemed excessively cheerful, and immediately threw himself at me: "Hey Dad, I've had a great idea. We could call Grandpa from somewhere, and he would come and join us."

"We'll have to wait and see," I said evasively. This was not the right moment to upset him, but I was grinding my teeth that Grandpa had managed to undermine the sacred feeling about our departure and turn it into an ordinary holiday prospect.

"But Dad, we could do that, couldn't we?" Ben didn't understand my discomfort.

"Now isn't the moment to discuss it!" I raised my voice. And quietly, so that Grandpa couldn't hear, I whispered in his ear: "People can't come and join us in the Back of Beyond. Don't you know that?"

The next day, I was waiting outside the school at ten in the morning. Benjamin ran out the door and up to me so fast that his hair was streaming behind him. I was his father, his everything. And I was grateful for that role.

Chapter II

The Journey Leads First Along Asphalt Roads

Father and Son Find Lodgings in the Czech Borderland

What words can I use to convey how nothing special happened that day? How can I express the ordinariness of our departure? We put as much luggage in the car as we could fit. Benjamin waited down in the street while I closed the windows and locked the apartment, and then I sat down at the wheel and started the car. Vacation wasn't only starting for us, and there were big columns of cars trying to get out of Prague.

Benjamin sat in the back seat unusually silent and didn't speak until we had been on the road for half an hour, and as if he had just woken up from a dream. "Dad, will we get to the Back of Beyond tomorrow?"

"I don't know. Maybe we're already there," I said.

"Here?" He was puzzled, "But we still know where we are, here."

"Yes, but nobody else knows we're here at the moment. And nobody knows where we're heading. And so, actually, we're already off the radar, we're in the Beyond. D'you see?"

He nodded, but he probably had his doubts. I wasn't even convinced by my own words. Although I was pretending that I didn't know where I was going, in fact, I had chosen quite a luxury hotel in the Šumava Forest on the Czech-Austrian border as our destination for the day.

And so, I could only guess whether this was the beginning of something new, liberating, a voyage of discovery; so far, it didn't seem to be. Only later would it turn out that the first step was really followed by a second, a third, a hundredth, and that I had never made a more fateful decision in my life.

That day, the clouds finally broke up, and after a week of rain, the sun was beating down on the overcrowded highway. Cleansed, the landscape was radiant in green and gold, but a rising mist still obscured the view in the distance. In any case, it was a sick landscape, spoiled by the omnipresence of human beings. Only after we had been on the road for two hours, and reached the foothills of the Šumava Forest, did the ratio of land to civilization even up. The little country churches on the hilltops and the isolated farms and mills brought back memories of the time when this was a poor region, and people had to sweat to make a living. But even here, we could see concrete factory halls on the edges of small towns and on the slopes above the town squares, and instead of avenues of trees, there were prefabricated tower blocks. This was the lasting, coarse impact of the communist form of civilization, which had swept away poverty and affluence, uprooted love for work, and created a suffocating equality. I comforted myself with the thought that maybe in a century or two these wounds would heal but immediately fell back into the darkest skepticism, asking myself what humanity could possibly be like after two centuries, when it was behaving with so little restraint and growth was so rapid and unstoppable.

The rather small hotel stood on the upper slope of a hill where the highest part of the range started. The slope was not dramatic but formed a kind of dividing line, offering a view far into the hills. I parked on a flat area in front of the recently renovated hotel. As a small boy of around Benjamin's age, I had been here for a few days on holiday with my parents. Back then, there had been no ensuite toilets and showers in the rooms, only basins. We had arrived by bus and the road had ended at the hotel. The virgin Šumava had stretched beyond it, with its deep forests and treacherous bogs but also its strictly guarded border zone. Beyond the hill was a forbidden world and anyone approaching—even within ten kilometers—had been the object of suspicion. These days we breathed more freely here, but the greater part of the forest around the hotel had fallen victim to ski lifts, and all the way up the slope, there were small but disruptive buildings.

We found our small, comfortable room with a shower and television and carried up some of our things from the car. "Dad,

Dad! What do you want to do here?" Ben pestered me.

"What do you think we'll do? We'll go on trips. There are lots of woods and streams here…" I saw this answer wasn't satisfying him, so I added, "And maybe we'll rent bikes and go somewhere on them."

"Yeah, bikes!" he cried, delighted, "I want to go biking right away." I persuaded him to be patient and wait until tomorrow for the bike ride. But I realized yet again how unrewarding and perhaps even harmful it could be if I were the only company he had. Maybe I would have done better to send him to summer camp.

From my childhood, I remembered that behind the hotel there was a narrow track leading into the woods. Beside it, there had been huge anthills, bigger than me as I was then. We set out in that direction. We crossed the ski run, and I was gripped by excitement, wondering if the anthills would still be there. I was experiencing a strange mixture of emotions and emerging memories, when just recently I would have thought that only old people had these feelings. At the same time, I realized that this persistence of things and events, which is so calming and scares death away by setting the order of the surrounding world above the life of the individual, was once taken for granted. The same pastures, the same shrine, the same cemetery, whole generations walking to church along the same avenue of trees. Until the last hundred years, when we had started to change everything at breakneck speed, making it almost impossible for us to leave any traces of ourselves behind. Our civilization will close over us as fast as foaming rapids swallow a stone, whereas before, our lives would have fallen into the quiet waters of a lake, where the play of ripples and circles could still be observed for years and decades.

It turned out that the anthills had probably been in the part of the woods felled to make way for the ski-run. We found only a single small hill and so I couldn't say to Ben, "Look, those are the anthills I admired myself when I was small" but had to tell him, "So you see how things have changed; what was once here has gone."

At supper, I took a look at the rest of the hotel guests. Probably because of the high prices, there were no ordinary Czech hikers here, no families with children, but at most some rich retired people with grandchildren. They were all dressed as if for the city and had apparently been circulating between the bar, their rooms, the restaurant, and the gaming room all day. Russians predominated—not the old, unvarnished Soviet kind on a group package tour, but the cultivated new middle class. They were duly uptight and haughty, but just a little bewildered. Who knows what Russian travel agency had recommended this place to them, when the countryside didn't interest them? During that long Bolshevik era, they had lost their feeling for natural things, and now they were rushing out into the big, wide world with borrowed manners, rich but not wise. Apart from the Russians, there were three older Austrian or German couples and some young over-dressed Czech friends of the waiters and receptionists. There was no hope of finding a friend for Benjamin here. It was completely obvious that he was going to be totally dependent on me here.

When we were returning to the bedroom, the receptionist looked up from her makeup and nail polish and regarded me with sympathy and perhaps even interest. She had a promisingly prominent bust.

The next day we rented bicycles. Away from the hotel on the forest paths and narrow mountain roads, we finally encountered normal people—whole groups of cycle tourists and only occasionally someone on foot—and we felt the refreshment of the vacation on our faces. Some of the children's high spirits seemed to have been passed on to the adults. In the afternoon, however, the weather took a rapid turn for the worse, with clouds descending and a cold wind starting to blow. Soon our hands were chilly on the handlebars, and we had to go back. By the time we reached the hotel, there was a heavy drizzle.

We had a quick meal and went back to our room where I took out the chess set, but Benjamin found it too hard. "If it's just going to go on raining here, Dad," he said, "there's no reason for us to stay."

"You're right, no reason at all," I agreed, "But I don't feel like packing up again so soon."

"Do you actually like being here with me?" He asked all of a sudden, with unexpected insight. I was disconcerted but pleased, because it showed that he was starting to be able to see with more than just a child's eyes and compare us on equal terms.

I couldn't lie to him, and so I gave him a warm hug. "You know what, Ben, sometimes a grownup can get a little bored for a moment being with a kid, but that doesn't remotely mean I'm not glad to be with you, or I don't like being with you. It's not always easy for me, being with you, but don't worry about it, because at the same time I can't imagine anything better for me than being with you. Having you as a son, being able to be with you and bring you up a little— that's what makes me happiest in life."

He gratefully curled up beside me, and I felt the warmest emotion flowing through his clothing into me. "I'm not bored being with you at all, Dad," he said, childish once again, "It's fun being with you."

Although the weather remained changeable and rather cold, we had some pretty pleasant days in the Šumava. Admittedly all we were doing was vacationing and so something quite different from what I had wanted, but at least I was free of the kind of tension that afflicted me in Prague. Around us was the cool Šumava countryside, and I felt on firm ground here as a Czech citizen in a Bohemia I knew well. In fact, this was a place where I was finally able to gather some strength for the coming journey. But I often found myself thinking how comfortable our era was, and how we were literally devouring everything, licking all the cream off the top, enjoying all of this prosperity, these possibilities undreamed of earlier, and even a lasting peace, getting fat, travelling, and consuming far more than Planet Earth could afford. It was as if history had reached its peak with us—just a few generations of unbounded hedonists—before we would destroy everything and this dream of ours would collapse with our great-great-grandchildren.

Each day I passed the young receptionist several times, and we always greeted each other pleasantly. I indulged in a small fantasy in which I would stop by her desk late at night. She would smile sympathetically, ask if my son was asleep yet, and then lead me into her little room. She would tell me that, when she eventually had a husband, she would want him to be the same kind of father as I was, and then she would let me come up to her from behind and cup her superb tits in my hands. I would take off her suit and under it she would be wearing the latest thong, and her whole young body would be exquisitely supple. I would take the middle string of the thong and run it between her buttocks and thighs—delicately and patiently, until she took off her panties and offered me her soft, moist womanhood.

As it happened, one of my pubertal experiences was associated with the Šumava. I had been here with two classmates at some gathering. We had been just fifteen or so, and at one forest pond—where we had gone despite being told it was off limits by the leaders—I suggested that we should go skinny dipping. At the time, all three of us had regarded a thing as natural as nakedness as the most closely guarded taboo. Even before I stripped, I was indescribably aroused by a burning inextinguishable lust that had not yet known a real climax. My red penis, still immature and rather strange to me, stiffened, and the same happened to the others. And so, we each hurried to a different part of the pond, where the water hardly came up to our waists, and we were choking with excitement. This experience, all that desire, has stayed in me forever. I still shivered at the memory even now and it lent the Šumava a touch of adventure for me.

On the fifth day, there was a change of receptionists. A different young girl was sitting at the desk, not as full-breasted but just as kind and courteous. All the same, I felt that our time at the hotel was up. We had become too used to it here, and if I didn't make a decision now, I might never make it. After all, life was peaceful here. I would send Benjamin out for the newspaper in the morning, idly page through it after breakfast, and then look at a map and decide on the destination for the day's trip. I would take a rest in the afternoon after our return and let Ben run around the nearby meadows on his own. Of course, staying here had its less-appealing aspects: I couldn't bring myself to turn off my cell phone, and someone was always calling me, including the parents, and these conversations were holding me back.

"Tomorrow we'll have one more trip," I told Ben at supper on Thursday, "and then we'll take off early the day after tomorrow."

He was twitching with excitement, but he was scared too: "The day after tomorrow? Already?"

"Do you think we haven't been here long enough?" I asked, "I didn't think we'd stay so long. Or don't you want to go to the Back of Beyond?"

"But you said that the Back of Beyond could be anywhere—even here," he answered promptly, and I could only agree. "You're right. Only we mustn't hang around here too long. Somebody might find us here. The grandfathers are calling us here…"

We packed the next evening. I tried to wash some of our underwear. Benjamin was in an anxious mood, but in fact it was really my mood he was picking up.

"Dad." He turned to me later, and I knew another difficult question was coming. "If Mom was still alive, would she come with us to the Back of Beyond?"

"I don't think so. If she were alive, everything would be completely different. Most probably we would be going to the seaside for a couple of weeks like every year."

"But I liked being with you and Mom by the sea."

In his words I sensed a mild reproof, as if he had doubts about whether I respected his relationship with his mother. "I know you liked it with her," I reassured him, "She was your Mom, after all. She loved you."

"Did you like being with her too, Dad?"

He looked at me searchingly, and I was afraid that, if I even gave a hint of anything negative, he would take it to mean I was pleased at her death. On the other hand, I didn't want to paint a false picture.

"Sometimes I liked being with her," I said, and in fact that was true. There had been times like that—at the beginning, before Ben was born, and later, when we had both been rejoicing at his birth. "But sometimes I was sad with her, because she was sad. That's not something you should worry about, though. For you, she was and will always be the way you saw her."

"I noticed she was sad sometimes," he agreed.

That sadness spread out in the room around us and pressed on our shoulders and on our chests. Her reasonless sorrow, that had caught up with us even here.

They Experience the Unfriendly Perfection of Austria

The next morning, we went downstairs to breakfast for the last time and there was still that tangible sense of safety. Anxiety was meanwhile starting to gnaw at me, but I knew I mustn't show the slightest sign of fear at whatever was waiting for us. After breakfast, I paid the bill to one of those pleasant girls, and we carried out the luggage, Benjamin taking the big backpack, which reached down to his knees. As we loaded the things into the car, I felt at least a small stirring of excitement at travelling and the prospect of the new, the future. Soon we were driving down the winding road. Benjamin was immersed in some thoughts of his own, while even my own eternally fretful ruminations were soothed by the quiet purr of the engine. There was movement here, and that had to suffice; unquestionably there was movement, and it didn't matter whether from the past into the future or in some unending vicious circle.

Gradually we came down from the Šumava slopes and headed straight for the frontier. As we got closer, I felt once again that sensation from communist times, when this had been the frontier between two worlds, impermeable and uncrossable, and no matter how hard we tried, we couldn't understand the laws of the world beyond it. In more recent years, a lot of nightclubs had grown up here, and they reminded me of my own need.

"Dad, Dad, they have hearts on the houses here, d'you see it?" Ben suddenly piped up brightly.

"Aha," I faked wonder.

For a while he was silent, in fact for quite a long while. Then he said, "Maybe it means that nice people live here, people who love everyone. Is that it?"

"I don't know, Benjamin," I was forced to spoil his pleasure. "I'm afraid the hearts are there just to lure people in and make money from them. A painted or lit-up heart doesn't necessarily mean that someone is sincere. You have to be careful and not let people play tricks on you. It's important to be able to tell who has a really good heart and who is only offering something fake."

"Well, I still think the people here really mean it," he said, clinging to his theory.

We stopped at the last Czech restaurant. While we waited for the food, I tried to explain to Benjamin what it had been like here when I was his age. I told him how only foreigners could drive through and only Czechs chosen by the communists could drive out. I don't know how much he understood, but when we were leaving the restaurant he asked, "Would those communists have shot us?"

"Not here. We would never have got this far," I tried to explain. "They used to check all the cars long before they got anywhere near the frontier. This restaurant didn't exist back then either. But it is true that if someone tried to get across the frontier secretly, going through the forest, they would shoot at him. They shot quite a lot of people dead."

We went through customs without difficulty. They didn't even want to see Benjamin's passport, which put him out. We were now driving through the Austrian borderlands. The landscape around us had not changed. As on the Czech side, it was mountainous with meadows and forests, and yet it seemed completely different— cleaner. The marks of human activity had changed. It wasn't just that the farms and buildings here were in perfect repair and spotless, but above all, because they were standing exactly where they had stood from time immemorial, as did their pastures, woods, and fields. Nazism had passed this way, and war too, but none of that had had as destructive an impact as communism on what might be called the continuity of human community. The war that we had lost behind the Iron Curtain had not been especially bloody—there had hardly been any shooting, but somehow the desolation had been all the greater.

The first Austrian town we encountered also amazed us (or

more precisely me) with its cleanliness and orderliness. What we call globalization seemed to have no purchase on the place—everything had been complete long before its arrival, and there was no room for it. Or for us for that matter. Here we were unwelcome and foreign, and all my self-confidence as a successful and affluent man seemed to evaporate. I kept expecting some uncompromising Austrian policeman to appear and inform me that I had broken the speed limit or was suspected of smuggling drugs or had stolen this expensive car, because Czechs just had to be poor.

We came down from the border hills into the valley of the Danube, and here we found towns just as ugly as any in our country —with industrial zones, huge parking lots, and temples of consumerism awash with all the things that had to be produced and consumed in greater quantities every year if the economists were to be happy and the people not to fall into depression.

After a few hours, we had covered a distance that in bygone times would have taken pilgrims weeks. From the Šumava on the Czech side, to the Danube, and from the Danube back up until the summits of the Alps were visible. What for centuries history had divided and distinguished was today connected and united by motorway asphalt.

I stopped the car in a rest area in the shadow of pines. It had become warmer, the sun shining through a thin tissue of cloud. Dozens of Austrian families had made a stop too. I pulled out a bottle of mineral water and some subs bought back in Bohemia. Although I had thought about stopping at a rest stop, I had somehow resisted doing so, putting it off even though I knew that in the end it would be inevitable. It was an inhibition stuck in my mind like a splinter, from the times when I had been poor and everything had been so much dearer here.

As the hours of driving passed, a massive rocky mountain rose up in front of us and after a while a long translucent lake appeared beneath it. I thought of the beauties with which this land had been endowed before it had been so densely settled and fettered by roads, one of them leading along the edge of the lake and so offering this vast ravishing picture free to anyone who could step on an accelerator pedal.

"Dad, Dad, let's stop here!" implored Benjamin.

I wanted to do as he asked but access to the lake turned out to be blocked by a narrow belt of private land. It wasn't until half-way along the lake that I found a small beach. I stopped—but inevitably in front of the driveway of a private plot, expecting someone to come and politely but firmly send us on our way.

Benjamin set about skimming pebbles on the narrow beach. I glanced at my watch. It was four in the afternoon and I had no idea where we were going to sleep tonight. It was warmer but the water in the lake was cold. Opposite us a limestone cliff, of a kind we would not have found anywhere in Bohemia, dropped directly into the lake. The pebbles on the bottom under the translucent water were also white. A little way on dozens of small yachts were anchored, as if this were not a lake but the sea. While Ben threw one stone after another into the water, I kept a nervous eye on the car. "No more pebbles, let's go." I tried to get Ben to move.

"But I'm hungry."

"Tell you what, we'll drive on further into the mountains and find a place to stay somewhere there and have a good meal," I suggested.

Once again, we were driving high in mountain country, superb on the eye but too neatly fenced and tamed for us to have been able to stop and put up a tent. And if yesterday I had been dreaming of sex-starved Austrian women with lush thighs and heavy sighs, today my manhood was in retreat, the sails had come down, and I was tossing about in anxiety and uncertainty.

"Dad, couldn't we stop here?" Benjamin was constantly pointing out some hotel or guest house, but it seemed to me too soon and too near the road, and so I carried on and on. In the end our road led quite high up into a pass and was obviously going to descend again on the other side. I decided to take a turn-off to what was some kind of little spa town. We drove into narrow streets thronged with vacationers

and it was clear there was nothing for us here. Despite Ben's protests I
drove right through and continued on. The road took us to what had
once been a mountain village but had become a tourism factory, with
perfect signage and perfect cleanliness—a kind of Alpine showcase
where cottages in historical style and with flowers in the windows
offered accommodation and all around stretched perfectly green
pastures full of perfect cows. Rising behind the village were perfect
limestone rock faces, while on the other side above the pass an
Alpine glacier gleamed dully in the afternoon sunlight. If I had been
ignorant of history, I would have thought that the people who lived
here were mountain men with pure souls, good and hospitable. Only
this was a country that had once succumbed to Nazism, which could
hardly have been confined to the towns. Here in the mountains the
people must also have marched and shouted, "Heil Hitler," and even
today there were plenty who voted for nationalists who liked to talk
of the "the good side" of the Nazi Reich. I therefore regarded the
locals with suspicion.

We drove up one of the asphalt side roads. An elderly lady shook
her head at us on the threshold of her house: No, we're full up here.
In a chalet on the edge of the village, with a superb view of the glacier
and green meadows, they also claimed to be full and told us to go to
a hotel. I wasn't sure I believed them. Maybe they didn't want to have
two suspicious foreigners—father and son—in the house. We came
out on the road beyond the village, but even here everything was so
perfectly clean and orderly that I felt guilty when Ben peed by one
of the small bushes. I identified another suitable bush for myself, but
when I got closer to it, I noticed something like a hunting hotel at
the top of the steep slope above it. The hotel had its own fenced land,
a forest, and perhaps its own deer for shooting.

"Dad, I'm hungry and my head aches," Ben complained for the
nth time. In any case there was a barrier across the road and so we
went back. We tried three more cottages but the result was always the
same. We got back into the car exhausted. "We'll go a little further
on."

Eventually we found accommodation in the little town under the forest, from where there was no view of the glacier or the cliffs. It was in a little hotel that evidently mainly served skiers in winter. The cramped room with a balcony was supposed to be our fixed point and security. We stretched out on the bed with our overclothes and shoes still on.

An hour later we were seated on the terrace of a local restaurant. Everything was made of heavy wood, possibly including our waiter. He was a fifty-year-old with a round head and rounded back, dressed in something that was nothing like a suit or a hunting vest. I immediately pictured him here in this restaurant under Nazism, standing to attention by the door and giving a Hitler salute. After all, it would have been easy to be a Nazi here, in the middle of flowers and trees, among respectable citizens. It would have been easy to host a summer gathering of the *Hitlerjugend* in this mountain air, too high up to hear the screams of the tortured, and far from the horrors that turned citizens into slaves anyone could humiliate, torment, or deprive of their children—or kill just for fun.

I ordered Ben a cola and wiener schnitzel and green salad and then a big ice cream sundae. He rubbed his freckled nose and bare head against my shoulder, and I saw the weariness in his eyes. I was on my third strong beer and conscious yet again that to have my beloved son with me was nothing to be taken for granted, and that despite all the fragility and vulnerability of life, nobody was going to come and divide us today.

They Camp in a Mountain Valley and Ben Prays for Mom

In the morning I wanted to stay in bed, but Benjamin was impatiently moving around the small room. Back in the Šumava, I could send him outside, but here he was completely dependent on me. And so, I got up.

"What are we going to do, Dad?" He was making me nervous with his questions.

"We'll hike into the mountains," I said, without knowing if there was a path leading up from here.

After breakfast, where the service was friendly and there was a great choice of food, we walked around the town. We bought provisions, and we found folding maps in the information center. The maps showed several dotted routes that probably led upwards. In the meantime, azure islands were appearing in the sky and the clouds becoming fewer. All this filled me with hope and longing and expectation. Back in our room, I speedily packed the essentials, and we set out. Benjamin followed me without questions or protests, which quite surprised me. Maybe he was better than I at appreciating the charm of the here-and-now, and it didn't bother him that we had no destination.

We made our way around fenced pastures for horses and reached the forest, where we walked up what was still an asphalt road to a few bungalows. Once again, we were going to end up blocked by a private piece of land, I thought, but instead a narrow path ran along the wall of one of the bungalows and continued steeply uphill through a beech forest. Everything inside me lit up, and I set off up the path vigorously. Few of the hundreds and thousands of tourists had ever come here, for the path was narrow and not particularly well trodden. Benjamin made stalwart progress, and even tried to walk ahead of me; we warmed up and started to sweat. The light

65

beech forest, full of sun, gave way to dense spruce, and the first rocks appeared. With every meter, I felt another piece of worry and depression falling away; after a long time, I enjoyed just breathing again, just being.

We went sharply uphill through the forest for about an hour before reaching the foot of the limestone slopes. Here scree, rock, and belts of wood alternated. Here and there, we had vistas of pastures and the little town, already far below us. From this vantage point, it even seemed a landscape without supermarkets, hotels, or cars, where one mountain face ran smoothly into the next, divided not by highways but only by the mountain streams flowing steeply from the slopes.

Sweating, we stopped for a snack. "Will we get all the way to the top from here?" Ben inquired.

"I don't know. I don't think we can get right to the top."

"I *want* to get right to the top," he protested.

"I don't know if that's possible."

I looked at his sweating face, his damp t-shirt and dirty hands (taking short cuts on the steepest sections, he had gone on all fours). He was here beside me, and I felt such affection and closeness to him that it made my heart thump. If she had lived, it wouldn't have been like this. I would always have kept on trying to compensate for her inactivity by shifting more of the childcare her way, and by trying to bolster her claims as a parent, I would have been renouncing him. It would have been an ordinary kind of missing out: at home over homework, at home by the television, on vacation in a bad mood that I would have had to conceal it from him. I thanked fate for giving us each other.

After another half hour, the path straightened out and led over rocks. It even started to descend slowly into a deep ravine, where the bubbling of a stream was audible from the bottom. We continued our zigzag progress over the chasm, until we found ourselves by running water. It was a very small stream, and the water in it was colored a little white. The path continued uphill, upstream.

"So maybe we really can get to the top," Ben said.

Once again, we were going up a steep slope. In the open places, where there was mostly scree, the noon sun was roasting, but when we were in the shady and moist ravine, there was an almost cave-like chill. It astonished me that we were completely alone here; everyone down below was wandering around souvenir shops or cramming into cable cars to get a few ravishing views of Alpine summits with no physical effort.

Suddenly the stream vanished, the ravine broadened, and we were walking through strange level glades in the shadow of great spruces. Here, the landscape had a melancholy and desolate look, and I realized that nobody knew about us and no one would ever get to know about us, if somebody robbed and killed us. I was relieved when we came out of these glades onto limestone rubble, and, scrambling over a high mound, we were amazed by a little lake about two hundred meters long. It was enclosed on one side by a rock face, and on the other side where we were walking, it was overgrown with spruce and dwarf pine and finally ended in a pebble beach and meadow.

"We'll make camp here, Benjamin," I said with excitement. "And tomorrow we'll bring a tent here."

"Yes, Dad," he cried gleefully. "Do you think there are fish in this lake? We could catch them and eat them."

We spent the whole afternoon by the lake. The sun alternately burned down on us and hid behind the clouds, and when it was at its hottest, we got up the nerve to swim in the cold lake and then dried ourselves on the white sand. Twice during the afternoon, a group of people came past us, and I started to have doubts about the wisdom of putting up a tent here. All the same, it was incredible that we were here. This time yesterday, I had been sitting behind a steering wheel, parched and with my confidence crippled in the middle of an all-too-perfect civilization, and today I was here, relaxed and happy in an unspoiled and natural site almost never visited by anyone. It was only in the late afternoon, with our return down to the little town and its cultivated cottages in wooden Alpine style, that a trace of anxiety and doubt crept back into my soul. I became conscious once again of the world as a place where a human body could become a bloody rag, from which the only escape was death, and death might not even come. It struck me that it was lucky that we hadn't conquered eternity and were not immortal, because the most terrible idea I could imagine was that we would be able to trap one another in a glass prism forever—and condemn someone to the hell of eternal immobility in full immortal awareness.

Benjamin seemed to sense the tracks of my thoughts, because he grabbed my hand, pressed himself to me, and gazed at me with devotion. "Dad. I love you, Dad."

The next day at breakfast, the manager asked for my passport, and when she saw we were Czechs, she told me we had to pay in advance—and asked me how many nights we planned to stay.

I said I didn't know precisely, but I would be happy to pay her for a few nights in advance. The card I pulled out so reassured her that she even smiled: of course, we could stay as long as we wanted—it had just been a thing required by the authorities, a local tax formality.

In the shops and restaurants, they also behaved very politely, but I knew that it was respect for our wallet, not ourselves. I could quite vividly imagine how repugnant to them we would have been, and how they would have driven us away, if we had been penniless and hungry.

But I still couldn't work out where that tight-fisted perfectionism came from. In the mountains, after all, people have always depended on each other, and life must once have been hard here. Maybe it had been precisely the hard grind that had made them so obsessively persnickety, bringing them incredible prosperity in a time when travelling to see nice views of the remnants of earthly beauties had become one of the strongest sectors of industry.

Before noon, we packed up and set out on the same route as yesterday, but today it seemed longer and a little boring. It was even warmer this time, and so I really sweated under the backpack, carrying the two sleeping bags and a tent. Benjamin ran ahead more boldly than yesterday, and I was afraid for him over the steep drops. Once again, we went through those mysterious little meadows, and they struck me as even more closed in than before, but then the lake water greeted us, calm and unpeopled. All the same, I didn't put the tent up immediately, but only towards evening, and I hid the little fire that I had promised Ben behind a boulder. It was cooling down rapidly, and the white cliff walls above the lake turned first pink and then silver.

"Dad, can I say a prayer?" Ben suddenly asked in the silence.

I was not surprised it had occurred to him here, when the atmosphere over the lake, the motionless rocks fading into darkness and the cloudless, dimming sky, all encouraged reflection. "You can pray whenever you like," I assured him. "But will you tell me what you want to pray for?"

"I want to pray for Mom. I want to pray that everything goes right for all three of us."

That disarmed me, the way that he had accepted my suggestion and now took it for granted. Suddenly, I understood why he so rarely spoke about her. I had been afraid he was hiding something, but, in fact the whole time, he had been assuming that she was still there with us. I stroked his head.

"You do that," I said, and there was a lump in my throat. "And if you talk to her, you can tell her that you are making Dad happy. That you're a good companion and very clever."

I walked off a few paces to the tent to get the sleeping bags ready for the night, so that he could be alone with his prayer. The first stars were coming out in the sky above the still visible edge of the rocks. The coming night would be clear and cold.

When Ben came back, we brushed our teeth and crawled inside the tent. I didn't know whether to return to the subject of his prayer. Instead, I said, "Now I feel like we're in a spaceship and sailing together through the endless universe—just us two and no one else."

"But what about Mom?" He reminded me. "Mom too."

"You're right. Her soul. That will always be with us."

"Dad, are there bears living here?" He suddenly took a different tack.

"Not here," I assured him. "There aren't any animals here that you need to be scared of."

"But what if I have to go to the bathroom in the night, will you go with me?"

"Of course, I will, Benjamin. You can wake me up whenever you need to." (But I thought he would sleep through until morning. It was me that would be tense and pricking up my ears, in case I heard some suspicious sound that would betray the steps of a human being.)

I zipped Benjamin's sleeping bag all the way up to keep the draft from his neck. I was using a torch on a headband, and its light flashed across the tent canvas as I moved my head. "And what about your prayer? Did it turn out fine?"

"Yeah, well, I don't actually know if God heard me. What do you think?"

"I think that if he exists, he definitely heard you. And I think he ought to exist, if only because of your prayer."

"But he didn't answer me."

"Maybe he answered you very quietly. Maybe he answered just with the feeling you had at that moment—if you felt happy and didn't feel lonely…"

Even in the sleeping bag he shrugged. "I don't know if I had any feeling," he admitted honestly, "I'm not sure I know how to tell."

"It doesn't matter. But now go to sleep, and I'll take a walk around the tent, so you can have a dream about something beautiful."

"Are you sure you're only going to walk round the tent?"

"At the most, I'll go to the lake and back." (The tent was about thirty meters from the edge of the lake.) I started to crawl my way out.

"Dad," he held me back.

"Don't worry, Ben." I bent down and kissed his forehead. "There's no reason to be afraid."

I came out into the meadow at the head of the lake and stood in wonder at the way the landscape had changed. The stars had multiplied and were reflected in the waters of the lake together with the rock face and surrounding trees, while the rising moon was shining through the trees. The power of the scene, its sense of culmination, overwhelmed me. At first, I was incapable of thought and just breathed deeply, and noticing how the whole universe came together in me here. For where else can the universe culminate if not in the place from which it is viewed? I—the observer— was the center of the cosmos here. Admittedly, there was always the possibility of God. But if God, then why so much pain and suffering? Why mothers whose children were slaughtered in front of them? Why millions of agonizing deaths? Why sparrows devoured by cats and mice swallowed by snakes and lizards snapped up by storks? Why the pincers used in Cambodia to tear flesh from the bodies of the tortured? And if not God, then why me? Why should millions of years of bloody evolution culminate in me—through my consciousness, only for that consciousness together with my body to fall forever into the void? Back then by the lake beneath the cliff, lit by an ever-brighter moon, I think I whispered, "I don't understand, God, I just don't understand."

Towards morning, I was woken by the drumming of rain on the tent canvas. Small drops driven by the wind were falling in rapid succession. I lay in my sleeping bag beside Benjamin, who was breathing easily, and I inwardly cursed this unexpected change. The interior of the tent suddenly seemed cramped and airless. Although it was only five, the dawn was breaking, and time seemed to draw out. Around seven, I crawled outside. It was only a fine drizzle, much less than it had sounded, but the low continuous cloud cover offered little hope of change.

Benjamin woke up after eight, and when I told him about the weather, he angrily punched the side of the tent.

"What are you doing?" I said, annoyed with him. "In the

mountains, you have to be ready for anything and not think the weather will always obey your wishes." In fact, it infuriated me too.

At a suitable moment, when the wind strengthened and the rain temporarily subsided, we rolled up the sleeping bags and the wet tent and started down. The limestone was slippery now, and in the places where the path narrowed over the drop, I went first with the backpack and then went back for the waiting Benjamin. He was bold and sure-footed, but I would have preferred to go around this stretch by another route or just wait for the rocks to dry out. I was terribly afraid for him.

"Will we come back here when it stops raining, Dad?" he asked.

"I don't know, Benjamin. There are plenty of other nice places. Maybe we won't be coming back here."

I shouldn't have said that. "Why, Dad?" Ben objected. "I'd like to come back here sometime. I'd like us to put up a tent here again."

"But maybe we can put it up somewhere even nicer," I soothed him.

"...But I liked it here, Dad."

"Me too," I assured him. "But it's not a reason for giving up on the back of beyond, is it?"

"But aren't we in Beyond already?" he wondered.

"It's true that last night we were a bit Beyond," I had to agree. "We were completely alone, and no one knew about us. But generally, we've only been travelling a short time, and lots of people come here to Austria to ski in the winter. Everybody can get as far as here."

Ben Finds Some Friends and Dad Gets over His Memory of Nazism

That afternoon and the whole of the following night, it rained steadily. In the morning, I found Benjamin had dressed while I slept. He told me he was going for a walk. I suppressed a stab of fear and just impressed on him that he mustn't go further than he could remember the way back, that he should take care when crossing the road, and should on no account get into a strange car if anyone invited him. And also, that first he had to have breakfast.

He nodded, but protested against breakfast. "I'm not hungry, Dad."

"It doesn't matter that you're not hungry. We've paid for breakfast…" I immediately realized that wasn't the best argument and added, "People have to eat in the morning."

He went off boldly down the steps, and I was gripped by angst. In my imagination, I pictured him leaving like this and never coming back, so that this trivial exchange about breakfast would be our last. I would look for him first in the surroundings of the hotel, then in nearby towns, and finally all through Europe, but I would find no trace, no hope of ever seeing him again. These scenarios got such hold of me that I had to sit up in bed and shut them down in my head, but the uncontrollable physical fear remained. When I recalled it much later—at a time when it would seem justified—the idea that it was a prophetic fear would chill me to the bone.

With misgivings in my heart, I went down to breakfast, where the lady of the house smiled at me and told me how clever my son was. I tried to copy her smile, "Of course he's clever." After breakfast, I went back to our room, flicked through the television channels for a while and then helplessly paced back and forth, entirely overcome by the appalling idea that I would never know what had happened to my son and would not be there in his moment of need, and that he would wait for me somewhere and maybe vainly call out to me.

After eleven, he bounced back into the room: breathless, wet, and happy. "Dad, Dad, I was playing soccer with some boys."

I looked him up and down distrustfully. "How come you haven't got dirty pants? Didn't you get a kick at the ball?"

"Sure, Dad, I kicked it. I even got a goal, when we were playing with a smaller goalpost," he gabbled. "They lent me everything. They're having a sports meet, Dad. I'm supposed to go back in the afternoon."

"You suddenly understand German, do you?" I was doubtful.

"No, Dad." He bridled and almost wept with frustration. "One of the boys there spoke a bit of Czech. Why won't you believe me?"

It was only then that I realized it was all true. Apologetically, I took his hand. "Okay, Ben. Sorry. I believe you now."

"So, can I go in the afternoon?"

"Sure. I'd like to come and watch."

"Hurray!" he whooped, "You'll see I can play just as well as they do. Their trainer praised me. Seriously, Dad. He knows a lot of Czech soccer players. He said Czechs were good."

In the afternoon, I let him go on ahead; I wanted him to figure it out for himself. After about half an hour, I set off after him. Already from a distance, I could see boys running around in green and yellow vests. Another two teams were sitting on the benches waiting for their turn, and four young coaches were running between then giving instructions. The turf was perfect, like everything else here.

It took me a moment to make out Benjamin. He was sitting on the bench and now he noticed me too. He ran up, followed by one of the coaches.

"Hi." Benjamin welcomed me as if he was at home here, and I was just a guest. "In a minute, I'll be playing."

"*Guten tag*," the trainer greeted me, and when I answered in English, he adjusted, "Very good," he pointed at Ben with a friendly laugh.

"No problem?" I asked from politeness, although I knew that

everything was just fine.

"Problem? … Maybe one problem," he said with affected seriousness, "Your boy is better than our boys."

"That will be a problem for me too," I laughed, "All he will want to do is just keep on playing."

I wasn't wrong. In the next couple of days, nothing but soccer existed for Benjamin. He went twice a day, and the coaches and boys accepted him with enthusiasm. Sometimes I went to watch, and it occurred to me that this was a different Austria from the one I carried in my imagination, the one that my historical memory foisted on me. These boys knew nothing about the past. They were clean and would remain so, if we adults didn't stigmatize them with our memory.

Too much free time started to create problems for me. I was always just waiting for Ben, aimlessly wandering around and consumed with my increasing desire for women. My world seemed to narrow to the folds of a skirt, pert breasts, tanned calves, and posteriors perched on bike saddles. But I was alone—uninteresting and almost too eager—with no hope of success. I was entirely lost in myself.

On the third day, Benjamin came back with tears in his eyes. He was carrying a lot of small presents, plus a little club flag and commemorative medal—the meet was over. I was getting cold feet about our journey yet again. Perhaps it is only my journey, I thought—and I've dragged him into something that he agreed to, only because I gave him no alternative. He was just a child, after all, an ordinary boy with a boy's longings, and these would certainly not include the desire to lose himself in the back of beyond. He was my beloved hostage.

Our time here in this perfect little town under the Alps was at an end. All the same, I took Benjamin on one more trip by car. We drove up the serpentine mountain road on a stretch that cost ten euros to pass. We soon found ourselves above the forest line; it would have taken hours of toil on foot, but now it was an easy and fast affair. The view was still fascinating, taking in the mountain faces and then the small tongue of the glacier winding its way down out of the rock fissure. Cows stood around on the slopes along the road. Their numbers must have been calculated to be precisely proportionate to the area of the meadows and forests here, and even the area of the ditch by the road and no doubt also the area of the grassy square in front of the mountain chalet.

At the top, we got out and walked to the panoramic viewing point, but Benjamin's thoughts were running back to soccer and mine were running ahead to the obscure destination of our journey. When we finally sat on a large boulder and unpacked our snack, I put my arm round Benjamin's shoulders and said, "I think there are still tons of places that we ought to see. Tomorrow we'll go a bit further." As I said it, the sea came into my mind. It struck me that its boundless waters might wash away all my doubts, and so we needed to head for the coast.

Ben Remembers His Home and Dad Heads for the Sea

The next morning, I loaded everything into the car, and we set off along back roads towards the main highway over the pass. I had to admit I was leaving a different town from the one where I had found us lodgings several days before. It was because they had accepted my son here--and with an openness that almost shamed me. My point of view had changed, and I had stopped being so prejudiced.

As for Benjamin, he didn't seem to want to leave at all. "Are we going somewhere where there'll be a soccer camp?" he asked.

I tried to explain that what had happened had been a fluke and that, even if there was another soccer camp like it somewhere, they probably wouldn't let him take part. But he stood his ground. "I want there to be another soccer camp somewhere."

In the meantime, we were rolling along the main highway south, where a broad belt of blue sky stretched above damp mountains. I played a cassette of songs, and all the fears of what was to come were gone. We were becoming children of the road.

Now, I had no inhibitions about eating in a rest stop and shopping in a nearby supermarket, which to my surprise was designed to fit in with an Alpine town. Evidently, they took pains with design here.

I was keeping an eye on the map. We could have reached the sea in a single day, but I didn't want to do that. I wanted us to arrive there like two thirsty pilgrims—not too fast or easily. That was why I chose a route over two high mountain ridges. The first ridge enchanted me right away, although these were in no way ostentatiously beautiful mountains. The slopes were overgrown with dwarf pine and grass, and the narrow road wound above the forest line; a stream flowed down, and instead of over-ornate guesthouses, we passed only a few mountain farms offering milk, honey, and cheese. But as soon as we got out in the fresh air a little further on, everything was fenced—

77

private pastures stretched almost up to the summits. Only at the top of the pass did the fences cease, enabling us to take a walk. On the further side, an even deeper valley opened up, forested at the bottom, and beyond it, a long ridge, which looked as if we could hike along it. A few solitary clouds had caught on the highest summits, but otherwise the sky was clear. I thought about putting up the tent somewhere on the slope, but it was still early afternoon and plenty of cars were driving through, and so I rejected the idea.

We drove downhill again, and the landscape started to change rapidly. There was no longer any possibility of camping; in the lowlands, we got caught in a traffic jam caused by the construction of a new road, and the slopes on either side were too exposed. I was waiting for Ben to start to complain, but he fell asleep, leaving me alone at the wheel. Finally, after about two hours of slow progress, I turned off up another ridge.

"When are we going home, Dad?" I suddenly heard a sleepy voice.

"Home?" For a few moments, I wondered what he was talking about. Then it hit me. For him, it still meant returning to our apartment on the edge of Prague—to the apartment that still held traces of his Mom, the traces of our cheerless life together. It made me very aware that, in my heart of hearts, I had no place I would want to return to in moments of grief or loneliness.

"Do you already want to go back?" I asked, full of fear of his answer.

"No Dad, I was just asking," he retorted irritably.

"Wait a minute, Benjamin. If you want to go back, then just tell me."

"I don't want to go back," he insisted in an even more peeved tone.

I was sorry I had driven him into hiding one of his wishes. I should have remembered that children don't make comparisons, and assume they have the best. Our apartment was where he had his room, where he found presents under the Christmas tree every year and did his homework and watched television. How could I have ever supposed that he would leave it all behind just like that?

After a while, I returned to the subject of home. "Anyway, I think we ought to buy a new apartment sometime in the future. In the old one, we lived with Mom, and so if we stay there, we'll always be thinking of her and that will make us sad. I mean, of course we must think of her. We'll remember her. But at the same time, we have to be happy, to enjoy life. To tell you the truth, Benjamin, I don't know myself when we'll be going back. It's simply up to both of us."

I also wanted to explain that there was no need for him to adjust himself to me. Maybe I was just giving myself an alibi, but it was important to me that he should feel relaxed and free at my side. "We're travelling together, and so what you want matters just as much as what I want. We'll decide on everything together." I fell silent, but he said nothing, so I continued. "Of course, I have more experience than you, and so sometimes I have to decide something for us both. I also have to take care to keep us safe, so nobody steals from us…"

"Could someone steal from us?" he echoed, astonished.

"Of course, they could. We have to be careful. People aren't all nice. There's a lot of bad in the world. In other times, and in other parts of the world, people kill each other, cause each other pain… We're very lucky to be living right now and right here. Because in recent years, nothing so terrible has been happening in Europe. But don't go thinking think it was always like that. Look at World War II for instance. All the people that perished. All the children that lost their dads and moms. All the dads and moms that lost their children…"

He leaned forward and gently touched my shoulder: "I love you, Dad."

I pulled off the road onto a flat area by the barred gates of a pasture. "Benjamin," I turned and hugged him. "I love you very much too. I'll always love you." (But as I said the word "always," I thought of my own parents, whose parental love had cooled as soon as I started going my own way and ceased to fulfill their ideas.) "When you're big, you'll make your own decisions on what you'll do, and I'll always support you. What I want is for you to do something you'll like and something that's meaningful." (I couldn't tell him my doubts about whether there was any such thing.)

"What I want is always to be with you," he said.

"I'm glad…I'm glad you think that." I wanted to explain to him that all children think something like that, but when they grow up, their attitude changes. Only I thought better of it and said, "This journey to the Back of Beyond is just ours; it's just the two of us, always together. And tomorrow we'll get to the sea."

They Camp beside the Highway and Dad Fears for Their Lives

Once again, we had driven above two thousand meters, but there was a ski resort in the picturesque pass with two lakes, and so putting up a tent was out of the question. Even in summer, there was a line of tourists for the chairlift.

"Let's go on the lift," Ben implored.

"No," I said severely.

"Why not? I want to!"

"Because it's getting late. It would be almost evening before we got back down, and we still have to find a place to sleep." As I said it, I was surprised at myself. It didn't matter, after all, what we were going to do and when and where we were going to do it. We could decide as we liked—we had a lot of time and no destination. So where was I rushing to now? I was succumbing again to that restlessness that had pursued me all my life. I had always put everything into trying to achieve something, and as soon as I succeeded, I just set another goal for myself. I was annoyed with my inability to rest.

"Okay," I gave in, but I couldn't rid myself of the feeling that I was somehow cheating, breaking a rule, playing the truant. I drove the car into the paid parking lot. The surrounding peaks were bathed in the afternoon sun, and the chairlift, despite all the modern tourism, clicked and whirred like an old clock as it moved up the slope. For safety, I took the backpack with warm clothing and all our documents, cards, and cash, and Ben ran up to stand in the line. After a few minutes, we were sitting side by side, our legs swinging over the green grass, as we slid quickly and quietly uphill. Ben was ecstatic, and I understood why.

Up at the top, the wind was blowing, and there was a great view of other rockier summits, while beside us wound a ski-run. "Can we come here sometime in winter?" he asked. "I'd like to ski here."

"There are a lot of places like this. But you're right, the skiing would be beautiful here." The mountain air calmed me down, and I stopped feeling like I was cheating. I put an arm round Benjamin's shoulders, and when we got off at the top, I wished that it would all last forever, and I even felt I had touched a small piece of eternity.

Later, down in the parking lot, Ben persuaded me to take him for a cola and a sundae. We had supper too, and it was after seven when we drove off. From the map, I knew we were coming down from the Austrian mountains. After another two hours, we passed a long-abandoned customs station and found ourselves in a different country, and I was a little sad for Benjamin, because his generation would never feel the excitement that we had felt at European frontiers. Highway asphalt is the same everywhere.

It was getting dark, and I hadn't understood the notices about tolls. I turned off the main route. Soon we were making our way through the narrow streets of our first Italian town. The houses here were not as decorative as in Austria; in fact, it was quite austere here. The road led through a deep, secluded valley along a mountain river. Limestone rocks and slopes rose high on both sides. The highway we had driven on earlier sometimes appeared above us and disappeared into numerous tunnels. It was as if someone had put a ruler across the valleys and mountains. Apart from the overpasses, there were two kinds of railway bridges—for old and new trains. It was a wretched, perforated valley.

We were driving downhill on a gentle incline along with the river on its time-honored journey from the mountains. Suddenly, within just a few minutes, I was overcome by a weariness I couldn't fight off. My eyes were drooping, and although I was keeping them open by force of will, the light in my mind was dimming, and I was afraid of falling asleep. In any case, I didn't want to reach the sea that night. A small rest area and turn-off to a track appeared to the right. I took it and drove along the track to the river bed. Now, at the beginning of summer, the river was flowing somewhere in the middle, while most of the sand and river pebbles were dry.

"What is it, Dad? Where are you going?" wondered Ben.

I turned off the engine and the lights. "I'm sorry, but I'm really tired. I can't drive any further today—I might fall asleep at the wheel."

"Are we going to sleep in the car?"

"Why? We'll put up the tent."

I went to take a look at the edge of a small forest. The vegetation was trampled down here, and considering that cars were roaring by only thirty meters away, the place was quite clean. People probably camped here sometimes. I moved the car right into the trees, so it wouldn't be visible from the road, and got everything ready by torchlight. With the car behind me, it was simple—we only took out the essentials, and we didn't even have to put up a rain sheet. Benjamin seemed tired as well. "Just imagine. As soon as we get up in the morning, we'll go straight to the sea," I said encouragingly. We had both eaten enough and went right to sleep.

I woke up in the middle of the night. There were voices and headlights lighting the interior of the tent. I registered all this in one subliminal moment, and my heart seemed to seize up with fright. There was no doubt that someone had driven down here and could well have noticed us. But who could want anything here at this hour of the night? My God, I thought, we're such easy targets!

I feverishly wondered what to do. If I crawled out, I wouldn't be so helpless, but I might run straight into them. If I stayed, they could easily pull out the tent pegs and beat us to death. Beside me, Benjamin was breathing evenly, but I was choking with fear. I was afraid even to move; the sweat was running off me inside the sleeping bag. I worked out that the people were probably speaking Italian, and it struck me that if they had bad intentions, they would surely be quiet. But even that sensible thought failed to calm me down. I was here with a child and even more helpless than if I had been entirely alone, under a highway embankment, a complete foreigner with no hope of any kind of aid. I would have given anything to have been sleeping somewhere in the safety of a hotel or in our Prague apartment, where all those dark corners that always exist despite the safety of homes could trouble only our dreams.

Another car drew up, the gravel crunching under tires and more headlights cutting through the trees. The three or four male voices that I could make out had started to discuss something. After a moment several other voices joined them. They belonged to the newcomers; the meeting must have been arranged. I had already bet on keeping still, so there was nothing to do but wait and pray to God, in whom we always hope in moments like this. I hoped, and I fervently wished for God to be up there among the stars and not just a figment of my desperate mind.

I don't know how long it all lasted. The men seemed to be having a pretty serious argument. At times, the voices were low and abrupt; at other times, there was loud cursing. I realized I terribly wanted to piss. But not even this consuming need could induce me to crawl out of the tent. There was a roaring in my head and my mouth was dry, but my beloved Benjamin slept on.

All at once, there was a slamming of car doors. An engine started up and one of the cars turned sharply and retreated up the track. The remaining men, evidently those who had arrived first, continued to discuss something. It occurred to me that they were debating what to do with us, and now they would kill us. Probably I should have woken Benjamin. If we made a run for it to the highway, maybe we would be safe. Only what was I thinking? Dashing out of the tent and escaping through the brush, when it wasn't even certain we were in any danger? That's just it—you are never really quite prepared to believe you are in danger, not really. Rather than make a fool of yourself by some rash flight, you bet on the power of prayer.

After about ten minutes (I no longer had much idea of time), the doors of the second car slammed too. It repeated the same rapid turn, and the inside of the tent and its surroundings went dark again. My worst fears had not been fulfilled. All the same, I still felt paralyzed, suffocated with fear in my sleeping bag. I ought to crawl out, I tried to tell myself. It would certainly be sensible to confirm what had actually happened and check that the car was okay. And to cap it all off, I was desperate for a piss. Yet one moment followed another into eternity—thousands of moments in which my brain center could have ordered my body to get up and out of the tent. Nothing happened, but of course it did in the end. Meanwhile, the darkness was thinning and a new day was approaching. All at once, as if without any will of my own, I extricated myself from the sleeping bag, pulled on my shoes and, after only a brief hesitation, unzipped the tent. The light was still dim in the forest, but I was surprised at how clearly visible the river bed and rocks already were. There was traffic up on the highway, and our own car was beside us with no sign of damage. In the safety of the dawning day, my experiences in the middle of the night seemed distant and unreal. Only the scattered sand and the tire tracks showed that it had not been a dream.

I had been very frightened, and now I was just as relieved. First, I had an incredibly long piss, and then I walked over the sand and gravel to the limpid flowing water from which the cold rose. I stood there at the very bottom of the deep valley, above me the embankment with the busy highway, and below me downstream, an overpass; but despite the tangible proximity of civilization, I was outside of it. At that moment, it was as if the two worlds—the river, rock face, and stones on one side and the highway, cars, and concrete on the other—had no intersection. And if there were any cranny that belonged neither to one nor the other, then that was where I was standing.

The chill reached into me, and so I went back to the tent. The pleasant warmth of the sleeping bag enveloped me. After a moment I was asleep.

Arrival by the Sea is a Joyful Event for Ben but a Disappointment for Dad

I was woken by Benjamin fumbling around in the tent. "What is it?" I almost shouted.

"I can't find my shoes."

"Really?" I impatiently bent down to his feet. "And what are these?"

"I didn't see them. Sorry, Dad."

He went outside to pee, and I slowly looked around. It was fully light, and a few flies were sitting on the tent canvas. The clock said nine. What had given me the right to be so aggressive with Ben?

"You slept well, didn't you?" I tried to make up for it.

"Hm."

"So today, we'll get to the sea." I pulled out my strongest weapon. (Only a few hours' drive would take us to the sea.)

"Will we be able to go diving?" he asked.

"Diving?" I found it hard not to be annoyed. I thought he would be pleased with the sea itself, but instead he had to think up something else before we were even there. At the same time, I realized I shouldn't try to force my own values and ideas on him. I shouldn't be like my own father, who used to punish the slightest deviation from his ideas by a bad mood and a retreat into inaccessibility, so that I had no option but to try guessing his wishes rather than spinning my own. "I don't know what the sea's like here, Benjamin," I said aloud. "If there's sand here, the water will be murky, and so you won't see anything. But if the conditions are good, I'll rent you a snorkel."

We had breakfast. I would have liked to make tea, but we had no water. We drank a little flat coke from a plastic bottle. Although the morning was already advanced, the sun hadn't yet penetrated down here under the high cliffs, and I wasn't sure whether it ever would, even now, in summer.

We packed up and set off. The fear I had experienced in the night already seemed no more than something very distant. The speed at which it had receded disturbed me. Was it possible that I hadn't learned anything? Would I refuse to take it as a warning and expose us to danger another time?

We stopped for tea in a little stone town. It was huddled at the meeting point of two equally deep valleys. It must have been a strange place to live. It was as if it lacked real three-dimensional space, or there were only two or at most three directions in which you could go. The locals seemed very grim—austere and forbidding, even to Benjamin. And they say Italians love children!

We drove on, always gently downhill, and as time went by, the valley opened out. It also became warmer fast; suddenly it was a hot summer day.

"When will we get to the sea? I want to be by the sea," Ben piped up repeatedly.

Dusty lowlands and the town of Udine in the middle of them did nothing to confirm my ideas of ancient Italy. Instead of seeing historical monuments, near Udine we spent a whole hour passing monstrous concrete retail facilities. We stopped and started in a line of cars with the air conditioning on full-blast.

"Dad, I don't like it here," Ben pestered, until I snapped back, "And do you think I like it?"

It was the afternoon before we came close to the area where there ought to have been sea. But the landscape remained unpalatable, and I started to lose hope that our arrival would be anything like I had imagined it.

Finally, I saw a sign by the highway showing a harbor. I turned off, and we soon found ourselves in something like a vast factory. It was all storehouses, warehouses, and train tracks, with no piers or cafes with a view of a harbor, or even any sign of boats.

"What about there? Go there!" Ben kept nagging at me, refusing to believe what I already knew, which was that there was nothing here that resembled our idea of a harbor.

After several minutes of searching, I spied a sign for a campsite. Where there's a campsite, there ought to be a beach, I reasoned, but it puzzled me that I couldn't smell the sticky presence of salt in the air. In the end, we found ourselves by the huge gate of a camping and motor home site. "Come on, let's get out and take a look around."

"Dad, Dad, the sea has to be over there." He pointed ahead of us.

I thought it would be too, but the camp was surrounded by a fence, and through the bars of the fence, I saw only an endless town of motor homes and large tents set up along asphalt roads in the shadow of trees. "Ben, we don't want to go to a camp like this. Do you have any idea how many people will be on the beach there?"

"But I want to go there," he whined. "We can just go and swim there. We don't have to put up the tent there."

I agreed that it was a good idea, but it turned out that you needed a chip card to get through the entrance, and it was only for people who were staying there. I silently cursed this mean-minded industrial culture, while aloud I tried to persuade Ben to let me drive a little further on. He resisted, already in a hell of a bad mood, and I wasn't at all surprised. To make matters worse, the sun was now burning hot on our heads, and the sweat was pouring off us. Why hadn't we stayed in the mountains, where we could drink stream water and there was a cooling wind?

We were soon back in the car, driving along the unending fences of yacht clubs, private properties, and I don't know what else.

We reached something that had probably once been a park. We drove onto a dirt track, which might earlier have been a bridle path for horse rides. Today, it was overgrown with nettles and bushes. I drove onto the grass and parked. A trodden path full of shit took us through the undergrowth to a narrow beach. It was obvious at first sight that the sea was stagnant and shallow here, like a pond. There was no sound of surf, no foam on the crests of blue waves. The water was green.

None of this bothered Benjamin. He rushed down to the water's edge like a lunatic. "Yay, we're going to swim, I'm going to jump straight in. Yay!"

"Wait, I've got to go lock the car," I interrupted his euphoria. At the car, I dug out a camping mattress, glasses, sun hats, and sunscreen with a strong UV filter.

The modest beach with its fine sand, where we were completely alone, ran around a shallow bay in which the water was as warm as coffee. At first, I was afraid Ben would step in something nasty in the water, but it was soon clear that the place was quite clean. There were small crabs and a shoal of fish between clumps of seaweed. Opposite us, about a kilometer across the bay, we saw the crowded beach of the campsite. A barely perceptible breeze wafted from the sea. This was not at all the way I had imagined it, but It was still incredible. I lay down naked on the warm sand, and soon gloomy Šumava and the chilly Alps seemed totally remote. Our distant Prague apartment, and the difficult time after the death of my wife, seemed even more remote than that. All the tension surrounding our departure was gone. I lay there in a kind of surrender, like in a spa, while the warmth took the edge off my mind. It made it easier to rest in the present moment —without past and without future—to let the whole burden of my existence go. But the sun was gradually sinking behind the trees on the coast, and the need to find a place to stay was becoming acute. We had no water, and after last night's experience, it wouldn't even have occurred to me to put up a tent there. It also made me suspicious that nobody else was camping there.

I sat up in the sand and called Ben out of the water. "Not yet," he begged, and so I left him there for a while and watched him messing around, and in fact, I envied him. In my own childhood, I would have sat here stiffly, at most skimming pebbles. I would never have managed to be so relaxed.

Eventually I got dressed and assessed the situation. There was no option but to go back and get a place in the huge campsite. I didn't want to, but we couldn't have stayed here, without water and without a shower.

Gloom descended on me at the big entrance gates. The people staying here had all come for several weeks' vacation. We were going to be here for just a short while, and this would just be an episode in our journey to nowhere in particular. I paid the outrageous price, and we drove in, looking among the rows of mobile homes and big tents for a vacant space. We finally found one in sector B12, under number 22. Looking around, I could see that our small mountain tent was going to be out of place. Dusk was falling, but the street lights were turned on. I soon noticed that everyone around us was speaking Hungarian. A Hungarian travel agency had most likely rented out the whole area. All the caravans and tents were the same, and obese Hungarian families sat around camping tables, stuffing themselves with food. We put up our tent (usually inconspicuous but here so eye-catching) and headed for the shop and showers, all signaled by arrows. For the time being, we only glanced at the bathrooms; they were enormous, built for hundreds.

At ten, I got Ben into his sleeping bag, and he fell asleep right away. I wandered around aimlessly. Little groups of young people were walking past, heading for evening entertainment. I longed to chat with someone adult. I went to the car and took out my cell phone, which had been switched off for two weeks. I thought of one male friend and two female friends I could call, but I hesitated. I knew that as soon as I switched on the phone, there would be messages—urgent calls from the parents, questions about work. I sat down in the passenger seat of the pleasantly warm car and hesitated some more. Eventually I switched the thing on, of course. Soon the messages started to pop up, but I deleted them unread. The person I thought of most was Petra. Suddenly, I remembered I had dreamed about her the previous night. A fragment of the dream came back to me. I had come to find her in a big villa, where some celebration was underway. At first, I was moving around in a water-logged cellar, but then I found my way up into a dance hall. As soon as she saw me, she ran to me, and we twirled each other around several times…I punched in her number.

"Petra," she answered in her quiet but slightly astringent voice. "It's David, hi."

"Dave, where are you?" she reacted protectively, and I immediately knew she cared about me.

"Right now, I'm with Benjamin in a huge, awful campsite in Northern Italy, near Trieste, I think."

"So, you're on vacation." She sounded relieved.

"Not entirely. We drove off...on what we call a journey to the Back of Beyond. We keep driving. I don't know exactly where yet. I don't know when we're coming back either."

She sounded a little alarmed, "Hey, but you do have a responsibility, you know!"

"I know."

"I mean, not to drag Benjamin into something that is actually your problem. And Dave...is what you're doing always safe?"

Her fears were disconcerting but understandable. After all, I had asked myself the same questions. "Don't worry, I'm taking care. And so far, Ben is really eager. We're happy together. Sometimes we remember his Mom too." I sensed that I couldn't communicate all I was experiencing to Petra anyway. I didn't even want to try. It was just our journey, and no one else could understand it. Rather than our trip, it was her I wanted to talk about. I needed to tell her I still loved her after all these years.

"I wanted to say," I began, "that I often think about you. Even before all this, I thought about you. You're still with me." I knew she wasn't indifferent to me either—or she wouldn't have let her pleasure show when I called. The problem was her faithfulness to her decisions, her dutiful integrity. She thought it wasn't possible to start over, and she was consistent about that. And in fact, it made me respect her more, because she was right. It was thanks to her dutiful integrity that our relationship could last.

"I haven't forgotten you either, Dave. I like to hear from you."

Hearing her quiet, unaffected voice, I became aware of her whole being. And I was immediately aroused. "But it can't all be expressed in words," I said urgently. I was choking with desire.

She laughed ironically. "So, let's tell each other whatever we can express in words. That's enough for me."

I respected her too much to say or do anything that might upset our relationship. "Well, maybe I'll call again sometime."

"Call. But please, don't forget about that responsibility. Don't go too crazy. I mean it."

We said goodbye, and I immediately switched the cell phone off. I remained sitting in the car. The Hungarians were still stuffing themselves with sausages, while freshly showered people were strolling back from the bathrooms. Tiny insects and two large hawk moths were flying round the lamp. I thought of the last month in Prague. I had called Petra back then too, but I hadn't felt then what I felt today. Had I been denying myself any open emotion out of loyalty to my dead wife? Going to prostitutes wasn't making love. So back then, Petra and I had mainly talked practicalities. She had been interested in Benjamin—how he was taking it. She had asked after my parents too; in fact, she had just asked questions the whole time. We hadn't talked about her at all.

I got out of the car, still aroused. I walked up and down the track, and then checked on Benjamin. He was sleeping on his back with arms flung out above his head, completely at ease. My arousal faded, and I went off for a shower, but on the way, I met a southern type of girl. She was walking in the opposite direction, with just a shawl over her breasts and a towel around her hips. Her brown belly and what I could see of her buttocks suggested the curves hidden by the towel and shawl. They were lavish and firm. She herself looked self-confident and provocative. Not that there was any chance of proving to her that I, a pale Central European, was the best man to deal with her secret places, to bring her to the point of frenzy, cries, and tears. We passed each other, and I went on to the showers. The cubicles were separated by metal dividers like in sports locker rooms. I waited until the shower at the very back was free. I stripped, turned on the water, and facing into a corner, I quickly jacked myself off. It cleared my mind, and I was once again capable of seeing sense and thinking rationally, but I was sure this would only last for a while, and I really needed a woman. There had to be a nightclub somewhere here. Only at the same time, I was afraid.

Soon I lay down in the tent beside Benjamin, but I couldn't get to sleep for a long time. It was partly because of the rather strong light from the nearby lamp and partly the distant sounds of music and evening entertainment. And all of it mixed with the incomprehensible voices of the Hungarians.

Dad Goes Looking for Physical Love when the Real Kind Passes Him By

The next morning, we went to the official beach. I bought Ben a raft and a snorkel. The beach was only just beginning to fill up with people and so, for the time being, it was bearable. The sea was more open here than in the bay, and the wind was whipping up the first small waves. A few small boats were at anchor beyond guard buoys.

Ben rushed into the water, and I watched him anxiously from the raised dune at the top of the beach. It was getting hotter and the fattened-up Hungarians started to arrive, but also a few superb women in skimpy swimsuits. I was once again gripped by erotic tension. I thirsted for it to be evening; I thirsted for the physicality of the female body, for its scent and smell, for its moist crannies. And I believed in my own determination. The southern sun was scorching my head and leaving only a steam of thoughts. Actually, only two ideas remained in it. One was that nothing should happen to Ben, and the other that it should already be evening.

A couple of times I ran into the water after Ben, and we swam out to the buoys. At noon, I wanted to get him to sit in the shade, but maybe for the first time on the trip, he defied me. He stayed up to his waist in the water, reddening from the sun, but at the same time shivering with cold and angrily slapping the surface with his hands. "You keep taking me away from anywhere I like."

"I don't want to take you away from anywhere," I tried to explain. "I'm just afraid that we still haven't got used to so much sun, and it could make us sick. I don't want you to be sick."

In the end, he obeyed me although reluctantly. In the afternoon, we went back to the beach. He made friends with some boys who had a ball. One always threw the ball as far as he could, and the others competed to get to it fast. Benjamin tried over and over again, but he always finished last.

The sun finally started to sink towards the west, and people began to leave the beach. I wondered how I was going to manage it tonight. I would have to tell Ben that once he was asleep, I was going for a walk. We sat down in the camp restaurant. "This evening, once you're asleep, I'd like to go for a long walk," I said, and to my surprise I felt a stab of anxiety. The way it looked to me I was betraying him, abandoning him.

He gave me an alarmed look. "But I don't want you to go somewhere."

I caught his hand under the table. "Don't worry, I won't go far."

He didn't want to hear about it. "But what if I want to go the bathroom?"

"If you want to go the bathroom, you know the way, don't you? The street light is on all night, like in the city—nothing can happen to you." I tried to convince him and myself. I looked him straight in the eye. "Benjamin, you have to understand that on this trip of ours, I'm with you all the time and…"

"Not all the time," he interrupted, "When I was going to play soccer you weren't with me."

"That's true. I wasn't there then. But otherwise, I'm always with you. I love you terrifically, you know that. But it's not easy for a grown-up to be just with a child. Grown-ups think differently from children and have different kinds of fun. Sometimes they need to chat together, or they need to be alone for a while to think about the things they consider important." However eloquently I spoke, I still felt I was cheating him. "You know I'm doing what I can to make sure you like our trip. We've been to the mountains; we went on the chairlift; now you've been swimming in the sea, and maybe… maybe," (an idea I had had this morning came back to me), "we'll be going on a big ship." It had struck me that we shouldn't stay on this deformed coast. I wanted more purity and more waves and here and there some rocks. We could take a ferry with the car and go somewhere to the south—to Greece, to Tunisia, to Turkey…Who knew?

"Wow, I'd love that," Ben brightened. "And will there be a pool on the ship? And a tennis court?" He must have seen something like that in a movie.

"I doubt it. But first we have to find out if there are any ships like that sailing from here. So, what I wanted to say," I returned to the original theme, "is that if I leave you for a couple of hours to sleep on your own in the tent, that's nothing compared to what we've experienced together and are still experiencing. Do you understand?"

"Sure I do, Dad. And can we go the beach again tomorrow?"

"If you like it there…"

"I do."

Darkness fell, and the Hungarians started to stuff themselves at their tables again. Next to us a family with nearly-grown children was feasting, a girl and a boy. Both were already fat.

At half-past nine, there was still a lot of noise, and Ben couldn't go to sleep. I sat next to him in the tent and told him a story about how a father and son had set out on a trip like ours, but two centuries ago. They had travelled in horse-drawn wagons or on foot. They often got lost in deep forests. They had to avoid soldiers going to the war. They were driven out and then taken in, suspected of smuggling and espionage. Although they set out in July, just like us, they only reached the Alps at the beginning of winter. As they went on, they were stopped by newly fallen snow. Before I could work out how they got over the snowed-up pass, Ben had fallen asleep.

It was the moment I had been waiting for all day, but now I suddenly didn't want to go anywhere. I would have liked most to stretch out beside Ben and dream of those far-off times. But I knew that my urgent need would still come back, and if I put it off tonight, it would be completely unbearable all day tomorrow. I checked once again that my beloved Benjamin was sleeping and headed for the main campsite exit. The night was clear and warm. I walked past a disco bar, rhythmic music blaring from its flashing neon interior. Ordinary discos had no attraction for me, and even in my youth I had tended to avoid them. Yet today, I thought of that first meeting of boy and girl, the initial tension that precedes the touching, the kisses, and passion. Though, what do the young know of passion? I wondered. Nothing compared to what I knew in my maturity. I walked alone along the road to the gate. I believed I knew how to bring a woman to the point of blissful madness.

The street in front of the campsite was pretty quiet, and I didn't know which way to go. I turned back to the reception office. A dark-haired woman with a masculine look was sitting behind the little window. I hesitated—ingrained shame inhibited me from asking, but she seemed so businesslike and neutral. I went up to the window. "Nightclub?" I asked.

She waved to the right, as if indicating the way to the station. "Porto."

I set off along the solid fence of the campsite away from the sea. The lighting became sparser, and fear started to assail me. I had left Benjamin by himself, I thought, here in all this vast hustle and bustle, and was exposing myself to danger. If someone attacked me here, what would happen to Ben? He had lost his Mom, and now he only had me. He was completely dependent on me.

All the same, a kind of inner engine would not let me stop. I had to confirm I was a man. I had to acquire some self-confidence.

Beyond the camp stretched a no-man's land of disintegrating warehouses between bushes and thistles. Just a little further, at an unimportant crossroads, shone the lights of a small bistro. Here was the turning to the port. I headed in that direction, and my anxiety grew. I thought that the nightclub where the porter woman had sent me would be part of the tourist zone, but it belonged to the port. Who else would control it if not the mafia?

I continued for another five hundred meters or so. A red light was glowing from the first floor of a house on the other side of the road. Don't go there, everything in me warned. You shouldn't go there. I turned around and started a slow retreat. Get back to Benjamin, who is by himself! After all, he's your little fair-haired cherub, your friend, your vocation. He has gotten over his Mom's death, everything has turned out quite well. But if you desert him too, his life will become one of incomprehensible suffering…I stopped again and hesitated. I couldn't be with Benjamin and, at the same time, smother a lust so strong it was darkening my brain. I would become careless, obsessed.

The best solution for this awful dilemma—the best that had occurred to me—was Petra. If she would only be untrue to that dutifulness of hers. Her children were nearly grown, and she could easily come out and join us. We wouldn't have to get married, just live together sometimes. But I knew that some women are immovable in these matters. And that what might at first sight look like an unbearable absence of imagination was in reality an unerring instinct for discerning which things could be and which should not be.

I returned to the red glow, feeling like a dumb, fascinated insect. God, let me survive this. God, let me get back to Benjamin, I prayed on my way to violating God's commandments. This time I had to do it—it was a matter of self-respect. I went through the door.

I found myself in a red and black interior. A woman in late middle age immediately came up and put a friendly hand on my shoulder. "Come and sit down." She led me to a bar and her behavior, which seemed to acknowledge my fears, calmed me. "Will you have something to drink?"

I ordered a coke. The woman brought it to me with a price list. It turned out that it was only around twice as expensive here as in Bohemia. In the meantime, I had regained my nerve, but as if to spite me, I had lost any feeling of sexual interest. Instead, I was more concerned just to get it over with and be back with Ben. I ordered only a half hour with one climax. The lady seemed to want to go on chatting with me and offered me alcohol, but I made it clear I was impatient. I paid, and in a corner of my soul even now I expected several tough guys to turn up, rob me of everything and then—if I was lucky—just throw me out. Instead, three girls appeared dressed only in see-through panties with suspenders. They smiled knowingly, winked at me stupidly, and turned to show their hips. One was a blowsy fake blonde—I rejected her right away. I hesitated between a brunette with wonderful curves and a long face, and the least pretty more mature woman, whose seductive manner seemed to me the most sincere. She would definitely provide the best sex and be the readiest to fulfil my desires, but a kind of pride compelled me to choose sex with the beauty. She took me off to a room, and it seemed to me that there was sadness and understanding on the face of the ugly one.

My first thought in that humble little room was that I already had half the business behind me. All that remained was the sex, and then I would rush back to Ben. I stripped behind a narrow screen and showered. Finally, I was getting an erection. I tried to imagine sinking it into her. The girl was waiting on the bed, naked. Her ass was what attracted me, but she turned to me head on. She gave me a condom and applied gel between her legs. I started to caress her. Just as she pretended smiles and desire, I pretended enchantment with her body, while in fact, I was only interested in one thing: thrusting it into her from the back and pumping hard. For a while I stroked her out of politeness and she started to touch my cock and give me head. I held her back and finally managed to turn her around the way I wanted to take her. She understood and opened her legs as wide as she could—at least they respected the customer here.

So, I pumped, but all my thoughts kept escaping back to Ben, and it took quite a long time. At one point, it even seemed to me that she was starting to like it and her gasps were genuine. Hard to say. When it was over, we lay beside each other for just a moment, and then she was taking off the condom and wiping me with a cloth. I got dressed quickly and didn't even shower. When I went downstairs, I found that two unkempt men had come and sat down in the meantime. They're going to rob me now, I thought, when the girl left me at the bottom of the stairs. I hesitantly walked into the center of the room and waited to see what would happen. But the men greeted me cheerfully. They were probably sailors. "Do you want anything else? Were you satisfied?" the woman asked from across the bar.

"Satisfied? Sure." I realized I was free.

I went out into the warm night and almost felt that I was flying. I had done it—I had overcome fear and nothing had happened to me yet. I started back with fast, springy steps, In the sky, the stars were shining, now once again for me as well as others. If not from here—I decided—then there would certainly be ships departing long-distance from Trieste. I imagined us sleeping out on deck under this sky, all around us the sea, and both of us dreaming of the other end of nowhere. And always, when the urge overcame me, I would be able to relieve it in some way like this.

I had a moment of embarrassment when I had to go back past reception, but the woman sat there in an attitude of complete indifference and evidently didn't even notice me as an individual. This was a factory, a conveyor belt with tourists who arrived and went through like chickens hung on hooks in the poultry farm, where it was just a matter of ripping their Euros out of them instead of their innards.

I was a little apprehensive as I unzipped the tent. What would I do if Benjamin wasn't there? … He was there. On his back and sleeping like an angel.

The Sick Son Longs for His Mom and the Journey to the Back of Beyond is in Jeopardy

We spent the next day on the beach as well. He played there with me and the boys, and it occurred to me that, in the evening, I might repeat my visit to that night club, now that I knew it was safe. But in the afternoon, Ben started to feel sick. We had just come from a late lunch; originally, I had promised him that we would go straight back to the sea. He began to complain that his head ached, and he felt ill. He could hardly manage to drag himself back into the tent. It was obviously sunstroke. It was only then that I realized how deceptive the ever-present heat was. You can escape from the cold by covering up or wrapping yourself up in a sleeping bag, but the heat penetrates everything, and the tent couldn't be aired out. The only thing I could have done would be to turn on the engine and switch on the air conditioning, but I definitely wouldn't have been allowed to do that here and didn't want to. There was nothing for it but for Ben to crawl into the overheated tent. In the meantime, he had already developed chills. I ran to buy clean water and gave him two aspirin with it. But there was a problem. When he drank a lot, he had to go and pee, and the bathrooms were several hundred meters away. Everything would have been a lot easier if we had been in a hotel.

The fever went down towards evening. Benjamin woke up from his half-sleep and looked at me with tormented eyes: "Dad, I want to go home to Mom."

Sorrow tightened round my heart. It took so little to dispel the illusion of happiness. Like every child, he needed his Mom most of all. He needed her without even realizing it. She was the only person who could take away a part of the pain in moments when things didn't work out for him, when he felt bad, when he was sick.

"Benjamin." I stroked his sweaty brow, "Mom is definitely here with you. She'll always be close to you. Wherever you are."

But Ben was working himself up to tears. "But I want her to show that she's here. I want to be with her."

The tears welled up unstoppably—more intense than I had ever seen in Ben. I knew that these were tears that had been building up over a long time. These were the tears that had not reached the surface when he was told of her death, or later at the funeral, or when we visited her grave. These were tears that there was no reason to stop, but I would still have given a piece of my life to have been able to stop them, to have been able to comfort my son. "I know, Benjamin." I hugged him and kept stroking his forehead. "I know you want to be with her."

Later, when the weeping had changed into irregular sobbing, I went on. "Now the main thing is for you to get well. You just have a touch of sunstroke, because you aren't used to such strong sun. After two or three days, it will pass, and you'll be able to swim again, and if you want, we'll go on the ship together."

"I don't know if I want to," he said truthfully.

"I'm not surprised. If I was feeling sick, I wouldn't know either. You only want to do new things when you feel well. But there's one thing we can do. Tomorrow we could find a guesthouse or hotel where you'll be able to rest better. Agreed?"

"Will there be sea by the hotel?"

"There has to be sea. We wouldn't want to stay in any hotel where there wasn't sea. I just hope that we'll manage to find one like that."

"Okay, Dad," he whispered and turned his back to me.

I stroked his hair for a little longer and then quietly slipped out of the tent. He didn't object, even though he wasn't asleep. Even such a small person already needed to have time for himself, to think, to dream, to remember.

In the night, he went to the bathroom about ten times, and in the morning, he was completely exhausted. He lay almost helplessly in the tent and stared at me with extinguished eyes; he didn't want to eat or drink. At least he no longer had a fever. I bought some yogurt and made tea on a gas camping stove. I wondered if we should pack up and look for some proper accommodation. But what if, in the end, we couldn't find any? I hadn't seen any hotels or guesthouses in the vicinity, and if there were some, they might be full. I couldn't risk exposing Benjamin to laborious packing and then finding myself out in the street with him in the noonday heat.

Time was dragging, and it was getting hotter again in the tent. "Dad, how about we drive home, and then come back once I'm better?" suggested Ben.

"Don't you remember what a long way that is?" I said. I tried to explain that it was really impossible. Yes, if he wanted, we could go back. But he shouldn't think that if we did that, we could continue… Probably he wanted to go back, but he was too keen to swim in the sea again. We decided that he would try to hold out. While we were talking about it, I felt a strange kind of depression descending. Outside it was a bright day, but I was starting to see everything as colorless, grey. There was no reason to be exactly here exactly now. There was no reason to be anywhere else either. I had stopped believing that the world could offer anything surprising that could change my destiny. If I hadn't found meaning in a Prague apartment, I wasn't going to find it anywhere else.

Father and Son Become Inseparable

So, we suffered with sunstroke for another two days in that monster camp. Benjamin no longer had a fever, but he was weak, and I didn't want to allow him to walk in the sun. We killed time between the showers, tent, shop, and restaurant. Sometimes, it took all my determination to make him get up and crawl out of the tent. You can only have a taste for life if you desire something, or if you get to some point of inner enlightenment and can free yourself from all desire. I had not freed myself from desires; I remained addicted to them. Having something to look forward to (at least a sports program on television), having somewhere to head for (at least the nearest brothel), having a reason to expect that the next day would bring something important or beautiful (at least a meeting promising a deeper relationship)—I needed all that for the passing moment not to seem pointless to me. But what was there to look forward to in a situation where I was expecting Benjamin would soon say that he wanted to go home? Even women were not arousing me anymore. I was gearing myself up to fulfill Benjamin's wish. The local attractions were losing their charm even for him, and he was going to lose interest in swimming in the sea or taking a sea voyage and just want to go home. So, I was gearing myself up to make a home for him of the kind that every child needs. It's not important for a child if his parent is being stifled by everyday banality.

Yet I think that it was then, over those two dismal stressful days, that a bond was forged between us that made us inseparable. Although I lacked a reason to be here, and he would have found it hard to find one either, I felt that he sensed how and what I was thinking, and that he was deciding about me too, and that it was for my sake that he was sticking it out. On the evening of the second day, we went out for a walk on the twilit beach. The sea was silent and neither of us was in the mood for talking. On the way back, he said, "Dad, go and have a walk if you want, when I'm asleep. You don't have to stand guard over me all the time." That moved me to tears.

On the third day, I allowed Ben to swim again. It was disconcerting how little things had changed on the beach. The same people, the same waveless sea. Only the sun didn't shine so brightly, and there were several white lines of clouds in the sky.

At midday, when the heat was becoming unbearable, I suggested to Ben that we should go to the port and find out something about ship departures.

"All right," he agreed, "But then I want to go swimming again," he insisted immediately.

Once again, we found ourselves in the confusing industrial zone that they called the port here. What now? I followed a truck and reached a barrier. A number of other trucks were parked behind it. A porter came out of his booth and took some papers from the truck driver. We had no papers, and so he sent us to a glass building opposite, but I couldn't see any information boards there, let alone a ticket office or schedule of boat departures.

"Dad, are we going to sail from here?" Ben pestered me with questions to which I had no answers.

"I don't know, Benjamin. You can see what it's like here. I just don't know."

We left the air-conditioned car and were almost knocked over by the heat. Behind the glass door was a dull corridor and staircase with no aspirations to architecture. I knocked at the first door and tried the handle. To my surprise, the door opened and I found myself in a small office. Two men were sitting at a counter. One was behind the counter—probably an official—and the second was a short, tanned figure who was handing something over to him. They both looked around startled.

"Excuse me," I blurted out, "I just wanted to ask if there were ferries running from here to Greece or Turkey."

The answer was simple: "There are no ferries running here." And when I just stood there, the official impatiently hooted, "Trieste, Pier 52."

I thanked him and left. "What did you find out, Dad?" Ben wanted to know.

"We have to go to Trieste. Nothing runs from here. It's probably just a freight port."

"But I don't want to go anywhere else. I want to go swimming."

I lost my temper. "So, go swimming. And we'll never get away from this place."

Annoyed with each other, we were just getting back into the car when the small brown man from the office came running up. "You want to go to Greece?" he asked me. "I could take you. Tomorrow."

My mind started working feverishly. The man probably wanted to make some money on the side by taking us on his freight ship illegally. What a wonderful possibility, a wonderful experience! Travelling among sailors—different from all the rest. But how on earth could I take such a risk? Alone with Benjamin among rough, dubious people, and when no one in the world knew where we were? My imagination quickly painted a dreadful story of how they would rob us, throw me overboard, and sell Benjamin. … I frowned as if regretfully. "Tomorrow isn't possible. We're waiting for someone else. We could only go at the beginning of next week."

He shrugged his shoulders in a gesture of disappointment, but also indifference, and walked off.

We drove back to the camp. On the way, I decided there had probably been no danger of a trick. In the era of cell phones, they couldn't know whether or not I had told friends I was travelling on their boat. I felt ashamed that, in the end, we had been forced to refuse a chance to get off the usual tramlines.

I looked in the campsite reception office to see if they had any ferry schedules. They had a reluctant air, as if it had nothing to do with them. In the end, they gave me a telephone number. This was starting to be a bore. I had imagined that our voyage would be a straightforward continuation of our journey, but so far, it had been a matter of laborious and rather banal practicalities. From the phone information services, I nonetheless gathered that there were ferries to the Greek island of Corfu running from Pier 52 on Mondays, Tuesdays, and Wednesdays at 19.00 and on Fridays, Saturdays, and Sundays around noon. Since it was already Wednesday, the next possibility was on Friday. Apparently, there were still places available, but to be sure, we had to arrive one day in advance.

In the afternoon, Benjamin messed crazily around in the sea again. As I watched his endless, constantly repeating games, it occurred to me that if we were leaving tomorrow, tonight I had a last opportunity to visit the local brothel. Not that I felt any burning desire this time. It was more like I coolly calculated that I needed to exploit a tried and tested safe opportunity that might not arise anywhere else in the coming days.

I sat down again at the top of the beach—a raised spot between remnants of dry grass. Quite a fresh wind was blowing from the sea today. Thoughts of the brothel failed to produce an erection and that prompted me to try to provoke one. I looked around at some of the tanned bodies lying closest to me. But I reflected that even if one of them would agree to sex, what was the point of orgasm without love? What kind of meaning and what kind of unique experience could be found in mere sex, when there were billions of people in the world, and so billions of orgasms?

I longed for love, painfully and desperately. If only Petra were here. Or if I could meet someone with whom I could find a use for all that piled up emotional potential, multiplied by years of deprivation. But I only had to look around, my eyes glancing off all those Walkmans, magazines, beach umbrellas, and sunscreens, to know that today the waiting would be in vain.

"So, now I'm going for a walk, the one you gave your permission for yesterday," I said to Benjamin that evening in the tent.

"All right, Dad," he agreed.

I headed for the brothel. I felt like a loser—the most degenerate of all. At least we were leaving tomorrow. I wished myself anywhere but in this recreation factory. Motion at least gave me the illusion of hope, even if I had no goal.

They Go to the Port and Prepare for Their Voyage

In the morning, Benjamin persuaded me to let him go swim by himself while I packed up, but I finished the packing fast and then waited for him impatiently. He came in only a little later than he had promised, but I still snapped at him, saying he wasn't responsible or reliable. Then I was sorry for my bad temper, and I couldn't see a way to make things right—I sensed that he took me seriously and took it as his fault. If I had apologized immediately, it would have confused him.

We drove through the port industrial zone again and followed the signs for the highway in the direction of Trieste. The weather was merciful; the sun stayed behind the clouds, and there was no extreme heat. I was tense because of my uncertainty that I would find Pier 52 somewhere in the big port of a big city, but the fast drive into the unknown was exciting. Ben was in the back seat, and I watched him in the rearview mirror. He sat up straight, staring ahead, and there was a kind of cloudless peace and resignation in his eyes. I hoped for this time in his life, that he could still leave his fate in my hands without restlessness or worry, but I couldn't imagine quite how he saw me.

I'm not a Dad, I wanted to say, I'm just a boy like you. It's not so long ago I was a child myself, and when I look back, I see the path that runs all the way from my childhood to here. I still have those experiences, griefs, and joys, my childish disappointments in myself. My soul is also the soul of a child and always will be, because it doesn't forget its childhood. Dear Ben, I believe that this is the only way I can be a comprehensible Dad for you—by remaining a child, by staying in touch with my memory. Because it's the men, who take themselves too seriously in their roles and regard themselves as real fathers, that are actually strangers in their own homes: feared, incomprehensible, untouchable… That was what I said to him and myself in my head, as I hurtled towards Trieste along the crowded highway. I noticed that the port and even Pier 52 appeared regularly on the road signs, and so I was reassured. The landscape was not so flat after all; there were limestone rocks, dry bushes, and the black burned stumps of trees.

We had plenty of time, but I decided to prioritize getting to the port and buying tickets. After a while, a city appeared on the right. The houses here were painted in earthy colors (white or reddish). It reminded me more of the Balkans than Italy. The highway continued at a respectful distance from the town, and the sign for Pier 52 kept pointing straight ahead, while the exits to the right were for the center. Finally, only Split and Pier 52 remained on the signs. Then we passed the last exit for Split, and only Pier 52 was left. The motorway eventually ended, and we found ourselves in a line of cars. Now that we were going slowly, I at least had a chance to look around. Occasionally, there were glimpses of the sea far below us. The large concrete houses on the slope—massive and ugly—were reminiscent of our Czech modern housing estates, although they must have had a superb view of the bay, the port, and the city. As always, I was appalled by the sight of so many windows in a foreign town. Again, I had to wonder if so many unique human destinies could fit behind so many windows. Or if each window just concealed the same stereotypical coexistence of a penis and a vagina, and the same desires in the form of a new television, soccer match, or popular series.

It was only then that Benjamin woke up from his resigned trance on the back seat. "Look, there's a boat. Down there on the sea. And there are others over there."

"The port we will be sailing from is probably down there."

"Can we swim at the port?"

"Definitely not. The water in ports is usually dirty. Boat engines run on diesel oil, and sometimes a little oil leaks into the water. There's also all the trash that people sweep off the decks. And maybe people flush the boat's bathrooms into the sea. And then there can be

110

different ropes and wires in the water that you could get tangled up in. No, Benjamin, ports aren't places for swimming."

"But why do people throw the trash overboard?"

We had now driven down the hill and were almost at sea level. The road widened again and doubled back towards the city, and so now we had the sea on our left. Only we could no longer see it, for once again we had driven into an industrial zone. It was much bigger than the one before, with disintegrating factories, cranes, warehouses, rail tracks, garbage trucks, and conveyor belts. There was nothing for it but to say goodbye to any vision of boardwalks full of cafes or a picturesque harbor with lots of little steamboats for excursions.

I slowed down so as not to miss an exit, but the signs continued to take us straight ahead for another five kilometers. Then came the exit road. We found ourselves underneath the overpass in a labyrinth of exits. The sign sent us further downhill. In front of us was a large open space with a porter's lodge and parked trucks. I got out and went to ask the porter, and he sent us even further down an inconspicuous track. There we encountered another big space with a row of ugly dormitories. A Greek flag fluttered over one of them. A few caravans stood here as well.

So, this was the Pier 52 proclaimed by motorway signs tens of kilometers in advance of Trieste. It was just an expanse of asphalt with dirty corners and bushes pissed on by stray cats, dogs, and human beings. Undoubtedly a paradise for harbor rats. Children were running around one of the motor homes. The plates indicated that they were Germans. I felt a certain relief. I wouldn't like to bump into any Czechs taking a vacation.

The office in the prefab hostel was just opening after the noon siesta. The warm, still air was stale with smoked meat and overheated plastic. The ferry did indeed leave on Friday at midday, but I was surprised to discover that the passage to Corfu would take a whole twenty-four hours (I had thought we would have been there by evening on the same day). They no longer had cabin spots, but they sold me deck tickets. I imagined us sleeping outside under the sky.

Unless of course the ship looked like this prefab… I asked the Greek at the window if he had a brochure with a photo of his boat. He fumbled around in a drawer as if looking for something, but then shook his head. He didn't.

Just as Hungarians had predominated in the camp, the parking lot in front of the hostel filled up with Germans. They were arriving with their motor homes, some had surfboards on the roof, and others had a boat on a trailer. We walked between them awkwardly. We couldn't get to the sea, for the gate in a barbed wire fence was locked, and so we set off for the city on foot. The sun had once again come out from the clouds but evening was approaching. Despite the grindingly slow passage of time in these inhospitable parts, I looked to the future with hope. After all, we were on the seashore, where one journey ends and another begins. To my surprise, Benjamin didn't complain about not being able to swim. He just kept on asking what the boat would look like and how big it would be.

The residential district around the port was not among the most affluent. The whole city spread out on a slope, and so we walked uphill. We passed a few grimy buffets. I wondered if there was a bus to the center, but I wasn't a great fan of monuments, and Benjamin would probably not have been enthusiastic either. We attracted the unpleasant attention of some staring youths. If I had been in Bohemia, I would have totally ignored them as just a bunch of young loiterers in a pub. But we were in a foreign land, and what's more, a port city, and so I was on my guard.

"Where are we going to sleep, Dad?" Ben asked over supper, "If that boat isn't leaving until tomorrow?"

I had just been thinking about it. To stay by the pier meant sleeping in the car, in the discomfort and dirt. But I didn't want to take the car anywhere else—because we would lose us our place in the boarding line, and I didn't trust the Greeks to have room for everyone. On the way from the pier, I had noticed one hideous hotel. It probably served poorer people on work trips or was just a hostel. "Maybe we'll stay in a hotel," I said hesitantly.

"Yeah, a hotel," Ben brightened, "Will there be a beach by the hotel?"

"A beach?" I frowned, "There are no beaches here. It's a port."

"But you said we wouldn't stay in a hotel without a beach."

I realized what he meant. Yes, I'd told him that when I'd spoken about a hotel in the camp. "You know Benjamin," I explained, "now we're in a city and just waiting for our boat to leave. I thought that instead of sleeping in the car, we could find a room somewhere close, and go back to the car in the morning. We're sailing to the island of Corfu. There are wonderful beaches there, and you'll be able to swim in beautiful water for as long as you like."

We checked into the old hotel. The corridors were dark and the plaster cracked in the room, but we had our own bathroom and bathroom, and in reception we rented a television so that Ben could watch Eurosport. Until about ten, he watched everything possible— boxing, soccer, and tennis—and then I sent him to bed. "Dad, does Mom know that we're going on a boat?" he asked, and from his tone, I couldn't tell whether this was just curiosity, or whether he felt that we should inform Mom before we did anything so unusual.

"That's not something anyone can say for certain—what it's like after death. If people are still aware of particular things like that, or maybe just know that we're here and remember them. But if you want Mom to know, then she does know."

"I want her to know. But I was wondering if she would mind."

"Mind? Why should she mind? The dead can't influence what the living do and definitely don't want to influence it either. She would only mind if we forgot about her. Then it would be as if you hadn't taken her with you. But as far as I know, you think about her often."

In the morning, the pier was busy. There were several dozen German families and a few Slovenians waiting as well. Officials were giving out numbers, and we gradually lined up at the gate. My pulse quickened with joy at how it was all working out. The ship was already anchored by the pier. The first to board were two trucks, then several motor homes, and then I was heading into the bowels of the ship.

When we left the shore and drove down the sloping bridge, I couldn't help remembering her—Benjamin's mom. Her life had not been happy, and maybe she was mostly to blame for that, but she had loved the sea. At the seaside, she had always revived. Only the sea could fill her with delight and freshness and relieve her of the weight of her existence. If she had been with us today, which of course was impossible, because with her I would never have set out on such a journey, she would have enjoyed that moment of boarding the same way I did.

We parked the car in the hold according to the instructions and hurried up to the deck with the backpack to find a good place. "It's a big ship," Ben exulted.

The passenger deck was in the bows, and we were one of the first to get there. I chose a bench under a roof but close to the railings. Suddenly we were looking at the asphalt expanse from above and across the water. The never-ending bustle of the town—all that dirt, heat, and stress—stopped affecting us. Here on the deck, in the shadow, it was pleasant, and there was a cooling morning breeze. But it took another hour before the boat was full and prepared for departure. In the meantime, the breeze had dropped, and we were being stifled by the greasy smoke from the ship's chimney. Waiting for the voyage was becoming unpleasant. I just want us to be off, I thought. "When are we going?" Ben asked aloud.

Finally, the propeller started to turn and the coast started to recede. The air immediately became cleaner—it was refreshing and flowed around us freely. We excitedly jumped up to stand by the railings. I put an arm around Benjamin's shoulders and pressed him to my side. "So here we go. It's only now that our journey to the Back of Beyond is really beginning.

Chapter III

The Journey to the Back of Beyond Starts in Earnest

They Sail on a Ship, the Sea Sets them Free, and Dad Finds the Word of God

We had been sailing out of the port fast, and so we could now see the whole bay and the city on its parched slopes like on a postcard. I had to admit that, from a distance, even a human settlement could look splendid and romantic.

In my head, I indulged the fancy that someone was following us, maybe spies or kidnappers, and they were now standing on the coast while we sailed away, escaping forever from our past and everything that bound us to it. The gulls seemed a symbol of escape.

After about an hour at sea, we relaxed and settled down—like all the others. A few charming young couples were on the boat with us. I envied them; they were lucky to have found each other so young and to be having the kind of travel experiences together I probably would never have now. There was also a bunch of Greeks, evidently returning from a family celebration, since I could see representatives of every generation from grandmothers in black headscarves to a newborn in baby wraps. Then there were several surprisingly quiet German families still up on deck.

For long minutes we watched the white foam in the wake of the boat. The water glittered blue, silver, and white, and seemed almost translucent. Benjamin tormented me with all kinds of questions— How fast were we going? How deep was the sea? Did sharks live here? Could I make it to the coast if we were wrecked? I had never before been on a boat for so long. At most, I had taken short trips from one island to another on vacation. So, I was just as excited as Ben, just as amazed, and just as intoxicated.

When our eyes had gotten sore from looking at the foam, we went to the rear where the captain's bridge was, and then down to the ship's restaurant. It was there, looking at the portholes, that we first realized the boat was rocking. It wasn't at all luxurious, but

117

all the same, there were two parties of young people here, clearly unimpressed by the voyage and dressed for the town.

"Can we go upstairs again?" Ben implored.

"I don't like it here either."

As the afternoon went by, the wind blew more strongly on the open sea, the waves grew larger and the rocking of the boat grew more pronounced. Ben wanted to walk around the boat by himself, but I was afraid to let him. We were sitting next to each other on an unrolled sleeping bag, his shoulder gently touching my arm. The sun, straight ahead of us, got itself bogged down in a belt of grey above the horizon and turned the outlines of the clouds first pink and then red. Later the white disk of the moon appeared, and the Greeks sat down to their evening prayer. I followed their example and turned to God. "If you exist, God," I said silently, "grant us a full and happy life, the kind we're experiencing just now, close to you."

As the sun set, the temperature dropped fast. The young couples squeezed closer to each other, the Germans brought out thermos flasks of tea and covered the children with blankets. I took our down sleeping bags out of the backpack as well as something to eat. "I don't want to go to sleep yet, Dad," Ben grumbled.

I let him stay up, and we spent a long time looking over the railings together again. The sea around us was now grey white and gradually vanishing into the gathering dusk. The moon had acquired a slightly yellow tinge, and the first star had come out close to it. The ship's engine rumbled on with undiminished vigor.

Eventually, I got Benjamin into his sleeping bag. He stuck out a hand and softly caught me by the arm: "Dad, I don't want this to end, not ever."

"How do you mean?"

"Our journey, I don't want it to ever stop. Our journey to the Back of Beyond. I don't want us ever to get there."

"I guess our whole life can be this kind of journey," I replied. I was speaking metaphorically although I knew he wasn't—and it was this one trip he meant. But it was important for me at the time to tell the truth without coming down hard on his ideas. "If that's what we want, a journey can be lifelong."

I left him by himself and went for a stroll. The ship was constantly rocking, but I was used to it now. The bustle around us had finally died down. The children of the Germans were asleep on blankets on the floor. Curled up in coats and rugs, the Greeks were dozing on their seats, and one young couple was most probably making love under their blanket. Their happiness filled me with pain, but I could see its positive value. As I stood on deck under a sky scattered with stars, I saw this pain as something that made my life unique. Yes, this is what I am—a man who has lacked a great love in life, but who has been freed by fate from a soul-destroying relationship and given a beloved son, Benjamin.

I was tempted to call Petra to share my feelings with her. I knew that, with every word she misunderstood, I might lose a piece of this special moment, but I still went to get my mobile phone. Benjamin was already asleep. Just the tip of his nose peeked out of the sleeping bag and he was talking steady tranquil breaths. I found my mobile and went back to the railings, but then decided to walk along the boat to the bows, where I was even more alone. I just wanted to tell Petra how I was standing in the middle of the sea, how Benjamin was sleeping, and how I had several stars above my head. I wanted to tell her that I felt melancholy but also wonderful and that she was the only person I brought to mind in moments like this. With a feeling of self-reproach for my inability to experience these moments entirely alone, I switched on the mobile and was about to punch in her number when I saw there was no signal—there was no signal at all at sea. I felt almost light-headed at this amazing discovery: circumstances had just forced me to be self-sufficient in a way that my own will could not. I immediately had another idea, and although I was later to regret it, at the time it seemed inevitable and the only right thing to do. I threw the mobile into the dark waters in front of me, and in that moment, it became a mere stone. I was flooded with a sense of satisfaction. My spirit soared like a bird.

The Sea Shows Them Their Nullity

When I returned, Benjamin was hidden right up to the hair. I rolled out my sleeping bag on the floor beside him. Lying on my back, I was very aware of the rise and fall of the deck. It made me feel ill for a while, and I couldn't fall asleep. Stretched out with my head in the direction of the voyage, I gazed into the darkness above me. Somewhere above my feet, the roof of the deck ended, and the starry sky began. A cold fresh wind flowed over my face. I imagined that it wasn't the ship but I myself floating and rolling on the waves. I was sorry that human beings couldn't feel as light and cheerful in the moment of death. It would make death something honorable and lofty—a real high point that the soul could reach in its earthly body and also the beginning of the true journey. I thought of my mobile phone too, and how it had must have already found its place somewhere in the depths on the sea floor, along with all those numbers, messages, and emails.

I woke towards daybreak as the darkness grew paler. The continuing roar of the engine and regular rolling on the waves seemed to hold out a guarantee that all was well with my journey, and it was proceeding just as it should. I stretched out a hand to check Benjamin, but to my alarm and horror I felt nothing but an empty yielding sleeping bag. I scrambled to my feet just as I was—in briefs and t-shirt. My heart was in my mouth, just as it had been recently in the tent by the river. The endless expanse of water around the boat had become a trackless wilderness. I immediately thought of more than one appalling explanation. Maybe someone had thrown Ben overboard, or maybe he had gone to look at the sea, leaned over the railings and fallen… Or else maybe it was a combination of the two; he had been leaning over and someone evil, standing close by, had given into temptation at that unlucky moment and tossed him over. This third version struck me as the least unlikely. I too had known sudden malevolent impulses triggered by an unexpected opportunity.

In fact, it was much more likely that Benjamin was somewhere on the boat and had gone to the bathroom or wandered away to look at the sea. But that still surprised me. I would have thought he would wake me and not go by himself.

I ran down the poorly lit steps to the bathroom one deck below: "Are you there?" I rattled the locked door. "Benjamin!"

"Yes, Dad," came an agonized voice.

"Are you okay? Were you feeling ill?"

"I felt like I was going to puke. And I have diarrhea, I think."

"Open the door for God's sake. Why on earth did you lock yourself in?"

He unlocked the door, and I went into the sticky stench of the cubicle. My heart was back to regular again, my biggest fear gone. I held Ben up, so he didn't have to sit on the squalid seat. He was sweating from his efforts to shit. Not even a touch of the fresh breeze from the plains of the sea reached down here, in the ship's lav. Ideally, I would have taken him upstairs and held him in a squat over the railings... "So, you've been sitting suffering here all by yourself? Why on earth didn't you wake me?" I demanded, "I would have come with you at once. When I didn't find you in the sleeping bag, I was really worried."

"I thought I wouldn't make it in time."

"Okay."

In the end, he didn't have diarrhea, just nausea. We went back to the deck in our t-shirts and briefs. In the meantime, the darkness had thinned some more, and the silver-grey sea had appeared again around the ship. Cold rose from the water, but we stayed by the railings. "You know what?" I said, "Let's sit here and look at the sea." I gestured to the nearest unoccupied bench, because the wind was strongest there. "I'll bring the sleeping bags over."

We sat with our faces to the wind and the paling horizon, huddled in our sleeping bags. "Does Grandpa Tomáš know we're here?" Ben asked all of a sudden.

"Nobody knows," I said truthfully, "Not Grandpa Pavel, or Grandma Běla, or Grandpa Tomáš…" (He hadn't mentioned any of our relatives since we left Prague, so now I waited to see what was coming.)

"Did they ever go a boat like this?"

"No way. They never travelled like this. It was a different time. Back then people were poorer. Most of them would never have had the money for this kind of journey. Then the communists came to power, and people weren't even allowed to travel." As I spoke, I realized that, even in earlier times, there were people who travelled. Those sorts of people, longing for adventure or a change, had always existed. They had moved to America, for example, or Israel. Even if they were poor. It was only superficial—the way the affluence of the modern period had blurred the difference, but while almost everyone travelled, there were still only some (no more numerous than before) who set out in happy uncertainty. Happy because only from this insecurity, the experience of being lost in the Back of Beyond, can the greatest of all certainties be born. And that is the certainty of the present moment in time. The certainty of being.

The sea was turning an unfriendly white and turbulent. Instead of a gentle morning breeze, there was a quite strong cold wind. The Greeks moved somewhere downstairs, and the Germans must also have been feeling chilly, but we had good quality sleeping bags designed for the mountains and went back to our places. I hid my head in the sleeping back and a comforting warmth spread around me. I wished to sleep, nothing more.

Waking again into bright daylight, this time I was sure something was wrong. I stuck my head out. Benjamin was where he ought to be, but the sky was covered in ominous white clouds, and there was a gale-force wind blowing. The deck rose upwards and to the side, and there was no one on it but us.

I was afraid I might have missed something. Was a disaster imminent? The ship seemed pretty large to me, and I couldn't imagine the waves here harming it. So why had everyone disappeared below deck? I looked at my watch. It was half past eight. I longed for the safety of the dry land that was waiting for us somewhere ahead, according to the company schedule, another four hours away. How wonderful it would be to stand on firm land instead of an unsteady deck and watch the raging sea from there. Where was that certainty of the present moment now? I was ready to give it up without hesitation.

I tugged at the sleeping Benjamin. "Hey…I think a gale could be coming. Everyone else has gone. We've got to go and take cover."

Confused, he started to struggle out of his sleeping bag: "Dad, I feel sick."

I wasn't feeling so great myself. I rolled up the sleeping bags fast. "Get dressed! Hurry! We've got to go down below!"

The restaurant was packed and made me feel even more nauseated. The Greeks were eating their own supplies, while the Germans looked terrified but were comforting themselves with laughter. I ordered two teas. The number of people was oppressive. I wondered how a crowd like this one would behave if something really happened. There was no sign of any crew member, anyone responsible for keeping order, but from the expressions on the faces of the waiters, it seemed there was no special need to fear. People had probably come down, because they had no warm clothes. All the same, I was afraid to go back up on deck, especially with an eight-year-old child.

After about an hour, the sunlight brightened behind the portholes, and the crowd in the restaurant started to thin. Benjamin and I went back up on deck too. The wind had dropped, and the only reminder of the gale was an unfriendly blurred silhouette of clouds on the skyline.

"Land, Dad, I can see land!" Ben suddenly jumped up and dashed over to the left-hand railings.

It was true. Parched treeless slopes—more white than yellow— had emerged from the blue-white mist. It was the coast of Albania, that strange land belonging to Europe and yet outside it. It was not all that far, but I couldn't see any highways or villages or any sign of hotel complexes. Of course, there had to be some settlements and roads. Slowly, we sailed around Albania through calm seas to the south. The wind disappeared completely, and the surface of the water became almost flat. Gradually we took off everything that we had put on that morning. It was hot.

My first impression of the island of Corfu, with its green hills under a clear sky, was of a kind of Pacific paradise. The sea washed all impurities from the shore and merciful distance, aided by the haze of noon, concealed all the scars of civilization that the local people must certainly have inflicted there. It was the island of our dreams. In the breathtaking moments as the ship sailed into the narrow straits between the rocky green island and the dry mainland, it was easy to imagine that we were somewhere far more remote, or here but in long-past times. Of course, soon we could see numerous small buildings on the coast (guesthouses and villas) and then a highway and a constant stream of cars. In the end, we packed up all our things and prepared to go down to the car. The Germans were already waiting by the steps to the hold.

A light-hearted holiday mood seized me. This wasn't oppressive Italy with its industry, malls, and big cities. Here it looked as if people could just live on sun and water. Benjamin ran from one side of the deck to the other in excitement. He pointed out yachts and motor boats and every beach he spied, asking me if that would be the beach where we were going to swim. I kept on saying I had never been here before and had no idea.

The boat was heading for a nearby harbor across a large bay dominated by quite a high rocky mountain, where the sun was blazing on scree and cliffs. After what I had seen in Trieste, the harbor looked picturesque like everything around it.

Reluctantly, we went down to the hold. The ship anchored, and the lit interior of the garage started to fill up with engine fumes. It was half an hour before it was our turn to exit, but then a truck blocked the way and foot passengers started to walk out in front of us. Finally,

I drove down the ramp onto the concrete of the harbor, turned off the main drag, and got out onto the quayside. The ground beneath me still seemed to be moving up and down. I walked unsteadily, Ben already pointing out a shoal of fish. "Is swimming in a harbor forbidden even here on this island?" he asked.

"Can you see anyone swimming here? Apart from the fish?" I was still feeling both excited and fulfilled. I had yearned to get out of Prague and set off on a journey, and this yearning could easily have stayed locked up forever in the deepest cellars of my soul, as often happens. It was true that, after several weeks of travel, we were now somewhere that we could have reached in a few hours if we had gone through a travel agency, but it was those weeks that separated us from the tourists around us. We had nothing in common with them—we were in the Back of Beyond.

Father and Son are Close to Paradise and Father Sees a Glimmer of Hope of Future Love

The tourist season was at its height when we arrived on Corfu. Hundreds of rented cars and mopeds were rushing around everywhere. Fortunately, we had our own car. Without it, we would have had a hard time finding accommodations, and even so, we had to drive halfway around the island before finding a vacant apartment on the further (western) side. The apartment wasn't even right on the beach, although we didn't mind this too much. Our villa was built on a slope accessible from the beach by steep steps. In the village (more a summer resort in fact), there were a few tavernas and shops, but not the kind of place where I could satisfy the sexual desires that the sun and sea woke in me.

Benjamin thought he was in heaven here. His days would begin not long after sunrise (here on the west of the island the first rays of the sun didn't make it over the green slopes until sometime around eight), when he would go to the shop for yogurt and bread for breakfast. Then he would run down to the sandy beach by himself and play, although he wasn't allowed to go into the water alone. When frustration got the better of him, he would run up to get me, and we would both go down to the beach together. The worst part of the day from his point of view was midday, when I would drive him home and think up study assignments for him, so he wouldn't forget how to count and write. During the day, we ate plenty of fruits and vegetables, and I would drink a little of the local white wine. In the afternoon, we would go back to the beach and to one of the three local tavernas. In the evening, we would tell each other stories of faraway countries and a father and son who had set out from Prague for the south several centuries ago. Then I would put him to bed and go for a run or a walk.

For me, too, the relaxed life here had something of paradise about it, but I had my doubts as well. Can this be enough to make a man happy? And if so, for how long? Forever?

From the terrace in front of our apartment, I could see the sea between the crowns of the olives. Even at midday, there was shade, and the sun only found its way through in the afternoon. I had no problem sitting there completely idle hour after hour. The minutes would flow by naturally and lightly, just as the sun moved across the sky, just as the warm wind from the sea wafted past, and the leaves of the crooked olive trees trembled, and the low waves played on the sea. The Mediterranean climate delights the senses by never overloading them (except with the heat, but in this spot on the island the heat could be avoided). I would sit with a thoughtful expression looking into the distance. And if that feeling forced on us by civilization hadn't been so ingrained in me—that sense that human beings must always be building something, getting something done, creating something—I would have been truly happy.

Every week, there were new neighbors in our apartment building. They were Britons with white skin that immediately turned pink or red and would still be water-logged after a week, as if marinated in real London fog. The British women were ugly, just as people say they are, but I was so randy that any view of a woman's backside or thighs was enough for me. But I didn't try to get acquainted with any of them. Late in the evening, I would just relieve my desires by myself, down on the beach, naked, ankle- or knee-deep in warm water.

The beach was divided into two parts by a rocky promontory that rose out of the sand and ran out into the sea, which rippled around it. Once, very late at night, I interrupted a couple making love behind it. They were lying on a rug they had probably brought for the purpose, and his backside was wriggling rather stupidly between her thighs in the moonlight. When I saw them, I was already so near that they noticed me too and turned their heads. In that fleeting instant,

I felt them hesitate, as if it had occurred to them to motion me to come over and join in. I had the same thought. If I had uncovered myself and shown them my erection, maybe they would have invited me—here, on the seashore, where inhibitions are easier to cast away, where what comes up from the depths can be allowed to flow to the surface. But I turned away and walked on.

The short, stout Greeks who served in the local tavernas soon got to know Benjamin and me and welcomed us with genial hospitality. Their thoughts and the way they moved were full of the easygoing mood of the Mediterranean. One time, Benjamin got a free melon and another time even a sweet tiramisu. He was now beautifully tanned and hardened, and, if he had suddenly found himself back in Prague, people might not have recognized him.

After two weeks of sunny weather, there were several wet days. One night, there was a tropical storm. The lightning was so frequent that everything was as visible as in daylight, and muddy streams of water flowed around the villa on the once parched ground. In the morning, we went to look at the stormy sea. Three-meter waves were breaking, rising close to the shore and flooding half the beach. The sand was damp and lumpy.

The sky remained overcast, and at midday, it started to rain again. For the first time in a long while, we got back into our car. I headed for the southern tip of the island. At first, the road led high up through olive and pine glades, but then towards the south we descended again. The southern promontory was low and sandy. To the left, we could see the coast of Albania again, not far away. On this side of the island, the eastern side, the sea was still calm and not choppy as on the west. The sun shone, and steam rose up from the road. Soon it was unbearably close. In the afternoon, we stopped at a taverna by the side of the road. At a nearby table, a party of eight was sitting and talking in Czech. They were discussing something about the standard of their accommodations. I had been expecting an encounter like this for some time, but it still took me aback and spoiled my mood.

"Dad, Dad! Those people are Czechs," cried Ben, which drew their attention to us. I moved my lips in a token polite greeting. "Don't yell like that!" I warned Benjamin, "It's best if no one knows about us."

"But why, Dad? Why shouldn't people know about us?"

"Well…we're in the Back of Beyond now."

It had been more than a month since our departure. My mobile was lying at the bottom of the sea, and the family, especially my father, was hardly likely to have accepted the idea that we had just disappeared somewhere and to have left it at that. The simplest thing would be to contact them, at least briefly. It hadn't been kind of me to leave them in uncertainty. It would be natural for them to worry.

But something had been stopping me from calling them. I didn't want to hear their views, their fears, their objections. I wanted to be on the road just with Benjamin—alone. And if I sent them a postcard, I would be giving away where we were. But then, my own attitude meant that I was becoming uncertain and worried myself. I could only guess what practical steps they might have taken—they might have started some official search for us, for example.

I ate up in a hurry, and even told Ben to eat faster, although the poor boy had no idea what it was all about. For the first time since landing on the island, I was nervous. On the way back, I bought a phone card. I was thinking of possibly phoning Petra that evening. Perhaps she would know something, but for the moment, I couldn't quite decide.

During the evening, I kept mulling it over. The last two weeks, free of all contact, had been the best for me. I was afraid that if I called, I would lose something. On the other hand, now that I thought about it, I longed to hear her loving voice again. Petra was a real friend—someone far away for most of the time, and yet close to me.

I went to a booth by the shore and dialed her number.

"Hullo?"

"It's David here."

"Oh David!" I could almost hear the sigh of relief, "Where have you gotten to? I tried calling you."

"You tried calling me??"

"Yeah, you have it turned off all the time."

"I don't actually have the cell phone anymore," I confessed cautiously.

"Someone stole it?" She sounded scared.

"No…I dropped it in the sea, from the boat."

To my surprise that amused her: "So you just drowned your cell phone. Maybe a fish ate it. Shall I try and call the fish?"

I was glad she made a joke of it and didn't ask any more. "Why not? Anything's possible."

"But tell me where you are. And how's Benjamin?" the anxious tone returned.

"Actually, I wanted to ask you whether people are looking for us. Some kind of missing persons thing?"

"Why? You mean you really haven't let anyone know? Not even the parents?"

"In fact, I wanted to ask if you could call them. Just to say there's no reason to be anxious about us, and we're okay. But on no account tell them where we are."

"And where are you?"

I hesitated. "We took a boat to Greece from Trieste," I started generally, but then decided to be more specific. "On the Island of Corfu. You mustn't tell them that."

"Wow, what a great assignment! The parents will just love me when I say you're alive and won't say anything more."

"But I'm sure you'll know just how to put it," I wheedled.

"Thanks a lot! … But you will be coming back to Prague when you've finished living it up there, won't you? Benjamin will have to go back to school."

She was expressing a thought I had been hiding from myself for the moment. It was already August. Soon I would have to decide. At the moment, it was still just a joke—a slightly more adventurous holiday than usual. But if we didn't get back for the beginning of the school year... "I guess I don't know yet, Petra."

"But you will be back eventually, David," she tried to reassure herself, "I know you're a sensible man."

"I guess I really don't know. But I want to tell you that you're the only person I could imagine being with us." (As I said it, I felt aroused.)

"Hm. I'm not actually planning on coming to Corfu right now. And I don't have any vacation left."

"Pity."

The telephone beeped, warning me that the card was running out. "Listen, the card's running out. Will you call my parents?"

"What am I supposed to do with you?"

"Petra... if you can't come with us now, and if we ever get back, I want to live with you."

"Well, that's something I'll..." Finito. The card had expired, the line was dead. I could swear I knew what she had been going to say. It held out hope because, yes, she had not refused me. It was something she would...she would think about. I left the booth with a feeling of victory.

In the night, it rained again, this time a mild, warm rain. Several times, I woke up and listened, pleasantly sleepy, to the soothing music of the rain; it reminded me of May nights in Bohemia. Here too the air was heavy with the scent of wet plants, and I imagined walking along the beach in the rain, naked—me and Petra or perhaps me and an indeterminate creature with a feminine body and a feminine soul. The femininity of her soul consisted in the fact that she would always offer me warm and unconditional acceptance.

The wet weather continued for another few days, and then the sky cleared again, but the sun no longer rose as high as after our arrival on the island and no longer had its earlier, lethal power. At the end of August, the number of tourists began to decline as well. In the afternoon, the beach was no longer as full, and after six, there was usually no one there at all. Only Benjamin wanted to stay there every day until sunset. His passion for the sea was inextinguishable.

The first days after my telephone conversation with Petra were the calmest and happiest from my point of view. The promise I had detected in her last words put me in a light and cheerful mood. Now, I walked on the beach with Benjamin more often than before, played with him in the water, and even bought myself a snorkel, so that we could go around the island looking for the most promising rocky inlets and exploring the undersea landscape. From childhood, I have suffered panic fears of suffocation, and so I would never have dared to dive really deep, but now I could at least imagine how wonderful it must be. While up above the surface, the wind blew, the sun shone, and the surf crashed on the shore; under the surface, everything rippled in the serene rhythm of a dance—unbroken and harmonious.

The sea here was not in fact particularly abundant with life; everything that could be eaten had been mercilessly caught. Altogether, we saw only about five species of fish. Once, we thought we glimpsed an octopus disappearing under a stone and a few lobsters marching across the bottom in the sand. Usually, I would get pretty cold underwater, and then I would enjoy lounging on the beach on the warm pebbles or sand. On the way back, we would stop for food in the evening, and I would drink wine on the terrace under the darkening sky, my legs wrapped in a blanket, since the nights were already almost chilly.

Time went by, and my doubts returned. Maybe I had failed to understand Petra. Maybe she had been going to say something quite different, or something more complicated. And even if she had really wanted to say what I hoped, there was still room for doubt. Petra lived a life that was very ordinary, almost boring. It was the kind of well-ordered nice life that lacked anything much in the way of imagination. It was a life that could hardly be led anywhere but in Prague. But I was on a journey to the Back of Beyond. I didn't know, I truly didn't know, where that journey would take me, and even less, where I would want to live afterwards.As the end of the vacation approached, I became more and more restless and felt an increasing inner tension. Externally, I devoted myself to the same actions, or rather happy inactions, but somewhere inside me, this paradise life had already come to an end. The situation was not so different from what I had experienced in June. Once again, I was facing a fundamental decision.

During those August weeks, Ben only mentioned his mother twice. The first time it happened was one late afternoon on the beach, and it was just an ordinary question about whether Mom was with us and whether she could see the beautiful colors of the sky too. The second time was different, and I was really grieved for Ben. We were snorkeling on the northwest of the island, and we spied a shoal of fish in a deep rocky ravine. Benjamin came up to the surface, beside himself with joy, and called out to me, "Hey, we have to tell Mom about this!" And of course, what he meant was that we had to tell Mom, the real Mom, and not some imaginary soul. In the rapture of the moment, he had forgotten that Mom no longer existed. Dumbly, I gazed at him from the water, and in that fraction of a second, I would have made any sacrifice if only my beloved son could have had his mother back again. And in the same fraction of a second, perhaps just because he saw my surprised and helpless expression, he realized the true situation. His joy vanished, fast as lightning. Without a word, he turned around and swam to the shore.

I caught up with him as he was crawling out of the water. "Wait, Benjamin. I'm not at all mad at you for getting confused like that. And I don't think it's strange. I understand."

But he just turned his back angrily, "Leave me alone!"

I left him alone. I went for a walk along the edge of the beach, while he flattened himself on the sand, face down. I understood him. I understood the terrible short circuit he was now having to come to terms with—it was as if he were losing her all over again. When he emerged from the water, she was still his, he was preparing to share his experiences with her, to tell her everything. And then, all at once, he had lost her. Lost her through my silence.

It lay between us all day until evening. We spoke only in short messages, Benjamin responding as briefly as he could, with "yes," "no," "Hm." There was nothing I could do about it, but it was if I were his murderer. As if it had been me who had failed to arrange things, so that the moment he came to the surface, his mother was waiting on the beach or at least somewhere at home in Prague.

Later I sat on his bed, put a palm to his head, bent down, and whispered in his ear, "I know just how you feel, and I'm terribly sorry about it, Bennie mine." In the end, he snuggled up to me, hugged me tight with his arms around my back, and we rested for a time in that warm embrace.

At the End of the Vacation Fateful Decisions Await Them

September 1st fell on a Tuesday that year. For Benjamin to get back in time for the school term, we would have had to leave the island on the Sunday. Sunday came, and I hadn't made any preparations for departure. In June, the decision had required the action of departure, but now inactivity was the decision. In the evening, I took Benjamin for a celebratory meal to a larger resort in the north of the island. Here, too, we could feel the end of the season coming. We sat on a big terrace by the sea, almost alone. Benjamin must have had an inkling of my thoughts, or been wondering about the question for some time, just like me. "Dad," he said suddenly. "What's the date today?"

"It's August 30th," I answered, simply.

"So, I can't be back in time for school, can I?" He shrugged with affected indifference.

"Do you want to be?"

"No, Dad, I was just asking. I don't mind."

He was no longer small enough for me to be able to read all his thoughts. I could see I was going to have a hard time deciphering what was behind his acquiescence.

"I won't mind if you give me assignments," he added after a moment.

I knew he had no reason to look forward to school. The boys there bullied him, and he didn't have a single good friend among them. But despite that, he had probably been expecting me to insist that he went back. It was automatic. From his earliest years, I had taught him that fun and games end where duties begin. Why would he believe it would be any different in the Back of Beyond? I didn't even know myself what I was going to do. "I'll give you assignments every day," I said, "But we won't be staying here long. Just another

135

week and then we'll be moving on."

He looked at me with surprise. He probably hadn't been expecting anything like this and had assumed that we would be going back, or perhaps staying here. But that we should be carrying on with the journey? "Where next, Dad? Aren't we already at the Back of Beyond?"

"I think we are. We're a little bit Beyond."

"I want to stay here, Dad. I like it here."

"I like it here too. But the summer is nearly over, and the restaurants and shops will be closing. We can only live this way in the summer. And anyway, it wouldn't be fun any longer just staying in one place." As I spoke, I realized that the decision had just been made. I couldn't take back what I had uttered. I couldn't say the next day that we were actually going back to Prague after all. All the same, I wished it was already mid-September. The first week, the people at the school would think we were just extending a vacation; the second week, they would assume Ben was ill. The third week, they would start to look for him.

On our return from supper, late in the evening, I went out to call Petra. I mostly wanted to know how she had coped with the parents. Of course, I also thought about our relationship, but now that I was at a crucial moment in the journey and perhaps my entire future life, I suddenly had no idea what to do with the affection I had cultivated for Petra.

"Are you back home yet?" That was her eager question when she heard my voice.

"Home? No…" I was taken aback at how little she knew about the seriousness of my plans. In fact, she wanted us not to succeed— she was on the side of all those careful bourgeois who are constantly trying to warn you off unconventional actions. On the other hand, maybe she was just ordinarily eager to see me. "We're still in Corfu," I said self-confidently. "In a week or so, we'll be travelling on to somewhere else."

She didn't even bother to conceal her shock. "You've gone really crazy, Dave, you're out of your mind," she repeated quietly, mildly.

"What about the parents?" I changed the subject. "Have you talked to them yet?"

"Yes, I have. I reassured them you were sensible and would certainly be back in time."

"And you didn't tell them where we were?"

"Of course not, Dave," she was affronted, "What do you take me for?" "So, they're not taking any action?"

"Not yet, they're not doing anything. Your father said he would wait until September 1st. But if you don't get back in time for Benjamin to start school, he'll start an international search for you. He was quite brusque. He's willing to sell them any line. For example, that you've abducted Benjamin and that you're mentally disturbed."

"He said that?" I couldn't control myself, "He's an asshole."

"Okay, okay, but I thought you were coming back. Now I can see that you really are mentally disturbed. What's going on? You just want to stay somewhere? What happens when the money runs out?"

"It won't run out."

"Fine. The money won't run out soon. But you're not a millionaire. You ought to think about the future."

It was only now, when I had gotten the essential information out of her, that I started to see her great affection and self-sacrifice. She was simply frightened for us, she cared about us. "You know what, Petra? I'd be sorry to drag you into something unpleasant for you. But all the same, please don't tell anyone where we are. If they ask you, tell them I didn't say."

I waited for her to answer, but she was silent, "So you won't tell anyone, then?" I repeated.

"I keep my promises," she said eventually, but her voice was empty and hollow.

I was moved. "I know, Petra. You're the most honest person I know."

"It's nice of you to say so, but I want to hear something else. Say you'll be sensible and come back. Missing just a week of school won't hurt Ben, and I'll think up some explanation."

I was beginning to regret having bought a more expensive telephone card. "It's impossible, Petra. I can't. I don't want to. Benjamin doesn't want to come back either."

"Don't drag Benjamin into it. Benjamin will be happy wherever you are."

"Probably. But I wouldn't be happy in Prague. Petra, if I came back now, I wouldn't really be myself. Instead of a father, Benjamin would have someone who doesn't exist, and he wouldn't even understand why we were coming back. Just today, I assured him we would be continuing on."

"Okay," she sighed, "I can see that…that," she was trying to say something fundamental, "that I'll probably have to fly out to join you."

I had been expecting anything but this. A few weeks before—yes, back then it had been what I wanted. I had longed to be on the island with her. I had longed for an end to the loneliness into which I had been cast long before my wife died. I had longed to experience that erotic intoxication of a relationship just beginning, to enjoy at least one more time that eager anticipation when two people already know it's going to happen, but don't yet know the place or the time. I had longed for that ease of a walk together after the first love-making—the stroll through the cooling night on warm asphalt, the bottle of wine in a local restaurant, the gradual charging up for the next act of love. Sure, I still wished for that today: it was a seductive and arousing prospect. But on the other hand, time had moved on. The calm I had savored here in the middle of the summer was gone, and the great and not entirely pleasant challenge of the next leg of the journey was looming. Petra arriving now, at the end of the summer, and what's more, with the intention of getting us to go back, could upset it all. And maybe it would turn out that the modern world ruled out such a journey and refused to recognize it…

"Wait…do you really want to come out to join us?" I asked, after a long pause.

"Yes, I do. What else can I do?"

"But you said you had no vacation time left."

"I'll sort it out somehow." (She seemed to be resolved.) "I'll take some unpaid leave."

I looked for other obstacles: "But what about Andrea?" (Andrea was her seventeen-year-old daughter) "Can you leave her?"

"Andrea? She'll cope. She has to. She's a big girl now."

I was at my wit's end. I couldn't bring myself to refuse her outright, and I didn't even know whether I wanted to. "You know what, Petra, I'm not sure right now. I'll have to think about it. Okay, I know it was me that suggested you come here. But I didn't think you'd want to persuade me to come back. I think the best thing would be if I called you again in a while."

She agreed and I hung up. I walked down to the beach along the surfaced road. The sea was splashing gently against the shore, and the cooling sand gave way beneath my feet. My throat was dry and slightly sore. I had a headache too, in fact. I was wondering about Benjamin. I had explained to him that no one else could come with us to the Back of Beyond. So, what would he think if Petra suddenly showed up? Maybe he would see it as a betrayal. Or maybe it would be welcome. It wasn't easy always being together, just the two of us. We could take a rest from each other, a diversion. All the same, I felt that the right thing would be to refuse. Everything else was just evasion. And then there was the dreadful possibility that Petra would turn up as just a friend, that she would reject me as well as try to persuade us to go back. In the meantime, I reached the stone promontory and climbed up on it. Today, there was no one on the other side, and the cold sand was not inviting. I squatted down close to the water and savored that wonderful feeling that the simple presence of the sea gives to anyone who was born in the middle of a continent. An idea struck me. I set off back to the telephone booth. I already knew what to say.

She took ages to pick up—maybe she was in the shower. "Yes, David?"

"Hi, it's me again."

"So, should I go to the travel agency tomorrow?" she tried to lighten it up. It wasn't easy for her either.

"Look, I've thought about it, and I would find it really unpleasant if you were trying to talk us into something. Come out and join us just for the hell of it, and I'll be happy that you're here with us for a while. Just come for the pleasure of the meeting (if it will be a pleasure for you). You're the only person I would say anything like this to. Believe me."

"You really put me on the spot, Davey," She sighed. "What's the message here? That I'm wrong to be worried about you?"

"Worries aren't wrong. We're sometimes worried about ourselves too. But you have to promise me you won't say anything to anyone before or afterwards. You can visit us in the Back of Beyond, and you'll like it here, you'll see. And then we'll be moving on."

"What on earth have I gotten myself into?" she lamented, and I understood her very well. She was such a respectable woman, and suddenly she was supposed to do something crazy. And on top of that, to deny it, to lie. "The worst thing," she continued, "the worst thing is that I'll do it."

"Why the worst thing? It's wonderful, isn't it?"

"I can't say it makes me proud of myself. In fact, I'm angry with myself. Really."

I wasn't sure that what we were arranging was a good thing either. I was feeling bad mainly on Benjamin's account. If he had had the idea of inviting someone out here, I would have persuaded him that it was impossible. What if he stopped trusting me? … It was all weird. Instead of joy and anticipation, I just felt awkward. "So, how shall we do this?"

Dad Struggles with Temptation

We agreed that Petra would go to a travel agency in the morning and make a reservation for the next possible flight. In the evening, I would call her again.

During the night, I kept tossing and turning, unable to sleep. I was either fantasizing about sinking into the white oval of Petra's body or waking up with a bitter feeling of betrayal. Beside me, Benjamin slept deeply and quietly.

Monday seemed to pass me by. I felt I was in a trance. Several times, the definitive question rose to my lips. "What would you say, Ben, if someone came out here to..." But I never managed to spit it out. Even though I expected his reaction would more likely be positive than not.

In the evening, I kept unconsciously putting off the moment when I would have to call. I needed to finish the wine first, I needed to have one more walk along the beach. In the end, I paced helplessly around and around the booth. In fact, I was growing ever clearer about what would be right. It would be right to refuse, to stay in the Back of Beyond with just Benjamin—as I had set out with him on the journey. But the desire to have a sympathetic woman at hand and to share my human predicament with her, at least for a while, was just as strong.

In the end, I decided to wait and see how the conversation went. Maybe there had been complications, and it would be easy for me to retreat. Only, as it turned out, Petra was happy and determined. "I managed to get a flight as soon as Thursday, but you'll have to get up early. I'm landing at eight in the morning."

There could no stopping her now. My mind went blank. "Really, that early?" I said with affected surprise. "When on earth will you have to get up yourself?"

"Around three probably. I'm out of my mind, aren't I?"

"Obviously," I said coolly. Right away I felt bad for not showing more appreciation. "How long will you be staying?"

She had an eight-day package deal. She was asking about the weather on the island, and what she needed to bring, and then she wanted more reassurance that we would be at the airport at eight, because otherwise she would have to go with the group. I tried to think of a way to find out if she was coming just as a friend, or if I could expect more. "I'm dying to be with you," I said, and it was not a complete lie. "I'm thinking of all the things we'll be able to do here together…"

But she ducked that one: "People on the beach will be laughing at me. I'm completely white."

"So, Thursday at eight," we agreed. I came out of the booth and walked down to the sea, but it was no longer the same sea, where all my longings could find a home and be accepted, soothed. Tonight, the sea could no longer relieve my soul—because I knew that what I was doing was wrong.

Later, in bed, I tried to fantasize about how it would be with Petra, but however hard I tried, I could only imagine embarrassment. Petra would be kind and warm but would reject my physical advances. She would use the extra bed in the living room, while I slept in the bedroom with Benjamin as I usually did. I would lie there long into the night, wondering if she was expecting me next door.

I also tried to imagine how things would go between her and Ben. In the end, I somehow fell asleep and woke up at nine-thirty in the morning. I sent Benjamin off for breakfast and went to see the landlady, to pay for a whole week. The wrinkled Greek woman in her black headscarf, whom no one would have guessed was wealthy, looked at me with surprise and suspicion. In her severe face, I read disapproval rather than satisfaction with the cash; she probably thought that such long vacations were godless. But she accepted the money, and said something loud that I didn't understand. I made an attempt at a smile and left.

In the afternoon, I suggested to Ben that later we should go see the main town on the island and the airport there. He enthusiastically agreed, which made me feel even more guilty about him.

We swam until five and then set out. As the car drove smoothly up the zigzagging road, it struck me as essential that I say something to Benjamin now. But he spoke first. "Dad, are we going to fly somewhere?"

I realized that we could if we wanted to. "I don't know yet," I replied. "But we'll find out where you can fly from here. And we'll go down to the harbor and see where you can sail from here."

"I want to fly in an airplane, Dad."

The local airport was quite small, but now in summer, it was busy. Hundreds of curious tourists were pouring out of airplanes, eager for sun and sea, while in the departure hall, hundreds of tanned "old hands," with their one or two weeks of experience behind them, prepared to board the same planes and smiled indulgent and experienced smiles at the newbies. I was on high alert, not wishing to cross paths with any party of Czechs.

Benjamin watched the arrivals and departures for a couple of hours, and when I eventually dragged him away, it was already getting dark. We headed through the overcrowded streets of the town to the harbor. Several magnificently lit steamers were just sailing in, with music playing and their lights reflected on the calm surface of the sea, which smelled of washed-up seaweed and rotting fish. Warmth and cold mingled in the air—traces of summer and winter, traces of life and of inevitable death. We found ourselves on the harbor pier at the very end. A challenge to continue our journey seemed to waft, scarcely perceptible, from the sea. Anxiety made me gulp. I was flooded with love for Benjamin. He was standing beside me, my son with his pure childish soul and his child's vision of the world, in which the highest, most unchallengeable place was mine—his dad. We sat down on the edge of the pier, our legs dangling above the stone breakwaters. I could feel Ben's shoulder and thigh against my side, and I pressed him to me with my right arm.

"Do you think I could do the long jump in the Back of Beyond,

Dad?" He asked unexpectedly.

"In the Back of Beyond?" Yes, I realized, he was going to have to be something in life. He was going to have to devote himself to something systematically so as to become somebody. But now I couldn't help smiling at the very tangible form that the Back of Beyond took for him. "It'll probably have to wait until we get back from Beyond," I responded. "One day we'll have to go back, even though we don't know when yet. Then we'll see what you ought to become."

"I'd like to be a long jumper or a soccer player, Dad," he insisted, "or a diver," he added.

For a while he fell silent, but then piped up: "In Austria, we were already a little bit in Beyond, weren't we Dad?"

I couldn't figure out where this was heading. "In Austria? A little bit, yeah… Why?"

"So even in Beyond, I could be a soccer player. In Austria, I was a soccer player."

"You're right. You can be anyone in Beyond, in fact. It's just that you can't decide it for yourself." The truth of that came to me. "Neither you nor I have any clue what we can become in Beyond. That's the difference between Beyond and everywhere else. Back home in Prague, someone can decide he wants to draw, for example, and so he'll start going to drawing class every week. But in Beyond, we know almost nothing about next week."

He gave no sign of having understood my answer. "Look, there goes a crab!" He pointed at the stone below us. We leaned forward, and the crab vanished into a crevice between the stones. We got up. It was completely dark now, and the lights of the harbor had become stronger. I headed to the main pier to look at the ferry timetable. The ferry to the nearest town on the mainland went every hour. The first at five o-clock in the morning.

We had supper in a harbor restaurant. We sat on the first-floor terrace with a busy road between us and the sea. Benjamin's mouth was red from spaghetti Bolognese, and he was drinking cola. "Dad," he looked up from his plate, "We're having a great time here, aren't we?"

Suddenly I was sure I didn't want Petra here. Nobody could visit us in the Back of Beyond, not even her. For the whole of our remaining time in the harbor, and on the way back, I couldn't think of anything else. I put Ben to bed and hurried to the booth. Of course, I knew how much I would be hurting her, but I had no option. My pulse was pounding in my ears. I was tense about the coming conversation, but at the same time, happy to have made my decision. Only Petra didn't pick up. Maybe she was already asleep, I thought. But I knew that the later I told her, the worse it would be for her.

I went out again to call before seven in the morning. Once I was awake, I couldn't get back to sleep anyway. But she still didn't pick up. And her mobile number was in the phone now resting on the sea bed. In the course of Wednesday, I must have tried her twenty times. My helplessness infuriated me, the way I had made my decision but still couldn't change anything. (It was only much later that I found out what had happened. Petra's mother lived close to the airport, and Petra, who often visited her, had packed up and gone there on Tuesday evening.)

After my final futile attempt, I paced around the booth for a while. I knew I had to do something. There was no way I could return to the apartment and sleep. There was also no way I could wake Benjamin early the next morning and go with him to get Petra from the airport. But it was also unimaginable for us to stay where we were, leaving Petra to spend a whole week on the island alone—angry or sad—while I just continued drinking wine here and admiring the sunsets and going down to the beach with Ben. Besides, what if she managed to find us? (Not that it would be so awful, I answered myself immediately—I might even be pleased—it would be a matter of chance then, and chance is everything in Beyond.) But I couldn't bet on chance. All at once, the only possible solution hit me: we had to leave. Pack up right now and sail away on one of the first morning ferries. Ben wouldn't like it, but at least I wouldn't be doing anything I couldn't explain to him.

On fire with my newfound solution, I went to walk on the beach, but instead of the kind of walk I had gotten used to here, it was a feverish pacing back and forth. In the very place where I had found so much peace, I was now shaking with nerves. I was reaping the harvest of a bad idea—a sin against Benjamin and against myself, against our life together on our travels. I felt like Adam when he had to leave Eden.

They Reap the Fruit of Dad's Sin

At night when we got back from the beach, I quietly packed up all our things and loaded them into the car. I was finished by half-past three. Then I went to call Petra just one last time; she would just be getting up, to be sure of getting to the airport at four. I wanted to tell her I would cover everything she had spent, and how very sorry I was about it. I knew that even if I got through to her, I wouldn't change my decision now, but at least I wouldn't feel guilty about leaving unanswered questions behind me. Anyhow, I didn't expect to get through.

After a while, I went back upstairs. All I felt was sorrow, as it struck me that I might never find so much peace again in my life. I lay down and wrapped myself in the light cover. By this time, the room was cooling down. I pulled the cover up to my neck and became absorbed in listening to Benjamin's breathing. At around dawn, I fell asleep briefly. I woke at six, my t-shirt damp with sweat and my chest sticky and reeking. I took a shower. Benjamin slept on with his head thrown back, unsuspecting, relaxed as a baby. I boiled water for tea and made breakfast. At four, I sat down on Ben's bed. "Benjamin." I stroked his hair and cheek—first gently and then more roughly. "Benjamin!"

He reluctantly half-opened his eyes, "What's the matter, Dad?"

"We have to move on, Benjamin. Further into the Back of Beyond. We can't stay on the island any longer, son."

"Why not, Dad?" He rolled onto his other side and yawned. "Why do we have to go right now?"

"Because our boat leaves at eight."

"But I thought we were going swimming today."

"We will go swimming. Where we're going there'll still be sea."

"But are we going to go swimming today?" He turned his face back to me, incredulous but already less disgruntled.

"Yeah, today. I promise you," I said.

He struggled out of bed and began to get dressed—that actually amazed me. We didn't have breakfast; our stomachs rejected the idea so early in the morning. As dawn broke, we were going down the steps to the road. The air was saturated with morning scents, with the unmistakable trace of autumn. My heart was tight with anxiety and pain. I saw that the feeling of happiness was just a fleeting phantasm and that everything in human life comes to an end.

We got into the cool car and set out along the quiet empty roads. The traffic only started thickening as we approached the main town. Delivery trucks and empty buses. It was already seven-fifteen. Almost despite myself, I glanced up at the sky, in case there was an airplane coming in to land. But Petra had said eight. I realized that everything could still be as we had agreed. We could easily have turned off to the airport and picked her up. I focused on Benjamin in the back mirror. He was sitting slumped back in the seat and gazing in front of him with empty, absent eyes.

The ferry to the mainland town of Igoumenitsa was already at anchor. I joined the short line of cars. The stir of activity this morning was quite different from the bustle of the previous evening. This was a workday, with Greeks commuting to work or transporting goods.

I only breathed freely once it was our turn came to board. I paid, and we were among the last to drive down onto the deck over an uneven pontoon. At that moment, I was so relieved that I even forgot my sadness. We parked and walked up to the top deck. I glanced at my watch. It was eight. I fixed my swollen eyes on the sky above the bay. Meanwhile, the ferry's propeller was churning faster, and the ship gradually moved away from land. An airplane appeared on the north side of the bay. Petra was probably really on it, and I imagined her looking down at the blue of the sea bathed in morning sun, the tiny boats ploughing through the waters of the gulf, the white foam on the waves. She was already feeling her nerves relaxing in the Mediterranean atmosphere, and her heart was beating faster in anticipation. As I put myself in her position, I felt sick. I had to lean on the railings, my jaw and throat tightening in tearful spasms. Whatever I do, I mustn't start to sob, I told myself.

"Look, Dad!" cried Ben. "An airplane. And it's coming in to land."

Chapter IV

The Journey Moves Further from its Starting Point

Father and Son Return to the Mainland

The ferry chugged out of the harbor and headed south through the straits. We sat on the upper deck silent and sleep-deprived. I had thought we would have breakfast on the boat, but the very thought of food nauseated me. Meanwhile, the plane was completing its descent and disappeared behind the roofs of the houses. Yet again, I could only think how strange it was, the way our paths never quite crossed. How close Petra and I were but how insuperably distant. Just now, she would be deplaning, walking towards the airport hall in certainty and expectation. Why was it Petra, of all people, that I had to hurt?

About an hour later, we were approaching the harbor on the mainland. Instead of another resplendent day, there were grey clouds massing in the south. Before we docked, the sun was hidden behind them and a peculiar greyness spread out. The coastal town was not as large as I had feared, but the local traffic depressed me. I started doubting the point of the whole journey and even wondered whether my father had been right. I felt insignificant and wretched in my own eyes.

We drove from the dockside straight into a busy street. I joined the lines of cars and tried to find a way out of the town along the coast. My headache was now acute, and sweat was standing out on my forehead.

"Are we going to swim here? Dad, where are we going to swim here?" Ben chose just the wrong moment to start pestering me.

This time—for the first time on the whole journey, I really went ballistic with him. "D'you see any damn beach here?" I roared. "Or maybe you want to swim in the middle of town! How about you go jump in the local canal? Okay, I'll stop here and you get out and go swim, if that's all you care about! Me? I'm driving on." It was something like that. I spat it out evilly, even turning away from the driving and seeing the guilt and confusion in his eyes. He said nothing, just sat there as if nailed to the spot. I would have liked to soften it a little, dial back what I had done, but I was under dreadful pressure and unable to think of anything conciliatory to say.

At a crossroads, I identified the right route, which was back the way we had come, so soon we were passing the ferries in the small harbor again. Then the road quickly left the town behind and climbed uphill along the coast—straight towards those rainclouds.

After a few kilometers of driving, I had calmed down again and felt the need to say sorry to Benjamin. I stopped at a small rest area high above the sea. The clouds had spread from the south to the whole sky and the air smelled of water. I got out, opened the door for Ben, and put an arm round his shoulders "There'll probably be a downpour," I said, although I had intended to start the conversation somewhere else. Empty plastic bottles, cookie packages, scraps of plastic bags, and pieces of used toilet paper lay around the edges of the dirt rest area between dry plants and thorn bushes. Below us, we could see a pallid sea with its white hem at the shore. After a moment, I recovered my nerve. "I'm sorry I yelled at you by the harbor. I love you very much, and I don't want you to be unhappy because of anything I said. I was just nervous, because it was all too much for me, trying to find which way to go in a strange town."

"I know, Dad," he said quietly, and it looked like he didn't want to hear any more about it. "D'you think we could get down to the sea here?"

A wind had sprung up with a light drizzle. We got back in the car and continued along the coast. Most of it seemed inaccessible, with small bays between cliffs. I didn't want to drive too far. After all, only one day's driving would take me to the other end of Greece, and I was afraid of that, because—what then? Maybe I wouldn't find a resting place anywhere, and quite soon, we would be on the outskirts of Prague. So, I took an exit to a little town that lay in a narrow inlet protected by an islet. Despite the strong breeze from the sea further up, the sea was almost flat in the inlet, just a little ruffled on the surface. The small beach was empty, however, and it occurred to me that I could finally let Ben go swim here, regardless of the rain.

He dashed into the sea, beside himself with joy, and I couldn't get him out of the water for a long time. When he finally came out, he was shaking with cold, and so I let him change in the warmed-up car. Then we found a room in a hotel opposite the church. While I was negotiating a price with the owner, his little son ran up to me and rudely tugged at one of my trouser pockets.

"What's that boy doing?" Ben asked angrily.

"He's being rude." (It bothered me a lot that his father didn't reprimand him.) "Now you see what it's like when little boys are badly brought up, and their parents let them do everything they want."

Compared to the lovely apartment we had had on the island, our room in the hotel was small and dark. The window looked only into the courtyard, and there was no balcony. It was also quite cold. What did I expect find here? Why did I have to be here?

I took just one backpack up to the room and sat down on the wooden marital bed I was supposed to share with Benjamin...What if Petra had come intending to give herself to me? Except that Petra was less a wild nymph than a she-elephant. Her contours dissolved and spilled across the bed like lake water. I longed for her, if it could really be called longing, because I was limp and chilled. Indeed, I was conscious less of longing than of comparison—a dismal recognition of how far I was from the great ritual bed of my imaginings. That imaginary bed was like an altar, rising up from a marble floor and perfectly flat—the kind of bed on which I could grapple with a divine she-devil, whose charms would set the candle flame blazing and extinguish it. My longing was for absolute union.

My thoughts were interrupted by the gurgling of water in the drain pipes. Someone above us had flushed, and the shit was hurtling down around us.

The Black Night Sea Exerts its Magnetism

Right beside the church, there was a school with a concrete forecourt. On my way to the car for the rest of the baggage, I watched the local schoolchildren coming out. Normally, they would probably have played on the concrete, but today there was driving wind and rain in the narrow streets of the coastal town. It meant I couldn't send Ben down there by himself, and even if I could have, it would have been very strange. His lack of a home might be a barrier between him and the local boys.

We struggled through the afternoon, both of us in a low mood. I gave Ben some assignments, but it was unpleasant sitting in the bedroom. In the evening, darkness fell quickly, and I saw anxiety and weariness in Ben's eyes. I sent him to bed. Then I went out by myself to the beach. The rain had stopped but the wind was now really high, and even from a distance there was an ominous thundering that amazed me. I quickened my step, and as I approached the beach, I was ravished by the sight. In the narrow straits between the islet and the rocks of the mainland, the sea was boiling, and large waves were smashing onto the stone breakwaters. I leaned on the railings and gazed into the foaming waters. There was something magical about the black night sea that drew me, tempted me to jump right into it (the same feeling you sometimes get standing above a big precipice). Yes, I felt an urgent attraction between the depths of the sea and the depths of my own being. I had just experienced probably the worst day of our journey so far, a day full of doubts and reproaches, a day when I had acted wickedly. But now it was as if I were being offered a chance to coalesce with something immense, almost infinite and almost eternal. What more could a wretched creature like me, standing on the shore, wish for himself?

I stood there a long time, unmoving. Neither the spray nor the cold bothered me. I thought about the things you think about at such moments. I wondered if there was still something waiting for me that would give my life meaning, or if I was just a link in a chain—a man who would bring Ben up to adulthood and then quietly get out of the way in the hope that at least his son would find what he had failed to find himself. I wondered if there was any meaning to be found, or if life held nothing but fleeting pleasures, small orgasms that give us the illusion of touching something, but immediately evaporate, forcing us to be just ourselves again, just miserable insects to be crushed underfoot. Or are our contemporary orgies of abundance supposed to be the content of life— sports matches, television programs, vacations, and careers, all intended only to make us forget? Is the life that has been given us too inexplicable for us to be able to admit, even for a single moment, its real gravity? In old age, in an old folk's home, on the threshold of death, will I be cursing the food and worrying about toilet paper just to avoid looking into my own uncomprehending eyes? Then a priest will appear in the door, take my hand, and tell me a fairytale about departure into nothingness, and I will be infinitely grateful to him…It struck me that maybe the people closest to meaning are those who have to fight for a mere subsistence, day after day, from dawn to dusk, by the sweat of their brows, who do things because they must. But that would mean that purpose is nothing but endurance itself.

The waves were coming from different directions, depending on the way they drove through the narrow straits, and so they clashed and broke on the shore unevenly. After a few smaller waves, one really big wave would always come. The water even washed the wall of the little fisherman's house on the islet. The light from the house glinted dully on the surface and replaced the light of the moon. The attraction exerted by the sea was so strong that, despite the risk, I took off my shoes and my pants and went down the steps to the beach. The wet sand was cold on my soles, and the first wave splashed me up to my thighs. The sand started to give way under my toes, and I was scared and retreated two steps. No light reached down here from the embankment, so there was just the sea and me. I had to keep telling myself that back in the hotel room I had Benjamin, who had lost his Mom and now relied solely on me, but even so, I took off my jacket and threw it up onto the railing. Standing there in my t-shirt without pants aroused me, and the possibility of bliss drove away my oppressive sense of meaninglessness. Look how simple it is, I thought. I squatted down so that the waves reached my jutting penis. As my eyes blurred and my semen mixed with the water under the dark sky, it seemed to me that there was another way out. That way our was abstract, unknowable, but all-embracing God.

The Sun Restores the Illusion of Eternal Summer

The next morning, I took Benjamin down to the embankment so he too could see the power of the stormy sea. The wind had dropped, but the waves were still hitting the dockside and roaring. Ben ran back and forth, looking for stones to throw into the surf. "Can I go down to the beach, Dad?" He turned to me.

"No," I said abruptly. "Not today."

I noticed that up beyond the rocks that dropped directly into the sea, there was a small cemetery, and I immediately remembered Benjamin's mother. "Come on," I suggested, "Let's go and see that cemetery over there. From there, we'll be able to see the whole bay and part of the sea. And you'll be able to say a prayer there for Mom. D'you want that?"

"Sure," he agreed, and we set off.

We walked up through crooked alleys to the cemetery, and I was suddenly reminded of the atmosphere of the place where we had buried her. The morning mist was gradually dissolving in the sky, and we found ourselves in the shadows of tall trees. Today, everything was redolent of yesterday's rain, as it had been back then, but here the air was thick with the scent of Mediterranean herbs. Below us the sea murmured, but here there was a calming enclave of peace. Dry grass grew in the spaces between white marble panels.

I gave thanks for the happy impulse that had brought us here, because this was absolutely the kind of place where we could encounter her soul, where maybe we were supposed to encounter it. Benjamin seemed to feel it too. He walked beside me, silent and serious.

"Which grave should I pray at, Dad?" He asked after a while.

"You don't actually have to pray directly. You just need to think about Mom a lot while you're here," I told him.

159

"I think about her a lot anyway," he replied, tearfully. "I haven't seen her for a long time now, you see. Sometimes I'm not sure what she really looks like anymore."

I knew exactly what he was trying to say in his childish way, and I felt a painful empathy for him. He had lost his Mom at eight, and for the rest of his entire life, she would be receding from him, dwindling into the distance, until eventually all he had left of her was a few misty memories and a feeling of emptiness...a feeling that his Mom was part of some other life, and perhaps she had never leaned down to him, never stroked his hair before he slept, never been his Mom..."I know, I know what you're talking about," I nodded. We'll just take a walk here."

"But I want to pray!" he objected angrily, stamping his foot, his face crumpling into tears.

I took him to the highest point of the cemetery, to a big white tombstone, and told him to pray there. I left him alone and went down to take a look on the sea beneath us. The sun had already cut a path through the mist, and the water was turning blue. In the distance, more and more rocky bays came into view, but my thoughts kept running back to my unhappy son. I was becoming aware that I would never be able to replace what he had lost. I would have liked to pray as well—for him. I was sorry that I just didn't know how.

When we returned to the hotel, we ate a meager breakfast consisting of tea and toast with jam and were glad to leave behind the dark room where we had both slept badly. As we got into the car, the school opposite was just having a break, and the cries of the Greek children reached us through open windows. They were like the shouts of children anywhere else in the world, but looking at that desolate square of concrete with its basketball net, I thought of the generous school playgrounds in the Czech Republic or in Austria. I gave Benjamin a questioning look, wondering what he would say to the noise, but he didn't look as if he thought it had anything to do with him.

It was now turning into a hot summer day, making up for the loss of the paradise of the island and taking the edge off my guilt about hurting Petra. I had always respected her, always thought about her from time to time, even if she was not the true love for whom I had always thirsted. Now, in a slightly self-excusing way, I told myself that at least she would have good weather and enjoy the sun and sea. I resolved to call her at the end of the next week.

Once again, we were driving high above the sea on a winding road, and on our right, we started to see dirty parking areas with lookout points. "D'you know what?" I said, "Today we're going to drive down to every beach we see, so we get to know this place properly."

"Hooray!"

We checked out around ten beaches this way, each with something that captivated us. First, there were beaches tucked away in narrow inlets. There the sea was calmer, and so we dared to swim further from the shore, and I was often a little scared for us. But one beach was long and open, with the sea coming in in regular waves. Individual vacationers and whole families were basking and swimming there, and it was as if we had returned to summer.

That day I also noticed ordinary local people, not just renters and retailers, but locals grazing sheep or goats. High up on the slopes, I caught an occasional glimpse of a Greek village between the dried grass and thorns. I couldn't work out what the inhabitants could be living on, and how they could prosper in this barren land, once doomed to poverty. I looked for destiny inscribed in weather-beaten village faces, but I wasn't sure I found it. I even asked myself what it really meant—to have a destiny. To me, a rich Central European with no ties to a native place, destiny seemed to mean a person being born into a single possible life, determined for him in advance—for instance there in that village on the slopes of parched hills...And then he either lives that destiny, or in some way liberates himself from it, and leaves it behind.

Several almost naked women were sun-bathing on the beach.

Ben Wants Dad to Marry and Dad Knows What He Doesn't Want

We found accommodation in a splendid apartment on the long beach. We had plenty of choice, because the whole villa was already empty. Only one of the resort's tavernas was still open, but peaceful Greek melodies wafted from its amps, and vines with ripening grapes climbed around its beams. We sat there in the dusk. At the other tables, there were only a few older couples, and the place seemed to me too adult, as if Benjamin did not belong there. Instead of running around with children on the beach, he was sitting with me at the table, quiet and well-behaved.

As often happened on our journey, his thoughts took the same direction as mine, even though he was still a child. "Dad," he said thoughtfully. "Now that Mom is dead, are you allowed to marry someone else?"

"Why do you want to know about that right now?" I asked, "Of course I'm allowed. Anyone who loses their wife or husband can get married again."

"But if Mom hadn't died, you couldn't?"

I wondered if he was trying to get at what my relationship with his Mom had really been like. "Yes, I could." I decided to tell the truth, "But first, I would have had to get a divorce."

"Mom used to tell me that believers didn't get divorced."

"Did you talk about that with Mom?" I was surprised. "Mom was most likely confused. Even believers sometimes get divorced. Once, a long time ago, they weren't allowed to, but now they can."

"Mom said that you were probably going to divorce her."

I was taken aback. I realized that for the whole time he had known more than I thought. "She said that? It's…It's not so simple. She shouldn't have told you anything like that."

"But she was very sad."

"I know. Mom had a lot of sadness in her. For years, I was trying to drive that sadness away, but really, she liked it. I realized she wanted to be sad, and so I stopped trying so hard, even though I was very sorry about it. But nobody can ever know how things would have been between us if she hadn't died."

"Maybe she'd have stopped being sad, and you'd have stayed together," he said finally, again like a child.

How much of her sorrow had she loaded onto him? I wondered. How much sorrow would Benjamin have to carry through life? "Maybe," I smiled, "Maybe."

There was silence for a moment, and I hoped he wouldn't return to the subject, but the theme interested him. "I guess there's no one here for you to marry."

It wasn't pleasant to hear my small son talking about something that was actually a sore point with me. I didn't want to look pitiable, deserted, and feeble in his eyes. "You know, that's not something you need to worry about as a child," I said to him rather severely. "When I get around to wanting to find a wife, I'll probably do it. But things like that are very complicated. Are you sure you wouldn't mind having someone else instead of Mom?"

"I wouldn't mind, Dad," he replied resolutely, but I had no idea what he was talking about. "I'd like you to get married, Dad."

"Well, I'm glad to know that." I patted him. "You're a good boy. But right now, we're together in the Back of Beyond—just the two of us together." As I spoke, it occurred to me that, behind this desire for me to find someone, there might be a longing for home, for a solid base.

"Would you prefer to go back to Prague, Ben?"

"No, Dad, I don't want to go back."

"Really?"

"What beach are we going to tomorrow, Dad?"

After this masterly change of subject, we never returned to the theme of marriage. Still, I tried to imagine how he might have reacted to Petra. Maybe it would have been a relief for him. Maybe he would have cast her in the role of Mom, and neither she nor I would ever have been able to get out of it. If I'd had this sort of conversation with him earlier, I might well have made a different decision—for his sake. But I didn't regret it now. Petra would have been a kind of solution but not a fulfilment. She would have been a comfortable middle ground with no highs, and I had worked out for myself that I wanted more.

Tormenting Desire and Divine Sex

We stayed a few days on the long beach, and I was seized by almost uncontrollable sexual desire. It was ignited by three mischievous German girls, whom I saw there all the time, and one wonderfully attractive woman who sunbathed naked. Not even masturbation helped me anymore. Even just after jacking myself off, or actually precisely after it, I felt a tormenting lack of fulfillment.

I was losing any ability to concentrate when Ben was saying something to me, and I was afraid to drive. It was like a darkness behind my eyes. In the evening, I would vainly walk along the beach and gaze at that attractive woman or some other, who might want the same thing as I did. I would vainly sit by myself in the taverna and vainly bathe in the moonlight.

The summer had not yet lost any of its strength. Compared to the island, where the cooler and wetter evenings had surprised me as early as the end of August, the climate here seemed hotter and dryer. After three days of futile sexual thirst, I decided to drive further on.

Once again, we went from beach to beach and hotel to hotel, and when passing through the larger towns, I looked hopelessly around for a brothel or at least a hooker standing on the corner. Here in Orthodox Greece, there didn't seem to be any. Or at least they were taking pains to hide away.

Benjamin seemed to sense my partial absence and lost himself in his own thoughts. Mostly he sat silently on the back seat, and whenever we parked by a beach, he would walk off by himself to paddle while I unpacked our things or looked for an apartment.

It was only occasionally that my thoughts strayed to Petra. She was not the object of my present fantasies—those were all women I saw on the beach, or at least the ones with whom I might have a chance. But as Thursday came closer, the day of Petra's probable return home, I thought of her more often. When Thursday came,

MARTIN VOPĚNKA

I told Ben that I would be driving to the nearest town that evening to get money from the ATM. I hoped I might find a brothel there too. As in Italy, only intercourse with a woman could give me back my lost equilibrium and clear my head. Ben did not protest, and so when evening came, I put him to bed and told him a goodnight story too—about a tomcat who travelled the world with his friend, a stork, and finally decided to stay in a dog kennel with a nice dog, and the stork was at first very sad about it, but then came to terms with it and came to see the tomcat regularly. I kissed Ben on his brow and, troubled by a bad conscience because I was abandoning him again and exposing myself to danger, I went down from the terrace to the garden and along the sidewalk to the car, all too aware that nothing must be allowed to happen to me.

This beach was in a big bay and the surrounding landscape was flat. The sea was almost motionless—like a lake. I started the car and opened the windows on both sides, because the car had been absorbing the sun. I drove down a narrow road between pasture and rushes and heard the croaking of frogs, and then I speeded along the main road to the town. My lust was suddenly less tormenting.

As I drove on in thickening traffic, I started to doubt whether I really wanted to go to the town. I wouldn't find a brothel and would just have to walk along busy streets. Maybe it was cowardice, fear of the unknown, but now my lust had not just diminished but vanished, and the trip to the town seemed to me pointless. I wanted to be close to Ben, to take a walk along the beach near our apartment, hoping I might just meet some wonderful woman who would become my destiny. I also wanted to call Petra to apologize and assure her of my respect and affection. I stopped by the edge off the road. Through my open windows came the chirping of crickets and the rattle of cars driving at speed. I hesitated a little longer, although really the decision had been made. Soon I was driving back through the warm September evening, and I didn't know if I should curse or bless myself. I suspected that the tormenting fantasies wouldn't stay away for long, but this time, when I got out of the car in front of our villa and walked along beside the motionless sea, I felt relief. Beyond the taverna at the other end of the beach was a telephone booth. I headed for it.

The telephone rung only three times before she picked up. "Petra," I heard her voice, it was really her voice.

"It's David."

Silence.

"Petra…I owe you the mother of all apologies."

"Do you, David? I don't see the need."

From her voice, I could tell that she had probably written me off. "But I tried to call you before you flew out. I was trying to call it off. You just never picked up."

"I guess it's because I keep to agreements."

"Oh yeah, and I don't," I said, flushing. I was prepared to be penitent, but I hadn't expected this kind of coldness. I felt resentful. "So, you don't want me to explain it to you?"

"There's nothing to explain."

"Okay then, Petra. As you like. But I can assure you I've been feeling really bad imagining how you must be feeling. I felt really sick…"

"David, please don't explain anything," she interrupted me, "I'm tired. I want to sleep." She was so brusque and severe—Petra, who had always offered me sympathy and understanding.

"So…goodnight then," I said, and moved to hang up. Just before I did, I heard her add, "But Benjamin…" but it was too late for me to check the movement of my hand. The "But Benjamin…" had sounded worried. She had probably wanted to ask if he was okay and signal that she hadn't completely washed her hands of us. That hard tone had been just self-defense. Suddenly I understood her. She had to defend herself when I had hurt her so badly. How could she have lived with herself if she had just let it go immediately and been nice again.

The next day, we drove on along that great bay, cut deep into the interior. The plain gave way to hills and the road wound around their flanks. Around midday, we came to a small bridge connecting the island of Lefkada with the mainland. I had read that originally it had been a peninsula, and the bridge went over what was in fact just an artificial strait.

The proximity of the open sea brought a little freshness to the sultry day—a warm but crisp wind was blowing. Only a few tiny clouds sailed in the blue sky.

I was very uncertain about crossing that short bridge. We had left one island a week ago, and our experiences there could not be repeated. There was no point even trying. But Benjamin insisted: "I want to see the other side. It'll be good there."

So, we crossed. "But don't go thinking we'll stay over there," I tried to bring him down to earth. "We'll just drive around the island and then come back here."

"You mean we won't even go swimming there?"

"You ever think of anything else?"

At first there was nothing to suggest that we would encounter anything extraordinary on Lefkada. The road zigzagged as before, and to the right, we saw the beginning of a bay with calm waters and circular nets for fish breeding. But gradually, we reached a great height and were looking down on an apparently wild coast. We drove through a village perched on such a steep slope that its   inhabitants must have had to climb like goats if they just wanted to shop, go to church, or visit neighbors. The white limestone that predominated on the island alternated with clumps of pine, and that pure rocky landscape without a trace of oppressive moisture freed the soul from its bonds. Far below us, the pale blue water hemmed the outline of sand dunes by the rocky shore. I felt like an aeronaut who has thrown the ballast out of the balloon.

"See that, Ben? It's fantastic. And the height." I tried to force him into the same reactions as me. When a sign appeared indicating a turn-off to a beach, I turned off without Ben having to persuade me. The road was very steep. I put the car in second gear and kept my foot on the brake. "Wow, Dad, this is steep," Ben piped up. "Will we be able to get back up?"

I was pleased to see that he could have doubts about technology, since his generation usual took its unlimited powers for granted. "I guess we'll find out."

The road ended in a small parking lot, but no one else was parked there. We were still high above the sea. The only access was a long flight of narrow steps. I was gripped by excitement.

We took a bottle of water and went down. The beach that we eventually reached was about thirty meters wide and perhaps a kilometer long. High, white cliffs seem to grow straight out of it. Regular meter-high waves were coming in from the open sea. It occurred to me that we could put up the tent here, but we didn't have enough water or food. "You know what, Ben?" I said aloud. "It's so beautiful that it would worth camping here. What do you say?"

"That would be great, Dad," he exulted, already starting to take off his clothes.

"But Ben, first we have to drive back up to buy food and water."

"What, now, Dad? Do we have to climb those steps again?"

"We do. But we're athletes, aren't we?"

"Why don't you go and shop, and I'll wait down here for you?" he suggested.

For a moment I considered the idea. Why shouldn't he wait here? But then I looked up and down the long empty beach, and at the steep cliffs and the open sea, and was appalled. Leave him here? Never.... "No, that won't work. I can't leave you here."

"But Dad..." he whined.

"No, definitely not. I would be too afraid for you. And in the end, you'd be scared too."

We returned from shopping in the afternoon. I had been wondering whether the beach might no longer be empty, but we were again alone in the parking lot. On the way down the steps, I realized someone could easily lie in wait for us here. There was only the one access route, and our solitary car in the lot clearly signaled our presence. I tried not to think about it so as not to start to worry.

I chose a place for the tent in a far part of the beach, somewhere between the cliff and the sea. The sun was gradually slipping down towards the horizon, and we raised the tent, half naked. Then we soaked in the waves for a long time, and I couldn't quite stop nursing the hidden fear that we were in a trap.

In the early evening, two women, or rather girls, appeared on the beach with backpacks. They headed in our direction and then started putting up a tent about fifty meters away from us. All of my fears fell away. After a moment, the girls stopped putting up the tent, stripped, and went to swim naked. One was horribly fat, but the other had a long dark braid, and as far as I could see from this distance, she was slim and sinewy.

I couldn't take my eyes off them. They splashed each other in the water, falling forwards and back, and unintentionally came only twenty or thirty meters from me (Ben was just exploring the rocky end of the beach). The slim one stood up straight, waved at me with a smile and called out, "Hello!"

I already had an erection, but this made me really hard. I found myself regretting that once Ben came back, I would probably cease to interest them. "Hello!" I answered.

Ben ran up. I heated up something to eat and made tea. Those two had probably expected another man to appear at my side and had written me off now. All the same, I was still hard.

Meanwhile, the red disk of the sun had expanded unnaturally and was about to drown in the waters of the sea. As I gazed at it, I suddenly thought that this was a night that had been waiting for me. And it wasn't just a theory, or a fantasy, but a kind of reassuring confirmation of what I had been thirsting for, for so long, and so vainly. Somewhere outside me and outside us, and perhaps even outside the real world, this night had already been set in motion.

The sun had not yet reached the horizon but sank behind a narrow belt of mist. Darkness was falling fast, and the incessant surf continued to blunt my sense of hearing, throwing wave after wave onto the sandy shore. This time, the sea seemed to me like part of the inanimate cosmos, like a perfect machine.

I tried to persuade Ben to get into his sleeping bag, but he was as fascinated as I was. I had to sit with him long into the night in front of the tent and tell him about the mystery of the universe, the solar system, the stars, the galaxies, and the unimaginable empty distances. Only when the silver moon had emerged from behind the rocks and was casting its pale but penetrating light on the beach, did I manage to get Ben to go sleep.

I stayed outside alone, my thoughts fixed on the neighboring tent. I imagined what would happen if I went there now, naked and aroused, and caught them fondling each other. In my fantasy, they would accept my arrival as something completely natural, and we would make a threesome of it, with not a trace of shame. It would be a feast of sex. At that moment their tent opened, and they ran out directly into the water. They romped about—throwing themselves into the waves and splashing each other. Now or never, I thought. I peeled off my briefs and ran into the sea by the shortest route, and then approached them parallel to the beach. I was not at all afraid; that lack of fear was what distinguished this night from all others before it.

They were the first to greet me. I was not unwelcome. I started to splash them, and they splashed me back and must have seen I had an erection.

The ugly one behaved more bashfully, staying in the deeper water from which only her large white breasts emerged. The slimmer one was no beauty either, as it turned out; her face was spoiled by lips that were too large and protuberant. But she behaved in a way that was self-confident, playful, and flirtatious, and I focused on her. At one moment, I found myself in a wave very close to her. The wave broke and retreated, but she remained lying on the sand and I knelt over her. We looked at each other wonder-struck and froze. A spark jumped between us (most probably the certainty that the other wanted it), and if her friend had not been there, we would definitely have fucked immediately. As it was, she jumped up, grabbed my hand, and dragged me away. We both broke into a run, my cock too stiff even to swing. We ran like we were possessed. When she could no longer keep going (or decided that we were far enough away), she suddenly ran forwards into my path and knelt down with spread legs, her palms in the sand. I saw she was no more than twenty and most probably did a lot of sports. She had a firm ass, only just acquiring a womanly curve. She stood on all fours, exposed like a mare, and if we had been in daylight, I might have seen the moisture dripping from her cleft. I sank into her.

I thrust with all my strength and had only the cool sea to thank for the fact that I didn't come at once. I tried to hold myself back as long as possible, although it still happened soon. At the last moment, I pulled out and sprinkled the sand beneath us. But before I had had time to soften, I slipped it in again and carried on pumping. For a moment I wasn't sure I regain my hard-on, but in the end, I did. Now, I finally had the time to savor my own consciousness of that unbelievable moment in which I was standing and naked and driving to the point of crazy ecstasy into a girl stranger who wanted it so much she was running with juice, although I too was a stranger to her, half just a penis ploughing deep into her womb, and half a god. After multiple lacerating orgasms, she fell to the ground and curled into a ball with her back to me. I lay down on her, covering her entirely, and at the same time, I penetrated her again. The drops of water on her skin had warmed up long ago and I could feel her heat. Now I was thrusting slowly and gently. After a while, she rolled onto her back and gave herself up to me entirely. Only the expression of her face remained inaccessible; her eyes were closed and her head turned aside, as if she wanted to experience it all without me. I caught her under the ass and rose to my feet with her. She embraced me with her legs, and I lifted her up some more and tried to use my finger to arouse her in her puckered anus, but she pulled away from that, maybe because she was already so hot again. She started screaming and swaying from side to side, until I was fired up again.

To show her I was about to come I started to scream as well, so she could decide whether to take my semen inside or let me spirt on the sand beneath us, but she just quickened her tempo even more. Then we were yelling together, truly, and our cries disappeared into the roar of the sea and quickly died away.

We fell onto the sand beside each other. The warm sea washed over my back, while she lay in front of me, closed and alien although limp and completely paralyzed, sent to me just for this unrepeatable night, just for this night.

After a while, I realized that this was the end of it for us. There was not going to be any later for us, no tomorrow. When this dawned on me, I rose heavily and walked away from her along the sand, full of bliss. About halfway, I turned around and saw that she was sitting facing the sea, her legs spread wide, letting the water drench her crotch.

I passed the tent containing her friend who had probably been masturbating and may have been regarding my blissfully charged body through a crack in the door. I was walking with my penis still enlarged, but now hanging down.

I slept late in the morning and was only woken when the sun had found its way over the rocks and was leaning on the tent canvas. Benjamin was playing in the water, and when I looked out, everything was as it should be. We were now alone on the beach.

Father and Son Go to the Parched Hills and the Illusion of Eternal Summer is at an End

A feeling of culmination remained with me for many days. Just as a mountaineer who has conquered a longed-for summit does not hurry on to climb another, I had no new exciting goals. I had realized one of my two old but ever-present dreams. I knew that the other, of finding the love of my life, would have to remain unfulfilled on our journey. After all, I was travelling with Benjamin and the idea was to experience all of it—the good and the bad—with him.

We stayed on Lefkada for almost a week and one more night in the tent. When we arrived in a civilized resort in the south of the island, I went to call Petra again. This second time she accepted my apology, and I explained why I hadn't been able to get through to her before her flight. She didn't want to talk about her week on the island. I asked what was happening at home. She hadn't spoken with my father, but she was sure that an official international search had been initiated. She had also spoken to my assistant, meeting her by accident in a store. The meeting had puzzled her a great deal, because the assistant had turned quite red and hurried away. Petra anxiously asked me whether I had taken proper measures to keep my finances safe from her.

I didn't trust her much myself. I knew that I should at least have called her from time to time, but that would have meant getting bogged down in banal business. So, I preferred to play the ostrich. Fortunately, the assistant only had control of around a quarter of my assets. It was only much later that I asked myself how I would have behaved if I had known back then about the transfers she was making—stripping me of everything I had entrusted to her. Would I have interrupted my journey? Would I have gone back to save at least something?

Petra asked me mainly about Benjamin, if he was well, and if he was still enjoying his travels with me. I couldn't really answer that last question easily. "You know, he can't really conceive of the possibility of doing anything other than being here with me," I tried to explain.

She argued with me. "Don't get me wrong, but I simply don't believe this can be good for him. A child needs a home."

I didn't argue back. I had no doubt that Ben needed a home, and I intended us to create one for ourselves at some point in the future. But for the moment, all we had was each other—our thoughts, feelings, experiences. That was our home.

After a calm, relatively short conversation, I said goodbye to Petra. She had stopped urging me to return or reminding me about mandatory schooling. I promised I would call her again sometime.

September was drawing to a close. We moved on, first further south and then east along the gulf separating Northern Greece from the Peloponnese. The sun became less bright, losing power, and the water grew cooler. After a few windy days, there was a dead calm, and the few people on the beaches managed to warm up during daylight hours. But there was a kind of sadness about the deserted coast. Long dried up leaves were slowly falling from the trees, but this was not autumn as we knew it in Bohemia, for here the leaves did not turn yellow, orange, and red, but just grey, parched by the sun. Occasionally, a leaf would waft onto the limpid sea water, which rippled only with the movements of our bodies, and less and less. After swimming, we often had to get dressed right away.

On one of these deserted beaches, where a few small boats were anchored in an inlet, Ben met a little British girl. Her parents had most probably brought her here at this late season for health reasons. They greeted me politely and with a smile but never started a conversation while our children played. The reason may have been that they sat on the sand fully clothed, while I swam naked. I told Benjamin he should at least wear his trunks when he was running about with the little girl. We must have seemed wild to those dignified British people: we were deeply tanned all over, while they were an underdone white. The little girl didn't go into the water. She built sandcastles with Benjamin.

I was happy that Ben had found a peer. They met regularly on the shore for several days. While they played, I took walks to look at the surroundings, but the parched Greek landscape already wearied me. It had been months since I had seen any of the juicy meadows I was used to. I missed gurgling streams with icy water; I missed the murmur of the spruce forests and the scent of forest soil and needles. Everything around me here, on both sides of the gulf, was just bare hills and rock faces.

After four days, the British people politely said goodbye. They were leaving the next day. I explained this to Benjamin. He was very sad. Later in the car, he showed me an address in England that he had written down. "And what about you?" I teased him deliberately. "Did you give her an address too?"

"I forgot," he lied, and I understood why. "But it'll be fine if I just write to her, won't it? I'll write to her, and you can translate it for me."

I couldn't rid myself of the feeling that, with the departure of the little girl, the place had been wrung of all new meaning. Anything more we could get from the sea would be just a pale reflection of what we had already taken. All the same, it is hard to come to terms with the idea that the best times are gone. You want more from the future.

Just then, I was having difficulty planning our future. With a pain in my heart like the pain you feel when you lose someone dear to you, and partly out of perplexity and partly out of longing for the damp Central European landscape, I turned off into the mountainous interior. Ben protested, but showed interest again when he saw the steep switchbacks we would have to drive to get up there. Soon the road narrowed, and holes appeared in the asphalt. We drove through the first village.

We were already quite high up. Far below us was a village with a parched riverbed, a quarry, and dirt roads, but here on top, nothing grew that could be called a forest either, only bushes or low oaks that the drought kept stunted. Occasionally, a solitary pine appeared on the slope. On the opposite slope, which we could not have reached from our side without losing almost all of our elevation, a small village squatted high up under the mountain ridge, with other roads leading away from it at an upward slant. When a small, inconspicuous exit appeared on our side onto a road even narrower and bumpier than the one on which we had travelled so far, I took it in the hope that it would take us to a parallel mountain village. We drove up almost to the height where the scree began, although not as high as the altitude of the village opposite, and a small basin opened up before us, greener than the surrounding slopes, with walnuts and figs. I slowed down and opened a window. A donkey was grazing behind the fence of a small orchard, while from the thickets above the road, came the bells of pasturing goats. We drove between dilapidated buildings.

There was not a single well-maintained house in the place, let alone a hotel or a taverna. It was out of reach of the bustle of the coast, and people were eking out a meagre existence in the heat and dry, far from offices and schools. We got out of the car and walked along dilapidated alleys, which could perhaps remember livelier times when bands of children had run along them and driven the flocks to pasture. Half of the houses were abandoned, with broken windows and doors off their hinges. We snuck into some of them. They didn't seem completely poor, with their carved wooden beams or an arched terrace above an overgrown garden and a view into the deep valley or the stone slopes of the mountains. Benjamin took a great liking to these houses and suggested we could repair one, keep goats and live here happily ever after. But the awful drought destroyed me. Maybe sometime in March the surrounding slopes would turn green, everything would smell of flowers, and the air would tremble with the buzzing of bees, but now you couldn't even to sit down in the grass, let alone run around the garden. From my Central European point of view, life here was impossible.

Eventually we found a small inn. A couple of older men were sitting there in peasant vests and with hats on their heads. Their eyes flicked over us indifferently and that was all; they were not going to make a single movement on our account.

"We'll speak quietly, so as not to disturb anyone," I told Benjamin, and we went inside and onto a stone terrace with a roof. Old metal chairs with cracked backs wobbled on the stone flooring and were not at all comfortable.

After a long time, a woman in black pants and a white blouse came over, probably the owner. It was hard to tell her age from her brown face—maybe forty, maybe fifty. We ordered cokes and, after lengthy attempts at communication, she made us a Greek salad. We each drank two small cokes, and I had a retsina, the aromatic local wine. It went to my head quickly, so driving was out of the question. I sat there indolent, reconciled to everything—as if I were turning into one of the locals. I felt sorry for Ben because he couldn't drink alcohol and sat there bored. I tried to send him off on reconnaissance, because the village continued up the slope, but he didn't want to go. I was just thinking I had to pay and leave for his sake when three emaciated kittens tottered in, and Ben threw himself at them with joy. I felt like getting drunk.

I called the owner over and used gestures to ask if she had a room for guests upstairs. For a moment, I feared she might misinterpret me and think I was saying I wanted to sleep with her. I hastily gestured to Ben and myself, and she nodded—yes, she had one room. I ordered another half-liter of retsina. It was almost six, and the sun was much lower; it was growing chilly. All at once a breeze sprang up, and I had to put on more clothes. Ben played with the kittens, dragging them around the inn and stroking them. It was as if I had grown into the uncomfortable chair beneath me. Balkan music played on the radio, and the whole place seemed to be taking an afternoon nap. There was nothing to tempt me here, but I felt no need to go anywhere.

Later—the evening shadows already falling on the slopes—I finally got to my feet. I called Ben, and the innkeeper led us up a narrow spiral staircase to a stone corridor without a trace of the coolness of stone. We went through a cracked door. The little room was the most spartan imaginable: a rusty metal bed frame, a tin washbasin with one tap that offered no more than a trickle of brackish water.

The innkeeper left us alone there. From the small window, we could see over the garden below onto another few houses and across to the opposite slope. The highest summit was still glowing pink with the last rays of the sun, but it soon faded, the pink turning to silver and the summit merging with the oncoming night. I threw myself down onto the mattress and the springs creaked. My eyes were closing of their own accord as a liter of white wine buzzed in my head. "Sorry, Benjamin," I mumbled. "I've got to take a rest."

I woke in almost complete darkness. The little window let in no more than a faint reflection of the starry sky. I realized I hadn't even taken the things out of the car. Benjamin was sleeping on the other bed in an unnaturally twisted position, with one foot on the floor; he had probably fallen asleep sitting up. I sat up and it took me a few moments to recover from the sudden movement. I staggered over to the open window. Outside, the crickets were chirping, and the shadow of a bat fluttered above the garden. Stars covered the night sky between the mountain ridges. There was no warmth rising from the stone beneath the window, but it was not yet giving out a chill. The air itself was cold.

There was something unreal about my presence at this particular moment in this precise place—in a small musty room in the middle of a dying village on the slopes of dry mountains, with wine lingering in my head and its aftertaste on my lips. I braced myself against the stone parapet and leaned out the window, which was only just big enough to let my head and shoulders through. I had no questions, and I had no words. Yet even so, the living God might still be coming down those rocky slopes, between the thickets and the sleeping herds, unnoticed and unheard, in human form.

It was just a pity that instead of waiting for him, I was obliged to stumble down the dark corridor, find the switch that turned on a weak bulb, and empty my bowels in the wooden toilet. Then I went back to the room and made Benjamin comfortable. I took off his shoes, kissed his brow, and covered him with a blanket. I also took off my shoes, as I had absolutely no intention of going to the car now. I lay down. I was still feeling pretty great rather than sick. I was no longer watching out for an approaching man, but my spirit still floated up above the untidy garden and silently stole along the stone walls.

In the morning, I was desperate for water and toothpaste. I asked Benjamin to go down to the car for the smaller backpack, but he was afraid to go by himself, so we went down together. Although the poetry of the night was gone, even with a hangover, I still found the atmosphere here calming. Perhaps it was the effect of the gradual disintegration of the place, which the local inhabitants neither helped along nor fought to prevent.

Down in the street, we were surprised at the change in the weather. There was a strong, gusty wind and a veil of silver-grey clouds over the sky. Plastic bottles rolled along the empty streets. Dust and fragments of twigs pricked us in the eyes.

We took just our jackets, toothbrushes, and toothpaste from the car. On the way back up the steep hill, I had an attack of faintness from hunger. In the otherwise empty inn, they gave us bread and butter, jam, and tea.

I was still vaguely wondering why we had to start moving again, why there was any need to drive or walk anywhere. Maybe we really could repair one of these deserted houses, I thought. Here we would soon kick the habit of hurry, and even boredom itself would eventually get tired and give up. We would grow into inactivity, and I would start to drink. Occasionally, God would visit us.

Ben's impatience brought me back to inexorable reality. No one was watching when we finally we got into the car, and the wind slammed the doors behind us. We sped off down the winding road. I began to see how high we had climbed. After a few hours, we were back down close to the sea, but the sky remained overcast and cold air blew in through the car windows. I realized that summer was over. Where could we go next?

Chapter V

The Journey is Lost in a Mist of Forgetting and Re-Emergence

They Encounter Ancient Civilization and Are Happy but Memories End

Out of sheer helplessness, I bought a special tourist map on which the ancient monuments were marked in green. Since childhood, I had hated this kind of thing—walking around castles and monuments, staring into cases where dead exhibits lay behind glass, perfectly lit and as if in formalin, where elderly ladies walked about spouting meaningless nonsense about long-gone times—but now I was apparently going to have to endure it with Ben. I discovered that not far from us, only about seventy kilometers along the gulf and then ten kilometers into the interior, lay legendary Delphi. As it happened, not even Benjamin was excited about the idea of us going over a hundred kilometers to somewhere where we wouldn't be able to swim or play soccer. All the same, we set out. The grey sea on our right side was ploughed up by thousands of little waves. Once again, we headed inland for the hills, but this time, the ascent was shorter and the roads less narrow.

Our first impression of Delphi only confirmed my fears. Everywhere there were parked cars or buses and stores full of replicas and souvenirs. Only the position of the little town on the slope, between rocks above a deep valley, gave any hint of the kind of emotions that might have overcome the pilgrims of ancient times.

I found a parking space with difficulty, and Benjamin decided that he wanted a coke and a sundae. I hesitated, wondering whether this might be the moment to take a stand, and when I should get up and show him that he couldn't always have everything he decided he wanted. But I didn't have a good enough reason for risking a sullen atmosphere just now, and so we ended up in the nearest bistro.

After about half an hour in which I tried to explain to Ben what ancient civilization was like and when it started, we set off on foot along the road out of the little town, following the stream of tourists.

Over the heads of a group of Japanese people, I soon saw the stumps of ancient pillars. Unexpectedly, despite the crowd of people, I felt the majesty of the scenery. The remains of the oracle, more extensive and better preserved than I had imagined, came into view at the foot of orange cliffs above the narrow throat of the valley.

I paid for our entrance tickets, and we dove into the labyrinth of paths in the fenced complex of excavations. As we walked between wrought slabs, pillars, and parts of statues, a curious calm descended on us. There was no doubt that we were passing the traces of a real civilization—much more authentic, refined, and profound than ours today. Even Benjamin felt it; he ran around between the slabs with interest and respect, asking me if he could touch them, and if the people who had once lived here had also walked on these paths. A kind of sacred tranquility reigned here, although we were weaving our way through tourists who had no humility and who were posing in front of cameras and eating snacks on the finely wrought slabs.

At one moment, Ben lost me in the labyrinth of paths. I walked faster and caught up with him a few terraces higher. He was sitting on the top of the stone steps as I came up them, or more precisely, on the little wall where the steps ended. His feet were dangling, and I suddenly found myself looking at him with new eyes. There he was above me, his fair hair only emphasizing the depth of his tan. I saw a bright boy, lanky and lean, and I realized how much he had changed on our trip. He was in a good mood and grinning, because he was looking at me from above. I caught him by the leg as if to pull him down, and he pretended to defend himself, and we pulled and struggled, and then he jumped onto my back and I walked on, carrying him—I remember it as if it were yesterday: the wild, wayward touches, his boyish body on my back, his laughter. It is also my last coherent memory of that part of the journey to the Back of Beyond, the last memory that follows straight from those that went before. Up to that point, I remember it all, spliced together like a film. At the end of the film, I run up the steps with Benjamin on my back, and I am out of breath and sweating; I am nearly at the top, my heart pounds, and my breath comes in gasps, but I keep going, experiencing joy, pure happiness. I am thinking of how we will bow to the majesty of the place when we reach the top; except then, the memory disappears…I don't even know if I reached the top.

This is all the result of a later event that deprived me of part of my memory, so the next leg of our journey—from Delphi to the green-painted railings on a Romanian railway station—is all broken and torn in my mind. Particular memories are surrounded by gaps. Isolated images, feelings, and thoughts rise up like islands out of the sea, or perhaps more like the tops of mountains out of low clouds. Sometimes, they are no more than mere fragments of experiences I never recovered at all, or perhaps never tried hard enough to recover, since some later events did actually re-emerge when I really concentrated or returned to the same place again.

But much has remained sunk in the mist, which over time has become impenetrable, and although I have sometimes gotten hold of a piece of information about these forgotten events—for example, from Petra, since I apparently called her again several times—it is as if I am hearing about a stranger. The film has been ripped, with nothing to glue it back together. All the same, at the end of the uninterrupted sequence, a feeling of happiness remains. Or precisely the memory of happiness, which also brings the grief of the knowledge that it is gone forever, that distant moment when Benjamin was eight, and I was not yet old.

Father and Son Head North—Neither Away nor Home

I don't know how long we stayed in Greece after that. Judging by what Petra later told me, it could have been two weeks, but I can't imagine what we were doing in those two weeks. Benjamin said something about a storm and torrential rain catching us on a beach. Otherwise, though, places and events had all run together in his mind, and I never considered it important to try and get more out of him. I guess I never admitted to him quite how big the holes in my memory were either.

Anyhow, I never entirely understood why we headed out of Greece north into Bulgaria, which, in fact, meant starting to go back. We could have gone on instead—straight to Athens and then to Cyprus or Turkey. I suspect that I was simply afraid, and not only that…Probably I hadn't been totally serious about the journey to the Back of Beyond. I didn't feel able to return to Prague yet, because I was still looking for an answer to the question of what the journey was all about, but I wasn't really prepared to go away with Ben indefinitely. Hence, that strange direction—through Bulgaria—a route that took us neither further away, nor directly home.

Of course, I might have had other reasons. A longing for lush mountain nature, full of streams and scented forests, perhaps, but also a fear of border checks, a fear that they were looking for us. Maybe I thought getting into Bulgaria would be relatively easy.

My fear of border checks, worry that we were in a data base of missing persons, was not unjustified. A scene in some hotel or other has stuck in my mind like a memory from early childhood. We are still in Greece. Benjamin is slightly sick and resting in a room somewhere upstairs opposite an elevator. On the second or third day, the hotel owner asks me to come down to the small reception desk. He is a tanned young man with a polite manner. He gives me a conspiratorial look as he turns the computer monitor towards me and taps in a search address. Photographs of various people start coming up on the screen. The hotelier clicks a couple of times, and one particular photograph appears, enlarged. It is of me standing with Benjamin—I have an arm around his shoulder, behind us is a high mountain landscape, and there are gnats around our heads. It's a snapshot that was taken on vacation the year before and sent out to all the relatives, including my father. I realize right away what this is about, but try not to give anything away by my expression. I look at the photograph without speaking. The hotelier looks at me, and then our eyes meet. In that moment of silent communication, I surrender completely. I feel like a Jew found in a shelter during the war, totally dependent on the good will of others. The hotelier probably has questions that he doesn't know how to ask in his broken English, but I also sense a certain admiration and sympathy there. After a moment, he reaches into a drawer and hands me our passports, and then a torn-out page from the guestbook, where our names are written. I don't know if he is expecting ostentatious thanks or just a silent nod. I take the passports and the page and bend my head. "Thank you."

Later, we are getting close to the Bulgarian border. The sky is covered in a shapeless mist, the road lead upwards, and the surrounding slopes are turning the colors of autumn I know from Bohemia. At every moment, I have to stop and go to the bathroom—that's how nervous I am. I try to calm myself with the thought that even if they catch us, nothing much will happen. At most, they will send us back to Prague. In a way, an enforced return would not be such a defeat.

My nervousness communicates itself to Ben; he complains of feeling sick from the turns and the ascent. I go for a walk to a river, full of muddy water flowing down from the Bulgarian mountains and the clay Bulgarian lowlands. Pieces of cement and iron lie on the bank, left there after the construction of a nearby bridge. Then, a piece of memory is missing. Then we are actually driving up to the border. The Greeks let us through without problems, and we enter the Bulgarian zone. Everything here looks shabby and severe. Ahead of us, there is a line of Bulgarian cars: they are all old wrecks with exhausts that belch stinking gas, and Ben is taken aback. I explain that in communist times, people used to drive in cars like that in our country too. Bulgaria is a poor country, even more affected by communism than we were. In the meantime, we have moved one car's length ahead. "Just keep calm, that's the main thing," I instruct Ben, feigning confidence, but in reality, I'm more nervous than he is and desperately want to go to the bathroom again. I look around to see where I might go, but Bulgarian border guards and customs officers are walking around everywhere. They all behave as if they are doing people an amazing honor by allowing them to enter Bulgaria. Evidently, Bulgarians don't need anyone else there.

After about an hour of tense waiting, we finally get to the window. The forbidding customs officer scrutinizes our passports, and I'm running with sweat because my need to urinate is so strong.

"Dad, Dad, tell him we're on a journey to the Back of Beyond," Ben advises me from the back.

"Just be quiet!" I say. The customs officer wants to see the papers for the car and some confirmation I don't have. I give him a baffled, desperate look. The coming moments are probably going to be critical. But the officer just sends me to an office where I'm supposed to buy the confirmation. I am supposed to leave the car here as it is, even though it is blocking the others. "Come with me," I tell Ben— the last thing I want is to leave him here.

"Where, Dad? Where are we going?"

"Quick, look sharp! I'll explain later."

Around ten minutes later, we get back with the confirmation. The barriers lift. Like in a dream, I drive through the shabby Bulgarian side of customs. Almost immediately, I stop by the edge of the road and run into the bushes.

Bulgarian towns and villages bear deep scars from communism. We pass houses built in the time of collective farming. They are oversized and insensitive, but now, long after the fall of communism, often dilapidated—without windows, without decorations, maybe without water and heating. The villages in the mountain valleys have lost their traditional character. There are no longer herds of cows and sheep pasturing on the slopes, or horses whinnying on village greens, and it's rare to see anyone offering honey, milk, or cheese for sale. The people look bewildered, as if they still haven't grasped why the supply of money from the state, which devastated the place under "real existing socialism," has suddenly dried up. The factory halls deserted, the railway stations squalid, the houses of culture—once bastions of communist propaganda—crumbling and blackened. Who wants to pay to maintain them today, when most people's immediate worry is finding the cash and the necessities to get through the coming winter?

I remember a little town in the mountains surrounded by forests. Disintegrating elevated pipelines lead along the highway, and the town is encircled not by cottages but by prefabricated apartment blocks. A pipe from a homemade stove sticks out of every window. Wherever you look, there is wood; it's piled high against every side of the concrete blocks. This region has enough timber, but the communists installed central heating using Soviet oil. We see no church, let alone villagers on the way to mass. They have been cheated and robbed. They have forgotten how to love their herds, their farms, forests, their streams running down from the mountains. They believed they could live a life without love and without faith. They believed that communism was more than God.

They Play Chess in the Fog of Forgetting

We had been on the road together for four months. Always together, always alone. I wondered if Benjamin would still be able to form friendships with his contemporaries. I had torn him out of his childhood and lifted him up into my adult world. In Greece, where we had enjoyed ourselves by the sea, the journey had still been not unlike a long vacation, but now that autumn had arrived and we were driving across Bulgaria, we must have experienced some hardship and discomfort. My memories of this time don't give me any kind of complete picture of our relationship. They are fragmentary scenes, like a movie without music, a flower without a scent, or then again, a scent without a flower. Considering the scenes, and the gaps in them, I have become aware of just how many layers there are to reality, and how many dimensions to each moment. Maybe you are just walking up a hill through dewy grass, for example. But apart from the dewy grass and feet walking on it, there is weariness, rapid breathing. There is the desire to be up there on top, and there is the doubt as whether this labor has any meaning. There are ants and butterflies, and all the weather on that day—the bright dawn, the first morning clouds, the expectation that it will warm up in the afternoon, and the evening storms. There are the rustlings of the trees and the buzzing of insects, but also the rumbling of the engine of a truck transporting timber, a village at the bottom of the hill, and whole mountains. There are all the people that come into your mind that day, there is love or its absence, fear for a son or joy in his progress, his difficulties in school and his successes. There is hunger and thirst, the stickiness of parched lips; there is the taste of sweat running down your face and the cooling touch of a sweaty t-shirt.

The dimensions of reality are endless, but my memories from that strange time mostly have just one dimension. Perhaps that grass underfoot, or one of Benjamin's questions, but no longer the place where he asked it…Perhaps the woodshed at the end of the village, but not the path that led there.

It doesn't bother me that I have forgotten facts—where we went, where we slept, or what we ate. It bothers me that I have lost more than a month of life with Benjamin. A great deal of time has gone by since then, of course, and has brought with it, countless important moments and impulses, but I will miss that month painfully, forever.

At some point in the second half of that month, Benjamin and I found ourselves in a musty chalet in the middle of the woods. I have no idea how we got there or where we went afterwards, but everything else rises up from my memory, even the smallest details. We had the sleeping bags rolled out on plank beds, and the surrounding woods were fading into the mist and low cloud. There was a dense but fine rain. The water was dripping from the rotting roof and leaking inside through several holes. Outside it was cold and wet, but the mountain air was cleansing and sent fresh oxygen surging through our veins. I walked across the meadow on the edge of the forest to a stream to wash the food container and get some water. A black bird fluttered from a thicket, brushed against the grass, and sent droplets of water flying. I brushed against spruce branches and water cascaded from them onto the sodden earth. All at once, the rain became stronger; I ran back to the chalet but was wet through by the time I reached it.

Benjamin took my advice and stayed wrapped up in his sleeping bag. We ate lunch, and the rest of the afternoon, the whole evening, and the long dark night stretched out ahead of us. I sat down next to Ben on the plank bed. *This is my beloved boy*, I thought, pleased at how patient he was, how he had grown, how he had grown up. "This is terrible weather, isn't it?" I said. "And just imagine how the birds, deer, foxes, and all the other creatures that live here have to put up with it all year round. Even in winter, when the snow falls."

"But it's clean here," Ben said. "The animals don't have to put up with smelly cars, and there isn't anything to disturb them…"

For a child, lighting a fire in the middle of a mountain hut and making tea on it is like being in a real-life movie. I thought how different Ben's perception of time was now, how even the smallest observations and activities were enough to keep him from getting bored. I was the one who stamped about impatiently, watching every brighter spot in the clouds with hope.

In the afternoon, we carved chessmen out of wet bark. The rooks were square shapes, the pawns were circles, the bishops were triangles, the queens were narrow rectangles, the kings were broad rectangles, and the knights had long beaks. Spruce bark meant black, and beech bark meant white. We sat down at the moldy, rickety table, our legs wrapped in the sleeping bags. Outside, the rain murmured, and it felt like we were the only two people in the entire world, the last two, completely devoted to each other.

"I love you, Dad," said Benjamin.

"I love you too, Benjamin," I said.

"I don't want you to die, Dad."

I didn't know what to say to that. Once, he had said that when I died, he would look after Mom instead of me. Back then, he had known nothing about death, of course, while now he had his own experience with it. Now, I interpreted what he said as meaning that he didn't want me to leave me as she had done, didn't want to lose me too, to be alone. In the end, I said, "Benjamin, I'm not going to die for a long time yet, don't worry. When I die, you'll already have been grown-up for a long time. It's many years ahead. It's your turn now, son. Play."

He moved a bark circle, but he didn't change the subject. "I don't want you ever to die. I want you to always live with me."

I stretched out a hand to him across the table, brushing several pieces with it and jiggling them. "I promise, I'll try to live as long as I can. I don't have any desire to die—I enjoy life."

"Mom didn't enjoy life," he said, like an adult.

"Play, for goodness's sake, concentrate. That's not a bishop but a knight."

It was getting dark fast. I added wood to the fire, and the smoke rose up to the opening in the middle of the roof. Only seven of the carved chessmen remained on the board. They were my king, queen, bishop, and two pawns (I remember this incredibly precisely) and his king and knight. He wanted to play to the very end at any price. We didn't speak of death again, but it was there in the gathering dusk around us. I realized that if I had never taken him on this journey, if I had never had the courage to do it, I would never have experienced this moment. We would never have been the last two people in the whole world in the murmur of the rain, in the fog of forgetting. The flames of the fire flickered and cast dull gleams on our chessmen. Now there was just my king, queen, two pawns—four twisted pieces of spruce bark—and his king.

They Cross the Danube with both Gangsters and Truckers

I would probably never have remembered the border crossing between Vidin in Bulgaria and Calafat in Romania if I hadn't been back there years later. Of course, I had a vague sense of its connection with my journey to the Back of Beyond,, but nothing more. Suddenly, my memory opened up. I drove along the huge, dirty Danube in a state of high excitement, one memory emerging after another. It was so sudden and unexpected, there was a lump in my throat. I was sitting at the wheel as I had been back then, but now I was an aging man, and there was no Benjamin in the back seat. Yet it seemed to me that if I turned around, he would inevitably be there. My beloved Benjamin. Love flooding my heart, I had to stop on a dirt track leading to the river. The back seat was empty, obviously, and there was nothing there but my personal stuff and an unfolded map. I wished as never before that time could be folded back, and I could start again from its midpoint. I wanted an eight-year-old with me.

Even that first time, it made a deep impression on me, the huge river that divided the landscape into two parts like a great natural highway. I turned around to ask Ben what he thought, but he was listening to music on his Walkman and hadn't noticed the Danube with all its momentous power. At the time when we were travelling, the river was a more absolute dividing line, since the nearest bridge was a hundred kilometers away in the former Yugoslavia. On the other side, there was just a ferry, too expensive to be used by the locals. On my second visit, the banks had already been linked by a provisional bridge.

The people in the villages lived their whole lives here—modern rootlessness hadn't spread to the place back then, and not even socialism had managed to alienate the river from the fate of its people. So everyone here had great respect for the river, which accompanied them from birth to death, which carried away the good and the bad alike—joy and grief, hunger, sickness, vanished youth...but also provided a kind of comfort, brought hope, and flowed away beyond the horizon of every day cares. Anyone who came to the river to catch fish, anyone who experienced a first kiss on its banks, anyone who longed to travel to faraway places as he gazed at its currents, somehow took from the Danube a little piece of its longevity and was united with it.

On the other hand, in Bulgaria back then, anyone hoping to find sparks of pleasure or colorful life on the banks of the Danube— wicker stalls or docks for summer pleasure steamers—would have been in for a sad disappointment. The town of Vidin had been just another monument to socialism, one of many like it. The endless, broken-down highways led us past the blackened walls of quickly prefabricated blocks. The people who lived there knew nothing of the river. They had been attracted from all corners of the country to the local factories and docks. I was sorry that we hadn't stopped earlier on, when we were still driving through villages. Now there was no alternative but to keep on driving in the direction given by the signs. The cratered highway led us into a desolate industrial zone, to a customs office where not a single regular car was waiting, only a line of heavy trucks. I began to worry about where I was taking Benjamin. This was a world unto itself, closed, with laws of its own that I knew nothing about. But one of the drivers gave me a friendly wave, indicating that I should go on ahead. A customs officer in uniform looked at our passports and gave them back to us, but kept on sitting there without raising the gate. After about ten minutes, during which nothing at all happened, he decided to let us through and raised the gate. I parked by the entrance to the customs office. Ben's cassette had just come to an end, so he started to show an interest in what was going on. "Where are we, Dad? Will we have to wait long? I want to see the river."

We got out and went into the office. Truckers were standing around with masses of papers. The presence of a child caused a stir and a degree of solidarity. "*Malodyetz*," an older grey-haired man gestured at Ben, came up, and ruffled his hair rather rudely. Taken aback, Ben turned around with a look that appealed to me for advice.

"The man says you're a fine boy," I soothed him. "He likes you."

The man reached into his pocket and brought out an electronic game. "*Vazmi!*"

I found this sort of kindness very unpleasant. It couldn't be refused, and it created a distasteful obligation. I thanked the man and gave Ben a discreet poke in the ribs. "Say thank you."

Ben liked the game, and it came in handy. While he played, the man grinned at me conspiratorially. I breathed a sigh of relief when the customs officer asked us to come with him to the car. He gave the car only a cursory inspection and sent us forward. We went through another barrier and ended up on a concrete ramp. In front of us flowed the greenish waters of the Danube, which lapped lazily around the reeds and the concrete. A few plastic bottles floated in circles, and others were stuck in the muddy bank.

Benjamin was overjoyed at the prospect of going down to the riverbank. I tried to dampen his enthusiasm, since I wasn't sure it was allowed. In the end, I went with him, and no one raised any objections.

After about an hour, an official with a pouch turned up and asked for money for the ferry. It was so much that I was sorry we hadn't driven to the nearest bridge. I also tried to find out when the ferry was going, but I didn't get an answer, except that we should wait.

So, we waited. It was the end of October, and the wind was blowing off the river. I had long ago explored the few meters of concrete bank that were fenced off by barbed wire, and there was no sign of the ferry. The day was almost over, and Ben wanted to go to the bathroom. I took him to the local outhouse, and it turned my stomach. I had to keep hold of his shoulders to stop him stepping in a pile of shit. When we got back, two black Italian BMWs were lined up behind us. They sat there silently—the engines switched off—and there was something sinister about them. Through the smoked glass, I glimpsed the unmistakable faces of gangsters.

"Look, Dad, another car. The ferry must be getting here soon," Ben brightened up.

"I don't know. Maybe." I led him to the car. "Get inside—it's cold." I quickly shut the doors behind us. Then, I followed events behind us in the mirror. After about half an hour, the door of one car opened and a fat, colorfully dressed godfather got out. With the gait of a man who doesn't do much walking, he walked around us to the front, where he stood facing the river, his hands on his hips. After a while, he was joined by a young, shaven-headed colleague, also perfectly dressed. Through the open doors of their car, I glimpsed a small, heavily made-up prostitute. I began to sweat and wished that one of the trucks would drive up. Instead, an even fatter and more fashionable godfather emerged from the second car. For a time, they all stood facing the river, and then they returned to the car. I wondered if there was a studio shooting porn near here, or if they were operating a network of brothels.

"Dad, I don't like it here anymore!" grumbled Ben.

I wasn't surprised. All this waiting hadn't brought him anything interesting, unless, of course, I told him what the Italians were all about. Maybe that would amuse him.

"You know what, Benjamin, we've just got to be patient here," I said. "Those people who've arrived, they could be criminals, and I don't want them to notice us. And we shouldn't pay any attention to them either."

"Criminals, Dad? How do you know?" he asked excitedly.

"I can tell, believe me."

"So why don't you report it?"

"What could I report? They're not committing any crimes right now. Or at least, there's no way of telling if they are."

"But you should tell someone they're criminals!"

"Except I don't have any proof. I just think they are, because of the way they look. Criminals like that are usually really clever, and not even the police can prove anything against them. You can't accuse people when you don't have any proof."

This didn't satisfy him, but he stopped insisting. Meanwhile, the mafia guys had returned to their cars and put the radio music on loud. The fattest one had narrow-tipped shoes made of crocodile skin. The sky had become more overcast, clouds overtaking what had earlier been a half-clear sky. Finally, I heard engines, and dozens of trucks came up from behind. The car ferry was heading our way from around a blind bend in the river. After long hours of inactivity, the whole place sprang into action. Officials let down an iron bridge and guided the trucks onto the deck. It filled up quickly, and I began to worry whether they would let us on at all. I started up the engine and edged forward, behind me the gangsters. We parked the cars close beside each other, tightly squeezed between trucks. I had the feeling it would be dangerous to stay in the car. What if one of the trucks tipped over? So, we got out, and I led Ben up the steps to the back. But he was more interested in the criminals than the river.

The ferry engines started up, and the ferry moved forward into the center of the river, its quiet, powerful current gurgling not far beneath us. The water's surface was disturbed by shallow, almost invisible eddies. I wondered what I would do if someone threw us down into the water or if the trucks flipped over and the ferry went down. Would I be able to swim to the side with Ben? I was afraid of the river and afraid of the Italians. It occurred to me that maybe they trafficked children, and so I held Ben's small hand tight and silently begged him to forgive me. Although the temperature had fallen and a sharp wind was blowing across the river, furrowing the otherwise calm surface of the water, Benjamin's palm was warm.

Many years later, I was driving across the new bridge a little further upstream. In the middle of the bridge I stopped, got out, and looked down, absolutely stricken by memories. The water was the same greenish color, and the eddies circled in the same unobtrusive, treacherous way—it was the same water, but still, it was different, just as I was the same but different. Something that, for years, I hadn't recalled even faintly, had come back to me as if a magic wand had been waved, and now I couldn't believe I had ever forgotten it. When I shut my eyes, I could see a ferry full of trucks moving alongside the bridge, and at the back, a father and son, standing close, leaning in to each other.

They Quarrel and Want to End the Journey

The point from which my memory more or less came back, because it had to, was the railway station in the little spa town of Baile Herculane. We parked in front of the station at the side of the main road and went to buy something to eat. I was surprised at how clean the station was and at its unified style, rather art nouveau. The cast iron railings had been repainted in green, and the small concourse looked like a spa pavilion, which would not have looked out of place anywhere in Central Europe. Otherwise, it was just a minor halt with one platform and one set of rails.

That day, Ben and I had been getting on each other's nerves since morning. He had gotten it into his head that he was missing his grandad and kept needling me about it. "But why can't Grandad come out and join us?" Or, "I like going on trips with Grandad." Or even, "When are we going to go home? I want to go see Grandad on Sunday. I don't like it here anymore."

I was at my wits' end. Now that we were going north and a little west, the journey had nowhere much to continue. In the end, I lost my temper with Ben and said, "So I guess it doesn't bother you that Grandad wants me to be sent to jail?"

"What d'you mean, jail?" He gave me a baffled look.

"Because it so happens that Grandad's told the police I've kidnapped you. So now they're looking for us everywhere."

He still didn't get it. "But why? Why would you go to jail?"

"Well, I've stopped sending you to school. There's a law that makes parents responsible for seeing their kid goes to school. If they don't, it's a crime."

"But Mom died."

"Yes. So that makes me the only one responsible for you now."

There was silence for a while, and I drove on in peace. Then, a small voice piped up from the back. "But if I don't go to school, I'll stay ignorant."

This infuriated me so much that I burst out crazily, "So what the hell is that supposed to mean? That you'd rather be in school now? That you want to tell the police and have them arrest me?"

It was the station that eventually calmed us down. We walked along the open platform. I bought us ice creams at a stand, and we sat on a bench and waved at a passing train. It was quite a warm autumn day, fallen leaves on the ground everywhere. Very high hills rose around us, slopes vivid with orange, yellow, and brown. The clouds were thickening, and soon it started to drizzle.

Of course, I was already feeling sorry for thundering at Ben like that. He had only said out loud what I knew myself—the journey to the Back of Beyond was at an end. Now, it was just a matter of thinking up some grand culmination for it, so we could tell each other it wasn't a journey from nowhere to nowhere and that we had achieved something special.

We walked back to the car. I turned off the main road to the spa center. It was obvious enough from the look of the people on the platform that this wasn't a "pearl" of European spa tourism; after all, this was a country just beginning to recover from merciless dictatorship and impoverishment. There were ordinary villagers loaded down with a pile of bags filled with everything possible. Then there were members of the dreary middle class of the Romanian towns—people dressed in the fashions of thirty years ago, with saggy luggage, and physically all unappealing, especially the women. Meanwhile, there were nouveau riche types sitting in a nearby bistro and making it tastelessly obvious that they considered themselves superior to everyone else. Taxi drivers in ancient Dacias waited for them in front of the station.

I stopped by a hotel that looked entirely new: stairs and railings in pseudo-classical style, a restaurant that was mostly glass. The price was acceptable, though despite the copies of the cards stuck on the door, they wouldn't take plastic. We took a room for two on the first floor. The bathroom door handle immediately came off in my hand.

The floor was uneven, the mattresses on the beds terribly soft, the toilet leaked, and one of the bathroom taps wouldn't turn off.

On the other hand, when I leaned out of the window, I saw these superbly colored hillsides. A solution came to me: as soon as the weather improved, we would make a several-day trip to the more remote mountains here. It would be a really great experience to end our travels with a true culmination.

In the Fall They Set out for the Cooling Mountains

The decision to end the journey was a relief. I felt a certain peace as well as eager anticipation for the culminating trip to the mountains. My sense of helplessness was gone and with it all the tension of recent weeks. Once again, I was looking around with hope and gratitude. That included the hope that Ben would accept the decision.

We walked around the spa town the next day and eventually discovered that there were no colonnades with fountains, that the local hotels had no pools of curative water, and that the curative spring just flowed from a concrete pipe that ran under the road into a mountain river (it was there, on a concrete embankment, that the hotel guests poured it over themselves). At this point, I judged the moment was the right one. "You know what, Ben," I started slowly, "I've been looking at the map, and there are very high and wild mountains—even wilder than the Bulgarian ones—starting just a few kilometers from here. As far as I know, there are bears and wolves there, but right now, in the fall, we don't have to be scared of them, because they have plenty of food in the forests. So, I think that if we go and take a look at these mountains—now, in the fall, when nobody's there—we'll finally be in the Back of Beyond in just the way we wanted. We'll reach that real Back of Beyond, and then we can go home."

I waited tensely for Ben's reaction, but instead of either brightening up or showing disappointment, he just said, "Do you think we might get to actually see a bear?"

"Probably not. And I wouldn't really want to."

"I'd like to see a bear."

"Don't be silly. We'd be afraid of him…But I just want to know you agree with the plan—to go to these mountains and finally declare ourselves in the Back of Beyond?" I insisted on an answer.

"Sure, Dad. And then we'll go home."

During the night there were showers, but the next morning, the sky cleared to a pale blue. It was colder and a wind was blowing. It worried me a lot that Benjamin was eating so little. He didn't like any of the food here, and now that his skin was paling and the power of the Greek sun draining out of it, he looked very skinny.

I also had trouble putting together food for the mountains. We still had some instant soup, pasta, and powdered drinks from Prague. I managed to find some long-life salami, peppers, and cheese. The bread was poor quality—white.

I packed one big backpack for myself and a small one for Ben. The sky was bright, and the wind brought a refreshing cold edge to the air. Early the next morning, I paid and we set off in the car along a small road leading upstream along the Cerna River. The traces of the town soon disappeared into the landscape, and wooden chalets appeared on the slopes, under beechwood with golden crowns glittering in the slanting rays of the sun. The river was lined with white limestone rocks.

After around fifteen kilometers, I stopped the car, and we clambered down a crumbling path to the limpid water. It was a place where you could jump from stone to stone right across to the other bank. Here, in the middle of nature, we both felt good, separately and together. Somewhere deep down, I could already detect a shiver of fear and foreboding about the unknown, but for the moment, I could suppress it. Benjamin jumped around among the boulders and played on the piles of sand brought by the current. Suddenly he squatted down on his haunches and looked serious. "I like it here," he said. "It's a pity Mom can't be here with us."

I could understand why she had come into his mind here, beside the pure mountain water. She was just as pure in his memory—she was the purest thing he carried in his heart, and her place could never be filled. "That clear water is what reminded you of her, wasn't it?"

"Mom loved water."

"You're right. It's surely no accident you started thinking of her here. Maybe her soul, which can still see you, has flowed here with the water."

"Really, Dad? Then I'll splash myself with it." Before I could do anything to stop him, he plunged his arms into the water up to the elbows.

We climbed back up to the car. It was still warm inside, making me very much aware of the wonderful base it provided, all of its modern comfort. We drove on another five kilometers until the highway divided into one last asphalt highway and a secondary dirt road. The dirt road was full of puddles. According to the map, this was the route we needed to take.

I drove at twenty kilometers per hour at most and had to keep almost grinding to a halt in front of potholes. Or sometimes just to look around. The valley was not as rocky as at the start, and the river wound between meadows hemmed with alders and bushes. We passed a few picturesque farmhouses. A shepherd woman in a shawl waved to us, her dogs turning around from the sheep and barking at us. The sun was still rising in the clear autumn sky, and everything suggested we were travelling through a land of happy people.

"D'you think we could live here with Mom, too?" asked Ben as we passed another farmhouse.

"How do you mean, live with Mom? Like before?" I didn't understand.

"Like if we lived here, you and me, then Mom would be here with us… if her soul is swimming in the water."

Whatever Ben meant, I had in fact been dreaming for a moment of a small farmhouse with a pasture and unfenced garden, with a full hayloft and a mass of cut logs ready for the long, cruel winter. But I knew this was just the fantasy of an urban person, with no idea of the drudgery, the discomfort and dirt, the getting up before dawn and mucking out the stalls…"Benjamin," I said, "if we lived here, we'd have great memories of Mom, but you shouldn't think of a human soul as having to be any particular place once the person has died. A human soul is more something you become aware of when you're alone and thinking of the person. If you remember the person when you look into clear water, then you may get the feeling that her soul is actually in the water. But you can remember the same person just as well when you're looking at mountains or even when you're just sitting at the table at home. The funny thing is, I was just imagining what it would be like to live here together. Only we wouldn't know how. We don't know how to keep a horse, how to cut the hay, how to repair the roof…"

"I'd know how to look after the sheep and horses," Ben said. "The dog would help me guard them." It just didn't occur to him that there might be anything difficult about it. He saw the sunlit slopes, he saw the freely grazing horses, he saw the wooden water trough, and it all seemed to say that life here would be simple and would just continue on of its own accord, without effort.

The road was constantly rising, and eventually a view of bare mountaintops opened up through a side valley on the peaks of mountains. They were rounded rather than rocky and looked easily negotiable, but right at the top they were covered in a white frost that hadn't yet melted since morning. "Look!" I pointed for Ben. "Tomorrow we could be right up there." I could almost feel the cold that I saw on those heights. We were approaching the cooling mountains in the late fall.

"How are we going to get there? Are we going to drive the car right to the top?" he asked.

"Of course not. We'll leave the car in the last village. Someone will probably let us put it in his barn. We'll go up to the top on foot."

"But couldn't we go there in the car?"

Soon we drove into a village. There was a lot of mud everywhere and heaps of plastic trash along the road. Huddling alongside the richer farms were some tiny wooden shacks with just one window. We passed a two-story school, and the local children pointed at us. "Would you like to go to school here?" I teased Ben.

"But I don't know anyone here, Dad," he said with a whimper in his voice.

"Calm down. I was just joking," I told him.

In the meantime, we had come to a kind of combined farm and loading station. Two large trucks piled high with timber were parked there. Several timber workers were standing there with long axes. A man with an air of self-confidence—the owner or boss—was keeping an eye on everything from a lookout above the yard. I stopped our car a respectful distance from the trucks.

"What do you want to do, Dad?" asked Ben in some alarm.

I was nervous too. The prospect of trying to come to an arrangement in a strange place wasn't at all pleasant, but in my judgment, we had an opportunity to leave the car right here.

We walked around the timber workers, who cast us curious but essentially indifferent glances. For them, we were something like space aliens—inaccessible, incomprehensible, foreign. The boss let us come up to his lookout. I greeted him deferentially, and the gesticulation started. I pointed at me, at Ben, and then at the mountains. "*Munti*," I said. Then I pointed at the car and his house, and said, "*Garage*." The boss waved his hands authoritatively, shaking his head—"*Nu munti. Nu munti*," and added some words that were unintelligible but most probably translated as, "You can't go into the mountains now in the autumn." He also gestured at Ben as he warningly repeated: "*Nu munti*."

I pointed again at our car and tried to explain to him that we had all the right things there, a tent and sleeping bags, food…To add weight to my words, I pointed at myself and lied: "*Alpinist. Munti*."

The boss did not approve, but he was no longer so indignant. After a moment, he motioned to us to follow him into the inner yard courtyard, where drivers were sitting drinking coffee, and hens and geese were wandering around on the trampled earth. The boss led us to a roofed patch without walls, half filled with logs. He pointed at a free space and said, "*Automobil*."

I indicated that I would pay him, but he just waved a hand and had the gate opened. We drove into the inner yard and then very cautiously into the open woodshed. To this day, I can hear the words with which I soothed the frightened Benjamin; I can hear them as if I uttered them only yesterday—"You see, the car will wait for us here. And from here, we'll go straight home."

Strict with his own people, the boss started to treat us like guests. He invited us to a table and had smoked meat and onions brought to us. I had to drink a glass of brandy with him. I noticed his deep wrinkles and the conspicuous tendons that testified to his heavy work. His wife appeared—an ugly, overweight woman dressed in a style that was neither rural nor urban. She wanted to take Ben into the house, but he wouldn't hear of it. She brought him fresh milk and bread with honey.

The sun had reached its high point and was beginning to descend. The wind had dropped and the air had warmed up. I pointed at my watch and then at the mountains, but the boss made it clear that we had to wait for a while. The same thing happened an hour later. I was starting to get nervous and wanted to go to the bathroom. After another half hour, an empty truck arrived from below. The driver came inside and the boss took him aside for a long consultation. The shadows were lengthening, and Ben kept on and on, asking when we would be leaving. Finally, the debate ended, and the driver picked up our backpacks. Apparently, he was giving us a lift.

So, we drove off. Ben forgot his earlier suffering and looked around the cabin with enthusiasm. The hours we seemed to have lost waiting in the yard were now being returned to us, as we realized how long the initial hike would have taken. Eventually, the driver stopped in a place where a fierce mountain stream ran down from the left. We got out, and the truck moved off. It was a minute or so before it vanished around the nearest bend, and even longer before the rattling of its engine died away. It was only then that we were truly alone, thrown back into relying on our own resources in the middle of the immense mountain forests. The cold was rising up from the stream, and a frog jumped across the road; the air was steeped in the scent of leaves. My mind wandered to old age and death, which would come one day, as inevitably as autumn had come to the mountains.

Father and Son Come Close to their Final Goal but are Prevented by Fate from Taking the Road Home

Our first steps up the steep slope, on a scarcely visible footpath, brought us cold and sweat, relief and anxiety. It was certainly sobering. Ben's backpack turned out to be too heavy for him, and so I had to take out his sleeping bag and carry it loose, because there wasn't enough room for it in my backpack yet. Dusk was gathering thickly in the virgin beech forest where the path led, and I urged Ben to walk faster, fearing that the day would end before we could find a suitable place to sleep.

When I remember them today, at a distance of many years, our ramblings through the Romanian mountains seem full of that eternal contradiction between spirit and matter. It was as if we touched the vault of heaven, but our feet kept us bound to the wet, cooling ground. There was something fantastical about being up here—father and son—on the threshold of winter, when the shepherds had long ago driven their flocks back to their homes in the valleys. We had to cope with chill and wind, strain, hunger and cold, but the autumn sun made up for it, flooding the deserted mountains in golden light. A touch of hardship made our experiences more worthwhile, and the wind whipped pure happiness into our faces.

Towards the end of that first day, we climbed up through a pine forest as the light finally faded. Benjamin stayed close to me; I only had to take a few faster steps and he would be calling out in alarm, "Wait for me, Dad!"

I would never have dreamed of letting him get lost. He had grown up in a city, surrounded by an advanced civilization that enables individuals to behave like God almighty without actually being able to repair the things they use, or even to understand the principles on

209

which they work. Here, in the deep and still wild woods stretching across numberless valleys and ravines, once lost he would be lost for good. Of course, I told him what he should do if he got into any trouble. I told him he should always go down alongside running water until he hit a road to the village, but that there could be fallen trees or long crevices in the ravines. "When it gets dark you shouldn't go on," I added. "You should wait where you are until the dawn."

"Dad." He caught my hand. "I'm scared."

As the first star appeared in the sky, we came out of the freezing damp of the forest into a small clearing—probably once a pasture— which was now thickly overgrown with ferns that thrived on a soil saturated in the droppings and urine of animals. In the middle of the ferns stood a tiny cottage, not much taller than an adult man. Inside was a little black kitchen with a collapsed stove and one room with two straw mattresses on wooden beds. Musty-smelling blankets and a shepherd's vest still lay there. It was hard to judge how long it had been since anyone lived here: maybe a year, maybe five years. Finding a base like this was a relief.

In the evening, we chatted about how people used to live. I felt deeply moved to think that people still farmed like this here. I also thought how remarkable it would be to be someone who was born here and grew up here but later left for the city, studied, and became someone else…surely the traces of his unselfconscious childhood in wild nature would remain in his soul.

Benjamin fell asleep around nine, and I listened to his tranquil breathing. I was unable to sleep. For the first time in our entire journey, for the first time since our departure at the beginning of the vacation, I thought about what I would do when I got back. For the first time, I looked forward to going home, and for the first time, I actually saw the city I had abandoned as my home. I thought of how we might find a comfortable apartment with a view of old Prague, and it even struck me as possible that I might still meet the love of my life. Now, near the end of the journey to the Back of Beyond, I felt that I was ready.

The next day, we didn't have the same luck finding night quarters. At first, we passed several other shepherds' huts, but there were none above the upper border of the woods. Grassy slopes, with just a few reassuringly easy rocks, gradually brought us closer to the main mountaintop. Benjamin trudged on courageously and did not complain at all, even though he had to carry his backpack, and we had nothing but smoked meat and damp bread to eat. I praised him and was proud of him.

After midday, we found a sheltered, sunny place where the grass was dry and warm. We lazed there for about an hour, talking about the weather and finding the wind direction by holding up licked fingers. That wind direction eventually turned, and we had to go on. I started looking for a place for the tent well in advance, and so I headed into a rocky valley in the lee of the wind. It was a place with odd acoustics, sound splintering strangely on stone, and I was gripped by anxiety at the solitude surrounding us. The sweat quickly cooled on our bodies, and the cold got its teeth into us. Darkness fell at six, and the tent provided only very limited comfort. I told Ben all about the hardships and discomforts that mountaineers had to endure, in the Himalayas, for example. But Ben was dreaming of the sea, recalling how he had dived and run around in the waves. "It has to be summer now somewhere on the planet, right?" he said.

"Sure, but would you want to us go there after this?"

"I don't know."

In the morning, the tent was covered in frost, and since there was no hope of the sun thawing it before noon, I had to scape it off. I stretched my painful spine, dealt with the frost, and went to a stream to get water for tea.

That day, we climbed up a scree slope and a rocky gully, where I once again felt the oppressiveness of the solitude, but then we swung up above the surrounding slopes, and I saw the immense forests of the foothills stretching away to the blue horizon. A few minutes later, we were on the very top, faces to a wind that confirmed our victory. The space around us was full of nothing but clear air and for a moment my heart seemed in contact with the secret of creation. If I remember rightly, it did not take the form of God but was more the abstract inter-relatedness of all with everything. I embraced Benjamin—for the first time as if he were a man—my equal.

So now we can go back with a clear conscience, I thought. But we didn't go back, and it wasn't me who set our new direction.

"Hey, look Dad, in the distance over there, there's a castle on a hill," Ben pointed.

I looked, and it was true. On the highest mountain of the range opposite, which was connected with our range by a high plateau, stood a building resembling a castle, or perhaps just a tower. "You're right. There's something like a castle there."

"I want to go see it. Can we go there, Dad?"

"D'you have any idea how far it is? That's two days' walk away, for you maybe three."

"But I really want to go there."

"No, Benjamin, it's too far," I said, but I was of two minds. It struck me that I shouldn't try to end our journey to the Back of Beyond prematurely. What if its culmination was, in fact, waiting for us over there? "And don't forget," I continued trying to persuade both of us, "that we'd have to come back the same way. And maybe it's not a castle at all. When we get close, we might discover it's just something boring."

"Well, us finding out would be the point," Ben insisted. "You were the one that kept telling me this trip to the mountains had to be really worth it."

I could see his determination, and his newly acquired strength, and suddenly I had no wish to bring him back down to earth.

Later, my mind would often run back to this conversation; it still does. We were standing on a summit at a height of two thousand and two hundred meters, and we were just a step from returning. If he hadn't just happened to look in that direction, or if I had just stuck to my objections for a moment longer, everything would have been so different. But I gave in.

212

"Okay, we'll see," I said hesitantly, but then I added more decisively, "all right, we'll go there."

That day we went on until dusk. We camped on the high plateau between the two ranges. A copious stream flowed across the plateau, though it had no visible source other than the meadows around it. As the evening arrived, we crossed the stream and put up our tent in a bend, close to the bank. Ben's legs were numb from the crossing, and I rubbed them with a sweater.

The next morning, we went straight on. The building on the horizon was larger—now we could identify it with certainty as a stone tower, but it was still quite a long way away, and the weather was beginning to deteriorate. First, a light smokey film spread over the sky. Then, a hostile wind rose and drove beech leaves across the plateau. They swirled around us, although there was not a tree in sight. I felt as if we were part of an oil painting on the canvas of some old master, but then the sky grew dimmer minute by minute, and the horizon became a blur. A thick curtain of clouds emerged from behind the summits.

The mountain with the tower had disappeared from view, and before we knew it, a sharp icy rain was whipping into our cheeks. "Walk in front of me. Quick!" I called to Ben, who was lagging behind. We were now crossing the hillside that connected the ranges, and there was nowhere to put up a tent. The wind was driving the rain almost horizontally, and water was running down our necks and into our sleeves.

"Dad, I'm real cold."

I was gripped by panic about what I had got him into. Alone, I would just have gritted my teeth and quickened my pace, but I was with eight-year-old Benjamin, who couldn't go any faster. "Ben, please, you just have to keep going. It's going to be tough, but we'll get through, believe me," I told him. In fact, I had to yell in the raging wind. "Just keep close to me, that's the main thing, and you can shelter a bit behind me."

But Ben was sobbing. "Dad, I don't want to be here."

I was desperate. I even considered throwing my backpack away and carrying Ben. "Benjamin, just listen to me!" I bent down to him, cold water dripping down my forehead. "We're going to be soaked and cold. I'm sorry, but it's true. But in the end, we'll get down somewhere, and we'll get warm. When you climb into a dry sleeping bag, you'll be warm in a moment. You bet."

I succeeded in calming him down, and we went on, side by side. The happiness of recent days was forgotten. Now we were suffering earthly hardship with no end in sight. But it in the end it was finite, of course, like everything in human life. Today it is just a memory.

I know I made many mistakes that day, and we were very lucky. The sensible thing would have been to put up the tent, even on the crossing and to wait. Instead, I took us across a main ridge, where I couldn't see my way, and then down by what I wasn't sure was any kind of path. The rain seemed to be exploding directly out of the cloud surrounding us, with visibility down to a couple of meters. Water flowed under our feet, taking small stones with it. I held Benjamin tightly by the hand. The desire to get him to safety was what was driving me on, although it was also what made me take risks. What I thought was a path could suddenly have become a drop. My mind was dulled by the wind and empty of anything save the will to get us down. Somehow, I succeeded despite my mistakes, and a little lower we hit a real path. Here, the rain and wind were less severe. Dwarf pine appeared and then low spruce. We were coming down on the opposite side of the mountains to where we had started, and the vegetation here was completely different. Benjamin was mute now, walking on mechanically and trembling with cold.

It was then that we heard a clattering—the sound of a wood or metal spade or something like that— the sound of a human habitation. It filled me with gratitude, and love and tenderness. I realized just how much I belonged to the world of people.

Fate had been good to us. It had led us out of the gale and to a farm where we were given a kind welcome. The sinewy brown farmer lit a fire in the stove, and after an hour we were warmed up. Two grimy boys, maybe five and six years old, eyed us from the corner of the dark kitchen. Cows pressed against each other in the stable, and pigs grunted in their enclosure. The farmer's wife, the small, wrinkled mother of the boys, bustled about the muddy yard.

They made beds up for us in the room next to the kitchen. They insisted we lie under their clean, white quilts, even though I showed them our sleeping bags. They heated water in a cauldron on the stove so we could wash. Before that, we had supper, and afterward, the farmer brought out the moonshine. We communicated using eyes and gestures. It seemed that we shouldn't expect to be going anywhere soon, because the weather would be bad.

Benjamin was silent the whole time. He only started to chatter when we were under the quilts. "How do they do any shopping here?" "What do they do if someone is ill?" "Where do the boys go to school?" "What do cows eat in winter?"

I couldn't always answer the questions. "I don't know where they go to school. Maybe there's a village a little further down. Or maybe they don't go to school—how would I know?"

The bed was hard, the quilt heavy, and the air in the room chilly. They had a dry toilet in a shed under the cottage. There was a chamber pot under the bed.

The next day it rained, and the mountains remained hidden in cloud. Again, they gave us milk, eggs, and all the best their farm could provide. I gave them some money; at first, they refused it, but when the farmer saw my determined expression, he accepted. I was relieved that we were not going to be a burden.

Benjamin was keenly interested in the work around the animals. The boys took him with them, and I heard no more from them for a while. The farmer chopped kindling by the barn. I went and tried to help, at least handing him the wet logs. The air was cold and wet.

In the next few days, the weather failed to improve. The boys pastured the cows in gumboots and raincoats, and I dragged logs with the farmer. The biggest problem for me was hygiene. Hot water for washing wasn't available every day—it couldn't have been.

Instead of toilet paper (ours soon ran out) they had old newspapers in the bathroom, and I was always stepping in droppings in the yard. I also sensed that the farmer's wife was uncomfortable around me and didn't like being alone in the cottage with me. Otherwise, they seemed like people who never had an evil thought. Everyday toil in harsh conditions isn't conducive to underhanded intentions.

It took about five days for the weather to start to improve. For all that time, they housed and fed us and were very patient with us, considering that we were definitely more in their way than any kind of help. I was reassured only by the thought that I had probably paid them well.

Benjamin was quick to get used to a new life; he got up to milk the cows, carried water, and gave swill to the pigs. A tacit understanding formed between me and the farmer. I noticed that neither he nor his wife ever physically punished the children, but they didn't pamper them either, and only gave them dour, brisk instructions. There was something very serious about those boys. The burden of survival through heavy labor was already written into their faces, and in this sense, they were prematurely adult, but in language and expression they were behind.

Benjamin became so absorbed in his surroundings that not once did he ask me when we would be leaving or how we would get back to the car, but I was always asking myself such questions. I enjoyed my walks across the wet, cropped grass to the end of the forest, where the damp moss grew on rotting wood, or up the slope where streams gurgled and were led through an ingenious system of channels, but I was constantly worrying about my next move. The car was on the other side of the mountains, autumn was threatening to turn into winter, and I was afraid to take Benjamin back to the mountain.

I think it was on the sixth evening that I went to the farmer and drew him a plan on a piece of paper. I showed him my car, the mountains, and his building, but it took a long time for him to understand what I wanted. In the end, slowly and awkwardly, in a stiff hand, he wrote down the names of several villages and towns, one of which was called Caransebes. I tried to convey the suggestion that I should go myself and leave Benjamin with them—and would that be acceptable? The farmer again failed to understand, and so I drew a little Ben figure on the plan, by their farm, and my own figure, crossing the mountains and then coming back around by the highway in the car. Then he got it: "*Da, Da, Da,*" he nodded in agreement.

In the evening, I sat down beside Ben, as he lay curled up under the quilts. The only lighting in the room was a candle, which kept throwing erratic shadows on the walls. "Our car is right the other side of the mountains," I said.

"Mmm," he mumbled, as if he didn't want to hear about it.

"To get to the car, we would have to go back by the same route, because it would be a terribly long way around by road." He said nothing, so I went on: "I don't want to take you up there again—you know how dangerous it was. I'd rather you waited here, and I went and got the car by myself."

"Okay Dad," he agreed without the slightest objection, although there was a lump in my throat at the prospect of leaving my beloved Benjamin behind. "Are you sure you won't be scared here? And you won't be angry with me later, that I left you here?"

"No, Dad, I like it here. Hey, d'you think we could have pigs and cows in Prague?"

"No way. You know that very well yourself. What would people say if we kept a cow in the stroller room by the hallway?"

He burst out laughing with that blissful, childish laugh you never can forget.

"When I'm gone and you're waiting," I continued after a moment, "remember I could be delayed. I don't know how long it's going to take. I'll drive to the nearest village, and then we'll go home."

"Okay, Dad." He rolled on his side and curled up even deeper inside the quilt: he was going to sleep. "I'll wait here for you."

That was the conversation we had the night before I left. I felt bad afterwards and couldn't sleep.

217

The next day, the whole mountain face was visible. I packed up and explained my plan to the farmer one more time. Then I pressed more money on him. I had to set off as early as possible, to be able to get a good part of the way before it got dark. Anxiety and sadness descended on me; after all, I had been with Benjamin continuously for several months. When I wanted to give him a goodbye hug, he was nowhere to be found. He turned out to be already pasturing the cows down by the forest. I went to find him.

"Benjamin…"

"Dad," he said, and pressed against me. But he was calm.

"I'll get across the mountains quickly," I assured him, although he hadn't asked for assurance. "I'll be back in a couple of days. You're a clever boy. I love you a lot."

Chapter VI

The Hell of Loss and the Purgatory before Entering the Paradise of the Heart

Dad Crosses the Mountains Alone on the Verge of Winter

I walked uphill with a bounce in my step and a certain lightness. After five months in which I had been tied at almost every moment to Benjamin, who was, after all, only a child with a child's capacities, I felt a sense of release and freedom. Before my wife died, I had done a lot of sports. The physical effort involved in sports had been a partial substitute for my unsatisfying sex life, giving me a chance to take some pleasure in my physical self. Now, it was as if I were returning to that self.

I passed the wooden water sluice gates above the farm and crossed the stream above them. The path continued up between little groups of spruce. That day, the sky above the mountains was grey-blue, with pale clouds massed on the horizon. The air was cold and sharp. The broader path soon turned back downward, and I tried to figure out the way I had come with Ben. I set off on a narrow track, now full of mud after the many days of rain. Under the summit, I found myself walking on fresh snow. It seemed to have thawed during the day but was now frozen. Before noon, I stood on the snowy, rounded mountaintop. The undisturbed coat of snow heightened the quiet and my solitude. The grey slopes of the range opposite were also covered in white at the top, lending them dignity. Below me, the farm where I had left Benjamin was no longer visible. For the first time, I was assailed by doubts. What if the farmer hadn't really understood what I meant? I had left Benjamin with people who have a different language and way of thinking. How would he communicate with them?

To my right, on the highest point of the ridge, rose the mysterious tower that had brought us here. Even from a distance, it seemed likely that its whiteness was the result of frost in the spars between slabs. According to the farmer, it was a meteorological station. It was baffling to me why anyone had considered it worthwhile to build such a thing in these uninhabited mountains.

I set off across the snowy plateau. My steps on the virgin snow were hesitant and uncertain, although it was only a ten- or at most twenty-centimeter layer. I wasn't used to walking on untrodden snow, and my initial euphoria quickly gave way to anxiety, but by dusk, I had managed to cross the connecting ridge. On the way, I remembered how we had struggled with the rain here, and I couldn't believe that we had managed to get so far, my brave Ben and I. The memory made me ever more conscious that nothing must happen to me. His fate was bound to mine.

I put up the tent in the saddle between the two ranges, in a spot where the snow had not settled and the grass remained quite dry. Twilight came on fast in the mountains, although it was only five. I could think of nothing but Ben. Maybe he was having second thoughts about staying behind and wanted to be with me. I was angry that the dusk was falling, and I couldn't continue on my journey. It was strange—I had set up the tent in one of the most ravishing places I had ever seen, surrounded by a garland of mountains, but I was shaken by doubts. Around seven, the cold drove me inside the tent. I used my headlamp for light, and the walls of the tent seemed to imprison me with my thoughts. Who was I really? A model, loving father, or a crazy gambler, wanted by the police for abduction, who had dreamed up a journey to the Back of Beyond, because he had nothing to give his son? I tried to conjure up my future life. In two months, it would be Christmas. But if there was one thing I couldn't imagine, it was celebrating it in our current Prague apartment. The atmosphere of last Christmas, when we were still together, crept back into my mind. I had been nervous, internally dissatisfied, full of tension. She had been sad, but clinging to the annual ritual of togetherness. Benjamin had insisted on being happy.

Later, the wind rose outside, whipping at the walls of the tent. Although I knew what it was, I held my breath. What if a bear came this way? It was the lowest place on the ridge, and a bear path could easily run past it. As if to spite myself, I started to want to urinate, and it was obvious that I wouldn't be able to sleep until I got out. But all at once the prospect scared me. When Benjamin had been with me, I had been forced to be courageous—I couldn't afford to show even a hint of fear. Now I seemed to be falling to pieces. I curled up in my sleeping bag, half sitting, and every second took forever. The call of nature grew ever more urgent. Now I really had to go. I turned off the headlamp but still delayed for a moment. In the end, of course, I unzipped the tent and ran outside. "My God!" I whispered and quickly pissed into the darkness. "My God." As soon as I finished, I dived back into the tent, as if it would really have protected me from a bear. My heart was thumping, and I was breathing fast.

I don't remember whether I got any sleep at all that night. My thoughts kept flying away into the past. I remembered how sweet Benjamin was when he was learning to walk and when he was saying his first words, and how he used to run to me with outstretched arms and a blissful expression on his face. I remembered my own childhood. My classmates from first grade came back to me, and the dreams that I dreamed at that age. Some of those dreams had been hair-raising, leaving dark traces in my childish mind.

In the end, the darkness thinned, and a white patch appeared in the east. I didn't have the patience to make tea, so I just drank water from the bottle and ate a couple of mouthfuls of cheese and a few biscuits. I packed up the tent and hurried on in the faint light before daybreak.

That day, tiredness started to get to me. In the afternoon, the snow softened, and my feet sank into it. I went too far downhill several times and had to toil back up the steep slope. Originally, I had hoped to get right back to the car that day, but at dusk, I was still high up, almost at the highest place on the journey. I had been drinking only water all day and eating little. Moisture had gotten into my boots as well, and they were starting to rub. Of course, the thought that I was already on the way home kept these privations in proportion. I planned to pick Benjamin up and leave immediately—

even during the night. On the other hand, I remembered that we were still on a wanted list and might not make it out of Romania into Hungary. There were still too many uncertainties waiting for me and too many tasks that all had to be successfully negotiated…Get down to the car. Pick it up. Find the right road around the mountains. Get to the farm and, above all, to Benjamin inside it. Get safely across the rest of Romania and make it past another three passport checks…

This time, the night was full of stars and, after midnight, the silver radiance of the moon. Then towards morning it became overcast, and on the threshold of day, the snow began to fall. It was a fine, powdery snow, its dry flakes sliding slowly down the rounded sides of the tent. In the morning, I brushed the snow off the canvas, chucked all my things into the backpack just as they were, and hurried on. There was something sacred about snowfall on these deserted mountains. I continued on along the ridge for only a little longer, and then I was finally descending towards the beech woods. Soon I was below the snowline, but the mud under my feet was frozen and flakes like tiny feathers were catching in the tracks of sheep hooves. In just these few days, the leaves on the trees had thinned and lost their color—this was already a winter forest waiting for its first delivery of snow. Once I was down among the trees, my mood lightened—my goal was close. It was just that I was afraid of bears.

I passed the chalet hut where I had slept with Benjamin, and a burning love flooded my heart. My feet were sore from blisters, but I quickened my step and almost ran down the slope. The road from the settlement that the truck had taken us along seemed unending, and this time I was out of luck—there were no truckers on it today. I reached the village in the late afternoon. The only thing that was keeping me on my feet was the vision of a comfortable car, which would take me wherever I wanted to go.

It was standing in the wood shelter just as I had left it. At that moment, I felt triumphant. In my imagination, I was already getting out of it to greet Benjamin. I would never have dreamed that soon I would be further from him than I had ever been in his short life.

That feeling of triumph can be so deceptive and misleading.

It took them a long time to find the boss. In the meantime, I stood around in the unwelcoming yard. So far down below the mountains, there was no ice, and inside the farm everything was hatefully wet. As soon as he saw me, the boss starting furiously gesticulating: where was my son? I tried to explain, and he seemed to understand. He even invited me to stay the night, but I wanted to get away fast. He had his people open the gate. I got into the car, and it felt unreal to be holding the gear lever again. I put the car into reverse.

With that reversal onto the bumpy and muddy highway, my memories end for good, and that includes memories that have reemerged more recently. My impatient wait in the yard, where, at first, I didn't even take off my backpack, and then my meeting with the boss and starting the car…these are the last events for some time that I can recall with any certainty. I have managed to discover quite a lot, but none of what I have objectively discovered has ever connected with anything that I've been able to find in my own head. This means that I have simply had to reconstruct part of my story, by trying to imagine my feelings and guess my motives, as if I were someone else.

I can well imagine what I was experiencing and what I was thinking as I drove down the bumpy road back to Herculane Spa. It was getting dark, and the farms, herds in the pastures, and woodcutters transporting masses of wood for sale were disappearing into the gloom. Most probably, I stopped for a moment outside the settlement to change my clothes and shoes, and most likely, the warm air from the ventilators made me pleasantly sleepy. Probably, I felt more in harmony with the surrounding landscape than when I had first driven here with Ben. Now I had it under my skin—its scent, its cold, its colors and shapes. But as soon as I drove onto the asphalt highway, my conversation with it ended. I switched my headlights to high beam, fiercely asserting my separation. I put the car into fourth and pressed my foot down hard.

At the Herkulana Spa, I must have stopped for food and drink, but I assume it was just a snack that I bought somewhere at a gas station, before driving on immediately, this time on better roads. Nothing could induce me to stop and rest, even though there was no chance of me seeing Benjamin that same day. It was frankly unlikely that I would be able identify the route from the last village to the mountain farm, and maybe I wouldn't even find the last village. Clearly, I gave in to the uncontrollable urge to go on that takes hold beyond the edge of exhaustion, and that I know so well. In this kind of state, you pass up one opportunity to stop after another, and no moment is the right moment to call it a day. I drove through the little town of Caransebes, where the scanty lighting gave me no sense of safety. I kept on following the names of the villages that the farmer had written down for me in his stiff handwriting. The roads there were narrow and badly paved, and it was too late to find a bed for the night. I drove on without any idea of what, in the end, I was doing. Now only thirty or forty kilometers separated me from Benjamin, and all my thoughts were with him. It was one o'clock in the morning, and the roads I was travelling on were surely empty even in the daytime. Mine were surely the only headlights piercing the darkness far and wide, and mine were surely the only hands turning the wheel of a car. But these are mere guesses. Only the final instant is fixed in my memory like the lash of a whip. There is a small light in the darkness, there is an impact, a somersault, perhaps a desperate thought of Ben… The darkness that followed the blow to my head will stay with me to the end of my life, when I sink into it again. It is a darkness unlike emptiness, because somewhere inside it is an awareness of human existence. It is a darkness saturated with life, but absolutely black.

He Awakes into the Hell of Loss

There was darkness. And a small lamp glimmering in the darkness. Its light flickered like a flame in a draft. I seemed to be thinking in some way, asking where the breath of wind came from, where the draft came from?

Every so often it repeated. The light of the lantern flickering in my head, or suddenly emerging from the distance and doubling up near the place where my consciousness was located. In fact, it repeated pretty often, perhaps all the time. Since then, I have often wondered whether this is what death feels like, but usually I have concluded that it might be more like what precedes death. After all, time itself didn't stop. One moment could have merged into week, a month, or a year, but not into eternity. And what's more, the lamp—its persistent light flickered, it moved further away and then nearer again, and that movement had to be taking place in time. I believe that for human beings, death is a liberation from the captivity of time. Eternity is not something a human being could ever possess—it must belong to the emptiness of God. Otherwise, it would turn into an endless hell, the soul paralyzed in immobility but still perceiving second after second for unending ages—that is my idea of hell. But when I return to the little lantern in my thoughts, to that haunting will-o'-the-wisp that flickered in the darkness, then I can imagine it might just be part of God's plan to imprison someone bad with his bad deed, which would keep circling for a long time around his immortal mind, on the threshold of non-existence.

It was dark, and the little lamp glimmered and flickered, and it all lasted a long time. I wasn't in pain; I didn't have any real thoughts or self-consciousness. When I opened my eyes, I was dazzled by the light of an electric bulb. Above me (as far as I was able to separate myself from and recognize what I was in that moment), there was a cracked ceiling. I looked at it for a while, and then I fell asleep

again, maybe for an hour, maybe for a day or two. Then, I opened
my eyes again and looked at that ceiling. In fact, it was very pleasant,
having nothing in my head and just looking. All my thoughts and
experiences, everything that formed the gravity of memory, was lost
to me. I lay there with the ease of an infant, who is already himself,
although he knows nothing at all.

Later, I noticed movement. Sometimes somebody appeared,
placed something on me, or took something away. I had no opinion
on the matter. The figure in a white coat leaned over me and looked
me in the eyes.

Later still, there were sounds. First a hubbub and hum, and
only subsequently speech, individual voices. I would rather not have
heard them—I enjoyed just staying on hold, without any kind of
responsibility for my fate. But I was already beginning to sense that
I had been someone and that I must have arrived here somehow.
Anxiety was knocking at the door. *Who am I?* I asked myself. *And,
where am I?*

As I was regaining consciousness, pain made an appearance too.
First dull and distant, then intense and even cruel, located somewhere
on the inner side of my skull under the right temple. It made the
slightest movement of the head unbearable, if I had happened to
want to move. But for the time being, I did not.

But I did at least move my eyes from side to side. When I did, I
found my world was no longer just a cracked yellowing ceiling with
dried circular stains from old water leaks. It was also a cart by my
bed, a neighboring bed with someone else (whose presence I could
only sense on my right), and it was an IV stand with an infusion, that
was slowly, regularly flowing into my veins.

It was the sight of that stand, the tubing with the transparent
liquid that would soon become part of my blood, that made me the
most anxious and prompted self-pity. I felt as lost as only a human
being can be. Beyond everything, lost even to myself, to my life, to
my past. Lost in the passing moment, but awake enough to know
that the passing moment wasn't everything there was, and that I

was not really meant to be lying here on this bed, and that on the contrary, to be here was a dreadful mistake.

Luckily, I was soon falling back into the embrace of sleep that wrapped me in a kind darkness where a flickering little lantern kept coming towards me. In that darkness, I lost any conception of the borders between myself and my surroundings.

After a time, the pain started to recede, as if it were returning to the state in which it had been at the beginning—dull and diffuse. Eventually, I got up the nerve to move my head. I remember that moment as one of the most painful in my life, and not only because of the stab of agony in my temple. I bent my head towards my chest and saw my body covered in a sheet—a miserable body that once had capabilities other than just lying here like this. That body belonged to me, yes, me. Only I didn't know who I was.

I started to weep, and someone noticed and came up to me. It was a dark-haired woman, tall and kind. She said something in an incomprehensible language, but I thought it was a language I ought to have known, and my inability to understand just deepened my despair. The woman called out something, another man and another woman came up, and they were all talking to me at once. I saw them in a blur through tears that had nowhere to run from my eye sockets. Someone wiped them away, and for a moment, I could see clearly. They were smiling, they were happy, and I felt like a child in the family circle. Yes, at that moment—and I knew of nothing but the passing moment—they became my family. They cared about how I was.

The following days seemed to confirm my role of child in a newly acquired family. I was completely dependent on them in all my functions: they washed my ass and genitals, they pulled my covers off without shame, and attached instruments to my body or changed the sheets under me. They continued to be very kind and considerate, especially the tall woman, who came most often. I had no shame either. On the contrary, I experienced my helplessness as a certain kind of sensual pleasure.

We rejoiced together at my progress: when I first raised my hand; when I grasped an object they gave me; when I first sat up. I began to register the events around me and to understand their tasks and the pattern of their visits. The tall woman would appear together with the man in the white coat, who had the smooth, yellowish cheeks, which were the first things I had seen when they wiped away my tears. They often visited me—especially the woman—even when they had work at neighboring beds, where two other people lay surrounded by even more machines, and I had no doubt that something much worse had happened to them than to me.

Yet, there were long periods when I didn't see either of them. There would be other people moving round the room, mainly women. These women also knew how to look after me, but they were not my immediate family. As I saw it, I had been entrusted to them for just a short time—like when someone comes to babysit a child.

After a time, they disconnected me from the drips and started bringing me liquid food. I sensed they were going to want something like independence from me, when in fact it suited me to be a child, for whom other people have to do everything essential.

Now the doctor started to come in the company of a small man with a pleasant smile. I thought of him as a decent, good-humored fellow. Later he would come to see me alone. Whenever he showed up, he would put his hand on my shoulder and say something in greeting. Then he would speak in soothing gentle tones, sometimes standing, sometimes sitting down beside me, but always turned towards me so I could see his face. Slowly and deliberately, he would utter words whose meanings I did not know. One day, he brought a box of wooden cubes, pyramids and balls, and I grasped what he wanted me to do. I picked the pieces out of the box and put the ones with the same shapes together. The man showered me with praise, and I was very excited by my success too, because I sensed the trace of a memory in it, and knew I had mastered something I must have learned in a different time than the now in which I was imprisoned. My ability to tell one object from another—which this smiling fellow valued so highly—was like a ray of light from the past, or a distant voice. It promised an imminent meeting with my own destiny, a meeting that I also feared.

Looking back on it many years later, I must admit that in the course of my stay in that intensive care ward, I didn't really try that hard, and if it hadn't been for the joy of my then-family at every sign of progress, even the slightest, I would have made no effort at all. My initial anxiety and feeling of being lost had receded and been replaced by a state of dependence, in which I felt as unencumbered as a child in early infancy. I guess I was given the chance to re-experience in adulthood what happens during the first months and years of life, that for some unknown but evidently good reason does not remain in our conscious memories. If I hadn't experienced such a state and retained living memories of it, I would probably assume that we forget, because these early memories are incompatible with how we see ourselves as adults, upsetting to our sense of dignity and self-respect. Yet, with my personal experience, I don't see it that way. I believe that, thanks to my memories of dependency and helplessness, I find it easier to overcome the barriers that separate me from other people. When I look into a baby stroller in the street, and a carefree little human smiles at me from under the covers, I can immediately imagine what that little human is experiencing, because I can imagine myself lying there in his place. In a way, I feel sorry for the little human, because I think how many hard and actually pointless tasks are waiting for him in the future.

One day, they brought a bed on wheels. My whole family was there—the doctor, the tall woman, and other women I knew well. By that time, I was able to sit up without assistance, and then they helped me roll over onto the rolling bed and pushed me out the door. First, we went down an empty corridor, but when we got past other glass doors, there was a bustle of activity. Half-naked people in bathrobes were walking around, uniformed nurses in white and blue were moving between them, and there were also people in overcoats, pants, suits, and shawls. I was rolled into an elevator, and we finished up in a quieter area. They took me up to the door of a small room with four beds. People were lying down on two of them, a gaunt brown man was sitting on the third, and the fourth, newly made, was ready for me. The room was crammed so full of beds that I had to stand up, and they helped me to walk over to mine. Those were my first steps—the first my memory reaches back to. They supported me from both sides, otherwise my weakened legs wouldn't have carried me at all. Fleetingly and unintentionally, I glanced out the nearby window before rolling down onto the bed. No clear image stuck in my mind, but only a sort of baffling tangle of buildings.

They showed me something, trying to explain, but I didn't understand them. In the end they left, one after another, the tall woman last of all—I think she wished me luck. She closed the door behind her, and I was left without a family—among strangers—in a room stinking of sweat, urine, and disinfectant. Although there was a draft coming from the barred windows, the room was overheated, and the air was dry.

The first minutes and hours in my new environment were as disturbing as my first moments after waking up. Again, I was overwhelmed by anxiety, a sense of being lost. An old man, unknown to me, wheezed next to me on his bed, while from the door, the brown man eyed me curiously and mumbled something. When he started moving towards me, I thought he was going to kill me. Instead, he stopped to stare out of the window, under which I was lying. I could see his sinewy crooked legs and right up to his bony ass, his black genitals swinging above the radiator. I realized he wasn't going to kill me, because he had his own worries and his own pain. He didn't care about me.

I must have slept for a time, because in the meantime darkness had fallen outside. I wanted to go to the bathroom, but I knew nothing of bathrooms; I didn't have a single memory relating to bathrooms. All the same, I somehow had an inkling of their existence. The contents of my head hadn't been wholly erased. Some habits and experiences remained in it.

But I had no idea where to look for a bathroom or any strength to walk to one. A chamber pot stood next to the bed for this eventuality. I realized what it was for and stretched out a hand to it, until I was crippled by pulsating pain as the blood rushed to my head. It took me several minutes of desperate effort before I managed to grasp the pot, and then a few more before I could lever it under me and at least partly sit on it. Finally, I did my business in front of the whole room. It didn't feel as right and natural here as in my old room. These men were not family. It was unpleasant to have to relieve myself in their presence, to be helpless in their eyes. When I think about it today, I am almost sure that the drastic move saved me, forcing me to get beyond the infantile ease that might easily have led to permanent degeneration and forgetting. Once my state had become unsatisfying to me, I was going to have to mobilize all my physical and mental resources.

The challenge to mobilize came right away, that evening. The door to the room sprang open, but nobody came in. Instead, the old man got out of the bed next to mine and hobbled out into the corridor. Meanwhile, a young man with a dreadfully bulging eye and bandaged head sat up in his bed. Everyone went out into the corridor—even the gaunt brown one. I decided I would go too—I had to, but once again it took me a few minutes even to sit up, and in the meantime, they brought me supper in the room. My gorge rose at the boiled meat and sauce and gummy rice, but I decided I was going to eat it.

While I ate, I sat with my face towards the window, but I could see only darkness beyond the parapet. Street lighting glimmered from below. I finished the food and pushed back the rolling table on which they had brought the meal. I supported myself on my hands and then stood up; it was only one step to the window. Shifting my balance, I leaned my whole weight against the glass. I was looking down from a great height onto a busy street in an unknown city. The street led almost right up to the building in which I found myself, and it ended nearby in a busy crossroad. Cars, trucks, and trolley-buses flashed past on that main street, while a tram moved along the street that intersected it at the crossroads. My God, a tram. I had seen one somewhere before. It felt as if only the smallest of steps would take me there. I reached out for the memory, but I just couldn't get a grip on it. It was the same feeling as when you forget someone's name, it gets lost somewhere inside, and you can't retrieve it no matter how hard you try, although you know you knew it yesterday; although you know for certain that you remembered it only yesterday.

There was certainly much more to see outside than just that main street with its busy traffic, but it was that street that attracted me. It was so alive, so real. I had no doubt it was the setting for real life, the kind that I had once lived but was now separated from by an abyss of many stories, an abyss of missing memory and cold glass. Soon I rolled back down on the bed, but even there, I couldn't leave that unanswered question alone—where and when had a tram been a natural part of my life? The more effort I put into wondering, the clearer it became that I was somewhere other than where I was supposed to be, where I belonged, and that I was lost and alone.

The first hint of an answer came in the night. I woke into darkness, and the window pane above the bed drew me with its magic power. The darkness was monotonous and dank, the clouds probably low over the city. I extricated myself from the bed and leaned on the window, as I had in the evening. The traffic had died away, the street was almost empty. After a while, a night tram crossed from left to right. I could even hear the metallic scraping of the wheels on a curve. I dropped back down on the bed and sank into semi-consciousness. An image swam up in my mind, not just an image but a whole long-ago feeling, a whole atmosphere, my whole childish consciousness. I am standing on the corner of an apartment block, I'm a small boy, I'm watching ants by the wall and waiting for my Dad to come back from work. He'll be coming on the Number Three Tram. Yes, it's the Three. I'm waiting with Mom. We live in…. in Libeň. It's Prague Eight, Prague…

But in the morning, my head was blank again. I knew that

something important had happened, but I couldn't recall what. I started watching the street again, full of cars, trucks, buses…And trams, bringing with them a past that just kept on slipping out of my grasp.

For several days, I put everything into thinking. My inability to remember oppressed me with such urgency that it kept me from anything but broken sleep. I returned again and again to that one thing: tram, tram. I stared out of the window every moment I could. I had the feeling that I needed to see every single tram that passed by or the memories would elude me forever. In the meantime, I was recovering fast. I was given slippers, a towel, and a dressing gown, and I started to venture out into the unfriendly corridor, as far as the austere cafeteria, where there were only the plainest of battered tables and chairs, no more. It was the meeting place for a whole community of bathrobes, men and women who seemed as lost as I was, and very miserable.

I was now able to reach the bathroom and able to appreciate that I was on one of the highest floors of a tall building built so badly that, in many places, it was falling apart.

The next afternoon, the small smiling man, who had visited me before, came to see me. He smiled again, greeted me loudly, and seemed to be congratulating me for being able to walk again. He pointed at himself and repeated something that I had once failed to understand but grasped on later visits: it was his name—George. Then he pointed at me. He wanted to hear my name. I think I somehow indicated I didn't know. George then went out into the corridor and brought in two men in uniform. He said something to them, and they took a photograph of me and looked thoughtful. I couldn't work out why they only photographed me and paid no attention to the other men in the room.

Later, I often wondered why I didn't even try to speak in those first days and perhaps weeks. For reasons unknown, it simply didn't occur to me. Maybe I regarded this ability as simply lost to me. I didn't understand what they were saying but had no basis on which to judge that what they were speaking was a foreign language. Which meant it was logically pointless and useless for me to say something. In any case, in the state I was in back then, I was completely incapable of figuring out that, despite everything, my own thinking was happening in words, and then comparing these words with their speech and identifying the difference. Actually, I wasn't really thinking in words all that much. My perception of the world was immediate.

I formed no connections with the other men in the room. We were surviving alongside each other, each submerged in his own suffering. The thin brown man was physically in the best state; he used to go and play cards in the corridor. Like me, he spent long periods at the window, leaning on the parapet and gazing down on the bustle outside. But it was impossible to tell whether all that activity attracted him, or he was more content here. I sensed that his life so far had not been happy.

The boy with the swollen eye used to look out the window too. He would nervously come up to it and then walk away again. He couldn't stand still.

The old man, my neighbor, mostly just lay on his bed. During the night, he tossed and turned and mumbled in his sleep.

I would gaze out the window whenever I could find the strength for it. Now, I registered more than just the busy main street and started to see the whole picture: a monotonous town built on a plain, without visible dominating features, hills, or towers. There was just one church tower in the distance that was higher than the surrounding houses and a pylon with a floodlight that lit some building or station. But for the moment, I knew nothing about stations; I continued to dwell on my trams.

From the cafeteria, where I went three times a day, there was a view of the other side. There, the town ended in pastures and fields. The pastures were interspersed with factory halls and groups of grey houses; the countryside seemed to mix with the town. In the distance, a herd of horses were grazing. It was a much more peaceful panorama than the one from my room. It challenged me to nothing and reminded me of nothing; it was the view of forgetfulness.

On what I think was the third afternoon, the corridor suddenly came alive with the clatter of footsteps and a bunch of people burst into the room. They brought with them the chill of the outdoors but also the stench of peasant food and musty clothes. A grandmother in black skirt and stockings, a thick-set son in a peak-cap and blue waistcoat, and a whole large family, maybe ten people, had come to visit the old man. They embraced him and unpacked all they had brought on the bed: homemade sausages, bacon, onions, apples, bread...Family had come to see the boy as well—most probably his parents and a brother, but they wore city clothes. Nobody had come to see the brown man. He moved the one extra chair, on which he spent most of his time, up to the window and gazed out of it, not down into the street but into the distance or up into the white clouds. I had a feeling we were in the same boat, but it wasn't a feeling I wanted to have. I didn't want to belong with him or for my life to be like his life. Surely that couldn't be my destiny; surely it ought not to be. Even physically, the man repelled me...his bony legs, his tan and natural brown indistinguishable from engrained dirt, his stink of hostels and workers' canteens. Perhaps it was his destiny to live out his life here, deserted by everyone, remote from everything. But I wanted more.

After a while, the country people noticed me and offered me some of the food they had brought. They meant it sincerely, and it didn't for a moment occur to me to refuse. With great gusto, I ate an apple and a piece of bread. They also gave food to the brown man, and he wolfed it down in his corner. They turned to me and spoke to me, the words tumbling out. They were so warm that, in the end, I started to smile, I think. And I was sorry that I didn't know how to say anything to them.

That day, I wouldn't remain alone. When all the visitors had left and the room had returned to its usual quiet, the tall, dark-haired woman appeared in the door, the one who had looked after me in the intensive care unit. She nodded at me in a friendly way, sat down by my bed, and started to shave me. I felt a pleasurable tingling at the end of my penis.

She shaved me and kept on smiling. She put away the basin and took a toothbrush, toothpaste, and soap out of her pocket. Gently, she took me by the hand, and I got up. She led me down the corridor to the nearby bathroom. There, I brushed my teeth in front of her, and the whole time I felt that strange pleasure; it seemed to be bringing me closer to the past, just like the tram. Then the woman helped me undress and washed me in the dark, unappetizing shower with its ancient mat on the floor. She was wearing a blue coat. It was loose around her high butt. Although I still had no conscious memories, and nothing to teach me, I would certainly have worked out where to thrust my penis, if it had been erect. But it was not.

The next day, the woman visited me again. This time she led me to the elevator. She pushed a button, and the display started to flash. I knew what was happening: we were going down.

Downstairs, we found ourselves in a large, busy corridor. I sensed the proximity of the street, the closeness of the wide world, which until now had been far below me. I didn't understand where she was taking me, but I trusted her like a mother, who wouldn't ever take me anywhere that would be bad for me. We walked down the corridor, until we reached a glass door leading to a patch of grass. A cold wind blew through a crack. Through a rift in the clouds, the sun shone on the building opposite, but the grass was in shadow.

A car passed nearby. And another. Stray dogs lay on the concrete around the grass, and I was deeply affected by a sense of the reality of what I was seeing. But then my head suddenly started to ache viciously, and I had to lean on the glass of the door. The woman—in that moment, my Mom—became alarmed and quickly led me back. My legs could scarcely carry me, and she had to support me. In the room, I collapsed back onto the bed, exhausted but happy. If I had managed to get right down to the ground, then perhaps I would also eventually work out who I was and what had brought me here.

In the afternoon, George came and tried some new tests, but I had lost interest in showing him what I could do. What I had experienced downstairs was spinning in my head. My world was spreading out into the distance and demanding to be explored. When George left, darkness was beginning to fall outside, but this time, the sunset colored the sky. First it was inky blue, then, at the horizon, paler and with a hint of pink. Then it dimmed fast, blue turning to black and pink to violet. The streetlights came on. A tram arrived at a stop.

That was when it happened. The recent dream came back into my head. I am a small boy, watching ants, waiting for Dad. He is coming home on the Number Three Tram. I live in Libeň. That's Prague, Prague...In a single instant I remembered my whole childhood. The house where we had lived, my friends from the sandpit and classmates from first grade, Mom, Dad, their trivial warnings that stuck in my child's brain in the form of law..."Don't knock on glass." "Don't accept sweets from anyone." "Steer clear of Kadeřábek." And my name was is back too. I am little *Davidek*; I am David.

Before I fell asleep, more and more memories emerged. One seemed to ignite the next, as one died away another turned up, a third, a fiftieth, as when sometimes a whole chain of dreams rises into consciousness. All were early memories—from when we still lived in Prague's Libeň district (later we had moved to another Prague district), and I was in the first years of school. But for the moment, there was no kind of continuity. Between me on the bed in the crowded stale room, and me the child of my memories, lay the white darkness of oblivion. At first, I was completely absorbed in what was coming up of its own accord and did not try to get through that darkness.

I couldn't get through the darkness the next day either, when I had calmed down and was trying to channel the memories by consciously working on them. I just couldn't unify my own self into a single logical whole, whose past precedes his present. The fact that I knew my name, parents, part of my childhood, ultimately seemed to be no help at all. I wasn't able to discover who I had grown into and what my life had been built on in adulthood. I even wondered whether I might not have fallen back into a coma then and not woken up until many years later here—in another world, among changed people. But it didn't feel credible.

After a day full of hope, I fell into a depression. It seemed to me that I would never discover anything more. I would stay here forever, beside the brown man with the skinny calves. I would share his fate and, in the end, I would have no choice but to make friends with him. After all, the old man had his family; his people loved him and always thought about him. And the boy? I knew he was here only for a short while. The swelling was going down, and they had taken off the bandage.

In the afternoon, George came, but I wanted to sleep. He tried to make me do simple arithmetic but got nowhere. For the first time, the smile disappeared from his smoothly shaped face. He shrugged and said something important-sounding to me. Then he left, and I spent the rest of the day in bed. I didn't want to think about anything. I wanted to forget even the little that remained in my head and never to try to remember at all. The only person I wanted to see was that tall woman—Mom. But she didn't come that day. There was nothing to do but sleep.

In the morning, snowflakes were flying outside. It was the snowflakes that woke me out of apathy. They were floating down onto the town from grey clouds and had the same urgent message for me as the tram. I pressed my forehead to the cold glass and watched their journey down into the street, where they melted. I tried as hard as I could to decipher their message. It related to me so deeply that I would have liked to open the window and let them fall on my head. But the window was barred and could not be opened.

Before noon, the snow stopped, and I still hadn't managed even to touch what had seemed within reach. All the same, a few more memories had emerged: my first, unfulfilled love—a girl from the parallel class of my secondary school, with whom, on our last date,

I had walked through old Prague in the silent snow. That set off memories of the school—my teachers and classmates. This was not early childhood—here I had been starting to look for my real identity.

After lunch, the tall woman arrived. I had been longing to see her. She brought me warm socks and a shabby overcoat. She helped me put the coat on over my dressing gown and led me to the elevator. I readily followed her.

In the elevator, the woman pointed to herself and said, "Maria." I pointed at myself and wanted to say...I wanted to tell her, but the word, my name, remained stuck in my mouth. All the same, I realized how far I had come. I already knew my name; I almost knew who I was. What's more, Maria was so moved by my effort that she seemed almost to have forgotten to breathe. Once again, she pointed at herself, and she repeated her name. Then she pointed at me and lovingly took my hand in hers.

Once again, we found ourselves in the corridor on the ground floor. Today, the floor was muddy and wet. I had only slippers on my feet, but Maria led me in the opposite direction from the last time. We went around a porter's desk, and the next moment, I was face to face with the hustle and bustle of the town. There was a parking lot, and beyond it the street that I had seen from above. People were streaming in and out and were avoiding a kind of ditch with dark mud oozing around it on the way. "*Timisoara*," said Maria, and because she gestured broadly in front of her, I realized it was the name of the town. This was not Prague, then, where I had been born, but somewhere strange and unknown. In that moment, I also fully grasped that the building where I was staying was a hospital. Up to then, I had definitely had an inkling of something like that but had not consciously thought about it. From now on, I nailed down that thought: I knew I was in a hospital and something had happened to me. This state of ignorance and forgetting was not my natural state, but the consequence of some event. Without thinking, I glanced up at the grey hospital wall with its rows of identical windows. Maria noticed it, took me by the arm, and took several steps away from the building with me. We turned around and looked up. She tried to show me the window of my room. I was moved and grateful. It was only thanks to Maria that I had managed to get down here, to the world below. After a moment, I started shivering with the cold, and Maria took me back. Now I was sure I wouldn't be staying here. In the end, I would realize who I was and what had happened to me, and I would go home…Home. The word overcame me. We were already in the rear part of the corridor, deep inside the building. I embraced Maria, hiding my face in her shoulder. Her coat became moist with my tears. I felt an endless self-pity…something has happened to me, I'm in a hospital, I've lost my way. Nobody knows about me at home; I must have a home, after all. There must surely be someone who is waiting for me and misses me.

In the next few days, I did a lot of walking. I walked back and forth along the corridor and occasionally got a glimpse through an open door of the women's ward, where wretched, half-dressed women were lying. Often, I spied a whole thigh or a buttock or even a tuft of dark hairs. Although they in no way attracted me, I had an urge to see as much as I could.

Now that I knew I was in a hospital, I could understand what was going on better. The nurses went around the rooms and occasionally comforted a patient who was in distress or needed something. They carried out chamber pots and dirty sheets. The doctor appeared only rarely. He would rush around the rooms checking the state of the patients. Once he gestured to me to do a push-up and to turn my head fast. George appeared on our floor much more often than the doctor, several times a day. He visited other rooms, not just mine.

Once, I tried to go down the stairs to the floor below, but a nurse immediately noticed me and held me back. I understood that I could only walk around the hospital with Maria.

It was in the evening of the day when Maria had taken me outside that I first tried to speak, under my covers. In a whisper, I tried to say my name. At first, I couldn't do it, but then my tongue obeyed, and I heard my own whisper, "David." I tried it more loudly, but my vocal cords seemed to have dried up: I mumbled and rattled. It was easier to go back to a whisper: "My name is David," I whispered a whole sentence. At the same time, I became aware that the language I was using was Czech, while here people spoke a different language, unknown to me. I was horribly afraid that my origin would become known. At this point, I still couldn't think coherently. I didn't know the circumstances that had landed me in the hospital. I didn't know any circumstances at all. For all I knew, there could be a war on, and my country could be on the other side. Or, I could disappoint Maria by being what I was, and she would stop visiting me. I preferred to stay silent.

Once I was moving around more, the lousy hospital food stopped being enough for me. I was hungry all the time and was always going to look in the cafeteria in case there were leftovers. I also hoped the old man's family would visit him again, and I would get a decent meal.

In unguarded moments, I talked to myself. Above all, before going to sleep, I always uttered whole sentences under the covers. My vocal cords were working again, and I could make quiet sounds with them. I talked to myself in the corridors too, when none of the staff were nearby.

I talked the loudest in the shower. I started to shower several times a day, just so I could talk.

Maria took me on walks and eventually showed me the whole hospital. She also took me to a concrete yard when an ambulance was just arriving. The stray dogs reluctantly got up and jumped away from the wheels at the last minute. Their thin rumps and protuberant joints reminded me of the brown man in my room. Even their eyes seemed like his—resigned but cunning, perhaps a little dreamy, but without dignity: broken.

The ambulance men unloaded someone on a stretcher, and Maria pointed at me, indicating that they had brought me in the same way. Me? I was surprised. But from where? I needed to know. Where had they brought me from? Maria shrugged, as if this was her answer to my unuttered question. Then she smiled and pointed upwards to the sky with its broken clouds. She must have meant that I had dropped from heaven, or that I should thank heaven I was here and alive.

On the way back, Maria took me to the second floor. This time, we went by the stairs, and she supported me only discreetly. On the second floor, she unlocked a white-painted door and switched on the lights. The light inside was poor, and the room had no windows. It contained metal lockers—a mass of lockers. I waited to see what would happen.

Maria opened one of the lockers and started taking clothing out of it. The first garment that appeared in her hands was in green camouflage fabric—pants with a pattern like autumn leaves. There was something intimately familiar about them. Maria put them on a chair and kept on getting things out: a white t-shirt with an old brown bloodstain, faded black briefs, a warm, black fleece with another stain not so visible on black. Finally, sneakers.

With bated breath, I took individual pieces in my hand; I was near, so near, and although I didn't know what I was near to, whatever it was waited inside me and made me tremble all over. I realized that these were my clothes, but when I touched them, I felt as if I were holding the clothes of a dead man. Yes, I had died, but at the same time, I had survived.

It was so overwhelming that I collapsed on the floor with the clothes and ended up leaning against the metal of the lockers. Maria stroked my hand. I pressed the pleasant fabric of the fleece and t-shirt to my face and then the coarser material of the pants. Although they had been laundered, I could smell clay. That scent reminded me of something—most probably a burial, the digging of a grave. This time I thought it was my own grave: I had dug it myself in an unknown place, and now I had to find it again—find it!

After a while, Maria started to take the clothing from my hands, wanting to put them back in the locker, but I grabbed them and wouldn't let go. She knelt down beside me and tried to soothe me,

244

but I held on as hard as I could. It seemed to me that if the locker door were to close on those pants, t-shirt, and fleece, the man who had died in them would sink into darkness forever, and I would never be reunited with him. Maria's face, long like her body, appeared by my face: her large mouth and the black down under her nose, her prominent eyebrows and raven hair—the face of a woman in middle age, a woman who probably lived alone. I could no longer smell clay but a strong artificial scent. Then, suddenly, our lips touched. She rolled me to the ground and kissed and comforted me. The pants from the locker lay across my stomach, the t-shirt soaked in the blood of the man I had once been was by my head, and her breasts were pressed against my chest, the whole of her considerable female weight. She overwhelmed me, caressed and kissed me, as if she wanted to save me. Yes, she wanted to save me. She wanted to wipe away all that suffering, all the disturbing questions and all that painful groping in the dark. I felt a pleasure similar to that which I had experienced when she came to shave me, but this time the pleasure grew hard and pressed against her belly. It was so easy to pull off the dressing gown that was all I was wearing; so easy for her. She took my cock in her hand but I didn't notice that as anything separate—every perception merged into one, and I let myself be washed in the hot spring of salvation. Maria kissed me, astride me in the hospital locker-room, smelling of perfume, disinfectant, and passion, and the whole time she caressed me down there, too far for me to reach across her physical weight. What she caused in me, as I rose to the climax, might be called oblivion but was at the same time reunion—erasing the difference between me and the man who had died in my clothes. Together we climbed to heaven and together we shed tears of joy in ecstatic spasms that seemed never to end—it was our shared zenith.

Later, she rolled off me and gently wiped me with a paper handkerchief, all rosy and out of breath as she was, and as I was too. Then she carefully picked up the trousers, t-shirt, and everything else, and folded them back into the locker, but constantly stroking me—perhaps afraid I would try to prevent her again. But it was an unnecessary fear. I was calm and reconciled, as I watched her putting the clothes back where they belonged.

Even when Maria had said goodbye and I was back in my room, and even much later in the evening, when I had stretched out on my bed and was resting in a half-sleep, a deep sense of reconciliation stayed within me. The legs of those pants seemed to float close by, scented with clay. What had the man who had worn them been thinking about before something bad happened to him? What had he been longing for, what had he been trying to achieve? Where was he heading in a strange unknown land? Just how strange was it to him? I would have liked to understand him, to know more about him. It was he, after all, who a little while before had been rising with me on wings of delight. Did something like that happen to him often? Did he love women? Did women love him?

Even later, when I was almost asleep, a burial scene arose in my head: somebody's coffin lies at the bottom of the grave, I am standing on the edge of the hole, I am with someone very close to me and very beloved. With someone I know well.

I was woken in the night by the anxious thumping of my heart. I was sweating and frightened, as if the ceiling were about to fall in. Confused and disordered memories were trying to force their way into my head, but all at once I didn't want them. I was terribly afraid of them.

Shivering all over, I got up and looked down from the window on the illuminated empty street. The sight calmed me a little; during my stay here in the room it had become my security. My thoughts eddied less crazily, and a wedding swam up out of the chaos. Yes, it was a wedding and not a funeral. My wedding with my wife. In an instant, she was present to me. It was, in its way, wonderful news for me, a desolate patient in a foreign land, so I couldn't understand the lump in my throat and my quickened pulse. After all, I had just discovered I was a married man, perhaps also a successful one. For long minutes, I stood by the window, sunk in a past that was surging back to me at this late hour. And then I remembered that a child had been born to us. I had been there at the birth; I had seen the little head appearing between the bloody labia. It was a little boy. Our Benjamin.

It was all too much for me, and I had to sit down. I saw that I was not just some lonely hobo lost to himself. I was all the more lost for having a wife and child. They had to be living somewhere, and they might be waiting for me somewhere. How come they hadn't turned up here? How come they weren't looking for me? I felt angry with my wife for her incompetence, for her indifference. How could she just have left me here like this? She was hopeless, awful, awful…

I fell asleep and did not wake until morning. I was sweaty but much calmer. The doctor, accompanied by a nurse, checked us all, and I went to have a shower. I stripped off and turned the shower head on my reeking chest. The water flowed, and my heart almost stopped with alarm. My wife was dead. She had been killed in a car accident or something like that. Which meant I had to take care of my son. But why was I here then? What had I done for God's sake?

My one thought was to get away from here. Home—to my son. But I didn't even know how old he was—most probably I thought he was still a baby. Maria, it occurred to me. I had to tell Maria. She was the only one who could help. I turned off the water and threw my dressing-gown over my wet body. "Maria! Maria!" I called. I went down the stairs and looked into the nurses' office. "Maria!" Not finding her there, I hurried back to the stairs. Maybe in the intensive care ward on the fourth floor—where I had seen her for the first time. On the way, I looked into another nurses' office, but there was no sign of her, and I was frantic thinking how every minute I was looking for her, my son was waiting for me. In the end, they grabbed me by the arms. I tried to break away, but there was an attendant there who held me painfully hard. I managed to get one arm out of the dressing gown and made a break for the stairs with all my strength, almost naked. They pushed me to the ground and gave me an injection. Everything grew wavy and ran together. What had seemed so intolerable sailed away into the distance. I became indifferent. I slept.

At first, when I woke up, I once again had no idea who I was and where I was. The only thing that was certain was that I was lying down, and Maria was standing over me. She had a worried expression on her face. When she saw I had opened my eyes, she bent down to me as if to a child…I was satisfied that it was Maria I saw, and I went back to sleep. I woke up again during the night. My head was swimming, and when I wanted to get up to go to the bathroom, I couldn't do it. I wet the bed. I tried at least to sit up, but I felt as though I was tied down, although I wasn't. There was nothing for it but resign myself to my state. I calmed down and stared silently through the dilute darkness at the ceiling above me. Under me, I felt the wet sheet cooling, but it was beyond my strength even to move a little bit to the side. I resigned myself to that too; probably it was the injection affecting my mind as well as my body. Maybe it was because of the injection that I reached a state of absolute calm, and new memories started to float to the surface. The white darkness lying between the present and the past began to disperse. I saw Benjamin's first steps in a rather grim apartment in a Prague housing estate. I heard him crying when he first went to school. I saw my office, where I used to escape to work—successful, lucrative work. Sometimes, I had even pretended to have work to do, so I didn't have to go home. Now I felt remorse about it. My wife had died, and my beloved Benjamin had stood next to me at her funeral. I was everything to him now. The school year had ended. I had taken him on a journey to the Back of Beyond. I remembered the little hotel in the Šumava, the Austrian Alps, and Benjamin's sickness in the camp near Trieste, my fear for him and his measureless trust in my power to protect him. Then the paradise of the Greek island, our fun in the waves, our browning skin. But then the incomprehensible journey east and north and the feeling of exile, as I realized there was a warrant out for my arrest. Then a few fragments, but the white darkness thickened again. All I had were islands of memory, the most recent being the barrier and the notice saying *Romania*. And yes, of course—Timisoara, a Romanian town. This is where I am now, I realized. But where is Benjamin, my son? Where have I lost him, I, his Dad, who was supposed to protect him always. I felt I was close, very close to an answer. Benjamin had not lost his life, and I hadn't lost him. I had left him somewhere, left him, left him...

Nobody could ever have felt as deserving of his own contempt as I felt then. I lay there, immobilized, helplessness incarnate, but in full awareness of my guilt. It was as I had imagined hell, as I still imagine hell. I was in hell, as if chained to the bed—to my cross. I was the one who had failed. And there was no one here to release me. There was no judge, either, but there didn't have to be, for I was my own judge.

The night went on a long time, and I didn't expect anyone to appear in the morning, at least not on my account. And if someone came, what would I do? I could tell them who I was and ask for help. And they would call the Czech embassy. No one would believe me. They would think I had abducted Ben and maybe even killed him. They would send me back to Bohemia, and then I would never see him again.

I lay in my own sweat until morning. I hadn't made the slightest move, since it seemed to me that if I did, the arch of the sky would collapse and everything would be engulfed in rubble. The doctor arrived with two nurses. The nurses stripped off my covers. When they saw how soaking I was, they looked at the doctor. He gave them instructions, and they pulled me into a sitting position. Then they helped me get up and almost carried me to the washroom. There they washed me and smiled encouragingly at me. But I was feeling better. I had sweated my way through the hell of loss.

I managed to walk to breakfast by myself. I had to eat, to build up my strength. For the moment, I knew one thing: I had to get out of here.

George arrived before lunch. He grinned and evidently made some joke about the fool I had made of myself. But I didn't trust his smile. He had brought tables with numerous examples and wanted me to tap the answers with a finger on the table. I hesitated for a moment, wondering if it might be unwise to oblige him, but then I decided it would make no difference. I tapped out the right answers—to his delight.

I spent the day in unbearable tension. I found it almost impossible not to get up and run away immediately to look for Ben. Every moment I didn't do it felt like a lost moment, but I knew that I had to control myself. This was not yet the right moment, I repeated to myself. I mustn't do it yet.

I think they gave me some sleeping pills, and so I slept until morning. They discharged the boy, and a new patient came in his place. That meant the room was busy, but I hardly noticed the commotion, for my attention was fixed on the outside, on the Romanian town of Timisoara. I went over to look at the second side as well—over the suburban houses and factory halls into the pastures and fields—to the horizon, beyond which Benjamin might be waiting anywhere.

Maria didn't turn up until late afternoon. Outside it was getting dark and looked as if there would be snow. As soon as I saw Maria, I thought the right moment could be getting close. I got up, as if we were going downstairs, but she talked soothingly, tried to get me to lie down, and put a hand on my forehead. I turned my head away in refusal. "Maria," I said quietly, imploringly, "Maria." It was the first time she had heard me say anything. Her eyes glistened with emotion.

So, we walked to the elevator. Inside, she pressed zero and it cranked into motion. It was spacious—big enough to fit a whole trolley—but we stood close to each other, almost touching each other. She regarded me protectively with her dark eyes, but she was no longer Mom for me. On the contrary, I was a Dad—a father who had failed. A father who had to find his son. As the elevator went down, an idea occurred to me, and I pressed Two. The locker room with the clothing I needed was on the second floor. I couldn't leave the hospital in just a dressing gown and slippers. I took Maria's hand, and this time, it was me leading her. She probably thought I wanted to make love, because she blushed and acted shy. I felt remorse about her. She had saved me, opened the way for me. Only yesterday, she had been my everything.

She unlocked the door, and we slipped inside. I remembered the locker, but she locked the door behind us. She flung off her coat, and I saw her full breasts with dark purple nipples. At the same time, I saw that I was going to have to hurt someone who had helped me. But what was that compared to my guilt about Benjamin? I was wretched, the most wretched of all. I could not have been more wretched.

I took Maria's hand and led her to the locker that held my things. She leaned on the next door expecting an embrace. I opened the locker and this time I caressed and soothed her with my other hand. I stroked her face. "Maria," I whispered. I let my dressing gown drop and began to dress myself fast— the blood-stained t-shirt, the fleece... She startled in alarm and tried to stop me. "Maria." I wasn't thinking hard, but I prayed wordlessly to God that I would only wound her in her soul and wouldn't have to hurt her physically. "Baby, baby," I tried to explain and pointed outside. But she held tight—she was strong, and trained. "*Nu*," she protested, "*Nu, Nu. Nu!*" At that moment, I had an idea—an idea that suited my goal but was also something I wanted to do. I dropped the clothes and pressed Maria and her breasts to my chest. I kissed her on the lips and with my hand I reached into her stockings. She was ready, completely wet. We got down on the floor, she spread her legs and took off her stockings herself. I had to get my clothes and get out of the hospital, but the truth was that I loved her, and I wanted her. She deserved my love—right now, when I was no longer a child or a youth who needed help. I rubbed her wetness over her large, white thighs and entered her, my mouth on her mouth. I was not sentimental, but vigorous, and she came several times before I reached a climax. I couldn't allow myself any more rapture. I quickly came back to my senses. I slipped off of her and finished getting dressed. Briefs, pants, shoes. "*Nu,*" she lamented on the floor and curled into a ball. "*Nu, nu, nu.*" Now clothed, I knelt down beside her and squeezed her hand. "Maria…" I headed for the door, but almost tottered, because the love-making had taken so much out of me. I realized that what I was trying to do was sheer madness. I hardly had the strength to get down the stairs, I had no money, and I didn't know the way. I was also confused; my memory was still poor, and I doubted that I still had all my mental faculties. Later, I came to believe that it was only because of my impaired mental faculties that I ever embarked on something so hopeless. The worse of all was that I had no idea where Ben was.

The keys were still in the door, and behind the door, there was a lighted corridor. I closed the door behind me. I could have locked it too, but I didn't. I staggered to the stairs, and my sneakers held me up pretty well compared to those hospital slippers. I managed to get down to the entrance hall and made it to the main entrance. A refreshing current of air came from outside and met me half way, but I was sure anyone who encountered me would realize I was escaping. Even the porter would remember me. Except that the porter happened not to be there. That is how I found myself outside on the sidewalk, in the early evening shadows. I would have liked to stop and take a deep breath, but I had to get going. I skirted the ditch and walked as fast as I could, but still too slowly. I made for the main road. That distance tested the limits of my strength. Without thinking, I glanced back and saw the hospital building with its multiple lit windows. At last, the crossroads. I looked left and right and tried to get across. A tram was just approaching. I headed for the tram island. It was just a few meters away, but the tram arrived fast and the doors opened. I tried to run and made it to the island. The driver had seen me and waited.

Gasping, I staggered to the nearest seat, wanting to puke. To the left, I could still see the whole hospital and its lighted windows, but I was swallowed up in darkness, a white darkness, as the tram rattled along its worn tracks.

When I came around, the tram was going down a narrow street with low houses. The neglected quarter turned into a well-maintained little town park. In the window of one of the shops I saw Christmas decorations. How long had I been in the hospital? I wondered. A week? Two? A month?

The passengers were mostly wrapped in coats, some with caps, but I was just wearing a sweatshirt. I felt cold. Absently, I dug in my pockets to see if I could find some forgotten change.

My situation was desperate. It occurred to me I was probably going to die. Never again would I see Benjamin, and his trusting child's mind would never understand why his father had betrayed him. He would muddle through life without love, with a burdensome sense of wrong, in an alien environment among alien people. Maybe he would end up in some appalling children's home, where he would be bullied by ruthless inmates. Maybe he had already ended up there, while I was sitting in this tram. Maybe they had sold him into slavery, to drudge from morning to night, or to be sexually abused. And when he had served their purposes, they would kill him.

I huddled on the seat in painful cramps and couldn't even manage a sob. Maybe I wailed, because people started turning away from me and changing seats.... Perhaps the only thing left to me in all this hopelessness was to turn to God, the God whose existence I had always considered possible, but had seriously doubted. There was nothing left but to believe in Him. To believe He would look after my Benjamin instead of me. In my mind (but probably it was more a question of pure instinct), I clung to Him as my only hope. It seemed possible to me that He would hear me. I readily forgot about the sufferings of millions of people, sufferings that had mounted up over the centuries like a mountain, and were mounting up more and more as every second of earthly time went by. I forgot the violent and often indescribably agonizing deaths that even the pious have not been spared. Where was God when they created Auschwitz? Where was God when they separated the mothers from the children? It was a question any person of sober mind would ask. But I wasn't sober. I begged God to put right what I myself had neglected. I pleaded with him, overcome with despair.

The tram stopped in front of a large building. A lot of people got out with briefcases, and the driver got off, too, and went to change the coordinates. A chill blew in through the open doors and woke me up. I saw the sign Timisoara Nord. It was a station.

I lurched off the tram without even knowing why. Well, actually I did know why, subconsciously. A station was a place where people wait, all night long sometimes. A station has waiting rooms where people's lives crisscross; you can survive there. And what was more, trains depart from a station to distant places, and in stations you can hear the names of towns. One of them might tell me something. And if not, I could still get on a train, ride off. If not directly to the place where Benjamin was, at least in the direction of an illusion, a false hope.

The entrance to the concourse was very busy. People all dressed in the same kind of clothes and laden down with luggage streamed out and in. Every so often, a genuine lady in a luxurious fur, or students in modern fashions, appeared in the crowd. There were stalls selling newspapers, drinks, and fast food. I realized I was desperately hungry and even more desperately thirsty. I thought of going to the bathrooms at least to drink some water. An arrow pointed to a passageway and then down into the basement. Here all the bustle fell away. I found myself in a dark corridor reminiscent of catacombs, with very scanty lighting. There was a cubicle where you had to pay, five thousand lei, apparently a negligible amount of money. If you paid, you could get through a revolving barrier. The sink was beyond the barrier. I couldn't get to the water.

I went back up to the corridor, and the cold shook me. I noticed a young boy begging. Compared to him, I was still decently dressed. He had rubber boots on his feet, and his tattered pants gave out under his knees. On top, he wore an equally tattered shirt over rags wound around his chest. He was walking through the hall between the waiting people—with hunched shoulders and outstretched palm. His expression was one of stupor to the point of insensibility. Mostly he got nothing, and when he stopped by a group of four men, they repelled him with a kick in the pants and stamping. He slid away as reluctantly as the dogs in the hospital yard. But then, an old woman gave him money. In that moment, he was richer than me. I envied him and realized I was incapable of doing what he did. At least, I couldn't do it yet. I envied him for having lost his honor and dignity and everything that could have made him a human being—he had become a dog.

A train arrived on the first platform, and there was some kind of announcement on the loudspeaker system. I listened to the incomprehensible names. They conveyed nothing to me. I crossed the platform and scanned the dirty concrete floor. Someone could have dropped small change there or the remains of food. I took a look in the trashcans. Eating trash would have bothered me less than begging.

Opening off the platform was a packed waiting room. I went in and was enveloped in a greasy, sticky heat. It was overheated here, and I couldn't understand why the people sitting down didn't even take off their overcoats. Some Romani children were playing on the floor. Their mother was leaning against a big hold-all and every so often handed them pieces of bread. In a corner, two men were drinking and playing cards. I noticed a plastic bottle, still a little liquid at the bottom. It was standing by a radiator and I started thinking how I could get it without attracting attention. I sat on the nearest seat and waited for the right moment. When I saw no one was watching, I picked up the bottle and hurried out.

Inside, there was sweetened water, and so I drank it up with a sense that I was sating my thirst. For a moment it really gave me a feeling of satiation. Only coming out of the waiting room, I realized I was cold. There was no alternative but to go back. I sat down near the door and took a good look in every corner under the seat. At that moment, I was probably no longer even thinking about what I would do to find Ben. The question was one of sheer survival.

As the evening wore on, more beggars emerged out of the darkness—my competitors. One came into the waiting room and went around everyone in turn. He even stopped in front of me. The smartly dressed parents of a bespectacled boy gave him the remains of an unfinished snack. I had to content myself with a piece of bread I found in the gap between seats.

Time went by and the people in the waiting room changed. Those who stayed lay down on their luggage and dozed. Weariness began to overcome me. After all, only a few hours ago I had been in the hospital. From my current perspective, the hospital seemed exceptionally comfortable. And Maria was there, who had nursed me. Probably I should have tried to get her to understand. If she had understood what I wanted, she would have helped me. Except that there was a danger she would have gone to the Czech embassy or the police out of sheer good will. Then I would never have seen Benjamin again. I would have ended up back in Bohemia, in prison.

But why did I think I would see him again this way, I asked myself as my eyelids drooped. At that moment, policemen entered the waiting room. They wanted to see the tickets of the men drinking. After a while, they took them away. They left me alone, since probably I looked respectable. There was nothing for it but to rely on luck. Voices and steps hummed in my ears, the hum of the station. A white darkness thickened around me. It had rolled across the platform and from there to the waiting room. It covered me completely. It brought the greatest of all pleasures—oblivion.

Towards morning, I was woken by an agonizing headache. I had never experienced anything like it; it was as if sharp screws were stuck somewhere inside my head, and as soon as I moved, my brain ran up against their corners.

But I needed to move. I needed to drink. I put my head between my forearms and tried to stand up. I yelped with pain and had to drop to my knees. I was kneeling by the door to the platform, where the artificial lighting had already been turned off, and the first railway lines were emerging from the dimness. Commuters were coming to work, and country people were bringing goods for sale: vegetables, poultry…But I was kneeling between the waiting room and the platform. It seemed that my journey had ended. I was incapable of walking any further.

Eventually though, the pain diminished, and I resolved to make a radical move: I stood up. A new wave of pain crippled me again. Then it began to fade away. I staggered off into the grey morning. I felt neither hunger nor cold. Just a tormenting thirst.

The hall was packed with people, and the crowd slowly carried me outside. The pain spread out into my whole head and became dull. I found myself on the sidewalk. Without a conscious decision, I walked over the crossroads. I was going away; I had no idea where.

Later, I reached a bridge over a small, stagnant river. Clumps of mist rolled in the river bed. The greenish water, full of plastic bottles and pieces of paper, moved and attracted my eyes. I leaned over the parapet and pressed my whole weight against it. The water hardly moved, and everything screamed at me: drink!

I don't know what instinct for self-preservation suppressed that desire, which was also an instinct, but something made me take my weight back onto my own feet and go. I don't remember where and for how long I walked, and I don't remember any ideas running through my head. I didn't even notice the cold, and even the pain seemed to seep away into the mist around me. I walked until a church loomed up in front of me. It was in a garden behind a wall. A stone wall, and from that wall, under an icon, sprang a fountain. People were stopping and drinking. Wonder blazed in my mind: Had someone guided my steps here? Was someone keeping watch over me? This was not just about Benjamin. It was about my battered body, which was dying of desire for water. I was just thirsty.

I knelt down to the fountain and stayed on my knees a long, long time. The water was icy—I could only drink it a few gulps at a time, but I was still drinking when I was already full of water. The remnants of the mist were dissolving, and the winter sun was finding its way out from behind a white veil. I rose and slowly walked away. I didn't understand what I had to thank for this strange morning. Was I going to live after all?

On the left, I now noticed a large marketplace. Stalls were selling fruit, vegetables, nuts, and honey. And all kinds of second-hand trash: broken appliances, dead batteries, worn-out clothes. Chickens were running around in little enclosures. I headed between the stalls in the hope of finding some leftovers. I quickly found two rather rotten apples on the trampled ground. I wanted to put them in my pocket, but my hand was so numb I couldn't get my fingers around the fruit. I had to press them between my palms to shove them into the pocket. A little further on, I found a large carrot. It wasn't at all rotted; someone must have lost it. I hurried into a quiet corner and started to eat it there. It was difficult when I couldn't move my fingers, but I managed. After a while, I went back among the stalls. I found another apple there and a potato. I laboriously picked them up and walked off. I had now drunk and eaten and my most important need was for warmth. The sun was without heat—it was veiled in mist. I needed to get back to the station fast.

I found the path along the small river. As I got closer to the bridge, I felt an urgent need for the bathroom. This was serious.

I crept under the bridge and tried to unfasten my pants. I couldn't. Dear God, I thought, and it was the first time that day that I had remembered the name of God. It already looked as though I would have to shit in my pants. I imagined fouling up the only set of clothes I had. Did I intend to walk around the town naked? God! I thrust my whole palms into my pants and with all my strength pushed them away from my body. In the end the pants gave way: the button flew off; I could take a shit. But them another problem appeared: how and with what to wipe myself.

It was only now that I had a proper look around. Here under the bridge, above the stinking town sewer, were traces of others who had answered the call of nature before me. There was also used paper. In places the paper still seemed clean. The problem was that my numb fingers couldn't turn the paper around in a way that guaranteed I would only touch the clean surface. I noticed that a piece of newspaper was lying below by the water. Someone had probably used it too, but it was much larger. Still squatting, and with my pants down, I crept lower. And somehow, I wiped myself with the newspaper.

I felt hungry again. In my pocket, I still had an apple and a potato. I pulled up my pants, but now they wouldn't stay up. I had to hold them up with my hands on my hips. I tucked my fleece into my briefs and stowed the food in its belly; now my pants had less of a tendency to fall down. I climbed back up to the pavement and bit on the potato. It tasted fantastic—like real solid food.

On the way, my head cleared enough to get me thinking again about Benjamin. I had escaped from the hospital, but I was no closer to him. I had done nothing that might take me to him. All the same, a kind of fragment of hope remained in me. When I think about it today, it was an unjustifiable hope and could certainly be called faith. But it might just as well be called resignation; a dulling of the mind. I had no plan, and taking care of my basic animal needs was so huge a task that I didn't have the time or energy for despair. Strengthened by the potato, I went back to the station. There were somewhat fewer people streaming through than in the morning, fewer country people. In the waiting room, the heat was sticky. I curled up on a seat with a feeling of pleasant tiredness. I was soon falling asleep after work well done; I had made an expedition for sustenance, and I had been successful. Now I had come back. It was like a return home.

I don't know how long I slept, but it was not yet dusk when I woke up. I was thirsty again. I decided to try to go to the bathroom below to drink—with any luck they would let me past the barrier. Under my fleece, I still had one rotten apple. I decided that if I didn't get past the barrier, I would eat the apple.

In the hall by the ticket desk, I saw an unusual group of people. They looked like foreigners and had big leather travelling bags by their feet. They were having a dispute with a woman at the ticket desk; the conversation was full of gestures and very agitated. My eyes fell on one of the bags. It was a little to one side, unfastened…and inside, on top of the folded things lay a large flat wallet—it had to be full of cash. Having seen it once, I couldn't look away. In a single instant, hope battled inside me with skepticism, determination with fear, temptation with resignation. I thought above all of Ben, to whom I was not a centimeter closer since yesterday. If I had money, everything would change, and I would be a father again, a man. It was an opportunity that would probably never come again. Maybe my last.

But I also thought about all the poor wretches I had seen at the station, who were surviving here hand-to-mouth and day-by-day, not by stealing but by begging. Then suddenly I turned up, an affluent man even if I'd lost my way back to my wealth—and I didn't respect that rule.

Finally, I thought of the immensity of the risk. I was weakened and inexperienced; I had never stolen anything. What if they caught me?

I had to act fast. Everything was at stake: my son, his life. What could be weightier than life? Didn't the life of my child outweigh the wallet? What would be the will of God?

I edged up to the bag. The foreigners were still failing to reach agreement with the ticket-seller; probably they had been sold the wrong tickets. They were completely taken up with the problem. Surely, they would have understood that I had to…I had to!

I didn't even glance round to check whether anyone was watching. I had no choice. Now or never. I bent down, and then I slipped the wallet under my fleece with the apple. Slowly, casually, I walked away, just waiting for a hue and cry to start behind me. I was resolved that, if caught, I would tell them everything. I would tell them who I was, where I was from, and what had happened to me. I could no longer carry this cross.

But nothing happened. I reached the steps in front of the hall and only then broke into a run, or at least it felt like a run to me. A tram appeared in the distance and approached quickly. I forced myself to stand still. No one was chasing me after all. I waited for it.

A moment later, when I sat down on the tram seat, I felt even worse than when I had escaped from the hospital. A sort of animal terror shook me, my teeth chattered as if they wanted to fly off, taking my whole jaw, and they couldn't be stopped. I thought it was best to get off at the very next stop. There in front of me was the bridge I knew so well. I reached it and headed down the steep embankment under a pier. There I lay down among the turds—face down. My teeth were still chattering terribly, and I bit into a stone underneath me until they scraped. I dug my fingers into the wet clay. I writhed in the stale twilight, hidden from the sight of men and God.

To this day, at a distance of many years, even the most fleeting memory of my state back then makes me feel ill. For me, it is a remarkable proof of how deeply the commandments of civilization are rooted in us. So deeply, that breaking them brings the body to the very edge of collapse.

After a while, I calmed down. Now, I had to confront the contents of the wallet. It might be empty, and then I would be back where I had started. It might contain some money but not enough. Then it would just help me eke out my existence for a brief time longer. I sat up and shifted down to the concrete step above the water. The noise of passing cars and the rumble of trams came from above.

Eventually, I opened the wallet. I was shocked at how full of cash it was—local lei and dollars. My feeling of triumph was mixed with guilt. I had committed theft, major theft. Who was it I had stolen from? The wallet had several compartments. In one there were only receipts, but the photograph of a child fell out of another. A two- or three-year-old boy with blond hair, playing with dice and staring into the lens. I felt nauseated again. The man I had stolen from loved his child as I loved Benjamin. Maybe he had wanted to buy him something for Christmas here. I continued to rifle through the wallet absently and pulled a passport from a large pocket. It was a Hungarian passport in the name of a Peter Horváth. A not-particularly-sympathetic round face gazed out at me from the official photograph. Nothing about the man caught my interest or made me feel any affinity with him. I snapped the passport shut and prepared to throw it in the water, but suddenly I realized that thanks to the passport, I would be able to compensate the man sometime in the future. It was a relief. One day, I would send him an explanatory letter and money, and that meant it was not a theft but a loan. I started to count the bills. It came to eight hundred and fifty dollars and over three million lei (the local currency was hyperinflated). I realized these were my only funds for finding Benjamin, and I would have no others. The sum wasn't paltry, but from that point of view, it wasn't a fortune either. I felt like a hungry hunter in the wilderness, who just a moment before thought he had an empty magazine and now had found ten bullets.

I feverishly tried to organize my thoughts. I was no longer at the bottom of the abyss, and so now I had something to lose. I couldn't afford mistakes.

First and foremost, nobody should be allowed to see me with this big wallet, which didn't exactly go with my down-market appearance. I took out all the lei and stuffed them in my pants pocket. I slipped the wallet back under my fleece next to the rotten apple. But where? I ought to go for some soup and tea, I realized, but first, I had to buy some clothes. The day was nearly over, and the cold was creeping under the bridge. I set off for the market. That morning, I had seen stands selling clothes there.

It was dark before I found the market. The vegetable stands were already empty, but stalls with Christmas goods were open. I stopped a little way from one of them. It was selling candles and wooden decorations. A little gas lamp hung from a corner, and I was reminded of the flickering light in the darkness that had tirelessly circled above my vacant mind before I regained consciousness. It had been like this little lamp in the market, but it had been fixed on…on the back of an old jalopy. It had hung from some wood projecting out of a wagon and I…I had smashed into it at full speed. The market and stalls vanished—around me was an impenetrable darkness, demarcated by high-beam headlights. It was a last moment—just a fragment of it. But where? And what had preceded it? I had nearly touched something, but it slipped away.

I woke up into frosty reality and found myself sitting on trampled dirt. Above me, a lantern shone a welcoming light, and townspeople stood around the counter. One was a mother with a little girl, and I suddenly felt the glow of home, where those two would soon be returning—their warmth, that had so little connection with me. I couldn't help thinking about my Benjamin, I couldn't help thinking that he was probably cold, and afraid and hungry at this very moment. After a while, mother and daughter chose a tall candle in a wooden stand and went home, where they would light it.

The stalls selling clothes were still open. I chose a knitted sweater, socks, gloves, a hat, handing over a million lei with a heavy heart. A belt, to stop my pants falling down, cost a hundred thousand. And with shaking hands, from an old peasant, I bought a used overcoat for four hundred thousand. I put all of it on right away, and expected someone to become suspicious, but they were all very pleasant, as if a customer with nothing to wear and pockets full of cash were perfectly normal.

I bought soup in a buffet on the corner. Now that I was no longer struggling to survive, I felt bitterness flooding my body and an unutterable grief rising out of the open pores of my dilapidated soul.

That little lantern kept coming back to haunt me; its flickering light emerged out of the darkness for a fraction of a second and then stabbed into it. There was no doubt that I had crashed the car—I had hit a badly lit wagon. But I didn't know where it had happened and why I hadn't had Benjamin with me... Why had I left him somewhere? Or had he been thrown out of the window by the impact and never found? Something told me it wasn't like that. He hadn't been with me. If he had been, Maria would have known about him. I had been driving at night, and I had been alone.

I went to the bathroom and caught sight of my unshaven face

in the mirror. It had aged and shriveled. I recognized it, but I didn't know what to think about it. I put my hand up to my forehead and ran a finger across it. It had all happened somewhere inside. The white darkness that had swallowed a part of the past was inside there too, as well as what I called my own self.

I thought of Maria. What had she really seen in me? She had looked after me when I was an infant and given herself to me when I became a man. Like most Romanian women, she wasn't pretty, but I would have liked to tell her what I had managed to do over the last day, and how, even weak and debilitated, I had survived in an unknown town. I wanted to tell her how my will to find Benjamin had stopped at nothing, and how, right now, I was standing and seeing myself in the mirror of a local buffet—and was alive. I wondered if I shouldn't go back to the hospital and wait in front of it for Maria to come to work. I would grab her by the arm and pull her aside and try to explain everything to her. But would she understand my English? And what if someone else noticed me? I was in possession of a stranger's wallet and documents. Any check could mean the end. Cautiously, I ventured out into the evening streets. In a little corner shop, I bought a toothbrush, soap, toothpaste, toilet paper, and a plastic bag. As I walked through increasingly prosperous streets, I realized that I must no longer look destitute. I was normally dressed.

I stopped for a moment by a stone fountain. Foaming water sprang from it. Frosty air was rising from the fountain, but there was a relaxed, holiday mood around. People were eating and drinking in restaurants, some were just out for a walk, and colored lights were stretched above the sidewalk. I walked around a bookshop that had a map of Romania in the window. The map was expensive, so I hesitated. My funds were limited, but a map might jog my memory. I bought it reluctantly. At the cash register, I glanced at the newspapers on display. The date on them was November 6. I was assailed by panic that I would not find Benjamin by Christmas. What the hell was I still doing here?

I headed for the station. Thanks to the little riverbed, I found the way easily, returning along the bank to the shabbier part of town. The roads here were broken, and the corners around the river unlit. I was a little afraid that someone might rob me. I hurried on, feeling that I should have been somewhere else altogether a long time ago, but I was back here for the fourth time today.

Before entering the station concourse, I hesitated. I had stolen something this afternoon, and I might have stuck in someone's memory. The sight of me might bring it back. Of course, the foreigners were no longer standing at the window, and there was a normal line there. I joined it like a man who wants to go somewhere, not a ragged derelict.

I scrutinized the departures screen. Confusing letters flashed past my eyes and combined into unfamiliar names: Deva, Craiova, Oradea… and finally a word I knew: Bucuresti. Benjamin could be anywhere, anywhere. In confusion, I opened the map, but the words, lines, and dots made no sense. My head was not ready for them. I looked for a key to interpreting the map but was distracted from this futile effort by the piercing voice of the station announcer. In the rapid sequence of information, I caught the name Sibiu; I went up to the window and bought a ticket for Sibiu. It was not expensive.

The stream of people brought me down to a dim underground section and from there to the second platform and a shabby train. I glanced around and stepped on. Inside, a toilet stank and a connecting door hung on a single hinge. It was unbelievably over-heated. The train was almost full.

I sat down by the window on sagging upholstery in one of the last empty spots. Looking out onto the dirty platform, I was conscious again of the change in my luck. I was sitting in a train with a valid ticket, more or less in charge of my life, dressed and fed. The station clock showed eight-thirty. Then eight-thirty-one, eight-thirty-two. Hot air rose from the heater, and I almost choked on it. Finally, the train started to move.

I was leaving the station where I had found a strange home on the threshold of existence. I was leaving the town that had led me to the man I had been before, with the help of Maria, the trams, and the snowflakes. Outside, the lighted windows of houses flashed by, followed by strange corners with shanty-style dwellings, and then street lighting again, trams running out into the rural suburbs. And then darkness. The train sped between pastures and fields, but I was still watching for any hint of a shape that might jog my memory. Too much remained unanswered, too much seemed irretrievably lost, and even what felt almost within reach evaded my attempts to touch it, to remember. I had survived, but for that to have any meaning, I had to find Ben. Without Ben, my survival would be just an unwanted awakening into a hell of loss.

He Does Not Lose Hope—Despite Everything

So began my lonely travels around Romania, my hopeless searching. As the train jolted through the unknown landscape, weariness caught up with me. The word "God" slipped into my mind, but not the gift of faith. What I experienced was really just a desperate and futile need for Him to exist. Yet in front of God, if he existed, I felt shame. I had failed in the most important task I had been given in life, and now there was nothing left but a hope that in the desolate distance—in the unknown but precisely defined place inhabited by Benjamin— God would be with him.

When I eventually dozed off, I had a wonderful and at the same time disturbing dream. It was a dream full of light, but not sunlight. In that light, we approached each other—me and my Ben. He put his arms around my waist and pressed his fair head to my chest. "Dad," he said, "Dad, Mom didn't die, you know." Except I knew she was dead and couldn't bring myself to say anything comforting to him. I said nothing, and he continued. "She's always with me. That's what you said. If she wants, she can see me." I knew I ought to comfort him, and I wanted to comfort him, but I couldn't get the right words out. I felt like I was under a curse. And after a moment, Benjamin understood my silence.

The dream reminded me of how I used to talk with Benjamin about his Mom. My memories were still just coming back and many were still lost, but now I vividly recalled how I had created the illusion for Ben that his Mom had not died and could still see him. I only hoped the illusion had not deserted him. I woke up in the wagon with worse pangs of conscience than when I had fallen asleep. But also, with the certainty that Benjamin was alive. He had to be alive.

In the days that followed, I became an inhabitant of stations and trains. I moved from place to place, hoping that somewhere I would see something to put me on the trail of my own memory. Beyond the train windows, the small farms went by, the yellowing meadows and cart tracks. It was a still unspoiled countryside full of hard daily labor, sometimes bathed in faint sunshine, at other times dripping with light rain or covered in morning frost. I had a lot of time to devote to memories. Again and again, I returned to every moment of the journey to the Back of Beyond; discovered new connections with my previous life. I thought about my childhood, my parents, my marriage…and compared what I had done in my life with what I had wanted to accomplish. In less than ten years, I had certainly achieved a degree of affluence, but that modern kind of work—without tangible products or clear values, dealing in the virtual reality of shares and bonds—had brought me no real satisfaction. Originally, I had wanted to do research, to study something important, offer answers to fundamental questions of existence. Or else to work with people—to address their problems, teach them to think about themselves, give them advice based on profound understanding. Now when I saw a shepherd at a railway crossing and watched how he lined up his herd to lead them across to the other side of the track, I even envied him the raw cold that was creeping under his coat, and I envied him the summer heat, from which he would hide in the shadow of a tree. And most of all, I envied him his slow-flowing days and his clear head; the music of church bells and cow bells. But soon, my thoughts ran back to Ben. I was swimming with him in the Greek sea, sitting with him on the terrace of the apartment after sunset and telling him about the universe. If only that summer had never ended, we would never have set out for the west and even less the north, where my memories disappeared into white darkness somewhere on the Bulgarian border.

I was in no state to consider my options rationally—not even the possibility of calling my assistant. I had forgotten the number, but I could have easily gotten it at a post office. I could ask her to come, bring money, and help me in my search. Only I rightly suspected that the present situation, in which I was missing and most probably dead, suited her just fine. My imagination was so fevered that I even wondered if she would come and kill me. After all, it would be so easy to get rid of someone who was in hiding, who didn't exist. I imagined her turning up with her husband, a simple and docile plumber, and pretending to be friendly, and at the right moment, bumping me off. I would be found with a stolen passport in an unknown country—nameless.

That left my father and Petra. I often thought about my father. Now I understood what it meant not to know where your child was, and I realized that he hadn't known for half a year. Whatever his way of showing his love, he did love Benjamin, and somewhere inside, he must still have feelings for me, even if he didn't admit it. I apologized to him in my mind many times and forgave him many times, and I hoped that one day I would find forgiveness from him too. But I couldn't turn to him with a request for aid, or to Petra. Those two were too honest to be able to imagine any solution outside of the law. They trusted in the law, but how could I turn to the law, when I had broken it many times and was continuing to break it? They couldn't have helped me, and even less could they have understood me. They would advise me to go straight to the authorities and would report it all themselves to the Foreign Ministry.

More than once, I also wordlessly spoke to my dead wife. I told her about my predicament, what had happened to me and Ben, and I tried to imagine what she would say. In my mind, she was neither angry nor reproachful but simply serious, gravely insisting that I should put right what I had gotten wrong. Now that she no longer had to bear the burden of an unwanted life on earth, she was much calmer and wiser. She didn't call me names or weep, and I promised her I would never give up my efforts to find Ben, and that I would rather die than live with even the fraction of a possibility that he was somewhere and waiting. To that she said, "Just make damn sure you don't die!"

So, I jolted around from station to station. I slept in waiting rooms, with a ticket already purchased for safety, and used local bathrooms for my hygiene routine—which consisted just of brushing my teeth, washing my hands and sometimes my face. Naturally, I took no showers—I couldn't go to hotels, because the only passport I had was stolen, and I was saving it for future apology and compensation. I spent all the lei and was starting to exchange dollars. If, at first, I was a hunter who had found ten bullets, now I had only nine, eight, seven…and I had made not one inch of progress. I preferred not to count the days. To judge by the atmosphere on the platforms and in the streets of the smaller towns, where I always took a quick walk around, Christmas was close. I passed Christmas fairs and the specially decorated windows of what, by local standards, were very modern shops. Sometimes I ate in a McDonald's and almost felt as if I were back in Prague in Wenceslas Square. But I always hurried back to the station, having found not a trace of a trail. Often, I cried in the corner of a waiting room or in the empty wagon of a train not due to leave for an hour. Even more, I often I hated myself, so helpless, wretched, and contemptible.

In that first night spent on the train when I left Timisoara, I got as far as distant Sibiu. I got off at the unknown station, which was not particularly different from the station in Timisoara, just smaller. It was just getting light, and I dashed along several streets, convinced myself I had never been there before and ate in the station restaurant. Then I took the train back in daylight, hoping (but also fearing), that in the dark and in my sleep, I had missed something important. In the following days, I repeated journeys of this kind, sometimes more than once a day, always double-checking, obsessed.

On what I think was the fourth day, I found myself in the town of Sineria. The sky was cloudless and the winter sun highlighted details of the landscape. Remnants of mist floated above dewy pastures. Gentle hills rose to the north and south. The hills in the south seemed larger and, in the distance beyond them, almost like a mirage that might be nothing more than a silver haze, there were snowy mountains. For a moment, it seemed that I might have caught the trace of something in the air—perhaps some natural scent—offering a kind of promise. Eager for the promise, I went around the front of the local station. On the other side of a cul-de-sac were small bistros and pubs. A horse-drawn wagon and two taxis were waiting here. It was already well after noon and soon it would be starting to get dark. I hastily made for the center of the little town and crossed it first towards the north. The streets were crowded between 1950s apartment blocks. Young people in jeans and leather were standing around bars, boys in ugly colored tracksuits were kicking a ball, Romani children calling to each other across the street. I wondered whether, even here, Ben would find it easy to join his contemporaries and if they would accept him. Yet again, it seemed incomprehensible to me, all these people living here and probably pursuing their small daily goals as people do everywhere, even if here the pursuit was more wearing, and they were more submerged in everyday drudgery. I couldn't imagine them experiencing a great passion or making love completely naked.

I found myself between small houses and then the road went out of the town and up onto a kind of promontory about twenty meters high. Under it spread the many kilometers of plains between the southern and the northern hills. A white haze was rising and drifting above the alders and poplars. Under normal circumstances, it would be a tranquil view of small herds of cows and sheep and a solitary grazing horse. Only my circumstances were not normal, and right then, all it told me was that I had lost that hint of a trail again—that scarcely perceptible scent in the air had vanished, replaced by a moist chill. The light was dying and there was no point in going further.

Before night fell, I walked through the little town to its the other side as well, but there I found a busy state highway full of large trucks.

I spent the night in the local, heated waiting room. The station was a place where the tracks converged from several directions, and the room was almost full. I watched mothers with children and old country folk dragging their humble livelihoods along with them, God knows where or why. The heavy, sweetish air was almost unbreathable, so every once in a while, I went out onto the platform and stared at the sky, where first the stars kept multiplying and then the waxing moon took over. Stray dogs were lying at the end of the platform and a wretched beggar couple were walking around the station. Eventually, they came into the waiting room. He was black-haired, youngish, with an air of mental disability. His bare legs poked out from under a black coat that made him look a little like an imp, and there were ragged socks and worn-down shoes on his feet. His skin was dark, but probably from ingrained dirt rather than pigment. He was not a Romani. He was shaking from the cold and perhaps from hunger as well, but he still took constant care of his mate. He put his arm around her shoulders, pulled her dirty knit top higher up round her throat and left her in the warm waiting room, while he himself went out and soon came back with a stale slice of bread.

She was not old either, but as ugly as only someone with her way of life could be: her face was flabby, her hair stuck together, and she had only a few black teeth in her mouth. But he looked after her as if she were a queen. She returned his affection. She rested her head on his shoulder, took his blackened hand in her own, just slightly paler palms, and he stroked her hair and then went out again to find something more to eat. With his back hunched, he went around the waiting room begging for her, getting an apple, bread, and a little bacon, and bringing it all to her. Time passed, it was well after midnight, and the waiting-room was filled with dim light. I kept falling asleep and then waking up again. I felt as if a curtain of gel had formed around me. There was a roaring in my ears. But every time I woke, it was those two beggars who attracted my attention—they were so in love, so tender.

The clear weather lasted one more day. In the evening, it clouded over and, in the morning, there was snow. By that time, I was somewhere completely different—jolting along in the foothills of the mountains, although the mountains had disappeared, and the snow was coming down thick. The wind drove the flakes from south to north; they were settling over the clumps of ungrazed grass on the banks of a small river that wound beside the railway. I had a sense of snow drifting over the track and the journey, including the journey to Benjamin. The search was petering out. It also struck me, sadly, that travel by train was not enough, for the tracks went through only a small part of the country. I needed a car.

Later, when I had a hunch that I might find something important near the town of Hunedoara, I hired a taxi. The snow was thawing again—at least underneath the mountains. The short taxi driver gave me a questioning glance—where to? I gestured ahead. On the right was a gigantic steelwork—a relic of communist monstrosity. A little way further on, an ancient castle loomed over the town. The taxi driver looked at me at every crossroads, and I showed him which direction to go. We went into the bare hills above the town, where there were still remnants of snow. We climbed up a potholed road among snowy pastures, and suddenly I saw how futile it was. All I was doing was spending money, nothing more. "Back," I told the taxi-driver. "We're going back."

I can't even remember all the places I went to. Often, I got out at a place that seemed familiar, realized it wasn't, and then had to wait half a day for another train. One time it was only chance that saved me from being arrested. Police came into the waiting room, wanting to see documents. I showed them my ticket, but it didn't satisfy them. I acted as if I didn't understand, asked if they spoke English. In the meantime, they caught someone else—and let me be.

Another time, a persistent beggar in a bathroom grabbed me by the arm when I was urinating. I didn't know what he wanted. I was only slightly better dressed than he was. Probably he saw me rinsing my face in the bathroom and thought I was trying to compete with him. He had a strangely crooked face, and although I was a head taller than he, I was scared of him. I pulled sharply away from him and ran out onto the platform.

One after another, the days went by, and time flowed into a slow-moving river of grief. Nothing changed. My thoughts, which had only recently been getting more organized and clearer, were starting to collapse and splinter. My mind became dull, and memories so laboriously wrested back from my broken recall were slipping away again into the white darkness. Instead of the longed-for reunion, there was nothing but more waiting rooms, bathrooms, and cheap eateries, and beyond the window, the changing scenes that were always the same. Searching was already turning back into surviving. Still, I cannot say that I was left more unhappy than before, because in fact, something new did happen, just when I was admitting to myself that I wasn't getting anywhere, that my goal was beyond my strength, and Ben was lost for good.

It was while I was slowly coming to that conclusion in the fast-falling twilight, somewhere between the mining towns of Petrani and Simeria, that a travelling harmonica player got on the train. He went down the aisle between the seats, playing wistful but lively melodies and collecting small change from the passengers. That music of a lonely pilgrim lost in a strange land opened its embrace to me. I realized that we don't come into this world especially big or powerful, and there is a great deal we can't control and even more that we spoil with our efforts to control it, to influence it, to be important. Once, I had seemed powerful to myself, as an independent trader who could exploit the rise or fall of the price of stocks, but then I went off to the Back of Beyond—with a child who I loved, but who hadn't had a choice in the matter. Maybe I hadn't been serving his interests, only my ego. Instead of admitting my helplessness and humbly finding a way through in my heart, I had been arrogant. Now I was at rock bottom. Not a trace of power or arrogance remained. All that remained was the purest essence of love…The harmonica player had reached the back of the wagon, and his melody was leaping and somersaulting. It was cheerful, but insincere, just a way of getting people to forget about their everyday lives, which are mostly sad. And in that moment, I suddenly believed that while I had love, I had hope. Despite all my vanity, I had found an indestructible "and yet" in myself. It was as if I had received the grace of God.

Looking back many years later, as someone who never became a believing Christian or a devotee of any other religion, I have tried to reassess this experience of mine in a critical spirit. I have told myself that maybe this was just the kind of delusional self-deception that happens when reality is harder than a man can bear. If I had wanted to go further, I guess I would have found some studies about hormones flooding the brain, to protect it at such times. But for all that, the experience, this hope in the midst of despair, this hope in spite of all, was very real and present to me. And I can only maintain that to experience it is like seeing the light of divine grace.

Sinking into a half-sleep, I started to see Benjamin as a light, as a ship. He and I were sailing immense seas, entirely lost to each other. The distances were immeasurable and the seas endless, but only until the moment when the spirit of my love spread out over the waters. That love was not bound by the laws of space or terminal speed in the cosmos and could be here with me and there with Ben in the same instant. I had been humbled, I had sunk to the bottom, I had resigned myself, and receded into my own background. I wept. In my head, there was no lessening of anxiety and remorse, but my heart, full of love, was happy.

From such liminal states on the edge of consciousness, in which I merged with the universe, and all the questions of the meaning of life seemed solved, I would wake into the bare reality of stinking trains. But the change was real and permanent. I knew that if I found Benjamin and returned home with him, the experience of love as the last certainty at the end of the journey would remain in my heart. The world, as I had perceived it, had changed. Absolutely everything had changed. Nothing could be as it had been before.

Dad! Dad!

Back at the station in Timosoara, back at the starting-point yet distanced from it by the thousands of kilometers I had travelled on Romanian tracks, with swollen eyes and six hundred dollars in my pockets, and tormented by constipation and headaches, I had the last sensible idea that my pain-wracked head could come up with. I bought a pencil, unfolded the crumpled map on my lap, and then took a long time carefully shading in all the places I had already been. The unshaded areas were mainly in the north and south, but I knew that we must have come from the south. It struck me that I should go south to the border crossing between Bulgaria and Romania in the town of Rus, where the two countries were connected by one of two bridges. If we had come that way, maybe I would remember. If so, then I would hire a taxi and try not to lose the trail. I would invest all my remaining money in it, and if it didn't work out, then with my last ten dollars, I would buy a ticket to Bucharest, go to the authorities there, and tell them the whole story.

I bought a ticket, initially just to Craiova (it was more than five hundred kilometers with several changes to Rus). The train was leaving at ten in the morning, and once the sun was up, I set off downtown, which I knew quite well by then. The crossroad in front of the station was once again crammed with people, and trams and cars were coming from three sides. I remembered how the trams had brought me back the first shards of memory.... the old Number Three Tram in Prague Libeň. I remembered how awful it had been when I had fled from this crossroads with the stolen wallet, but then how much hope its contents had given me. Half of that hope had been wasted, but my feeling of reconciliation persisted.

I walked as far as the bridge over the stagnant river before slowly coming back. On the way, I stopped for a mug of hot chocolate. Christmas carols floated from the radio behind the bar, and it struck me that the very next day might be Christmas Eve. I headed back to the station fast. The train was waiting on Platform Three. I sat down in a left-hand seat, facing the engine. Inside it was warm, and there were only a few people so far. I stretched my legs onto the opposite seat and propped my head on my folded coat. It was difficult to sleep well in waiting rooms; I rarely slept more than three hours at once. I was tired.

I fell asleep before the train departed and woke a couple of hours later. The mist had lifted, and there was good visibility. Gone was the dull, flat landscape, and the mountains rose up ahead of us. The lower slopes were brown, but a little higher, they were flecked with white and, from around five hundred meters, covered in uninterrupted snow. I gazed at them with longing. What a relief it would be to lie down in all that loose snow. To concentrate only on love for Benjamin and gradually cool down, never to go anywhere again.

The train was going slowly, stopping often at tiny stations. The valley narrowed, and the forested slopes came closer. Now the train picked up speed downhill until it was rocking from side to side, and then immediately started to brake. It came into a station that was small but designed in an urban style. My eyes absently caught on green-painted railings.

Before I had time to think anything through or even remember anything, I had leapt up and was hurling myself towards the door. I jumped from the already-moving train at the last minute. My heart was pounding and I was somehow baffled at the whole incident: was it really possible that I would see him again?

I looked at the notice over the platform. It read Baile Herculane. Memories broke into my head so violently that they crashed into each other. I leaned against a bench. I blacked out.

I came back around immediately, even before a few bystanders who had rushed to my aid were at my side. It took me a long time to get my head in any order. I lurched around in front of the station.

Opposite me, I saw the stall where I had bought Ben cola, and there was the road we had come in on! Yes, we had been here. All at once, I knew almost everything and couldn't grasp how I hadn't known it before. I remembered the trip into the mountains, the yard where we left the car, and our wanderings together. For the moment, I didn't get any further; it was all too much for me. My newly acquired hope had an undertone of fear, for I knew that the snowy mountains lay between me and Ben. In any case, he might not necessarily still be there. When I hadn't returned, who knew where they had put him?

I would willingly have run up to the hills and never stopped, run day and night. The urge was strong, but I had to control myself even though inaction had become agonizing. I prayed. "God, let him be there. God, let me find him. God, guide my steps."

I went up to the nearest taxi-driver: "*Munti*," I gestured.

He didn't seem to understand: "*Munti?*"

I insisted: "*Munti.*"

I got in the car, and we set off. I couldn't exactly remember the route, and things only improved in that respect when we reached the hotel where Ben and I had slept. Here I remembered the whole spa town—its little river with the hot spring pouring out of the pipe under the road. We drove slowly between hotels that were not particularly attractive, but seasonally decorated, with Christmas trees in the front. It was strange to find myself in a familiar place that had only a moment before emerged from nothingness and that still seemed to bear traces of our presence. Here, Ben and I had prepared for our last big journey into the mountains—the journey to the Back of Beyond—before we were going home. It was hard for me to control my emotions at the thought of all I had lived through since then; the painfulness of the experience that separated me from the man I had been the last time I was in that place. The nearness of my unravelling drove me out of the paradise of my heart. I was shaking with uncertainty and tension.

Finally, we drove up a steep slope and onto the road leading along the valley of the Cerna River. So far, I had given the taxi-driver fifty dollars. He looked at me with distrust, but because of the money, he was loyal. We reached a valley under the mountains with a view of pastures and rocks. At times, the clouds broke to reveal the fading white blue of the sky. Above us, lay the snow.

It didn't take long before snow appeared by the road too. First just a dusting, then a more consistent layer. Clumps of grass, sticks, and leaves were still sticking out of it, but where the road forked, it was a good fifteen centimeters deep. There was snow on the road we needed to take too. It was freezing, and the taxi driver waved his hands. He pointed at the car and said something, most probably to the effect that the car wasn't built for these conditions.

I showed him another fifty dollars, and after a moment's hesitation, he took the exit. I could immediately feel the undercarriage scraping and the wheels slipping. A truck had driven up the road before us and left tracks that were too wide for us. We were skidding on the snow with one of the wheels. The taxi driver battled on for a while but gave up after about a hundred meters. I got out and was almost knocked flat by the pure mountain air. The light was fading, but the white landscape seemed to give out an early evening glow. The taxi driver lit a cigarette and silently stared at the snowy crowns of the trees. Then he sat down at the wheel and started to reverse. The wheels slipped: I leaned on the hood and pushed. The motor roared, and the car moved. A stinging smoke floated up over the road.

I took off at a fast walk. The snow crackled, and the truck tracks were a little slippery. It didn't take long for the valley to be submerged once again in holy silence. The dry, cold air rushed into my lungs, bringing a little joy. So much had changed. Just a few hours, not even half a day, and suddenly I knew where to go.

After about half an hour's walk, the first isolated building appeared on the right. There was a light in the window and a dog barked wildly in the yard. I quickened my pace. I was afraid that someone might delay me or even accuse me of wanting to steal; I smelled the scent of burning wood.

Then, silence again and the untouched expanse of snow mirroring the darkening sky. The rocks above were powdered with snow. The

road went over a stream. Not much water was flowing, and ice had
formed on the sides. A long upward stretch began. I was gasping for
breath and losing strength. I realized how weak I was.

The next hour of walking was very tough. I kept impatiently
looking around for the village. The effort warmed me up, and I even
had to take off my overcoat. It was dark now, and the stars were
shining. The Christmas landscape—still and silent—was cleansing
me of the dirt of the waiting rooms and trains. If I remember rightly,
my mind was empty, without particular memories or thoughts. I
connected to Benjamin, not with thoughts but with my whole being.
My new hope gave me the strength to carry on.

It was late evening when I approached the village. I was walking
by moonlight, but at that moment the moon was hidden behind
the surrounding slopes and its light fell only on the mountaintops.
I was hungry, thirsty, and exhausted, and the barking of dogs broke
out from all directions. To the side, I even saw the silhouette of a
dog. It scared me. Now, so close to my goal, I simply couldn't have
another disaster. The dog barked but did not attack—he ran along
the road with me. There was no longer light in the windows of most
of the cottages, but the flames of decorative candles flickered here
and there. A single street lamp illuminated the space in front of the
school.

I headed for the familiar building. My heart was pounding when
I knocked on the closed gate. Here, too, a dog started barking. I had
to knock several times before I finally heard footsteps in the yard. A
light came on. I hoped it would be the boss.

I was lucky. It was his imposing figure that stood in the gateway
in front of me. He stared in a puzzled way at my face and searched…
searched…and suddenly it came to him: "*Automobil!*" he said hoarsely
and with surprise and looked around towards the woodshed, as if he
thought it might still be there.

"*Da,*" I nodded.

"*Unde automobil?*" he asked, peering behind me.

"*Automobil kaput.* Accident. Problem," I explained, the

international words tumbling out of me. Then I pointed to the mountains and put my head in my hands. "Baby. My boy."

He began to grasp what I was talking about. He nodded to me to come inside. He led me across the familiar yard into the main room, and a stab of pain hit me at the memory of Ben. Here they had given him milk and honey. The man's wife and around eight younger people—probably sons, daughters, and their partners— were sitting there watching television. A large Christmas tree, splendidly decorated, stood in the corner.

Was it already Christmas Eve? I wondered. I was sorry for Ben and felt ashamed to be disturbing these people, but they were terribly kind. Whenever I think about it, there were so many people along my journey who deserve my most profound gratitude. I received more good than I could ever pay back.

One son knew a little English and interpreted for us, so I was able to explain to the boss what had happened, and what I needed: tomorrow morning, at the latest, I needed to set out across the mountains to find my son.

They shook their heads. They told me that getting across the mountains on foot in winter was impossible; I would sink up to my waist in snow. They brought me a piece of paper and got me to draw the route I had taken with Ben. I remembered it. I could use the meteorological station as a key landmark. They discussed it excitedly and the son finally turned back to me. It was decided: there was no way I could go across the mountains on foot, as I wouldn't even make it up to the ridge, but it the morning they would take their off-road vehicle, and we would drive down and then around the whole mountain range, as I had wanted to do. The father thought he knew which village we needed to go through to get to the farm where I had left Ben. He had purchased wood there the year before. There was no need for me to fear.

My eyes filled with tears. It was the first time since my escape from the hospital that someone had relieved me of a piece of my burden. These people were capable of finding Ben. They knew how to do it. Not me.

I covered my eyes with my hands, and everyone started to comfort me. The boss was especially moved; clearly, love for a son was everything to him.

After a while, I ventured to ask what day it was. They laughed. It was December 23. They told me I ought to take my son a gift. They didn't seem to have the slightest doubt that we would find him there. At the time, that somehow convinced me, but later, in the dim living room on the white covered bed, I was once again afraid.

At five o'clock in the morning, the farm came to life. A mooing, bleating, and whinnying rose from the stables, chains clanked and water buckets thudded. I got up and went out into the courtyard. I couldn't sleep anyway.

The boss and his son were already getting the off-road vehicle ready. We ate a quick breakfast in the living room, with nothing to show it was Christmas Eve. But then, the farmer's wife came and gave me a box of Christmas cookies, a knitted scarf, and a water pistol—for my son at Christmas. I was put to shame. They were all so good-hearted, and I was dependent on their goodness. I, who had been forced to steal.

It was still dark, and now moonless, when we drove back down to the valley. I had mixed feelings. It was somehow the wrong direction. I was going down when I should have been going up to find Benjamin—into the mountains. After about an hour, we drove through the sleeping Baile Herculane and continued along the main road to the north. I was overcome with anxiety. Inside, I was trembling, and my teeth were chattering slightly. We made fast progress, as there was little traffic that day. By the time the sun was up, we were past Caransebes and nearing the mountains from the other side. A white coating had formed on the horizon and was gradually thickening into clouds. Tiny beads of snow were falling and covering the frozen trail. Just don't crash, I thought. Nothing must be allowed to go wrong.

Eventually, we started to gain height. We came to a big village spread out along the road, and the boss went to ask for directions. He spent a long time getting advice in the trampled space in front of the church. Then we drove on. The road narrowed above the village but was smoothed from the dragging of timber. We went up through a forest and across a plateau where trees had been felled. Caps of snow lay on seedlings, and the beechwood on the opposite slope was perfectly outlined in snow. We drove over the saddle, and the road continued through the forest down the other side. Here, the boss turned off the road onto a forest track that also had tire marks. For the first time in a long while, he said something, and his son translated at once, "We'll drive as far as we can."

From then on, our progress was jolting, and at times we seemed to be tilting dangerously. I dug my fingers into the seat underneath me. On the steeper hills, the vehicle just barely managed to keep going, even with four-wheel drive. The boss liked to show off, but in the end, he had to stop and turn the vehicle around laboriously. We got out. My heart was pounding like a drum, and my legs seemed weighed down, like those of a condemned man who has to walk to the gallows. It really looked as if I wouldn't be capable of walking.

They helped me, and I soon found my strength again. We walked through an ancient forest, like a great temple with its mountain quiet and the majesty of its great trees. Yes, I was in a temple, and Christmas Eve was approaching. I prayed. Let it be a temple of divine mercy, let it be as they believe it to be, let us find the farmhouse and him, let me see him again in a moment.

We came out onto a pasture at the end of the woods. The mountains in front of us were sunk in white clouds. We walked through another little forest and...it was already familiar to me.

I broke into a run up a steep hill to a snow-covered building. The snow here was trampled by animals and logs, and above me, a mill was clacking despite the frost. There was a darkness in my head and anxiety in my heart, but I kept running. The gate into the yard was open. I saw three little farm boys plucking a goose. Even now, after many years, I know that there is nothing I would not have given to have that one moment. "Benjamin!"

He turned around in surprise. It took him a while to realize it was me. "Dad! Dad!" He ran to me, "Dad! Where have you been for so long?"

We hugged. "Benjamin." He seemed to me to have changed—to be older.

"Dad."

He extricated himself from my embrace. "Hey, look what I have here."

Chapter VII

Epilogue

Grown Old, Dad Recalls his Journey to the Back of Beyond

So ended my search, but not our journey. We celebrated Christmas Eve in the mountain farm where I had left Ben and found him again. It was the most moving Christmas of my life. It was the one to stand for them all—the one authentic Christmas. The farmer and his wife welcomed me with no fuss, taking my arrival for granted. These simple people had probably never thought something might have happened to me. They treated Ben as another child and waited for me to reappear. The boss explained to them what had happened to me in Romania. They crossed themselves in horror, but that was all. They had enough cares of their own. The boss and his son left as soon as they could to celebrate Christmas Eve with their own.

We stayed a few more days. I gave the farmer three hundred dollars; he didn't even want to take it.

Benjamin's calm turned out to have been superficial. He had pushed thoughts of my death, fears that I would never come back, below the surface of his mind, but they had still been there. Now that I was back, he started to be anxious. I only had to start walking to the woods, or even to the bathroom, and he would immediately ask where I was going and try to stop me.

After the New Year, I went down to the village with the farmer. He had friends there and arranged for us to be driven further down in a local truck; he paid the owner in cheese. We sat down together in the small cabin; it was moving to leave this quiet landscape as more snow fell.

"Are we going to come back to visit sometime?" Ben asked.

"Would you like that?"

He shrugged. "I don't know."

We boarded a train in Caransebes to Bucharest and the Czech embassy.

My dealings with the Czech officials confirmed my earlier misgivings. They treated me like a criminal and someone who was making work for them. They couldn't agree on what to do with us. Because there was an international warrant out for my arrest, they suggested I report to the local police so that a local court could rule on my deportation to the Czech Republic. I told them they had to be out of their minds, that there was no question of anything like that. All the same, there was a risk that they would separate me from Benjamin. They had to call the ministry many times on our behalf, and eventually, I managed to convince the deputy minister. After a week, they somehow managed to get the warrant rescinded and provided us with provisional travel documents. Poor Benjamin was drained: he kept waking up in the night and even wet his bed twice. They asked him if I had forced him into anything, if I had abused him, and how I had come to leave him by himself. And if he thought I loved him.

During that time, what kept me calm was that last sense of certainty I had found in the midst of despair on the local train—the certainty of love, which is greater than anything else. I had found Benjamin, and no one could take that away from me.

There was yet another unpleasantness when they discovered that the passport found on me belonged to the Hungarian Mr. Horváth. I told them the truth, and they wrote it down and looked at me as if I had leprosy.

Finally, they sent us to Prague. They put us on a plane, accompanied by a an official with power of attorney, under a special permit. In Prague, meanwhile, they had frozen my accounts, even those that had not been pillaged by my assistant. Criminal proceedings were initiated against me.

In the meantime, I had plenty of chance to talk with Ben. I described part of what I had been through to him. We talked about how we would soon go to see Mom at her grave, and how we would look for a new apartment, and how— because he had missed a term of school—he would have to enter the grade below, and how he could try athletics again.

But when we arrived in Prague, I was taken to a cell, under provisional arrest. And Benjamin taken to a psychiatric unit for examination. I eventually had to undergo psychiatric tests too. Fortunately, I had anticipated something like that and prepared Benjamin for it. We agreed we would stick it out. Although he didn't understand it all, he was brave.

There were constant difficulties. They released me after two days, but I couldn't get into the apartment, since I didn't have a key. I couldn't get access to my money either. Then there was the worst blow of all: I learned that my father was dead. When I was told, the journey to the Back of Beyond turned sour. Everything else could be mended. I could return the stolen money with interest, I could reward the people who had helped me, and I could apologize to those I had hurt. But I could never apologize to Dad. He had died believing he had lost his beloved grandson, in grief and despair that might even have caused his death. He had died on December 10, two weeks before I had found Benjamin. He had never learned that we were alive, and now he would never know. Even today, after so many years, it still casts a shadow over me and raises haunting questions in my mind. What is a man entitled to do? How much does he have a right to free himself from earlier bonds? Does he have a right to be free?

The court proceedings dragged on for another six months. Journalists began to take an interest in my case. I had a chance to speak publicly and formulate my feelings. I became quite a well-known person. I didn't care about it, but it allowed me to do things that were more valuable than following the movement of stocks and shares.

Otherwise, everything went back to its normal tracks. I fired the assistant, but I didn't sue her. I had no more desire to play the role of plaintiff than that of defendant. I challenged her to give at least some of what she had stolen to charity .

I became friends with a journalist who was writing about my

case. It became more than a friendship, but her world was not, and could never be, my world. I had returned from the Back of Beyond, I had touched rock bottom, and although I had lost neither the desire nor the ability to experience passion, my heart was calm. She lived for her causes—in an endless rush. My calm attracted her, but it was not something she really wanted. After a few months, we parted, but she somehow managed to arrange a presidential pardon for me. My case was set aside.

For me, the most important thing was that Ben had calmed down. He was going to school as usual, and he trusted me. Even the pain of the loss of his mom was healing. He just could never understand how his grandfather could have died. "Why didn't he wait for us? Why is he dead?"

My thoughts often returned to the people who had helped me so much. I wondered whether I shouldn't visit them, somehow reward them. But it seemed to me that I had no place in their lives. I had stepped into their lives, and they had helped me and saved me, but now I should just let them get on with those lives in their own way. So, I only sent money and a letter to the Hungarian Horváth. It was a real surprise when I got an answer. It was in Hungarian, of course, and I had it translated. He wrote that he was pleased that his money had most likely saved a human life and helped a father find his son. He had a child, too, and understood very well.

It was not until some years later that I partially changed my mind about stepping back into the lives of others. I went to Timisoara to see Maria. Benjamin was at a sports camp at the time, and because I was still always afraid that something might happen to me, I took an interpreter with me. I bought a pearl necklace and big gold earrings, and when I chose them, I felt sincere love.

We arrived in Timisoara by train. It was spring, and everything looked a great deal more cheerful than when I had been staggering about on the edge of existence. There were also signs of rapid economic development in the town. But I was still overcome by memories. When we were going into the hospital building, I was so agitated I could hardly breath.

Maria was due to arrive in an hour, and so we waited. As soon as she set eyes on me, she remembered. She put her hands to her head, called out, and then started lamenting loudly. I wept too. I embraced her. "Maria, you saved me. I've brought you this as an expression of my deepest gratitude," I said, and the puzzled interpreter translated. Maria had to go to work, so we arranged to pick her up the next morning and go to lunch. We eventually told each other our stories in a restaurant in the center of the town. She was single, and as far as I know, she has stayed single. I only hope it's not because of me. I suspect it's more because she does her work so conscientiously and with her whole being. She brings people back from darkness to light, to life—often even against their will. How could she have time for more?

Over the three days I spent in Timisoara, I managed to reconstruct the missing part of my story. I found out that I had been taken by Romani, unconscious, to the district hospital in Caransebes; clearly, it was their jalopy I had crashed into. They had reported nothing to anyone, just left me on the hospital steps and run away. The car was never found, and no one ever even looked for it. Maybe they used it as a shelter. In Caransebes, they had not known what to do with me, and so I had been transported to Timisoara. If I had been left there, I wouldn't have had a chance of survival.

Many years have gone by since then. I grew older, and Benjamin grew up. I never gave him a new Mom, not while he was still a child, but I did meet the love of my life—the sort I had always dreamed of. I met her at a time when I no longer expected any such blessing. It was in her company that I drove from Bulgaria to Romania over the new bridge between Vidini and Calafat—the place where Ben and I had crossed by ferry. She got me to tell her the whole story. Her understanding and her feminine charm, a kind of endless youthfulness, are just more proof-positive for me that nobody should ever give up hope. Just now, I'm waiting for her to appear beside me and put her hand on my shoulder. "My dear," she will say and gently caress me.

Today, when I look at Benjamin and see a grown man who has made a good life for himself and sincerely loves his wife, it fills me with satisfaction, but in my mind, he is still the small boy I took on a journey to the Back of Beyond. Memories of that journey fill me with love and sorrow. What can be more beautiful in life than to protect your child and share his destiny? Yet, these are also memories of a time when I was not yet old, that time I almost failed. I could have lost my Benjamin, I know. I still ask myself if I had the right to take that journey with him and expose him to danger. And what about my father? His unhappy death weighs on me to this day. But against all that, I hold up life. When I remember our journey, I think of a time when I loved, thirsted, lived. I truly lived. Who can say that of himself?

I don't know why it took me so many years to decide to write our story down. They might have made a movie about us if I had agreed, but I wasn't interested. Somehow, I had to wait until everything settled inside me. In recent weeks, I have often had headaches. That old injury never healed entirely. I get attacks of vertigo and short lapses of memory. I'm relieved that I've managed to put it all down on paper now. Of course, I would like to live many more years, and I would be happiest if I had never gotten old, but I know that nothing terrible is waiting at the end. It is just a matter of getting over the fear and finding hope where, objectively, there is no hope. That "and yet" kind of hope. Hope in spite of everything. Happiness, after all.

Travels with Benjamin

When it was finished, I decided to give the manuscript of my memories to Benjamin. It concerns him so much, after all. I was curious to know what he would say to it, but at the same time, afraid of his verdict. Three weeks ago, he and his wife, Marcela, came to lunch with us, and it was then that I handed him the manuscript. He did not hide his astonishment: "So many pages about our journey!" He exclaimed. Two weeks later he sent me a letter. He called it "Travels with Benjamin," and wrote in brackets: "That's me." He agreed to let me add it to the book.

TRAVELS WITH BENJAMIN (That's me)

Dear Dad,

I'm really grateful that you gave me your story to read. And it's a good thing you wrote it. It means I'm lucky enough to be able to see myself through the eyes of one of my parents.

For me, as a child, the journey to the Back of Beyond wasn't such a huge deal in my memory. Children live in the present. As soon as we got back to Prague, I started going to school again and got absorbed in my everyday pleasures and disappointments, and looked forward to new vacations and Christmases. Memories soon covered memories. It wasn't that those memories disappeared, but everything new that life brought was just as important to me. That doesn't mean I wouldn't want to remember. Thank you for what you have written. Now I understand better why I love you so much.

It wasn't always like that. I can remember standing over the grave at Mom's funeral and saying to myself—Why did she have to die and not him? Why did my dearest Mom leave us, while he—who sometimes yelled at her and often left us on our own—is still around? Before what happened to Mom, you really didn't take a whole lot of interest in me. You had your work, your deals, your sports, and you didn't much like being with us. Today I understand that, obviously. I can see the rational reasons for it. But for me, as your child, it was always painful to admit that you weren't happy with Mom, that she wasn't the love of your life, that you simply didn't love her. By the way, that doesn't mean I ever begrudged you the happiness that you've finally (hopefully) found.

As your son, I was first of all shocked by the openness with which you write about your sexual needs. I don't know why most children think that their own parents don't need it. There's no good reason to think that—I'm an adult after all, with my own experiences. But all the same, it seems terribly strange to me. On that journey of ours, I regarded you as my absolute security, as a Dad living only for the two of us, us two. Now I suddenly find out how much frustrated desire you were carrying around. That you masturbated and still had an erection. That you went to brothels and wanted to have sex with any woman who came near you. I know it's human. How could I judge you for it? But it still gives me a strange feeling.

In the first weeks after Mom's death, I realized that you did know how to look after me. You paid me the kind of attention that even Mom had never paid me—she was too sad for that. Her death visibly relaxed you a little. You seemed to be cheerful, full of ideas. I stopped being sorry you were alive and she was dead, and was just sorry she was dead.

Apart from you, I loved Grandad. I didn't want to go away and leave him for so long. If I had been able to choose, I would have wanted him to come out and join us. But I would never have had the nerve to resist you. As a child, I could see very well what you wanted and what you didn't want, what you found pleasant and what annoyed you. You got your way easily. In fact, you controlled me, manipulated me. At the same time, though, you really got me excited—crazy with enthusiasm. That journey promised so many new things. And it meant you would be with me all the time. I never regretted our leaving. And if you were often afraid for us, you managed to hide it perfectly. That was why I was never afraid. After all, I had you by my side. Nothing could happen to me.

My happiest memories of the journey are of that endless summer on the island of Corfu. The warm sea, the glowing sand, the undersea world, French fries, bicycles, my body in the waves. Even when I'm not actually thinking about it, that sun has stayed in me. It's still there every moment, it warms me and lights me up from inside. Anyone who encounters something like that in childhood will always have something to live off.

It's only now, after reading your memoir, that I realize we experienced something remarkable. The modern world today doesn't offer much in the way of such stories. Without my being aware of it, my experience on the trip to the Back of Beyond has definitely often helped me. Of course, I get some of the events confused, and some have run together in mind. I probably won't be able to fill the gaps in your memory.

I had no idea of everything you suffered before you found me again—you kept so much back. Oddly enough, it was easier for me. Children don't have such a clear sense of time. For the first few days, I was still waiting for you, wondering where you were. But there were so many new and interesting things on the farm, so many animals, so many activities. And those good-natured farmers accepted me so unquestioningly.

Everything around me was reassuring too: the sight of the rock faces, the streams, the rustling forest, the falling snow. And the everyday discipline…Of course, somewhere deep down, I was disturbed. "Dad is probably arranging something," I thought, "maybe that new apartment he has been talking about." To this day, I can't say for sure whether I was afraid for you.

What do you think those farmers are doing today? And what about *the farm? Do their sons live there or is it falling down? Suddenly, it seems stupid to me that we never went back to see them again. Our lives crossed so remarkably, so why should they never cross again? I'm curious to know how they look today, how they've changed. What they think and how they remember us. People often think of others but don't do anything. I've decided to change that and go visit them this year—at Christmas. I've already talked about it with Marcela, and we're both going. Would you like to come with us? I'm really looking forward to it.*

My dearest Dad, I don't regret anything we lived through together. It was wonderful being with you.

Your Ben
November 6, 2034

CPSIA information can be obtained
at www.ICGtesting.com
Printed in the USA
BVHW040630040522
635782BV00001B/40

9 781951 508012